D1126608

THE
POORHOUSE
FAIR

RABBIT, RUN

John Updike

THE
POORHOUSE
FAIR

❁

RABBIT, RUN

The Modern Library
New York

First MODERN LIBRARY Edition, 1965

THE POORHOUSE FAIR, © Copyright, 1958, by John Updike

RABBIT, RUN, © Copyright, 1960, by John Updike

All rights reserved under International and Pan-American Copyright Conventions. Published in New York by Random House, Inc., and in Toronto, Canada, by Random House of Canada Limited.

REPRINTED BY ARRANGEMENT WITH ALFRED A. KNOPF, INC.

Library of Congress Catalog Card Number: 65-12450

THE MODERN LIBRARY

is published by

RANDOM HOUSE, INC.

Manufactured in the United States of America

Acknowledgment is made to Penguin Books, Limited, for permission to quote in THE POORHOUSE FAIR from *Luke 23:31* of E. V. Rieu's THE FOUR GOSPELS.

RABBIT, RUN was written with the help of a grant generously given by the John Simon Guggenheim Memorial Foundation.

FOREWORD

The Poorhouse Fair was written in 1957 and was supposed to take place twenty years hence—that is, in 1977. I meant the future it portrays to be less a predictive blueprint than a caricature of contemporary decadence. Though I expected that some details would be rendered obsolete, I did not imagine that Hook's rhetorical question on page 120, "Isn't it significant, now, that of the three presidents assassinated, all were Re-publican?" might abruptly become impossible. I have let it stand, as a vivid anachronism. I thought, in 1957, fondly composing this latter version of the stoning of St. Stephen, that the future did not radically differ from the past; and this notion now seems itself a product of the entropic years of the Eisenhower lull.

Rabbit, Run was written in 1959, in the present tense. The time of its writing contained the time of its action. The songs and news that Harry Angstrom hears on the car radio in his drive south, on the night before Spring arrives, were what came over my own, more northerly radio that very night. I fell behind in this synchronization, but still worked with such haste that I felt impelled to rework all proofs heavily and, after the book was published, to make further revisions for the Penguin edition printed in England four years later. I thank the Modern Library for troubling to include these revisions in this reset text.

JOHN UPDIKE

Ipswich, Mass.
October 1964

CONTENTS

CONTENTS

THE
POORHOUSE
FAIR

If they do this when the wood is green,

what will happen when the wood is dry?

LUKE 23:31

E. V. Rieu translation

I

"WHAT'S THIS?"

"What's what?"

"Why, *look*."

In the cool wash of early sun the individual strands of osier compounding the chairs stood out sharply; arched like separate serpents springing up and turning again into the knit of the wickerwork. An unusual glint of metal pierced the lenient wall of Hook's eyes and struck into his brain, which urged his body closer, to inspect. Onto the left arm of the chair that was customarily his in the row that lined the men's porch the authorities had fixed a metal tab, perhaps one inch by two, bearing MR, printed, plus, in ink, his latter name. A reflex of pride twitched the corners of his mouth; he had always preferred, in the days when certain honors were allowed him, to have his name spelled in full, with the dignity of the middle initial: John F. Hook. On the adjoining chair the name of his companion, Gregg, was similarly imposed. With the eye it was not difficult to follow the shining squares all the way down the line.

"What birdbrain scheme is this now of Conner's?" Gregg asked noisily, as if the taller man might not hear. "Is he putting tags on us so we can be trucked off to the slaughterhouse?"

"Well, yes: what is it? A child must tinker."

"They'll come right off," Gregg said and produced from the hip pocket of his shapeless wool trousers a black bone jackknife of the old style, with a blade for removing the metal cap from bottles. With this blunt blade he adroitly began to loosen, not his own nameplate, but Hook's.

Gregg's small brown hands, the thumbs double-jointed and spatulate and the backs covered with dark lines as fine as hair, sought leverage with a quickness that recalled to Hook that his companion had been, before alcohol and progress had undone him, an electrician.

"Here," Hook said, hoarse as much from the discomfort it caused him to focus his eyes on action so near at hand as from disapproval. In truth he felt helpless. He enjoyed no real control over Gregg, though some crooked whim or weakness led the younger man lately to cling close to Hook's presence. It was Hook's misfortune to have the appearance of authority yet lack the gift of command. He sought a reason that would stay Gregg. "If we forget our place, they'll take the chairs themselves off, and we'll be left to stand."

"And then all die of heart attacks; I hope we do. It'll make a f.ing black mark in Conner's book, to have us all keel over without a place to sit."

"It's a sin to talk on so," Hook exclaimed positively, for death, to his schoolteacher's mind, was a bell that must find the students with their noses to the desk. "And," he went on, "it is a mis-take for the old to mo-lest others' property. The young now, the young have nothing, and may be winked at when they steal a foretaste; but those who have had what there is to be had are expected to be beyond such foolishness. We fellas so close to the Line"—he raised his voice on this last word, inclined his head, and lifted his right hand in a dainty gesture, the index and little fingers pointing upward and the two between curled down—"have our accounts watched very close." The disciplinarian's instinct—which was somewhat developed, though he had always lacked the cruelty to be the disciplinarian paramount—told him these words had been correct for the purpose; he had a shadowy sense that what Gregg sought in his company were elevated forms of thought to shape and justify the confused rage he felt toward the world that had in the end discarded him. Also, there was something in the relationship of Hook's teaching the younger man how to be old; Hook at ninety-four had been old a third of his life, whereas Gregg, just seventy, had barely begun.

"Ah, we can pick them off with our fingers any time we want," Gregg said with contempt, and, nimbly as a monkey on a rubber tire in the old-fashioned zoos, he turned and sat on Hook's chair, rather than the one labelled as his own.

"Modern day workmen are not what they were," Hook stated, satisfied. Standing on one porch edge, he rested his gaze in the comfortable depths to the east and north of the porch: shallowly concave farm plains tilled in scientifically irregular patches, the nearer lands belonging to the jurisdiction of the Poor Home; further off, small hills typical of New Jersey; presiding above, a ribbed sky, pink, betokening rain. The blurred click of Gregg's blades being snapped back into the sheath satisfied him still further. Pain ebbed from the muscles of his eyeballs as they lenghtened to suit the horizon, and he felt positive pleasure. Despite the low orange sun, still wet from its dawning, crescents of mist like the webs of tent caterpillars adhered in the crotches of the hills. Preternaturally sensitive within its limits, his vision made out the patterned spheres of an orchard on the nearest blue rise, seven miles off. Beyond and beyond the further hills, he knew ran the Delaware. His life had been spent on that river, white in morning, yellow at noon, black by supper. On the other side had stood a green rim: Pennsylvania. In those days —it would have been in the fat Taft's administration—when he had freshly come, direct from normal school, to teach at a building of then less than a hundred pupils, walking to work had taken him along a path from which, down the long bank through switches of sumac and sapling oak, glimpses of water had appeared as white and smooth as a plaster wall. The path ascended, passing beneath a red oak where children had attached a knotted rope and on the trunk had nailed a ladder of slats. At the highest point three shacks housing the humblest elements of the town commanded a broad view. The bank was so steep here the tops of the tallest trees clinging to it were lower than one's own shoes. The river's apparent whiteness was dissolved in its evident transparency: the contours of bars of silt and industrial waste could be easily read beneath the gliding robe of water. A submerged bottle reflected sunlight. Occasionally, among the opaque fans of corrugation spread by each strand of shore growth, the heavy oblong of a catfish could be spied drifting. The family in one of the shacks did woodcutting; the air at this place in the path where Hook usually paused always smelled of sawdust, even in winter, through the snow. And across the width of water a curtain of trees hung, united with its reflection, unmarked by a house or puff of smoke. To Hook Pennsylvania had been the westerly wilderness, and when he crossed the bridge at Trenton it surprised him to encounter houses and streetcars as advanced as those in his native state.

His eyes had a thirst for water, but no amount of study would turn the blue-green hills into a river, and even were the intervening land shaved as clear as a table top, the Delaware would be hidden from him by the curvature of the earth —eight inches to the mile, as he recalled it. His education was prominent in two places: Roman history, which he had received in the grammar school of his day, and nineteenth-century American politics, talk of which had filled his father's home.

Closer to where he stood, on this side of the rough sandstone wall the women were beginning to move about on the dark grass, picking up sticks and carrying tables; foolish women, the dew would soak their feet.

"The sky suggests rain," he said, returning to Gregg in voice while not moving.

"The f.ing bastard I have half a mind to snip every one of these rotten tags off and throw them in his birdbrain face."

These wild words were not worth answering, and an answer, no matter what, would involve him deeper with Gregg. He felt distaste for Gregg: he was like a student who, having been given the extra attention due the sheep in a hundred that has strayed, then refuses to know his place, and makes of the older man's consideration a cause for a displeasing familiarity. Yet Gregg's physical aspect, and specifically the small, stained, wrinkle-hatched, dour and dangerous face that left no impression of its eyes, inspired persistent affection, reminding Hook of Harry Petree. Against Harry Petree's memory Hook abruptly shut his mind.

He said, "Aren't the women foolish now, to be setting up for the fair with a storm at their elbows? They'll be bringing in those tables before noon. No doubt Conner put them up to it."

The sense of moisture ascending was everywhere: on the sandstone walls, some stones wet and others without clear reason dry; in the odor of the freshened grass; in the amplified sound of the grackles in the maples to the left and the chatter of the women down below; in the hazy solid movements of the women. Tens of thousands of such mornings had Hook seen.

The deepening of the sky, however, above the southeast horizon, where it should be lightest, and the proclamatory weight of the slow wind that fitfully blew, were peculiar to this day.

"A bit of ago," he stated, "the sky was savage red."

Gregg raved on, "What we ought to do is take one of these tabs every day and mail it to him, a different tab every day; the post office can't refuse our custom."

"Such talk," Hook sighed, lowering himself philosophically into the chair to the left of Gregg, his customary position.

Since Gregg was sitting not on the chair labelled his own but perversely in Hook's, Hook correspondingly occupied a wrong chair. When George Lucas came around the porch, from the side beneath the maples, he unthinkingly sat beside Hook, as he always did. "Have you noticed these tags?" Hook asked his other friend.

"The damn bastard Conner," Gregg shouted across, "I have half a mind to strip every one of them off."

Lucas was a fat man, yellowish in complexion, with a brief hooked nose. Young by the standards of the place, he had been a truck farmer in the southern wedge of Diamond County. His land had been requisitioned by a soybean combine organized by the Federal Department of Conservation. With the money they paid Lucas he had begun a real estate business in the nearest town, where he was well known, and had failed. He knew land but displeased people. Hook himself, charitable and gregarious to a fault, found it hard to enjoy association with Lucas, not because of the man's bluntness, but because he seemed preoccupied still with the strings of the outer world and held himself aloof from the generality of inmates. His friendship with Hook, Hook felt, served some hidden use. As a legally declared bankrupt Lucas had come to the poorhouse less than three years past, the winter of Mendelssohn's funeral. He was forever digging in his ear with a wooden match to keep an earache alive. "No," he said, "where are the tags?" As he said this an instinct made him lift the wrist beneath which the silver rectangle glittered.

"They put these on the chairs so we won't lose our way," Hook stated with irony.

"But this ain't mine, it's Benjie's chair," Lucas was saying, having read the name imbedded in the arm.

"A child like Conner must tinker endless-ly," Hook continued, deafened by his own chain of thought. He felt his wrist being lifted and his wine-dark lips quivered with being startled as he gradually brought his eyes to bear on the man inches from him.

"This is my chair," Lucas said. "You have it."

"Well, Billy is seated in mine."

"Come on then, Gregg: get up," Lucas said.

Furious, Gregg screamed between held teeth, "That son of a bitch I'd like to stick one of these tags down his throat and listen to the f.er scream when he tried to pass it."

Bending and bowing in a variety of friezes, the three men each moved up one chair in the long row that with the earliness of the hour was full in a bar of dull bronze sun.

"Rain," Lucas said, seated again.

"Goddam it I hope it pours buckets and washes out the whole damn business. We'll see then how high and mighty Conner thinks he is."

"And have no fair?" Lucas said. "The women love it so." His wife was also at the Home.

Settled in his own chair Hook felt more in charge. "Depend upon it," he said, "there are no workmen now as there were in my day. The carpenters of fifty years ago could drive a stout nail as long as my finger in three strokes. The joints that they would fit: pegs and wedges cut out of the end of a beam to the fine-ness of a hair, and not split the wood though they were right with the grain. And how they would hunt, for the prongs of the old-time carriages, to find a young birch that had been bent just that way. To use the wood of a branch was considered of a piece with driving two nails where one would hold. They cut nails, you know. Then wire became common, and all their thinking was done for them by the metal manufacturers."

"Now it's all soybean plastics," Lucas said.

"Yes: to make a juice and pour it into a mold and watch it harden. What is there in that? Rafe Beam, my father's handy man, could split a sunflower seed with his hatchet so you couldn't tell between the two halves. He used to say to me, 'Aren't you fearful of standing so close?', then he'd touch the blade to my nose, so you know gay-making, and show me the end of his thumb between his fingers." He demonstrated and smiled.

"Dontcha think," Gregg called to Lucas, "we ought to do

something about this putting our names on the chairs like branding f.ing cattle?"

Hook resented this appeal, across him, to the other man. Lucas, deep in his ear, showed no disposition to answer, so Hook announced, "Caution is the bet-ter part of action. No doubt it is an aspect of Conner's wish to hold us to our place. An-y motion on our part to threaten his security will make him that much more unyielding. They used to say, 'A wise dog lets the leash hang limp.' It might be more politic, now, if we breathed a word to the twin, and hear his explanation. You may be sure of this: tear yours off now and a new one will be on before noon."

"The twin," Gregg said contemptuously. "He knows less what goes on in Conner's brain than we do."

"Ah, don't be that sure," Hook said. "We old fellas, we don't know the half of what goes on."

"The twin isn't even half a man he's half a moron. What I think is we ought to go up to Conner in a body and say, 'O.K., Birdbrain Conner, treat us like humans instead of stinking animals or we'll write our grievances to the government in Washington.' The post office can't refuse our custom, we aren't sunk that low yet."

Hook smiled thinly. The sun had so risen that the shadow of the porch eave was across his eyes, while his lips and chin remained in the bronze light of the haze-softened sun. His lips appeared to speak therefore with individual life, "We must bide our time. Any size-able motion on our part will make Conner that much more in-secure. Now Rafe Beam used to recite,

'A wise old owl
Sat in an oak.
The more he heard,
The less he spoke.
The less he spoke,
The more he heard:

Let's imi-tate
This wise old bird.' "

Lucas, grimacing, had been digging into his ear, and now, watery-eyed from the pain, studied his two companions. Then, his eyes on the sulphur end of the matchstick, he said, "If you want, I'll go up to Conner and ask what his idea was."

Hook's sole answer was to draw up to his height in his chair; his face lifted entirely into shadow. The corners of his lips were downdrawn as fine as pencil points. Lucas had no fear of Conner; it was what everyone had noticed. Hook had momentarily forgotten.

"You give him this," Gregg said, and he held up and vibrated a skinny white first, yellow in the sun, "and tell him it came from me."

CONNER'S office was approached by four flights of narrowing stairs, troublesome for these old people. Accordingly few came to see him. He intended in time to change this; it was among the duties of the prefect, as he conceived the post, to be accessible. It had not been he but his predecessor Mendelssohn who had chosen to center the executive in the cupola. Why, Conner could guess from the look of the man in his coffin and the layout of the buildings. Though the fourth flight, the last and narrowest—tan unpainted stairs rising between green walls barely a shoulders'-breadth apart—led only to the cupola and alone led away from it, once this brief diagonal descent had been made, a man could easily thread unseen through the fourth floor—half of it the closed doors of the bedridden—to the rear stairs, and thus reach the out-of-doors, and sneak behind the pig buildings and along the edge of the west wall into the adjacent town of Andrews, where Mendelssohn was well-known as a daytime drinker. The altitude of the office assured that it would seldom be visited, except by Mendelssohn's subordinates, who understood him. Further, the view commanded from the cupola was inclusive and magnificent. From what Conner had seen in the coffin—

the ponderous balding head, the traces of Jewishness in the vital nostrils and the smile the embalmers had been unable to erase from the lips like the lips of a gash long healed, the faint eyebrows, the unctuously, painfully lowered lids—Mendelssohn had in part thought of himself as God.

Conner thought of no one as God. The slats of light from the east and south windows, broken into code by the leaves and stems of the plants on the sills, spoke no language to him. He had lost all sense of omen. Rising as early as Hook, he had looked at the same sky and seen nothing but promise of a faultless day for the fair. Young for the importance of his position, devout in the service of humanity, Conner was unprepossessing: the agony, unworthy of him, he underwent in the presence of unsympathetic people was sensed by them, and they disliked him for it. The ignorant came to him and reaped more ignorance; he had no gift of conversion. The theatre of his deeds was filled with people he would never meet—the administrators, the report-readers—and beyond these black blank heads hung the white walls of the universe, the listless, permissive mother for whom Connor felt not a shred of awe, though, orthodox in the way of popular humanist orators, he claimed he did. Yet there were a few—*friends*, he supposed. Buddy was one, the twin, tapping out budgetory accounts at his porcelain table in the corner of the spacious room. Frequently Conner could feel Buddy's admiration and gratitude as a growing vegetal thing within himself, fed by his every action, especially the more casual; the joking words, the moan over a tangled business, the weary rising at the end of the day to pour, out of a wax-paper cup, a little drinking water on the roots of the decorative plants—like the Venetian blinds, a post-Mendelssohn innovation. Moving in, Conner had found the office bare, drab, dirty, unordered: a hole where a tramp napped.

"Conner? Hey, Conner." It was Lucas's habit to come halfway up the last flight and then shout, his voice highly acoustical in the narrow enclosure. Conner did not know how to correct him; there was no bell; he did not know how they

did it in Mendelssohn's day, nor did Lucas, Lucas and his
wife having entered the place a month after the new prefect.

"Yes, George. Come on up." He frowned for Buddy to see
and kept his hands on the piece of paper he had been reading,
a letter from an anonymous townsperson. Buddy's hands
ostentatiously rapped on, not compromising his noise for their
visitor. The twin's brain in boyhood had been soaked in thrillers, and to him Lucas was the Informer, indispensable yet
despicable.

Indeed, that Lucas, in the midst of such general hostility,
should be comparatively natural with him made Conner himself uneasy. The man perhaps thought he was winning kindness for his wife, though there was no evidence that he was;
impartiality with Conner was a crucial virtue. By way of
comment on his puffing, Lucas said, "A lot of stairs. You'd
think you were hiding."

Conner smiled mechanically, his eyes glancing to the letter;
help not hinder, I myself, and *rights* leaped from between his
fingers. He lacked the presence, however, to hold a silence.
"Martha getting her cake made?" he asked, clipping away
minor words in embarrassment at being conventionally cor-
dial.

"She's fussing at something, I know."

"You must be glad," Conner said, "that she's on her feet
again." He felt this remark instantly as fatuous; of course
Lucas was glad. Yet he had meant it well, and he felt irritation
at the invisible apparatus that, placed between himself and
any of the inmates, so scrupulously judged the content of expressions that were meant to be carelessly amiable.

To his relief Lucas removed their talk to the plane of business. "They noticed their names on the porch chairs downstairs."

Conner's heart tripped, absurdly. He should have given up
hope of pleasing them long ago; it was enough to help them.
Ideally, his dedication wore blinders, but he was too weak
not to glance to the side for signs of approval. The sculptor
has his rock and the saint the silence of his Lord, but a man

like Conner who has vowed to bring order and beauty out of human substance had no third factor; he is a slave, at first, to gratitude. In time, he knew, this tender place grows callous; he had heard the older men whose disciple he was discuss, not entirely in joking, mass murder as the ultimate kindness the enlightened could perform for the others. "From your tone," he said to Lucas, "I take it their noticing should cause me anxiety."

"Well, they're confused. They can't read your purpose."

"Who is this they?"

Lucas poked something small and wooden into his ear and made a face of pain, his clayey skin eroding in rivers suddenly.

"You needn't name them," Conner added.

"Hook and Gregg were the ones I heard talking about it."

"Hook and Gregg. Poor Gregg, of course, is one notch removed from dementia. Hook is something else. Tell me, do you think Hook is senile?"

"In the head? No."

"Then there must be a rational cause that has set him against me."

"Oh, he's not against you. He just talks on the first thing that comes into his mind."

"And I'm always in his mind. What better friend does he think he has than myself? Hook's been here fifteen years; he knows what it was like under Mendelssohn."

Lucas looked startled to be feeling the edge of an apologia that was, Conner realized, principally excited by the preposterous and insulting letter he had been reading. "He speaks real well of him," Lucas said, with an odd steadiness of his eyes. "I have no opinion; I came here after you."

"Half the county home acres were lying fallow, waste. The outbuildings were crammed with refuse and filth. The west wing was a death trap. When Hook, last autumn, ate that unwashed peach, he would have died if Mendelssohn had still been in charge."

"Doesn't anybody realize," Buddy interjected in his somewhat frantic boy's voice, "what Mr. Conner has done here?

This home has one of the five highest ratings in the north-eastern sector."

"I read that on the bulletin board. It makes us all proud." Lucas's hands went to the side of his head, and his face crumpled again. This over, he asked soberly, "But now what was the idea about the nameplates?" *Dogged,* flashed on Conner as an adequate summation of Lucas.

Conner wondered if it were wisest to be silent. Words, any words, gave a person a piece of yourself. Swiftly, reasons marshalled against this unworthy impulse:

You should not make shows of authority.

Lucas, fat and blunt and coarse-pored as he was, soiling the order of this office and the morning's routine, deserved polite-ness, as one of the unfortunates.

If Conner fudged, Lucas would convey the fact to the others.

The question was not, as it seemed (so strong was Con-ner's impression this moment of defiance and ingratitude everywhere), an impudence to which there is no answer.

There was an answer; everything Conner did he did for a reason; his actions were glass.

His motives occurred to him; he stared at the shine on Lucas's taut hooked nose and then shot his gaze to the stripes of blue at the window, saying, "There have been complaints, *a* complaint—one of the women came to me, in regard to her husband—that on rainy days the men who work on the farm can't find chairs on the porch, or at least the chairs they think of as their own. The vacant chairs are scattered, so some are unable to sit with their friends. It's childish, of course. Men-delssohn, I'm sure, would have laughed her away. But I—my duty is to take all complaints seriously. Part of my policy has been, within the limits of the appropriations, to give the residents here some sense of ownership. I think especially of men like Hook, who have known a share of respect and prosperity. It strengthens, is my belief, rather than weakens a communal fabric to have running through it strands of private ownership. Lucas, I want to help these men to hold up their heads; to retain to the end the dignity that properly belongs to every member, big or little, of humanity."

He pivoted in his socketed chair and saw that in his typing corner Buddy was blushing jealously, to hear his superior speak with such fervor to an interloper. The boy (so touching, his blurted proclamation of their fifth-place honors) had perhaps assumed that the image of the thread of private property and the hope concerning dignity to the end had been a confidence shared between just the two of them. It would not do for Conner to explain, by even so much as the tone of his eyes, that in this instance, without disbelieving his words, he was using them more for their impact than their sense, more to keep Lucas at a distance than convey a creed. When Conner had been Buddy's age he would have been repelled by any revelation to the effect that within the outer shell of a man's idealism is fitted a shell of cynicism; within this shell, another, contracted compared to the first, of idealism, and so on down, in alternate black and white, to the indivisible center; and that it is by the color of the star here alone that the course of a man's life is set. Obliquely mitigating his unintended offense to Buddy, Conner mentioned his name in continuing to Lucas, "Mr. Lee, with a few of the other women, took much trouble in fixing each man's favorite chair. In some cases the old men themselves sat in a new place every day. The present arrangement is a work of love on his part. And yet Hook takes it as a cause of complaint. This is the reward Mr. Lee receives for the devotion he brings to his work in this institution; his talents would earn him three times his present salary in private or semi-private industry."

"Well, I'll tell them," Lucas said, though his attention for the last minute had been turned toward the inside of his head.

Perhaps still appeasing Buddy, Conner asked sharply, "What in hell are you doing to your ear?"

"A little soreness." Lucas went on the defensive; his head bowed and the pink inner skin of his cumbersome lower lip showed.

"For how long?"

"Not long."

"A day? Two?"

"I guess longer."

"You've been running an earache for longer than two days. What medication have you received?"

No answer.

Conner answered for him, "None."

"I've had a soreness, off and on, for some time."

He might have been speaking of an animal he had befriended. "Well, could you go to the west wing *now*, please? And throw the matchstick into the wastebasket. *This* wastebasket. Good God, you'll give yourself otomycosis." Conner hated, more than anything, pain dumbly endured. Oppression, superstition, misery—all sank their roots in meekness.

Lucas, turned into a child by this undeserved streak of rebuke, left as commanded. Conner, grieving for the bad temper brought on by the uneasy conscience unjustly forced on him by Buddy's sulk and the letter on his desk, rose and stood by the east windows and looked down through parted blinds to people foreshortened on grass. On the east, south, and west sides, the cupola had big windows, sets of three with round-arched tops, the middle one taller than the two flanking. The metal supporting the Venetian blinds muddled the stately lines, and the semi-circles, each fitted of five pieces of hand-worked wood, peeked above the manufactured horizontals like the upper margin of a fresco painted where now an exit has been broken through. On the fourth side, the north, the steep stairway climbed from the floor below, contained within the external silhouette of the cupola, so that the door came into the room, making on each side of it an alcove, in which a simpler window had been let. Light at all times of the day came into the room; each standing object in it became a sundial, which no one there could read. The man, Walter Andrews, who seventy years before had built the mansion had meant this for the piano room; the system of supports and joints above had been left free, diagonal rafters and slender crossbeams where music could entwine, and the musicians grouped around the piano below could play on and on, feeding the growing cloud above without having their noise press out from the walls and crowd them. The piano was still in the room, underlying terraces of green steel cabinets. There was no way of getting it out; it had been hoisted up and set on the bare floor when the room was unfinished. Where the east set of windows were the next day placed, the wall was open on blue air, the ends of the golden boards making a ragged hole in which the romantic black piano-shape appeared, a miracle, the ropes too thin it seemed, the workmen apprehensive, a breeze blowing, the points of the tapered legs tracing a fugal phrase *largo* on the emptiness as the huge instrument gently twirled in its secure cradle of rope. The piano within, the workers completed the well-knit wall, Andrews giving no consideration to the day after tomorrow or to the species that would follow his.

The tall space above, crossed with stained beams, catered to a kind of comfort not proper to executive and clerical work. Conner came from a world of low ceilings, onion-gray or egg-blue, made still lower by fluorescent structures. The space below made him uneasy, too. "Damn these people," he said, his lips an inch from the sharp blond edge of a subtly curved slat of the blinds. "Now down there's Hook, making his rounds like the mayor of the place, talking to everybody, stirring them up for some crusade."

To Buddy, watching, the profile of his superior was incisive against the luminous blinds: the little round nose above the long bulging lip of an Irishman, in saddened repose. In his rush of love Buddy had to speak, any words, and the first words came to him from what was bearing on his mind, "Don't you think we could dispense with Lucas? He learns more than he tells, and physically, you must admit, he's a monstrous error."

"AH, Mrs. Jamiesson," Hook said, "don't the apples shine in your cheeks this morning? That's what Ed Hertzog used to say, when greeting the women after church service."

She was tacking an oilcloth frill to the front edge of the bare table she had set in the grass, and he was standing in her way. "Could you hold that there with your fingers?" she asked him.

"De-lighted, posolutely delighted," he said, mimicking someone else, a normal school chum, forty years dead, named Horace Frye. His downward vision was so poor he set his fingers along the naked edge of wood, and when Mrs. Jamiesson went with her hands for the hammer and tacks, the scalloped strip fell, the unfastened end of it into the drenched grass. As if managing a baby and his spoon she laid her tools aside and gripped his hand and brought the cloth to it and pressed his fingers against the edge. He let her drive one tack and stood away, his eyes on the top of the silver maple by the west wing. "That sound," he announced, "is music to my ears; the carpenters in my day would drive a coarse nail with three swift strokes."

"Well I guess I'm not one of them," Mrs Jamiesson said. She was a heavy woman whom homeliness had trained to a life of patience and affection. It was a wonder to her mother that this daughter, with the freakishly protuberant jaw, had married and held the man and raised a family. The waspish temper she had inherited from her beautiful mother Mary Jamiesson had repressed, a luxury she had to do without. Yet a lively tongue never quite dies. "It's a rare sight for me," she went on, "to see a man do any work; else I guess I'd learn something."

Hook did not miss the sense of her remark, only its application to him. "It's the admini-stration," he confided. "To let a man choose idleness or labor, on the ground of whim: why in Mendelssohn's time such a thing would never be seen. Able-bodied men like Gregg and Lucas—it's a wonder they haven't grown too lazy to lift the food to their mouths at mealtimes."

"Lucas has the pigs, though." Mrs. Lucas was a companion of hers.

"What day's work is that, to carry the garbage from the kitchen to the trough?"

"Well it's more than some do," Mrs. Jamiesson observed.

Uneasiness crept over Hook. The woman's implication—that women did the work of the place—was disagreeable to him, like a scent which raises the fine hairs on an animal. "Isn't it strange now, the only muscle which never tires is the tongue," he said, and moved on, forgetting who had begun this train of remarks. The long-grass lawn, now that the sun had moved higher, turned toward yellowness; in the center of the main walk, two old men were slowly unravelling electric cords, cardboard boxes of colored bulbs behind their legs. A stepladder lay flat in the grass. One of the men fumbled at a snarl as if this were his sole task for all the time remaining in God's scheme. A robin scolded *wheep wheep* in the tree nearby. Beyond the south wall, the landscape extended itself generously; deliberate stands of trees were dotted like islands over the land; a few houses, outreaches of Andrews, intruded their colors on the left edge of his aimed vision. He coughed and stated, "Now I can remember," and noticed he was standing alone. He moved closer to the men on the walk. The one not fiddling with the snag was removing bulbs from their beds of tissue paper and laying them, so that no two of the same color touched, on the bench. "Now I can remember, as a boy, how you could go to the top of a hill and not see a house in an-y direction. "Now"—he coughed again, since the heads of neither had moved—"there can't be a foot of earth east of the Alleghenies where a body can stand and not be within hailing distance of a house. We have made the land very tame." Hook cocked his head inquisitively. He decided he had picked two deaf ones. Their names escaped him.

Turning away, he felt like a rise of unplowed land which approached from below swells unexpectedly and in a spattering of daisies makes a join with the sky. All the movements of preparation around him gladdened him. He was glad of Gregg's absence; the man had gone to the kitchen, to wheedle a second breakfast. There was one lack, one shallow pit in the surface of his pleasure: he had no cigar in his hand. He allowed himself four a day, and in the discussion over the tags had neglected to light his morning one; he did this now, a White Owl. The barn odor filled his mouth; he posed, cupping the elbow of his cigar arm in his other hand, the other arm braced gracefully against his abdomen.

The wooden tables—their eating tables before the dining hall was fitted with square tables of synthetic marble purchased from a renovated cafeteria—were arranged partly along the main walk, but principally in two alleys at right angles to the walk, straight across the grass. Because the old people did it the lines were not absolutely straight. Hook strolled down one of these alleys, angling the cigar this way and that in friendly fashion. By Amelia Mortis's table he halted. She was a short old woman, in her eighties and thus not far from Hook himself, who wore an ancient stiff bonnet and had a goiter hanging around her neck. Each year she made from rags a few quilts, perhaps six in all, which she sold each August at the fair. Last year a man from Trenton had bought four.

"Do you expect your sharper from Trenton again this year?"

"I hope to heaven not. It makes it so dull to have them sold so quick."

"That fella, dollars to doughnuts he was one of those antique dealers, and peddled them for thrice what he paid you."

"Last year it was so disappointing; he bought all I had left and there was nothing left for me but to go to bed and miss all the music." Her voice had a crooning quality, as if it originated deeper than most and rose through a screen; she had a tendency to let the ends of her sentences impatiently drop, which led Hook to bend toward her.

"I wager," he said, "he made a ver-y hand-some profit."

"I like to see the young couples have them, but you know how they care only for the new things. I was the same way myself."

One of her quilts, folded, rested on the table. The remainder were in two boxes labelled with the name of a dehydrated milk. At the end of a year of threading and biting and matching, she stretched the simple arrangement of them on the table into a full morning's job, refolding, patting, replacing them in the boxes, dawdling and turning until she felt quite dizzy and had to beg for a chair. Of the quilt displayed, one square was of a cloth on which a green hill had been printed, covered with uncommonly large flowers, and a river wound at its base, and on its crest had been planted a small open temple, the blue of the sky showing between the pillars. This figure had been repeated over the fabric. The square of cloth next to this one was evenly dark, the color of purple vetch. Next to this was a coarse plaid weave, many colors but sober, the largest stripe a green, making in the section a cross. The first square of the next row, beneath the temple and hill, seemed silk, a blue that appeared to retreat beyond the surface of the cloth, dotted with warm rectangles and crescents. The next patch was savage red; violently strewn across it strange golden forms like a carved alphabet or furniture molding. Another square showed children running carrying a pail. Another was brown corduroy, another green cotton. Another—here Hook disbelieved. The violet ground, the five yellow ovals around a blue five-point star, within a brown square, again and again, were too much like his childhood bedspread for belief—the very dusty grape tone, the nameless flowers seen so squarely from above. In the confused way of recollections from that time he saw himself as a child wandering among the rectilinear paths of the pattern, searching for the deeper-dyed thread that occasionally, in the old woven cloth, would arch above the others. In the rough-walled room lit by kerosene, the wick kept thriftily low, he saw the coverlet waiting for him; it was evening, he was a child. His parents were down below; his father's voice shook softly up the stairs. He felt no great resentment, for as a serious-minded child he feared the dark but knew that he must sleep, when the time came each day. Studying the cloth Hook felt the small condensed grief—that the past was so far, the end so near—secreted safe within his system well up and fill his head so exactly the thin arcs of his eyes smarted with what they contained. He blinked rapidly, erasing the glow of that kerosene lamp.

"Now how Mendelssohn," he said, "would have stroked and patted this quilt."

"Wouldn't he though? He gave me such encouragement."

"It was his way."

"He was like McKinley," Mrs. Mortis exclaimed, invoking a girlhood idol of hers, "for dignity, yet he was never too busy to drop a kind word." Her face in the shadow of the bonnet was uplifted rhapsodically. "That's how you know them, John."

Her high tone, and his old debater's instinct, prompted him, above his fundamental agreement, to enter a qualification. "They say, you know," Hook said, "that in regards to administration, he would let a few things slip. But in his day there wasn't such idleness as you see now."

"Ah, and often I can picture him in the mind's eye saying grace," she continued, her goiter bouncing like the breast of a clucking chicken, "with his eyes downcast so gracious, and his voice booming out so even the deafest could hear; in his coffin, I remember saying to Mrs. Haines, he looks like he's come to the end of a prayer, his nostrils still full of its breath. My heart told me to stoop and kiss his hand, but the line was pushing."

"He had a natural faith—"

"You know them when you come across them, rare as that is. Oh, we've had our time, John."

Hook did not think it was a woman's obligation to tell him he had had his time. Amy Mortis was a woman of his own generation—she would have been marriageable to him— and along with the corresponding virtues she had the talkativeness, the presuming habit, the *familiarity* of such women; calling him "John." He enjoyed conversing with them, but not as much as they with him, nor for as long. Yet as with his late wife, he was too weak, too needful of her audience to break away, and instead lingered to lecture.

"Now, that McKinley was nothing but Mark Hanna's parade uniform; the man he beat was twenty times his greater, and he did it on the strength of New York and Boston money. Bryan."

"Yes, one of those wanting to steal everything from the rich and give it to the poor and now that they've done it, are we better off? Are the poorhouses empty? Why, no: they're building more and still they're crowded. I feel so sorry for the younger women, having to share those tiny rooms. Young Bessie Jamiesson lying down at night with Liz Gray, who hasn't washed herself in human memory. And the Lucases and that bird keeping for themselves a room that would do for four humans."

Having forgotten what he wanted to say, Hook shook his head negatively and thoughtfully pulled on the cigar. The metallic cloud, as good as any sensible masculine argument, hung in the air between them, then snapped away. Taking his time within the won advantage, he pronounced, "Were Mark Hanna still running the country, good lady, our kind would be dead long past."

"Yes and wouldn't it be an improvement," she said with great readiness, as if she had been impatiently watching the sentence take form in his head. "We hang on and hang on and spend our time on such foolishness"—a scrabbly motion indicated the quilts—"when if we had any sense we'd let the Lord take us and start us off fresh."

"You don't antici-pate, then, any difficulties, on the other side?"

The suggestion in his tone that there was crudeness in her religion irritated her. She said, "Well, if there are for me, few'll pass," showing that in asking her rights she could be as testy with the Lord as with any other man. "I've been as good as most."

"Ah, yes," he said, breathing admonitory smoke, before the comedy of her spunk occurred to him, and his mustache broadened, and he promised her that if, as was likely, he got there before her, he would certainly save her a place on the settee. Making this guarantee he bowed with cocky gallantry above the nearly dwarfish figure of the good lady. There vibrated between them something of the attraction he had of old exercised on members of the opposite sex.

THE ENTRY DOOR to the west wing whispered shut behind Lucas and he was frozen. There was white on both sides of him, extending like the repetition of a few beds in double mirrors, with increasing dimness, to the end beds by the Palladian windows, which shed on the linen a pearly, generalized light. The west wing did not get the sun directly until the latter part of the day. The figures beneath some of the sheets made faint movements; a skeletal arm lifted to gain attention, a pink scrubbed head turned listlessly to take in the new entrant. The sheets did not seem to have beneath them persons but a few cones, from the points of which the folds sloped apparently to the mattress, and Lucas thought of parts of bodies—feet, the pelvis, shoulders without arms—joined by tubes of pliable glass, transparent so the bubbling flow of blood and yellow body juices could be studied. The impression was upon him before he could avert his eyes. Incapable of any retreat he looked on the floor, fearful above all of accidentally finding among the composed faces of these ailing and doomed the face of an acquaintance, someone with whom he had shared a talk on the sunporch, or walked into Andrews with. On the floor his helpless eyes noticed the marks made by the soft wheels of the stretcher-wagon. Even more than black death he dreaded the gaudy gate: the mask of sweet red rubber, the violet overhead lights, the rattling ride through washed corridors, the steaming, breathing, percolating apparatus, basins of pink sterilizer, the firm straps binding every limb, the sacred pure garb of the surgeons, their eyes alone showing, the cute knives and angled scissors, the beat of your own heart pounding through the burnished machinery, the green color of the surgeon's enormous compassionate eyes, framed, his quick breath sucking and billowing the gauze of his mask as he carved. Carved. Surgeons bent over you like

lions gnawing the bowels of a deer. Lucas had watched his
father die of cancer of the bowel. It was the family death, for
males.

Many of the heads suspended on the white waves were
turned to him by now. Lucas, with his big body and strange
skin, was not inconspicuous. Dr. Angelo came up to him
silently. "Yes?"

The doctor was a middle-aged Italian, highly handsome,
though his head was a bit too big for his body, and his eyes
for his head. It was as if the years of service and fatigue that
had subdued his Latin mannerliness to mere staring, indeed
dazed, gentleness had also been a drag on his lower lids:
his green irises rode a boat of milk, under a white sky. Thus
his eyes were targets.

"Conner thought I should come here."

"Why did Conner think that?"

"No reason, except to get me out of his way."

Angelo waited, the beautiful mouth smiling regretfully beneath the two ovals of gray hair symmetric on his upper lip.
He held some cards in his hands but showed no sign of being
interrupted. "Is the difficulty rectal?" he at last suggested.

"Oh, hell, no. No. It's just my ear. A little itching that
comes and goes now and then."

"Could we have a look? Come over here, Mr.—?"

"Lucas. George R."

"Yes. You have a wife. Did her legs improve?"

"Wonderfully. We're both wonderful. The ear doesn't pain
at all now, but I guess that's always the way."

"Mm." Angelo led the way to his office, a brown desk
shielded by frosted glass partitions, but open in the front. One
entire pane was papered with licenses, permits and certificates
of authority from state and federal bureaus.

"This ear?"

"The other."

Angelo inserted the nozzle of a brass funnel painfully deep
into Lucas's head and murmured with a trace of pride,

"Definitely inflamed. How have you been irritating this canal?"

"I try to keep it clear of wax," Lucas admitted, his voice made flat, loud, and hollow by the cold metal in his ear.

"How is the other?"

"First-rate. Never a twinge or anything."

"May we see?" And the frightening operation was repeated. Lucas wanted all metal to keep away from his body. With a certain brutality the icy intruder in his head squirmed, and Angelo's wet breath beat on the side of his neck. "Nothing," Angelo decided finally.

Lucas was sufficiently relieved to observe across the aisle from the office a gaunt woman, of seemingly prodigious length, switching her head back and forth on the pillow, as regular as a pendulum.

"Let's try this," Angelo said. A soft rubber mask was clapped over the bad ear; he winced. "Tender?" Angelo asked.

"A little, but you know . . . nothing." It occurred to him, with a muffled inner jolt, that his ear was quite badly off; would have to be lanced. He had heard rumors all his life of this operation; nothing was more painful. It was brief, they said, a mere moment, an atom of pain, but of such pain as couldn't be bettered; the prick pierced all the layers of numbness right through to the ultimate, blue-hot sheet of pain that set the limit to suffering.

Angelo threw a switch at the side of his desk, by the radiator. "Just tell me the numbers you hear."

Lucas figured that if he passed this test he would be let off the lancing. At first it was easy. The voice was a woman's, very slow and ticky, like a phone operator's. He repeated after her, "13 . . . 74 . . . 5 . . ." Her voice grew higher as she sank into a lake of viscid substance. "12," she called, "99." In the strain of listening the rustle of blood in his head created static. "Uh, 99." His tongue had become queerly cumbersome; his heart fluttered high in his chest. He missed the

woman's next two cries, so deep and tiny had she grown.
The head across the aisle turned left, then right on the pillow,
like a wing-beat. Lucas ventured, "80?"

Angelo impatiently tore away the rubber cap. In his anxiety Lucas had pressed it hard against his skull; his ear
smarted.

"Grace," Angelo called. "Grace!" To the girl who appeared he said, "Lucas. George R., please."

His eyes settled into fixity. The two irises enlarged and
merged into one great opaque black pupil circled by consider-
ate green, which shield pressed against Lucas's chest. Wriggling under this weight of attention Lucas's mind desperately
sought to gain a glimpse of the phantom Grace and whatever
cruel instruments she was bringing. How could he know what
grim message the simple syllables of his name, in Angelo's
mouth, had spelled to her? Smiling tirelessly, Angelo explained in monotonously intoned detail the clinical nature of
his aural morbidity. Lucas caught none of it, except when
Angelo, in specifying the location of the worst redness, made
a circle with his thumb and forefinger and with a finger of the
other hand rubbed the wrinkly part of the thumb skin and
said, "Right in around here. Between seven and eight o'clock."
A queer trick, his making the ear a timepiece; there was
something insane in so much explanation.

All Grace brought was a blue card. Making swift marks on
it. Angelo asked if he had ever had that upper molar pulled.
Two years ago it had been noted as dead and liable to abscess.

"It never gave me no trouble."

"A submerged infection doesn't always declare itself to the
nervous system. There are instances of an abscess at the root
of a tooth—up in here, you see—" he touched one half of his
mustache—"inserting poison into the bloodstream until the
host suffers a coronary. Will you make an appointment please
with Dr. Duff's secretary, you know the office? The second
door to the left as you leave the ward." While saying this he
fussed in his desk. "Now. Steady, please."

He came at the side of his eye with something long and thin. Lucas reared away, half-rising.

Angelo smiled. The heavy beauty of his face loomed beyond a small rod of cotton-tipped wood, which he held up for Lucas to see. "We're going to apply a little zinc to ease the irritation." He did this, inserting the warm gray unguent with a careful twirling motion that tickled intimate turnings dangerously near, Lucas felt, seats of pain. But Angelo, godlike, resisted the temptation, so understandable to Lucas at this moment, to prod a sensitive spot. He was soon done. He gave Lucas a small silver tube, several wooden wands, and a wad of cotton wrapped in orange tissue. The ointment was to be applied three times a day. If the trouble did not vanish in four days, return. Rolled on inertly by the sound of his voice, Angelo asked if Lucas were ready for the fair today, and said something implying that Lucas and his kind seized this annual opportunity to import hard liquor and get "a load on" behind the north wall.

Lucas had never heard of such a practice. "What year did this happen?"

Angelo looked surprised. "*Every* year. Don't you know about it? I forget, you're a married man."

"Oh—" Lucas felt himself expected to smirk. "I know enough. Being married doesn't mean you never lift your arm."

Angelo, for a moment uncertain, like a joking priest who has perhaps misjudged his company, laughed aloud in relief. "A patient some years ago told me that was the custom. He wanted to know if it wasn't a good idea medically. I told him it was a good idea *cos*metically. That poor fellow's gone now. In fact his insides had been gone when he came here. I was afraid for a minute the rest of you had profited by his bad example."

"Well, no," Lucas easily lied, "we try to keep up the old traditions."

Angelo liked this, and they might have gone on and on, for the thought of corruption put a sinister bloom on the doctor's manner, but luckily for Lucas there was a distraction. The woman flapping her head across the aisle called "Miss. Miss." Angelo's ponderous eyes wavered, and heavily he pushed away from the desk.

Lucas left the three-sided box—box no doubt for some the entry to smaller boxes, more intricate chairs, and the final straps beneath the violet bulbs—light-headed. Passing Grace, the nurse, he saw she was a beautiful girl of twenty or so, her body firm as a half-green apple. He seemed to skate through the white cones of the doomed, and felt himself, mirrored in the waterless eyes watching, a cruelly vital toad. He was so rejuvenated he played hooky, ignoring Dr. Duff's door and making no appointment.

HIS WORDS with Amy, and the patch of frail grape cloth, reminiscent, in her quilt, had affected Hook poorly. Her speaking so plainly of death stirred the uglier humors in him. In the mid-mornings of days he usually felt that he would persist, on this earth, forever; that all the countless others, his daughter and son among them, who had vanished, had done so out of carelessness; that if like him they had taken each day of life as the day impossible to die on, and treated it carefully, they too would have lived without end and have grown to have behind them an endless past, like a full bolt of cloth unravelled in the sun and faded there, under the brilliance of unrelenting faith. Amy, with her sharp short view, had disrupted the customary tide of his toward-noon serenity. He consoled himself by contemplating the southeast horizon, where, in support of his prediction, luminous leaning cumulus clouds were constructing themselves.

Not that the sun was diminished yet. On the meadow beyond the wall, low where Hook stood, a rabbit paused, a silhouette of two humps, without color. When the creature lifted his head his chest showed its sharp bulge, and a lilac redness was vivid within the contour of his translucent ear—as Hook saw him he had but one ear.

In the wide darkness surrounding the constricted area Hook's eyes could focus on, stars began to dance. They shut off and on with electronic rapidity, midges of dazzlement, and when he sought to give them chase, they removed their field to a further fringe of the sky his eyes made, and with a disconcerting sensation of insubstantiality he realized he had been concentrating into the sun, and that he had had little sleep the night before. He retired early but slept little, waking at queer hours with the feeling of no time having elapsed. Hook shielded his spectacles with the cigar hand and moved the three steps to the wall. Once he had a hand placed on the abrasive tepid surface of a sandstone, he lowered his lids.

The wall, its height slightly waving, like a box hedge, enclosed four and a fourth acres. On the north the rear of the stone barn served as a section of the wall, near a wide gap once for wagons, marked by two pillars, in the mortar of which the hinges of the double metal gates of the old estate were still fixed. There was a less wide entry, more for men than vehicles, also gateless now, at the front—the east—leading into the central gravel walk. On the northeast corner, nearest Andrews, a small gate was kept padlocked, though in the estate's days it had seldom been; Mr. Andrews had intended the wall and the look of the buildings to say "Mine" more than "Keep Away." The Diamond County Home For √ the Aged lorded over a considerable agricultural plain in New Jersey. The main building, the home, was inexactly an embroidered cube, with a shallow, somewhat hovering roof, topped by the airy cupola. The west wing, once a ballroom, looked added-on but in fact was a portion of the architect's and the second Mrs. Andrews's conceptions. The substance of the great high house was wood painted a tempered yellow weathering toward orange. To the credit of the old carpenters their work still appeared solid, without being thickly made. Along the eaves fancy trim hung, lace wheedled from pine planking. Five lightning rods were braced by spirals of hand-forged iron. The sixth had partially collapsed and pointed diagonally. Maple, horsechestnut, cherry, walnut, apple, and oak trees had grown old on the grounds. There were several broad elm stumps as memorial to the blight.

Hook prayed, requesting that the spell be allowed to pass and that his children he restored to him in Heaven. The face of his daughter occurred to him, when she was twenty-two and not married a year. He asked that he be guided to act rightly on this day. Warm color touched his lids. His mind seemed a point within an infinitely thick blanket.

Steadied, he dared open his eyes. The grass had peculiarly darkened, growing waxier, in anticipation of the rain. The cigar had died beneath the conical ash. A sense of being menaced made him look up. Gregg approached rapidly, limping as he sometimes did though his legs were sound, out of sarcastic anger or excess of energy.

"Where the hell did Lucas get to?" he asked. "Conner must have made the bastard Garbage Supervisor and we'll be lucky if he ever tips his f.ing hat to us."

Hook was pleased to have an answer. "Well: ask Conner. There he stands."

Gregg, nearsighted in the way of small people, had difficulty making out the plump figure of their prefect, where he stood at a distance, by the porch steps.

THE REVERBERATION of descending all those stairs still sounded in Conner's legs, making them feel disproportionately big. From the window, he had watched Hook perform his rounds among the old people, tried to return to work, been wounded again by the complaining contents of the letter, and had let the humid importunate atmosphere Buddy was giving off get on his nerves. The air on his desk cooled; the slats of sunshine dimmed and disappeared. Returning to the window, he observed, through the blinds, a few flimsy clouds, perfectly white, strung like wash on the vapor trail of an airplane too high to see or hear. So near the ionosphere, so far from his fellow-modern watching below, was the aviator that relative to that breadth of blue his progress was imperceptible; yet the length of his trial, intact through half the firmament, bore witness to the titanic speed he was making, alone, in that airless cold.

A few clouds dropping their shadows shouldn't matter. Certainly the immense bowl above could not be filled. But Conner pictured the fair occurring in unblemished weather, like the weather on a woodcut. The weather of this one day would be, he felt, a judgment on his work; these people, having yielded all authority, looked beyond themselves for everything—sufficient food, adequate shelter, and fair weather on their one day of profit and celebration. He would be blamed, and strangely felt prepared to accept the blame, for foul skies.

He should be with them, his people. By default Hook was capturing the domain. Conner's jealousy deepened. And the aura of holiday, the general dislocation of duties, infected him, and he began the flights of stairs, but not so suddenly Buddy did not communicate, through the simple pink oval of his face caught in the corner of Conner's eye as he seized the doorknob, amazement.

Once out in the open he wondered how he could help, then realized it was not in his position to help. The emotion that had led him down had been proprietorial and aristocratic; one of the ancient men he included had spoken a word and he had followed and been abandoned on the steps, in the sunshine. He was in command only figuratively. In the long era of Mendelssohn's indifference the old people had worked out the business of the fair so they needed little interference. On the third Wednesday of August, such and such was done, regardless of who reigned in the cupola.

Conner stood by two men screwing, with painful slowness, colored bulbs into sockets strung on long cords. They were maneuvering this chore in the dead center of the main walk. Surely they needed at least advice or one of the nimbler men—Gregg, for instance, who had been, come to think of it, an electrician in Newark—to mount the shaky ladder lying on the lawn, stained by dew, when the time came to string the lights on the posts. He asked aloud how they proposed to get them up. The two went on fumbling without replying.

Conner proceeded down the walk, to where the tables began across the grass. He observed that the tables were poorly aligned, and suggested that a few be shifted slightly. Neither fastidious nor silly, he himself helped, physically, move the tables. He wondered what kind of impression this made and did not see how it could be other than good. His intentions were wholly good. Refreshed, he stood a moment by the stand of Tommy Franklin, who filed peachstones into small baskets and simple animals. Tommy himself was away; his handiwork littered the table casually, strewn on the silver boards like brown pebbles taken from a creek-bottom by the handful.

He was conscious of Hook and Gregg at the end of the alley, conferring by the wall. Under their gaze he turned to Mrs. Mortis; she was sitting in a chair and looked unsteady with her absurd towering bonnet. He asked her how she was feeling.

"No better than an old woman should."

"An old woman should feel fine," he offered, smiling: she seemed more accessible than many of the others. "Especially one who can display these lovely quilts."

"They aren't the best I've done; it's hard to get figured rags; so much of this new cloth is plain. It's all made for the young, you know; they want the simple dresses to show off their figures."

Some of the patches she had used seemed so fragile and dry he feared the sun beating from above might shred them. She herself seemed that way; the wire hoop giving her bonnet shape was wearing through; the exterior had faded while on the inner side the pattern was preserved clearly. "Wouldn't you prefer a table underneath the trees? You're in a rather exposed position here."

"Well, if I weren't exposed who'd see me?"

"I meant simply up by the walk, in the shade."

"I'm usually situated here."

"If you prefer it . . . though of course there's no difference. I only thought you looked a little pale."

"What do you expect at my age? You expect too much from us old people, Mr. Conner."

His cheek smarted, but he had never found the reply to blunt injustice. "I do?"

"You expect us to give up the old ways, and make this place a little copy of the world outside, the way it's going. I don't say you don't mean well, but it won't do. We're too old and too mean; we're too tired. Now if you say to me, you must move your belongings over beneath the tree, I'll do it, because I have no delusions as to whose mercy we're dependent on." The goiter, from which he had kept his eyes averted, swayed disturbingly: inanimate but still living flesh.

"That's just the way I want no one to feel. I'm an agent of the National Internal Welfare Department and own nothing here. If it is anyone's property it is yours. Yours and the American people's."

"The American people, who are they? You talk like Bryan; Hookie's always talking him up to me."

"There is no reason," Conner said, with a sensation of repetition that made him stammer, "unless you want to, why you should stand under the sun for ten hours."

"This isn't an all-day sun."

"Whether it is or not, let me and one of the men move your table and chair underneath the trees." A shadow with the cooling quality of treeshade fell over them. He looked up while she studied him; the cloud obscuring the sun had a leaden center. In great vague arcs a haze was forming in the sky. Near the eclipsed sun a cirrus cloud like a twisted handkerchief was dyed chartreuse; the phenomenon seemed little less eerie for being explicable, as iridescence.

"The chair's not mine; I borrowed it for a second, until the giddiness passed."

He pressed, "It will take just a minute."

She smiled absently, then said, girlishly direct and flirting her head, "If you think up there in the shade I'll take off my bonnet because I make this place look like a fool, I won't because when they come from in town they expect to find fools out here. Anyway I'm half bald."

Vividly, comically conscious of his own thick hair, from the black roots of which the heat of a blush poured down over his face, Conner said, "You're nothing like a fool." In these words he committed his worst error with her. He felt in the air between them her patience with him snap. Previously she had been trying him, tentatively, testing him against her memory of Mendelssohn. The game lost, he spoke more in his own voice. Haughtiness showed. "You have free will. I'm not trying to steal your bonnet from you, or your usual place; I had only your welfare in mind. But we'll let things as they are."

He continued down the alley of tables, obscurely obliged to speak to Hook. It was Hook, after all, who had compelled him to venture down into this unsafe area hours before he was needed. Self-denying by doctrine, he walked against the slope of his desire, which was for retreat into the buildings and up the narrow solacing stairs to his office.

Yet the spot where Hook and Gregg had been standing was vacant, or seemed so until with a shock he saw the cat. A caramel tom, it held one useless foreleg crooked before its chest, and its face was mashed and infected. An eye was either gone or swollen shut. Three brown snaggle-teeth hung slantwise beneath a rigidly lifted lip.

It looked like the work of an automobile. Another cat could not have produced that crushed effect. The modern cars, run by almost pure automation, became accustomed to the superhighways and sped even on decayed lanes like the one curving past the poorhouse. Conner wondered that the animal had lived. To judge from the advance of the infection the accident had occurred days ago. A disease seemed mingled with the wounds.

It was uncanny, considering the smallness and inhumanity of the face, that there should be distinctly conveyed to Conner, through the hair and wounds, an impression of a request, polite, for mercy.

Though he didn't move, the cat abruptly danced past him, bobbing like a cheap toy, keeping to the long grass near the wall. Conner wondered how he had gotten within the wall.

HOOK'S BLOOD felt thick and dark with this hurrying and confusion. His eyesight seemed further impaired; he saw nothing, in the sense of focus, but received an impression of green as his eyes by habit searched the ground before his feet for obstacles. Gregg beside him was a malevolent busy force in whose power he had unaccountably been placed. Hook felt incapable of leaving the smaller man's orbit. It was better to remain with Gregg than to stay behind and risk association with the cat. Gregg had seen it wandering in the field beyond the wall and like a boy of twelve had scrambled over the wall and captured it. Hook wouldn't have thought he could have captured it, but the creature offered no resistance, merely limped a few yards and then waited. Gregg cradled it in his arms and dropped it over the wall, near Hook's feet; Hook saw that the animal was hopelessly out of order. What did Gregg want it for? To torment, no doubt. He recalled how some of his students, in the days of the smaller school, had beaten a flying squirrel with hockey sticks during recess. Breaking up the screaming ring he had found as its center a gray pelt wildly pulsing with the parasitic life that refused to loosen its grip, and had had to dispatch it himself, weeping and trembling, with a hatchet brought up from the basement, while the pupils were within with their books. As he imagined it there had been a storm brooding that day; children invariably became unruly under the approach of wet weather.

They were hurrying because Gregg, on fire with his idea, was going to the kitchen to beg scraps for his new pet. Hook, bewildered by the sudden introduction of the animal into his morning study, had gone with him a distance, but at the corner of the big house, he realized it would not do to accompany him further. "You proceed," he said, "I want noth-ing to do with such monkey business."

"Okay, Hookie," the little man said, rudely using a nick-name Hook had overheard before but always chose to forget, "You stay here and keep an eye on the tiger. Don't let the cops see it before I give the word."

Fanciful talk. Gregg imagining that a lame cat on these acres would be observed. Superimposing his memory of diffi-cult students on Gregg, he perceived the true motive for his act: it was a disturbance of accustomed order. In abruptly vaulting the wall and dropping at Hook's feet this live respon-sibility he was making a sardonic comment on the elder man's brittle ways, which could not comfortably deviate a hair from worn paths. Hook smiled to himself. It was different now; teaching school, he had been bound to the students, but here there was no law forcing him and Gregg into association. It did not occur to him that, though Gregg in part may have been teasing his stately old friend, it was Conner's authority the cat's presence flaunted.

Obediently—in a life as empty of material purpose as Hook's, there was little substance to resist any command— he fixed his gaze on the spot far down the wall, where they had been standing. Though his sight possibly deceived him, there was no cat there. He was principally pleased. At his age it was not difficult to believe he had imagined the entire inci-dent, and the cat in his misery was phantasmal. To strengthen his case against Gregg's certain reproval, he scanned all the distant terrain this side of the wall, looking especially under the tables and around the feet of the women. Nothing but trod lawn. The sky in the southeastern quarter was unmistak-ably darkening now; the thunderheads had moved up into the sky, grounded no longer on the horizon but jutting from the dense atmosphere like blooms trailing their roots in murky water.

In fact at the moment he first looked the cat was within yards of his feet, and while he inspected the distance the cat had passed his ankles and gone and hidden among the sheds in the back of the house. Hook, blind in all directions but the forward one, was vulnerable to approach from below. He was amazed when a voice by his side spoke.

"Good morning, Mr. Hook."

"Eh? Ah, Mr. Conner; pardon my not responding. I would make a better lamp-post than a spy."

"Are you admiring the view?" Conner was a head shorter than he, with a smooth face that had little harm in it, discounting the sureness and appetite of the young. His eyes were a remarkably light brown.

"Why, yes. It seems overcast."

"I'm hoping that the clouds will be blown around to the west."

A corner of Hook's mouth dimpled at the folly of such hope. The rain was upon them now, in his mind. "The rain would be a great dis-service to the preparations," he admitted.

"WNAM predicted fair and cooler at six this morning."

"These forecasters, now,"—Hook waggled a surprisingly shapely finger upwards—"they can't quite pull a science out of the air."

Conner laughed, encouraged to be striking sparks of life from this gray monument, which had held so abnormally still as he had approached it. Then he insisted, a bit priggishly, "Everything, potentially, is a science, is it not? But it takes many years."

"More years than I likely can wait."

Conner good-naturedly held his peace. It seemed a draw. Over by an open window of the west wing a nurse laughed. The tops of the walnut trees were beginning to switch. Hook coughed. "In my boyhood, now, the almanacs would predict the entire weather for the year, day by day. Now they think it bold to venture to say what will come within the next hour. The reports in the paper seem concerned more and more with *yesterday's* weather."

"Perhaps the weather is more variable than it used to be."

"Yes well: the bombs."

Conner nodded quiescently. He was sleepy; he rose at six,

after perhaps five hours sleep—he never knew precisely, the near boundary of insomnia was vague. He hated beds; they were damp and possessive, and when he lay down, words, divorced from their objects, floated back and forth, like phosphorescent invertebrates swaying in the wash of the sea. Day came as a reprieve. This had begun recently with Conner, in the last few years. In his sleepless state, then, he was susceptible to the contagion of his companion's pacific mood.

The figures on the front lawn, at some distance, moved in soothing patterns, silently bumping and pausing. Legs made x's when two passed each other. The activity was as ill-planned as that of an ant colony, but for the moment it did not exasperate Conner to watch. In the frame of mind of an old man idling beneath a tree, he was grateful for slow spectacles. Hook relit his cigar, now short. His eyes crossed in a look of savagery behind their magnifying lenses, and the gasps of his sucking lips assumed, in the enveloping hush, high importance. Moisture walked out from his mouth along the skin of the cigar; the nipple burned; smoke writhed across Hook's face and was borne upward.

Standing so close, and, due to Hook's eyesight, unobserved, Conner could examine the old man's face as intimately as a masterpiece in a museum: the handsome straight nose; the long narrow nostrils suggesting dignity more than vigor; the dark, disapproving, somewhat womanish gash of the mouth; and the antique skin mottled tan and white and touched with rose at the crests of the cheeks, stretched loosely over bones worn by age to a feminine delicacy. It was not the same person—compact, jaunty, busy, menacing—Conner had watched from afar, from above.

"Mr. Hook, have you seen a cat on the grounds?"

Hook's head moved not at all. In time he pronounced, "A cat with the one eye missing."

"Missing or shut. That's the one. It looked as though a car had struck him."

"Ah, isn't it a judgment, though, the way these highways are extermi-nating the wildlife? By the time you are as old as I am—not that I would wish such a fate on any-body—the sight of a rabbit or squirrel will be as rare a treat as the glimpse of a passenger pigeon in my boyhood."

"How did the cat get within the wall?" Hook gave no evidence of hearing. "By rights, it shouldn't be alive at all. Pathetic-looking thing."

"They cling to life extra-ordinarily. My father had a female, Becky, whose hind legs were removed by the mower, yet she lingered another six months and furthermore bore a litter of kittens. But indeed I don't believe her suffering was worth it."

"That's my feeling."

Gregg, unnoticed, had come back from the kitchen with meat scraps wrapped in orange paper. Quick to see Conner, he hid the parcel behind a post of the porch and joined them, overhearing that they were talking of the cat. He had to brave it: "What's this about my cat?"

"Why yours?" Conner asked.

Then Hook hadn't told who had brought it within the wall.

Hook said serenely, "The animal has made a get-away."

"Have you seen it, Mr. Conner?" Gregg asked politely, and continued, less politely, "I guess the damn thing was coming to the fair."

"Yes, I saw it by the wall, and it ran past me. Someone, I think, should put it out of its misery."

"Or else put a tag around its neck," said Gregg, alluding too subtly to the nameplates on the porch chairs.

"What?" Conner had difficulty understanding the excited enunciation of this man.

"Probably it'll be the only goddam thing to come to the fair today, with the storm," Gregg went on, nearly crazy with his own boldness in the face of the fact of Conner's being right there. "If I could catch it," he cried, "I'd wring its f.ing neck."

"If a group of children were to find the animal," Hook spoke out of his memories, "they would make uncommon sport of him."

The idea sickened Conner, children soaking the dying animal with kerosene. He lacked most men's tolerance for cruelty, their ability to blur and forget rumors of it. He wondered if Gregg were ugly enough to make good his insane threat. Perhaps he was; a net of dark wrinkles had been thrown across his face, and his features seemed bright things caught in his net. Conner asked him, "Why would you harm the animal?"

Gregg was taken aback. In tides as variable as those of astrological influence, sense and caution flowed in and out of him; comparatively lucid, he realized he was facing the tyrant of the place and had been saying whatever came first to his tongue. Now Conner had taken him up, ready with a trap. "Why because," he answered, inspired, "it spreads disease."

Conner blinked; this was true.

"Among chickens," Hook interceded, "I've seen the fever brought into the pen by a fox spread so there weren't a half dozen standing by morning."

"Yes, and to humans too," Gregg went on, cleverly sensing he had found a sore spot of Conner's. "Don't they carry typhoid? If Alice sees it, sure as s. she'll let the stinking thing play around in the kitchen." His eyes glinted, and he did a dance step, unable to keep his feet from jubilating.

The cat had not gone far, once it felt unpursued. While the men talked, it returned, having smelled the parcel Gregg had laid behind the porch pillar. Alice had not tied the parcel, so it had unfolded of itself. The scraps—pork, minced—smelled neutrally to the cat; he recognized them as life-stuff, unconnected with pleasure. Dutifully he nosed the chunks, searching for lean; his bowed grave head half-lost in the collar of upstanding orange paper.

"Look there," Gregg cried softly.

As the three men watched, the tomcat, jiggling his head, got the smallest piece between his teeth, on the side where they were not smashed. But the arc his jaw could make was too small for chewing, and the piece dropped back among the others. The thin yellow tail swished twice. For a moment he licked a hump of gray fat, then lost interest wholly, looked up, saw the men, bolted off the porch, and hobbled around the house into the shade.

"Who put the meat there?" Conner asked.

"I brought a little up from the kitchen," Gregg admitted, thinking that now he was in for it.

Conner realized how badly he had misjudged the man; the culpability of the distrust he bore these powerless old people, whom complete material deprivation had not deprived of the capacity for such acts of kindness, was borne upon him. He wished there were some feasible way of abasing himself before Gregg, and he tried to compress all the affection and humility he felt into the gentle-spoken, "I'm afraid it's beyond help."

Relieved to hear in the tone that he would not be punished for trespassing into the kitchen, Gregg did not comprehend the point of Conner's words.

BUDDY, feeling jilted—especially so when, less than an hour after Conner left, sunlight drained it seemed forever from the windows of the cupola—became unable to bear his solitude, and started downstairs, in Conner's cold tracks. The twin had an unspoken terror of being alone, terror so keen that, abandoned, he unwillingly animated dead things—the green steel cabinets, the buried piano, the upright objects on Conner's desk top. These summoned presences intimidated him; he expected at every moment the window to smack its lips and the water cooler to gurgle uproariously. The stairs themselves had a dreadful capacity of closing, the walls meeting the instant before he gained the broad landing. The bannister uprights and their shadows rapidly crisscrossed in a secret conversation that grew shriller as the speed of his descent increased. He broke into the open air of the porch flushed, under the eyes of several inmates, with the pink blank beauty of a Greek sculptor's boy.

Happily Conner was looking for *him*. His superior was walking down the porch, beside the receding bright-tagged chairs. "Buddy. Good. Are you busy?"

"I came down . . . the soft drink truck might arrive. He came last year before noon."

"There's a diseased cat on the grounds. The thing's in pain and should be killed."

"You're sure?"

"That's a curious question; I'm fairly sure of what I see, yes." He glanced up nervously at the blackened half of the sky. "I'm going back up until noon."

To Buddy it seemed that today Conner was always escaping him. It was the work of the fair; the decrepits had everything their way today. He protested aloud, "What do these people want a holiday for, every day is a holiday for them?"

Conner didn't answer him, except by describing where last he had seen the animal, and the direction in which it had run.

BLOND and teenage, Ted, the driver of the soft drink truck, hummed a Spanish tune in duet with the radio:

> "Eres niño y has amor,
> qué farás cuando mayor?"

It was mostly what you got on the radio now. Ted even got a little tired of all this Latin stuff. Every other movie star was a Cuban or mestizo or something, as if you had to be brown to look like anything. Some guys he knew wore "torero" pigtails standing up from the back of their heads and sprayed their hair with perfumed shellac. Ted'd be damned if he'd do this. They could call him a Puritan all they wanted.

Turning into the curved road, the asphalt of the edges crumbling into grass, Ted had a creepy sensation of heading into death's realm. The county itself was out in nowhere—farm stuff. A poorhouse in the middle of it was twice as bad.

From a Spanish movie Ted had seen he remembered a scene showing skeletons trying to get a young man and turn him into one of them. Ted wanted to get out of this territory fast. He had another delivery before lunch, twenty miles away, not far from his home and near a luncheonette where the girls from high school, including his, gathered to eat pizza and BarBQs. He had fixed his delivery schedule so he could be there when she was; having juggled the list made him nervous. He wasn't sure there was time enough if this took long. He wasn't even sure he could find the damn place. In the movie the idea was that after you die you're not really dead until a year or so and a scientist right before he died took a drug so he would be able to walk around. Then this colony of dead people he founded had to get the body of a young man or woman every eleven days and until they needed to eat them kept them in a cave. This young guy and girl were in there together and they fell in love. These two lying chained in the cave brought Ted to thinking of his girl, Rita, and of Rita's belly, which she had shown him the night before last. She belonged to some girls' secret club in Newark called the Nuns where they took vows not to let men touch them. But if they wanted they could let men *see* sections. She had often undone her blouse before, but the night before last was the first time she had lifted her skirt and slid her silver pants down and lay there on the back seat of the car while he kneeled beside her, his hands folded in obedience at his chest. Her eyes and mouth, three shadows in a ghostly face, looked up at him kind of sadly while below, even paler and more luminous, the great naked oval between her waist and the middle of her thighs held in its center one black shadow. Remembering seeing it, the true thing, chased away all the skeletons of that lousy movie.

Finding the place turned out to be easy. He drove under some trees and the land opened up and there it was on the left: a hell of a big yellow house back from a wall. Old people were crawling around like bugs on the lawn. To give them something to talk about he speeded, squeezing the brakes on just at the entrance, so all the cases piled high behind him clattered in gallant style. The radio sang

> "Será tan bivo su fuego,
>   que con importuno ruego,
>   por salvar el mundo ciego—"

He switched off the ignition and with it the radio. "Hey. Amigos. Where does this stuff go?" He caught a look at himself in the side mirror. A brownpaper cigarillo hung from his lips and his crushed cap was tilted steeply over his forehead. When he set his forearm on the sill his bracelet scratched on the steel.

"Where's Buddy?" one of the women asked nobody in particular. She had a thing growing around her neck as big as a bag of groceries: God. Ted hadn't known there was a garbage dump like this left in all of New Jersey. He even felt sorry for them, living to be so old. He hoped somebody shot him when he got to be thirty.

"Some-one re-sponsible had better fetch him," a tall gent said, not moving himself.

"Aah," a small crusty-looking one said, "what's the f.ing use? Buddy doesn't know his head from his a.h. Why do they order this p. anyway? Who in hell drinks it?" This one had a tongue in his head at least.

"Other years it goes under the trees," a woman said.

Ted asked, "What trees, señora?"

The dirty-faced man broke in furiously, "The trees down there in the meadow, forty miles away. What the hell do you think, what trees? The trees there; Jesus what the hell is your company hiring dumb kids for?"

Ted's heart raced angrily. Though his girl and the distance he had to go to her pressed on his brain, he took his sweet time inhaling sour smoke and stared the dirt-face down. He saw himself at this moment as an elegant snake. "Si," he said at last, as if in the silence he had wrung a confession from his prey. His smile, he felt, was beautiful in its serenity. "And how do I get up there, old man? Fly?"

"Fly if you can; you look the type. If they can't hire anybody except little pansies why doesn't Pepsi-Cola give up? Want me to back it up for you? Fly!—did you hear him?" The other old people made no motion to control this nut; they acted like he was their spokesman.

Ted swung down from the cab. "Look dad," he said, "you're very good, but I don't have all day. A woman's waiting for me in Newark."

"You're from Newark? I know Newark. You ever live near Canby Street?"

"No," Ted said, and blushed lightly; the quick fawning overture had made him feel, in front of these people, big and vulnerable to ridicule and slow.

"Did you ever get a drink in a place called the Ten Spot, on John Street where the old trolley tracks used to curve? Lenny Caragannis used to run it."

"I don't remember. . . ."

"Before your time? Or are you lily-pure?"

To Ted it seemed that with this sudden searching turn the man had penetrated through his presence backwards into the chambers of his life, and the few treasures there—his mother's profile, the tolerant face of the brick wall across the alleyway from his bedroom window, Rita's skin glowing white around the cushion of tense hair—were exposed in their poverty.

Dirt-face drew very close. "Whyncha take me back with you? You're a tough kid. You're no company man, are you? You're not in love with the company. Let's go back together. Listen. This is a hell-hole of a dump. You know what they do? They put tags around your ears like pigs. Hook, the kid's going to take me back."

"He'll be sorely repri-manded if it is discovered," the tall one said.

"Come on," Ted pleaded, blushing more deeply, "how do I get this junk in?" He was addressing the others over Dirt-face's head.

"Back it up through the gate," the nut insisted, dancing and brushing against Ted's shirt, "right into the porch, and then we'll be off. You and me, kid. Bang. Bang."

"Is it wide enough?" Ted asked the tall man, who looked as though he had some authority.

"Last year they backed it through," a woman said. More old women and men were slowly gathering from everywhere.

"Now don't start to cry," the small man with the dirty-looking face said. "Why the f. does your company hire kids that can't drive even a kiddy-car? Can you only drive forward? Ram it into reverse."

Ted stepped away from him, plucked the tan butt from his mouth, let it drop at his feet, ground it into the gravel, and said effectively, "O.K."

"Slam her through, dump the p., and I'll get in the seat beside you and crouch down. Then step on it. Don't look back. Do you have a gun, kid?"

THE ONLY GUN within a mile was in fact in Buddy's hands. A .22 purchased by a gardener many years before, when foxes and groundhogs could still be seen in the countryside, the gun was kept, with a few cartridges, on a shelf of a locked closet on the second floor.

The wand of the barrel drifted pleasantly at Buddy's side as he passed between buildings and trees the many colors of which were all, under the stress of the lowering clouds, tending toward the tint of the metal. The color of the barrel seemed the base color of all things. With the lethal weapon balanced on the hooked fingers of one hand Buddy became the center of the universe. In Conner's entrusting him with this task he saw proof of the man's affection, not dreaming how much Conner would have hated to do it himself.

He stalked beneath the windows of the west wing, tall windows designed for a ballroom. He scanned stumps, overturned boxes, corded wood, and half-collapsed sheds leaning sideways, with rhomboidal doors. The thrillers he used to read for recreation began to infest his head. His stealth became exaggerated. At a corner—there was something dramatic and treacherous about a wall changing direction—he paused, fingering the bolt and testing the clip, that it was secure. The springs of the mechanism had grown stiff with rust. The clip probably wouldn't feed the next bullet into the bolt, if he missed with one shot. Buddy stepped around the corner, and there was the cat, not twenty feet away, in the center of an open area strewn with chopping chips. It astonished him how close things looked in this foreboding atmosphere. The cat's face—he could see every whisker and wet streak on it—loomed like a china plate in a shooting gallery.

Holding one leg off the earth, the cat, while staring at Buddy, didn't act as if it noticed him. Just as Buddy had the broad forehead steadied in his sights the animal looked casually away, giving him a piece of neck.

"Meow," Buddy crooned, "mm-row-w-w."

The cat looked. Its working eye was a perfect circle, rimmed opal. Suddenly suspicion dawned in the cat; not a strand of fur moved, but a cold clarity, as if from without, stiffened the forms in the vicinity of the rifle sight; the flat nose and clumsy asymmetric cheeks crystallized in the air of Buddy's vision. With a sensation of prolonged growing sweetness Buddy squeezed the trigger. The report disappointed him, a mere slap, it seemed in his ears, and very local.

If his target had been a bottle, liquid wouldn't have spilled more quickly from it than life from the cat. The animal dropped without a shudder. Buddy snapped back the bolt; the dainty gold cartridge spun away, and the gun exhaled a faint acrid perfume. Buddy thought, *If he had made the river, the secret would be in enemy hands.* Going up to the slack body he insolently toed it over, annoyed not to see a bullet-hole in the skull. Chips of wood adhered to the pale fluff of the long belly. The bullet had entered the chin and passed through to the heart. Buddy couldn't imagine how he had missed by so much. Defective weapons, sabotage.

THE SOUND so small to Buddy echoed around the grounds, its loudness varying from place to place, causing curiosity where it was heard. Ted, who had backed around and aimed his truck the best he could toward the narrow gap in the east wall, wondered about it but didn't ask any of the old people for an explanation. The less he had to do with them, the better. The crowd they made menaced him. A few were outside the wall, near his front tires; the rest had bunched inside, leaving a lane between them for his truck. As soon as he had started up the motor they had fallen into position respectfully, as if what they were about to see was a great feat, a modern miracle. Dirt-face hovered near the cab, whisking back and forth with the maneuvers of the truck, flirting with the giant wheels that could crush him.

The gunshot suggested to Ted that he should hurry. The pack of Mexican cigarettes squaring out his shirt pocket and the graceful look of his own hand on the wheel were reassuring reminders of the world waiting for him. His truck was still at a slight angle to the opening, but if he went forward in first once more they would get the idea he couldn't drive at all. On the left side he had enough room: six inches. On the other side there was a thin mirror, but the sleek shape of these new GM trucks left a percentage of guesswork in estimating clearance. Ted had found, in driving, though, that you always had a little more room than you thought you did. "Plenty of room," Dirt-face said, "what's the matter? Foot freeze? Shall I climb the f. in there and do it for you?"

Ted pushed the reverse switch and delicately pressed the accelerator. "Straighten the wheels, kid. Straighten up and you're in." Ted had learned on an old hand-shift truck; automatic transmissions had the one defect of maintaining a certain minimum speed or stalling. It would make him a fool to stall in front of this mob. "More," Dirt-face called, "more." Halfway through, a faint rumbling developed on the right side, where Ted couldn't see. Just grazing. Ted corrected the direction of the front wheels, while the murmuring motor maintained a creeping backwards direction. The scraping sound intensified, but a foot or two further and the body of the truck would be safely through. With a perceptible pang of release the body eased through, and a rock clattered on the running board of the cab.

As those watching on the right side could see, the slow pressure of the metal wall had caused cracks to race through the old brown mortar, mostly water and sand, and a coherent wedge-shaped section, perhaps eight feet long, collapsed, spilling stones over the grass. "Jesus Christ, kid," Gregg screamed, "you better give up. You're nuts!" The destruction was principally on the inner side. For the wall, so thick and substantial, was really two shells: what surprised the people standing in silence was that the old masons had filled the center with uncemented rubble, slivers of rock and smooth fieldstones that now tumbled out resistlessly.

THE TRUCK had pulled up while Conner was climbing the stairs; the subsequent quick clatter and soft rumble of the collapse did not reach the cupola. Buddy's rifle shot had sounded in here like a twig snapping. Conner had no regrets about ordering the animal killed. He wanted things *clean;* the world needed renewal, and this was a time of history when there were no cleansing wars or sweeping purges, when reform was slow, and decayed things were allowed to stand and rot themselves away. It was a vegetable world. Its theory was organic: perhaps old institutions in their dying could make fertile the chemical earth. So the gunshot ringing out, though a discord, pleased the rebel in Conner, the idealist, anxious to make space for the crystalline erections that in his heart he felt certain would arise, once his old people were gone. For the individual cat itself he felt nothing but sorrow.

Given his post, he had accepted it. Irishly, he had hoped for something dramatic, but the administration of order had few dramatic departments. The modern world afforded few opportunities for zeal anywhere. In the beginning there had been Mendelssohn's mess to set right: the west wing was con-

verted into a decent hospital; Dr. Angelo was begged from
Health and Medicine; there had been painting and building
and bustle the first summer, and into the winter. But over two
years had passed; this was his third fair. Many of those who
had greeted him here (how assiduously he had attempted to
learn the names of that first batch!) were gone now, but the
population of the place had grown and was growing. There
were rational causes: lengthened lives, smaller domiciles, the
break-up, with traditional religion, of the family. The pam-
phlets and pronunciamentos he daily received in the mail,
from official, semi-official, and unofficial bureaus, made it
clear and reasonable. Swelling poorhouses had a necessary
place in the grand process of Settling—an increasingly common term that covered the international stalemate, the general economic equality, the population shifts to the "vacuum
states," and the well-publicized physical theory of entropia,
the tendency of the universe toward eventual homogeneity,
each fleck of energy settled in seventy cubic miles of otherwise vacant space. This end was inevitable, no new cause for
heterogeneity being, without supernaturalism, conceivable.

Despite these assurances, however, the limits of being a
poorhouse prefect chafed a man dedicated to a dynamic
vision: that of Man living healthy and unafraid beneath blank
skies, "integrated," as the accepted phrase had it, "with his
fulfilled possibilities." Conner was bored. He yearned for
some chance to be proven; he envied the first rationalists their
martyrdoms and the first reformers their dragons of reaction
and selfishness. Two years remained before automatic pro-
motion. The chief trouble with the job was the idleness; not
merely that there was so little to do, and that he had to make
work, concocting schemes like tagging chairs, but that idleness became his way of life. He was infected with the repose
that was only suitable to inmates waiting out their days.

The very way, for instance, he had rather enjoyed the balm
of standing by Hook's side for those moments this morning.
Or the way he stood by this window content to gaze at nothing, or what amounted to nothing—the red-tin roof of the

west wing, the sheds and pig buildings below, segments of west wall showing in the intervals between trees, and the little gate to Andrews, unlocked today for the fair. Someone was passing through, tacking from wall to bush: Lucas. He was sure it was Lucas, even from this distance. He was carrying something in a small paper bag, too big for candy, too small for food. While Conner was trying to make it out Lucas passed from sight beneath the guttered edge of the red roof.

On the glossy varnish of the window sill the canted pane of glass installed to minimize drafts laid a peculiar patina, a hard pale color neither brown nor blue.

Conner had chosen to stand by the west window because the spectacle of preparation on the east lawn scratched his eyes; he didn't wish to be made to feel that he should go down and play shepherd. Buddy was with them; little could go wrong. It was futile anyway; the coming rain cancelled everything. The western sector of the sky was as yet unclouded. Between the tops of the trees and the upper edge of his window oblivious blue held the firmament. Then a cumbersome tumble and crash resounded, and Conner witnessed an appearance of the phenomenon which two millenia before had convinced the poet Horace that gods do exist: thunder from a clear sky.

DOWN FRONT Buddy was arranging with Ted that Pepsi-Cola would pay for repairing the wall—there was no cause for tears. Everybody had insurance. As he could see, the wall was rotten anyway. Buddy, dropping the shovel with which he had not yet begun to dig, had rushed to the accident and found its perpetrator oddly child-like. In a voice husky with apprehension the boy insisted that it had not been his fault and that he had to get to Newark in a matter of minutes or lose his job. The driver was rather handsome, in the rococo lower-class style, and Buddy instantly began to mother his innocence. The two young men were about the same height and complexion. An old man coming late to the confusion imagined at a distance that here was Buddy's twin, visiting.

Buddy in fact was more highly colored, five years older, and educated. Consciously superior but distinctly tender—still elated with his outwitting the cat—Buddy helped the driver guide his truck backwards along the walk. Then the two rapidly unloaded the consignment of soft drink, rapidly because a few drops were falling, speckling the turquoise tailgate. At the thunderclap the old people scattered, gathering quilts and preserves and crude toys and canes and pieces of patient embroidery. As they hastened toward the porch, under strings of colored bulbs now swung in the air, the fourth noise of the half-hour summoned them, encouraging their flight, the ringing of the lunch signal, a tall hammered triangle used in the days of the Andrews estate to bring in the hands from the fields.

II

THEY ATE in groups of four at small square tables of synthetic white marble purchased cheaply from a cafeteria that was discarding them. The rain falling across the high windows, high from the floor, had the effect of sealing in light and noise, so the tabletops shone garishly and the voices of the old people shrilly mixed with the clash of china and steel. Mrs. Lucas was saying of her parakeet, calling really, though her companions at the table were only noses away, "Poor thing has to have some exercise, you can't ask it to sit there like a stuffed ornament, in my daughter's house it had great freedom. It can't have that freedom here, but it has to have some; its cage is too small for it, poor bird, its tail feathers stick out and it can't turn around. In my daughter's house the cat caught it and took off its tail feathers—that's the final result of all the freedom they gave it—and when they grew in, nobody thought they would, they grew too long, so the feathers stick between the bars and it can't even turn around. It can't have the freedom here it had in my daughter's house, but that's too much, not being able even to turn around. So out

of simple mercy I let it out at least once in the day, in the fore-
noon usually. Oh she's cunning. I think it's a she, because the
coloring is dull, and a male, you know, has all this brilliant
plumage. I keep thinking I could clip the tail feathers with the
sewing scissors but they say no, it's like taking a foot or hand
off a human being, they lose their balance and don't feed and
grow listless. So when I come back from baking the buns—
and wasn't that futile, now that the fair's washed out?—I let
her out to do her tricks on the window catch and the picture
frames. She even swings on the geraniums, doing her little
acrobatic tricks. Oh, she's clever. If you let her out when the
faucet's running she'll try to fly through it like a waterfall.
Who was I to know *he'd*"—she snapped her head toward her
husband, who munched slowly, because each unmeditated
bite accented the soreness in his ear—"barge in right when
she was on the knob with a bottle of nasty stuff in a paper bag
and let the pretty little thing flutter out the door into the
hall?"

"It won't go far," Lucas said.

"And then he won't even chase it. How can I chase it, with
my legs?"

"We left our door open," he explained. "When it's got out
before it's always come back. If you leave the door open."

"There's always the first time," she said, speaking, like him,
to the other two, who acted as the channel of their argument,
"and how do we know this isn't the time it will get caught
fast, with its toenails? You know their toenails have to be
trimmed. I didn't know that. If I had known half the trouble
the bird would be I wouldn't have let her wish it on me. Anything my daughter doesn't want—she's on the move day and
night, never in the same place more than a week it seems—
she thinks, Oh Mom up at the Home will be glad for this. She
has nothing to do. She's grateful for anything. She has nothing of her own."

"Joan doesn't think like that," Lucas explained.

"Well she didn't think twice about wishing the parakeet on
us. She bought it for her boy and the boy tired of it after a

week, as you might expect. So, ship it off to Mom, and let her spend her pitiful little money on fancy seed of all sorts and cuttlebone. Let her clean the cage once a day. Let her worry with the bird's nails. They're more than a half-circle and still growing. It gets on its perch and tries to move off and beats its wings and wonders why it can't, poor thing. I thought I could take my sewing scissors and trim its nails myself; they're fragile-looking; you can see the little thread of blood in there. But evidently you can't. They'll bleed unless you know just where to cut. My daughter sent along a magazine, on how to take care of them. They'll bleed if you don't know just where you can cut. So we have to wait until *he* takes it into his head to go into town with the cage to the dog doctor in Andrews. It costs money, too. It's not free. They have free medicine for humans but for any little bit of animal care you have to pay, and they call this progress. I said, you know, if you tell them you're from the poorhouse, but no, he wants to pretend he isn't."

The Lucases' companions at the table were homely Tommy Franklin, who made small baskets by filing peachstones, and Elizabeth Heinemann, a blind lady he sometimes guided about and always escorted at meals. Tommy, fearing that the other woman's hurried talk would tire Elizabeth, and anyway feeling a need to put his voice before her, began softly, "Your talking about scissors reminds me. . . ." He was so shy of talking the Lucases fell silent, to hear him, and he had to proceed. "Last month I took the bus to Burlington, to see my brother, and I noticed when I got on this old woman talking to the driver. I didn't think about it any and always try to mind my business because you never know. . . . Though I was looking out the window darned if she didn't sit down right aside of me. I guess she figured, another old person. . . . Well, she had been a nurse, she said. And she goes into this long story about how years ago she was called in to care for an old rabbi who had pneumonia. The house was full of nice things, she said, very expensive and well-kept. The rabbi's daughter kept the house. But underneath this beard, which went down to here, according to their religion, was where this terrible mess connected with his disease was, she said. She said the first thing she did was to go to the store and buy scissors, and a razor, and *shave* him. The daughter, she said, howled something terrible. And when the doctor came he took one look at the old fella and his eyes popped and he said he would never have dared to do that." Somehow when the woman had told it, this sentence was more of an ending. Tommy glanced at Elizabeth; her eyes were brilliantly fixed on a spot past his shoulder. She had a long neck stretched tall by her perfect posture; at this moment her wide mouth was broadened further by a sweet smile of expectation. Confused and inadequate, he went on. "I asked her, didn't he try to stop you, and she said, he was very sick. I guess he was unconscious when she did it. So I had to sit there listening to her tell this all the way to Burlington. Your mentioning scissors put me in mind of it." It had turned out wrong; when the woman had told the story, there had been a righteousness in her action and a kind of justice in the close. His way it sounded simply as if he were against the Jews, when he had no feelings toward them one way or another.

"I guess she thought," Lucas said, "it being a Jew, it made no difference." He studied his food, boiled potato white on the white china on the white table-top. Potato, meatloaf and broccoli was the meal, big because this evening, if the fair were in full swing, there would be no supper. Lucas never found his appetite until dark, and after Angelo's fooling any pressure on his left gums made it ache above. Still he appreciated that Conner tried to feed them well. His thoughts predominantly were with his morning's purchase, a pint of rye, and the relations it would assume with his pain.

His wife, who during her recital had fallen behind, was eating rapidly.

Elizabeth Heinemann said, "Isn't it pretty, the rain? You never feel alone when it rains." Her clean neck elongated to bring her closer to the drumming overhead, which in the first movement of the storm was savage, though she wished it even louder, to clarify her confused inner world of tilting purple tumuli, a pre-Creational landscape fairly windowed by her eyes, the navy blue of a new baby's.

"DIDN'T I see Buddy's twin on the lawn?" an old man at another table asked.

"Buddy has no twin," Gregg said. "That's just what they say to excuse Buddy for being a moron."

"No. In a crushed-cap-like."

What the old man—Fuller—saw dawned on Gregg, and the tension of mischief smoothed the net of wrinkles on his small face. "Driving a truck?"

"I saw the truck. I didn't see him drive it." Fuller was wary of Gregg.

"How do you think he got here? Flew? You think fairies can really fly?"

"No, in a cap with his sleeves rolled up."

"Buddy's twin. He came up from Newark to see his f.ing brother. It was very touching. Gypsies had split them in the cradle. The only trouble with the twin is he got this job driving a truck and he can't drive a foot. He knocked down a big section of the wall out front."

At this point Fuller sensed that Gregg was having him on. He looked toward Hook, who he knew would speak the truth, but Hook was saying, "It was re-markable, the way the stone fence gave. You would think, now, that the few end stones would fall away and leave the rest stand. Yet a whole tri-angular section held together, the cracks in the mortar running in a straight line. Indeed it will cost Conner a pretty penny to have it repaired; the stone masons nowadays are used to setting nothing but bricks and the cinder blocks."

"Who was the young man I saw on the lawn then?" Fuller asked.

"Buddy's twin he means," Gregg said.

"Buddy's twin? Buddy's twin is in Ari-zona." Gregg's signals to play along were quite missed by Hook, who turned considerately to Fuller, known as soft in the head, and explained, "That young man drove the Pepsi-Cola truck here, and was nothing like Buddy. Buddy is educated."

"Educated how to be a pain in everybody's a.," Gregg said.

Fuller's broad downy eyebrows twisted a bit in perplexity. "Who was it who came from Newark, then, the driver or the twin?"

"The driver *is* the twin," Gregg said.

"The twin is in Ari-zona," Hook repeated, "in the south-west, where they are doing such wonder-ful things with ir-rigation."

"And who fired the shot?" Fuller asked, his soft brain affa-bly manufacturing a third image of Buddy, this triplet holding a rifle, for he knew that around the place the only person will-ing and permitted to handle a gun was Buddy.

Neither Hook, whose attention at the moment had been fixed and who was incapable of receiving side impressions, nor Gregg, then buzzing around the motor of the backing truck, knew to what Fuller referred. "The kid, the twin," Gregg answered quickly, "he had a gun in his pocket. He was a tough kid. He tried to kidnap me."

"A gunshot?" Hook asked.

"Out back," Fuller said. "It was why I came outside, now that I remember."

"That wasn't a shot," Gregg told him, "that was just your own head cracking you heard." Ashamed of having said this, he stood up and added, "I'll get dessert." As the youngest and best co-ordinated of the three, it was fitting that he should. He brought back four plastic dishes of peach halves, and ate his and the extra one while his companions were still chop-ping theirs with spoons.

BECAUSE he had not been naturally shaped for solitude—indeed a native gregariousness had been a factor in Conner's early dedication to a social cause rather than a more vertical and selfish career, in a science or art—he felt despairing as he proceeded down the deserted stairwell and was glad to come upon Buddy, his one friend in the place. With a bang of the outer door the boy emerged into the hall, drenched. His torso beneath the soaked adhesive shirt declared its forms. The collar was recklessly open; in the V the tan hollow at the base of his throat pulsed. His face was red with exertion and his wet hair hyacinthine. "That's done," Buddy breathed, taking Conner's presence there casually. "The soft drinks are stacked under the trees by the porch. Not that we'll have anybody to drink them, except maybe Noah."

Buddy's flip acceptance of the rain, Conner's enemy, cut slightly. He asked, "Why did *you* have to handle the cases?"

"Beyond and above the call of duty," Buddy sang: parody of Conner! "The driver of the truck, a lovely youth, was so abashed by his error of smashing down our wall that he would have been incapable of completing his delivery. His impulse was to hop astride his mount and flee to Newark, where he was planning, I gathered, to deflower a local bloom."

"Smash what wall?"

"The late Mr. Andrews's. Haven't you seen? It made an audible thump."

"No I haven't. Did you get the kid's name, or were you both too excited?"

"*I* was calm as the proverbial vegetable. He was the tot. He even imagined one of the inmates—one of the smaller men—was planning to hide in his cab and make an escape. I begged him to take several, but with a tremor of his bedewed lashes he declined. Behold, his name."

Conner took the wrinkled damp piece of paper offered him, scribbled in Buddy's somewhat studied Italic hand. "What do you think he'll tell the insurance?"

"Lies, nothing but lies. He spoke pidgin Spanish in his dangerous, composed moments."

"O.K. Thanks for everything. You better change, Bedewed. What happened to the cat?"

"Cross him off your list. Our secret is safe."

"Buried?"

"Not yet. I rushed to rescue our friend Ted."

"O.K." Conner let a frown show, pettishly, since of course

there hadn't been time. Now with the rain the cat must lie uncovered. A sadness of sorts pierced him, and he asked, "About the wall. Can I see the damage from the porch?"

"Nothing easier, alas. It's no mean hole." This last was called on the fly, since the boy was running up the stairs, removing his shirt as he went.

The warm sense of shelter given by a porch whose railing is spattered with rain insufficiently offset Conner's disappointment with Buddy, his feeling that they had met at incompatible angles, and his renewed awareness that it was still the fate of his kind of man to be, save in the centers of administration, alone. The rain, falling absolutely, with an infrequent breath of wind turning a section temporarily oblique, pounded the porch rail, and a spray so fine it was more of an aroma than a mist rolled in to the wall, dampening the yellow boards, making the tops of checker tables glisten, and tinting the wicker chairs a darker vanilla. The air turned white; a fork of lightning hung above the distant orchards, shocking each spherical tree into relief. Seconds later the sound arrived. The clouds above formed a second continent, with its own horizon; a bar of old silver stretched behind the nearly tangent profiles of the farthest hills and clouds. Again lightning raced down a fault in the sky, the thunder following less tardily. On the lawn before him there was no sign of the day's celebration save the empty aligned tables and the cords of colored bulbs strung on the poles. The fumbling old men had somehow done their job.

Through veils of rain the damage was indistinct: a discolored patch of some length, and a curious pallidity, as if the wall had been stuffed with oyster shells or fragments of plaster. It did not seem to interfere with the silhouette of the wall. While it could have been worse it was bad enough. With the shortage of craftsmen weeks would pass before a mason could be got out here. In the meantime the stones that littered the lawn should be collected. On the day of the fair the poorhouse was on view; his management would be incriminated in the apparent collapse and neglect of the wall, right where everyone entering could see. All his conscientiousness was denied by that section of stone. He hated the tongues of townspeople. A sentence from the disturbing letter of the morning recurred to him: *Yr duty is to help not hinder these old people on there way to there final Reward.* Their final reward, *this* was their final reward. How much longer before people ceased to be fools? It had taken the lemur a million years to straighten his spine. Another million would it be before the brain drained its swamp? An animal skull is a hideous thing, a trough with fangs, a crude scoop. In college, he had been appalled by the conservatism zoological charts portrayed. With what time-consuming caution had the tree-shrew's snout receded and its skull ballooned! He could picture the woman who had sent him the letter, her active pink nose, her dim fearful eyes, her pointed fingers crabbedly scraping across the paper—a tree-shrew, a rat that clings to bark. When would they all die and let the human day dawn?

He wished the rain more vehemence. In the volume of space above the lawn, set like a table for a feast, the impression was not of vacancy but of fullness; the feast was attended.

WITHIN the dining-hall most had completed dessert but few left. Where had they to go? Some days they hastened to get into the open, or gather by the television, or get to their duties. But today was what weather could not change, a holiday. They remained seated at the small white tables, enjoying the corporate existence created by the common misfortune of having their fair washed away. "Now in all Mendelssohn's years," Hook stated, "I don't recall inclement weather on a fair day."

"That bastard Conner's afraid to show his face," Gregg said. "Why doesn't he come eat the garbage he gives the rest of us?"

"Can't you picture Mendelssohn now?" Amy Mortis asked at another table. "How he'd have us all singing and shouting prayers and telling us how we all must die? Ah wasn't he the man?"

"Yet we'll see him again," the woman beside her reminded.

They were seeing him now. A great many eyes had lifted from their food and were directed by common impulse toward the vacant dais where the prefect had had his table before Conner came and deemed it arrogant to eat elevated above the inmates. These eyes conjured there the figure of the darkly dressed stocky man with spindly bird legs, nodding his large head with the great nostrils in the lean nose and the eyes pink-rimmed as if on the verge of weeping, and they were again seated at the wooden tables now on the lawn, eating in long rows on cracked and various plates, and afterwards singing in unison, "She'll be coming round the mountain" and then "Onward Christian soldiers marching as to war" and then "With arms wide open He'll pardon you." As the songs grew more religious the rims of Mendelssohn's eyes grew redder, and he was dabbing at his cheeks with the huge handkerchief he always carried and was saying, in the splendid calm voice that carried to the farthest corner and to the dullest ear, how here they all lived close to death, which cast a shadow over even their gaiety, and for him to hear them sing was an experience in which joy and grief were so mixed laughter and tears battled for control of his face; here they lived with Death at their sides, the third participant in every conversation, the other guest at every meal,—and even he, yes even he—but no. Today was not the day for talk of bad health. As the Preacher saith, To every thing there is a season, and a time to every purpose under Heaven. This was the day intended for rejoicing. Though for the moment the rain had obscured the rays of the sun, in another hour these rays would break forth again in the glory of their strength and from all the points of the compass people in the prime of their lives, carrying children in their arms, would come to this famous fair.

Conner, who entered the room at the side, had in nearly three years become enough attuned to his wards to perceive in the silence and the one direction of the heads the ghost posturing on the dais; he took a tray up to the counter with his

head slightly bowed, in the manner of a man, however insolent, who arrives late at the theatre.

Conversation commenced. The live prefect displaced the
dead. Buddy, entering in a crisp shirt and with his damp hair
combed flat, blinked at the clatter; one vast bright beast
seemed contained in an acoustic cage. The old people began to
stand and leave; Buddy and Conner would be left to finish
their meal in a nearly deserted room, while the kitchen help,
youngsters and matrons from the town of Andrews, waited
sarcastically for these last dirty plates to be handed in. Many
reported to work at noon, so the kitchen smelled of raincoats.

GREGG overtook Lucas at the spot where Conner and Buddy
had met a half-hour before. An oblong of water still stained
the crimson linoleum, worn brown where people walked.
"Where the hell have you been all goddam morning?" Gregg
asked. "Conner make you his Garbage Supervisor?"

"I went in town." Lucas's lower lip, shaped like one of those
rare berries that is in fact two grafted together, protruded
defiantly. He liked Gregg less and less, Gregg who had
never known family, who had never had a woman take the
best half of the bed, who still lived in a boy's irresponsible
world.

A coward in the face of blunt hostility, Gregg modified
his tone. "What did he say about the tags?"

"He said it was for our good."

"S. he did. When that pansy gives a thought to my good
I'll be a bag of fertilizer."

"It was interesting to see how his mind works. He said
some of the women complained for their husbands who
couldn't get a chair when they came in from the fields. So he
thought he'd put these tags on and make every chair somebody in particular's."

"God, what a birdbrain story. He's even a bigger nut than
Mendelssohn with his singing hymns. Christ, we get the rock
bottom here."

"Then he made me go to the west wing, when I hadn't complained, and Angelo jabbed at my ear until I won't be surprised if I go deaf."

"I hope you do. Then sue the s. out of them. You know what I thought? I fetched a cat into the yard this morning, and what we should do is take off the tags and make a collar for the cat—it's a hell of a sick cat, dead on its feet damn near—and sneak the cat up into Conner's office. He's scared s.less of the cat anyway; I was talking to him this morning."

"*You* were talking to him?"

"Why not? Hell, he came down nosepoking and I went up to him and said, Look out the cat don't eat you, Conner. Listen. I said, This place is full of wild beasts, Conner, bears and tigers as big as your swollen head. You should have seen him stare."

Lucas smiled. "And he didn't say anything?"

"Now what could he say? He's not my boss. Nobody's my f.ing boss here. You think I'm lying."

"Oh, no. Lions and tigers, I believe you, Gregg."

"Bears and tigers. What'd you go into town for?"

"When?"

"This morning, you said you went into town. Lucas, you're slippery. You look slippery and you are."

Wanting to hit Gregg back, Lucas picked up the handiest weapon, the truth. "I went in to get a bottle of rye. Angelo gave me the idea."

"Screw, you didn't."

"Screw I did. I have money. I do a little work around here."

"Being a pig's friend you do. So: Marty's little boy buys a bottle of rye."

Lucas's brain, had not the dull earache been occupying the best part of it, would have ordered his body to walk away, because Gregg's jealousy was driving his tongue beyond all reasonable bounds.

"So: the pig-feeder and the bird-keeper are going to set down in their nice little cozy room with all the holy pictures and get a load on. Son of a bitch if that isn't a picture."

"Martha won't touch it," Lucas said, meaning to show how he operated on his own initiative.

But the sound of the remark was so feeble Gregg laughed delightedly, with genuine good humor. "Well then, share it with me. And some others I can get hold of. Where is it?"

"In my room."

"We'll see you on the porch. Nobody will be sitting out in the rain. I'll steal a cup. Come on, we'll make a holiday out of this mess yet. Come *on*."

The image Angelo had planted in Lucas's mind had been that of several men drinking together on the grass behind the wall, which was unfeasible due to the rain, so he agreed.

HOOK made haste to be among the first to enter their common sitting room, Andrews's old living-room, furnished in black leather and equipped with a vast cold fireplace. On the central round table he knew the newspaper that the noon mail had delivered would be placed. It was there for him. Many of those who would have coveted it had gone into the smaller room on the other side of the hall, where the mail rack stood, to see what letters had come. Hook had this advantage: there was no one alive in the world who would write him a letter.

He settled on the sofa and unfolded the paper to the obituary page. After perusing these unfamiliar names he revolved the paper to the opposite page, where the editorial opinions were found. The chief one was titled "Two Horns of the Canadian Dilemma":

What shall be done about overweening Montreal? Public opinion is rising hysterically against our neighbor to the north. Two months ago the Dominion was pointedly excluded from any of the chairmanships of the Free Hemisphere conference held at Tampa. The increasingly austral orientation of our policymakers is mirrored by hatred voiced on every street corner against the Old Lady of the North. Now if ever is the time for level-headed review and reassessment of the causes and factors which have led up to the Canadian imbroglio at present facing our policymakers.

The St. Lawrence Seaway, precipitously approaching its china anniversary, created a new Mediterranean Sea in the nation's heartland. The Great Lake ports of Chicago, Detroit, Duluth, and others proudly expanded to fit their new role of oceanic ports. Despite the warnings of Eastern manufacturers Washington took no steps to discourage the precipitous shift of the nation's economic fulcrum from its traditional position in the Northeast—a shift that did incalculable long-range harm to New Jersey industry and shipping. Montreal bided her time. Not until the commitment of capital and manpower was irrevocable—and here is proof of the thoroughgoing cynicism of her motives—did our courteous neighbor to the north apply her strangle-hold. In the last six years tolls on the St. Lawrence locks have *more than quadrupled*. The American Midwest has woken and discovered itself locked in the humiliating relationship Paraguay in South America has for centuries endured in relation to Argentina, astride its sole artery to the sea. At the moment of writing it costs more to ship a ton of Nebraska grain from Chicago than from San Francisco, through the Panama Canal, to Europe!

The Canadian dilemma must be understood as having two horns. On the one hand

Hook had difficulty reading this. The light coming in the windows behind him was gravely muted by the weather, and he had to hold the paper to one side, to avoid the yellow shadow of his head; his face was tilted far back awkwardly so he would get the benefit of his bifocals. His attention moved to the political cartoon. An elderly lady, wrapped in shawls labelled CANADA, hypocritically smiled as she twisted Uncle Sam's arm, which was spiralled as tightly as a rope. Tears flew from his face. The caption was, "Don't Worry, Sam, We'll Get Those Kinks Out Yet!"

Hook folded the paper horizontally and laid it on his knees. Immaculately he interlaced his fingers and laid them on his abdomen, which sloped comfortably as he relaxed into the sofa's inclination. His eyes rested on the drawing of the old lady and she seemed very pleasant in her animation. Without forethought his consciousness faded and he slipped into sleep.

MARTHA had come to the room ahead of him. "No bird," she said. "No little bird," She was sitting on the bed, her lap spread disconsolately; all her public talkativeness (he knew her better than that) had faded away.

He looked automatically for a sign of green life in the thin-spun cage, the delicate door of which stood ajar. The little white bath, like a miniature saltlick, held a silent eye of water. The rain outside, steadily filming the panes of the room's one window, seemed to call to this eye. "I don't know what we can do," Lucas said.

"I know it's stuck somewhere. Its claws made nearly a full circle: *why* couldn't you have taken the poor thing in town?"

"Now Martha. Do you imagine someone trims the nails of the bird in the jungle?"

"That's the jungle. When you take them out of the jungle you become responsible."

"Well, I'll look around the halls."

"Oh my poor legs."

"Here." He went to the bed, plumped out the pillow, then took his wife's ankles and, operating gently against the slight protest of her body, lifted her legs to the bed, so her head fell back into the pillow. She stared at the ceiling.

"On my feet all morning making those buns that now can't be sold," she said.

He took the thin coverlet at the foot of the bed, unfolded it, and dropped it over her, saying, "The room's damp."

"It's the sudden drop in temperature," she agreed. "The twinges I can stand, but this constant dull ache. . . ."

"Close your eyes," he said, "and when you open them, see what's in the cage."

"No letter from Joan," she said with her eyes closed.

On the way out he lifted the bottle from the bureau lightly, not wanting the paper bag to rustle. In the hall he hid it in a niche, behind a statuette of a woman whose thighs swelled through a wet nightgown. One of her hands floated in the air and the fingertips of the other touched one hip. The cylinder her bare feet posed upon was plastered into the bottom of the niche, so she had never been removed, though the mantle of dust on her shoulders had grown black. The patches of dirt the upward-tending planes of the face had received, contrasted with the bright white of the sheltered spots—eyes, and beneath the nose and the lips—gave her a clownish anxious aspect independent of the modelling.

The parakeet must have gone to the left, for to the right, after three doors, there was a dead end, a window laced with chicken wire that could with great effort be opened onto a fire escape. The window and escape were Conner's innovation; in Mendelssohn's day they would have burned.

This was the third floor. To the left Lucas traveled down a bleached corridor, and came to a crossing, four staring corners sharp as knives. One wall still bore ancient medallion wallpaper; the rest was spray-painted ivory. He looked to his right, and there, fluttering at another window of wire and glass, was the parakeet, a dipping arc of green nearly black against the luminous color of the rain.

Lucas approached lightly but before he got very close the bird, of its own volition rather than from an awareness of being chased, darted to the right again, down another hall. By the time Lucas reached the end of this hall the bird had vanished. The channels of wood and plaster were again meaningless. The corridor the parakeet must logically have flown down had windows on the right and vibrated with shadows of the downpour outside. This row of windows gave the ef-

fect of a ship, an enclosed promenade; the clammy light fell
through still air, free of dust, as at sea. He softly walked down
the hall, next to the skin of the house; down below, the roofs
and foreshortened fronts of some outbuildings were visible.
Through the door of one shed he could see the rug of straw
spread in there, dry. The radiators beneath the windows
were heating; fog crept up the lower panes. To his left the
successive doors were closed; occasional thin cracks revealed
flecks of paint and cloth and dead matter. The corridor led to
the stairway. Lucas with circumspection moved around in
front of the stairs; in his stealth he felt enormously thick, cos-
mically big: his shoulders were Jupiter and Saturn.

The action of his feet became unconscious; the stately
mass of the upward staircase passed in front of him and to
his left. He stopped short, his coarse breathing suspended.
On a steel bannister on the fourth floor the bird roosted
fussily, shifting its awkward feet on the too broad perch and
fanning its wings for balance. The bird was so small Lucas
fitfully lost sight of its green in the multiplication of planes
created by looking up the stairwell diagonally. Then it flickered, and with a whir mounted the terrible volume below it;
hung there angrily, not so much beating its wings as shaking
them in a tantrum, above Lucas, who stared beseechingly at
the spinning pale belly, even stretching out his hands, to
attempt to catch the bird as it fell. The parakeet folded its
wings and dipped between Lucas's head and the leaning edge
of olive iron beneath the stairs, veered down another corridor, and with an abrupt backwards motion, landed, and like
any small gentleman walked through a waiting open door.

Desperate, yet convinced in minutes it would be over, Lucas ran down the hall, so unused to running he ran crooked,
his shoulder heavily brushing the wall. This was the west wing.
He had marked the door where the parakeet had entered and
threw it open. On a white bed beneath white sheets a sunken
invalid lay, dreamy with heavy injections, the sheet falling
away where the legs should have braced it. The parakeet was
perched on the foot of the bed.

what the invalid sees

THE GREEN FLOWER had sprouted unsurprisingly; the appearance of a bear seemed to follow from that. Now the bear growled. It seemed sorry for something, but then he was sorry too, and though there was no need to say so he smiled. The bear pointed; the flower leaped; the flower skimmed over the ceiling, and at a command from the bear the door closed sharply, saying "Idiot." The bear lifted its black arms and sank from view, and the flower bloomed on the bed, its bright eye frightening. He was glad when the bear came again. A chair fell lazily, and the bear was of course sorry about that, and ashamed. Then the bear grew very clever and plucked the green flower from a picture on the wall. He was so proud, he tried to show it, but of course if he opened his hands too wide the flower would leap again. It occurred to him that it all had been arranged to amuse him, and he laughed obligingly, so they would not feel sorry, and continued laughing when they had gone through the door, for them to hear, though curiously he was not sorry when they had left him alone again.

DOWNSTAIRS the strange thing was Conner's entry into the sitting room. He himself felt the strangeness keenly; it was a criticism of him. When the dining-hall had emptied quickly after his arrival, Buddy's chatter had grated unfeelingly on his sense that in two and a half years he had quite failed to get himself across to these people. And he felt, important within him, something he should get across, a message more momentous than his desire to be their friend, "friend" being perhaps less the word than "guide." So he courageously decided, today being a dislocated day anyway, to join them sociably. There was in his decision a shadow of the supposition that Mendelssohn—so much in the air since the rain began—would have done so. Once, however, in the room where he knew they tended to gather, he hesitated; the old people were grouped in the sofa and the chairs by the window, and a conversation held their interest. Only Mary

Jamiesson noticed that he had entered. The surprise her face showed him made it harder for him to declare himself; tightened the screw on his silence.

Hook was saying in a speechifying manner, ". . . received money from the hands of the northern manufactur-ers. Now that was what was said in my father's day."

"Look at an old penny, John," Amy Mortis said, "the next time you have one. That's the face of no grafter."

"Hav-ing your face on coinage," was the considered reply, "doesn't make an honest man. Else why would we hold the opinion we do of the Emperor Nero?"

Hook tilted his cigar with satisfaction at himself. His antagonist's goiter shook as she made a crude counterthrust. "You don't think then he should have freed the slaves? You think the slaves should still be that way?"

"Ah, they still were. Had the northern manufactur-ers been half so concerned with the slaves in their own mills as they were with those in the fields of the South, they would have had no need to make the war for the sake of munitions profits. But they were jealous. Their hearts were consumed by envy. They had taken a beating in the Panic of '57. The civili-zation of the south menaced their pocketbooks. So as is the way with the mon-ied minority they hired a lawyer to do their dirty work, Lincoln."

"They should have kept the niggers down then?" Amy said, restating her charge, with the implication that it had been evaded by the old debater.

Conner conceived of a way to postpone inserting himself into their circle. The room was damp and chilled by the change of weather. None of the inmates had thought to light a fire, though dry wood was stacked pyramidally by the great fireplace, a black carven thing shipped from Bavaria by Mrs. Andrews, as fruit of a flighty excursion. All he needed to light a fire was paper. He moved about, with only Mary Jamiesson studying him, searching; accustomed to his office, he was bewildered that a room could contain so little paper In a dark corner he did find, meticulously stacked on a table, some copies of a monthly publication of the Lutheran diocese titled *Sweet Charity*, forwarded to a male pensioner who had died the previous year in the west wing and to whom this musty stack appeared to form a monument. Conner took several of these white magazines and crumpled them.

"Not *down*," Hook said, "but not everywhichway either. Where do you think the freed Negro was to find work, if not on the home plantation? Now did the manufac-turers want him in the northern cities? Now if I may have a minute of your time, good lady, endure this old fella for the length of one anecdote. Rafe Beam, my father's hired man when I was a boy on my father's farm ten miles this side of the Delaware, came from Pennsylvan-i-a, and had been raised near a settle-ment of the Quakers. The Quakers among the city dwellers had a great repu-tation for good works, and in Buchanan's day were much lauded for passing the runaway slaves on up to Canada. Ah. But the truth of it was, this old fella who was the patriarch of the sect would harbor the Negroes in the summer, when they would work his fields for nothing, and then when the cold weather came, and the crops were in, he would turn them out, when they had never known a winter before. One black man balked, you know, and the old fella standing on the doorsteps said so sharp: 'Dost thou not hear thy Master calleth thee?' "

Everyone laughed; Hook was an expert mimic. The hiss of avarice and the high-pitched musical fluting of the hypocrite had been rebuilt in their midst, and Hook's face had sub-mitted to a marvelous transformation, the upper lip curling back in fury, then stiffening to go with the sanctimony of the arched eyebrows. Smiling a bit himself, he pulled on his cigar and concluded, "And no doubt he was a fair specimen of those so desirous to aid the Negro."

It puzzled Conner to overhear such lively discussions of dead issues. The opposition of Republican and Democrat had been unreal since the Republican administrations of a genera-tion ago. The word "Negro" itself was quaint. Dark-skinned people dominated the arts and popular culture; intermarriage was fashionable, psychologists encouraged it; the color bar had quite melted. The Enforced Reforms and Regulated Riots, so stirring to Conner's youth, might never have occurred, to hear Hook talk.

Silently Conner laid the paper and logs and applied a match. He pictured his presence being at last revealed by a triumphant burst of flame. The glossy stock of *Sweet Charity* burned reluctantly, however, and the dark oily smoke slithering from the air spaces between the logs persisted in curling into the room. After a minute flames were visible and it became clear the chimney would not draw; the flue was closed. In a hurry Conner poked his head into the fireplace, looking for a catch, and as rapidly withdrew it, at the scent of singed hair. The lever must be on the surface of the fireplace. There seemed to be only carved bearheads and scrolls and cherubs dotted all over with highlights. Mistrusting his eyes, his hands flittered across the black craggy surface, cold as marble.

"Buchanan, I suppose," Mrs. Mortis said, "was doing a first-rate job, eh John?"

"A ver-y unfairly esti-mated man," Hook slowly replied. "The last of the presidents who truly represented the *en*tire country; after him the southern states were slaves to Boston, as surely as Alaska. Buchanan, you know, had been the ambassador to Russia, and was very well thought-of there."

A small man with broad eyebrows, whose name, Conner believed, was Fuller, came over softly and whispered, "I think this does something." He touched a short chain hanging from the mouth of a bear, and Conner roughly pulled it. For a moment the fire continued sluggish and smoky, then the draft caught; with a jerk the smoke whipped inward, and the dry logs roared. "Birch," Fuller said, "has its own smell don't it?"

"Where is that smoke?" Amy Mortis asked aloud.

"We've built a fire," Fuller said before Conner could himself speak.

Conner wondered if the man knew who he was, that he should presume to protect him. But if he did not know who he was, why come to his rescue with the flue? All the eyes in the circle except Hook's and a blind woman's focused on him. He knew he should speak and took a breath to begin.

Staring at a beam of the ceiling, Hook announced further variations in his argument. "The panic of 1857 and not the Negro lay behind the attack on the south. When the shooting died the Negro became merely a cause for pecu-lation. The administration of Lincoln's man Grant was without a doubt the most crooked the nation had seen until the other Republican, Harding, came to power. Now he was around in my time: a man you would have thought dirt wouldn't cling to, as tall as a church door, and trimmed like Moses. . . ."

"Well you can't blame Lincoln for Grant," Mrs. Mortis said.

Hook's mustache broadened humorously. "They were as close as Baal and Mammon," he said. "Lincoln was no lover of morals. In private practice he was an atheist, you know."

"A Deist, wasn't he?" Conner said. "A Unitarian."

"Is Mr. Conner with us?" Elizabeth Heinemann cried beautifully, turning her head on her slender neck pathetically, as if she could see.

"Yes, dear," Mary Jamiesson said, "he's been building us a fire."

"I heard that someone was. Thank you, Mr. Conner."

"Thank you," Tommy Franklin echoed, and further murmurs sounded.

"You're quite welcome—I, I'm sorry that this rain has delayed the fair."

"It's not your doing," Mrs. Mortis said.

"You can't take the world on your shoulders," the blind woman told him.

"I can't?" Conner wondered, impressed that she should phrase it so.

Mrs. Mortis, acting slightly deliberate, as if her host's small boy had wandered unbidden into the room and it was not in her place to question his presence, continued to Hook, "Well, when I get up to the Good Place, I'll have Lincoln and your friend Buchanan stand side by side a minute and we'll see who has the longer wings."

Hook did not reply, merely smiled and let his chin lapse humbly on his chest. With Conner there, his manner stated, discretion was most politic.

Whereas his presence, Conner felt, excited Elizabeth. "What else will you do, Amy?" she asked after a pause; her vowels were of different distinct colors, the consonants like leading in a window of stained glass.

"Do where?"

"In Heaven. I don't think you were quite serious before."

"Not? Well you can think what you please. It's your right."

Elizabeth's voice rose in volume and she turned her head. "Do you think, Mr. Conner—is he still here?"

"Yes, I'm here." He was standing behind her; there was no handy chair to sit in, and it seemed to be assumed he would not be with them long enough to make fetching a chair worth the trouble.

"Do you think in the Afterlife we shall *see?*"

As the pause lengthened he realized that they *did* respect him; as up-to-date where they were old-fashioned, as educated where they were ignorant. Mute, they were looking to him now, for something which was, whatever it was, not the answer he must in honesty give. False solace must be destroyed before true solace can be offered. "I can't, for myself, believe it; vision is a function of the eyes, and when they are gone it must follow."

"Don't be afraid," Elizabeth said, smiling broadly, "of shocking us; this is America where, as Amy says, we're all entitled to our own beliefs. I *agree* with you. As a little girl I thought of Heaven as a place where I should see, but I'm no longer a little girl. I'm a woman old enough to have some wisdom, though of course an old woman's wisdom can't be compared to yours, Mr. Conner—or yours, Mr. Hook."

"I know noth-ing," Hook protested.

"As a little girl," Elizabeth Heinemann continued after waiting a moment for Conner also to offer a remark, "I be-

lieved that everything on earth would be in Heaven, right
down to my mother's knitting needles and a pin cushion that
was shaped like a pumpkin. I saw these things in a blurred
way all my childhood and then very intensely in the weeks
after my last operation, before all the work the doctors had
done slipped away, just failed to hold, and there was no hope
left. Well! Elizabeth! Why are you going on about yourself?"
Though she made these exclamations, it was with an eerie
evenness of tone. Perhaps, long handicapped in the human
game of response and reaction, she had lost interest in it;
there was a smoothness in the discharge of her inner accumula-
tions that compelled the silence sacred performances ask.
Conner, standing near and above her head, loved this woman
somewhat, for her external beauty, to the extent that the total
innerness of her life did not repel him; and he regretted it
when she, feeling in the silence of the others consent to go on,
turned to him in a voice and asked, "Mr. Conner, do you have
a picture of Heaven?"

"No, I'm afraid I don't really have a picture."

"I don't *either*. I no longer know what color was, or what
oblong means. And it doesn't matter, it doesn't matter," she
insisted, nodding her head reproachfully on the stem of her
neck and vividly smiling at a spot between Hook and Mary
Jamiesson. "The things you see, are to me composed of how
they feel when I touch them, and the sounds they make, for
everything has a sound, even silent things; when I draw near
an object it says 'yes' before I touch it, and walking down a
corridor the walls say 'yes, yes' and I know where they are
and walk between them. They lead me, truly. At first, when
this sense began to grow, I was afraid to have these voices
come into my darkness; this was before I had forgotten what
darkness was, when I still remembered the light. You see, I
could hear the walls talking, but didn't understand that they
said, 'Don't be afraid, Elizabeth; I'm here, yes,' like Mr. Conner speaking a moment ago. I believe"—her voice rose a little
out of control, and dropped modestly, and in that fraction
of a second Conner had time to grieve for the tremblings of

her mind, these shy hallucinations which, had only the universe been made by men, would have been true evidence instead of what they were, cartoons projected on a waterfall—"we live in a house with a few windows, and when we die we move into the open air, and Heaven will be, how can I say, a *mist* of all the joy sensations have given us. Perfumes, and children speaking, and cloth on our skin; hungers satisfied as soon as we have them. Other souls will make themselves known like drops of water touching our arms.

"Living here, where there is no cause to be jealous—for don't you believe jealousy is the one *real* sin?—I've learned how sweet a human presence is, how timid, and safe. Yet when I could see, as a girl, I hated people—hated them terribly. They could run without tripping, and eat their food without spilling—my own eating was so unpleasant, I imagined, for others to watch. My sister would read to me; I hated her. I believed my parents loved her and only pitied me. There were so many jokes I couldn't understand. I must have set my ears against them. I *know* I indulged my disability in order to hurt my parents. Yet when my sight fell away finally, all those busy angry patches I couldn't quite make sense of, everything changed. A voice wasn't a twisted face but something musical. I could sit in a room with my parents and feel their emotions washing my sides, and hear a thousand details in their speech they were ignorant of, and feel my being in the room turn them toward gaiety and reverence. For when I was a young girl in my teens my presence did that."

"You should not," Hook said, "take it upon yourself to deny possible blessings."

Tears started to her eyes at the unexpected accusation of pride and the finish of her fine voice was scratched by the emotion of her protest, "Mr. Hook, I've never denied; I've accepted everything."

"I meant," he stated slowly, "the blessings of renewed vision."

"But how can you picture Heaven and be sensible? Mr.

Lincoln in wings; a kind of tabletop, with distances between everyone that you must travel like an airplane to leap? No. Isn't it absurd? Mr. Conner thinks so. What Heaven can there be for our eyes when vision separates, and judges, and marks differences for envy to seize on? Why are we taught as children to close our eyes to pray? Please.

"Years ago, when I was still troubled, I heard a minister on the radio say, 'In Heaven there are no appearances.' For that moment that man was to me the voice of God. 'In Heaven,' he said, to me, 'everyone, everyone, will be blind.' And you needn't be frightened, Amy, because I know what it is and none of you do."

It is true, Mrs. Mortis had made a gesture of indignation.

SPRAY, cast up when the heavy rain pounded the flat porch rail, glimmered as if the sun, buried high overhead, were attempting to strike rainbows off the mist. The air had grown lighter since the first announcement of thunder; the thunder had moved off slowly to the north. Gregg, who had gathered three other men with something like his own reckless and defiant temperament, was growing impatient for Lucas to arrive with the bottle. The fear that Lucas had no bottle and had lied, slippery Lucas, and that he, Billy Gregg, had collected his friends only to seem a fool and a cheat, petrified into a conviction. "This crappy rain," he cried abruptly, "will screw Conner's goddam fair at least."

One of the men, August Hay, a Philadelphia derelict who years before had been an ice cream vendor in what was then Shibe Park, laughed; he laughed at anything. His face from the side was marked chiefly by deep creases streaming from the corner of his eye across the flat of his cheek. Whereas Gregg's net of wrinkles gave the impression of caging a bright and panicked energy, Hay's seemed to witness an old collapse. His gouged skin, the tip of his nose, his lower lids, blood-pink on the inner surface, all drooped. Hay and his two companions showed no signs of impatience; they had no responsibility in the affair; the porch was as good a place as any to sit out the rain. They talked among themselves, a distance down from Gregg. They had not seen much of Gregg since he had taken to Hook's company.

"I wonder," one of them said, "when Gregg washed his face last."

"Looks bad, don't he?"

"Bad."

"Shrivelled up, like. What does he do to himself to make himself so drawn?"

"How do you sleep nights, Gregg? On your belly or back?" August Hay laughed and the other two followed closely.

"What the hell are you talking about for Christ sake," Gregg asked, "what the hell are you sitting down there for?"

Hay laughed. "These are our chairs, Gregg. Can't we sit in our own chairs, Gregg?"

"Who the hell says they're your f.ing chairs? Conner puts goddam little tin tags on and you think you have no right to sit in any but the ones with damn tin tags."

"Whose are you sitting in?" Hay asked, and the three laughed viciously, for the chair was his own, prolonging the laughter past mirth, old street-boys tormenting the neighborhood weakling.

"Where's the booze, Gregg?" Hay pointed beyond the porch. "That's rain, Gregg. Can't drink that. Why'n'cha wash your face in it, Gregg?"

"Why don't he wash his hands?"

The water fell from the edge of the porch roof in strings; it poured off every acute angle of the ornate brackets. "Son of a bitch, son of a bitch, son of a bitch," Gregg said. "Like some bastard's drippy nose."

"Who is?" Lucas asked. He had appeared, holding the bottle in a paper bag.

"Hooray!" Hay shouted, and the other two echoed it as a joke, beating their hands on the wickerwork arms, which resounded very little.

"Where've you been, looking at the pigs?" Gregg asked Lucas, to whom he felt, nevertheless, gratitude.

"I had to catch Martha's bird," Lucas explained, glancing at the other men. He was short of breath, not only from the chase but from suspensefully putting the parakeet in the cage without waking Martha, who had been snoring under the coverlet. His palms still tingled with the sensations of holding the living bird captive in his hands. The rapid beating of the tiny breast and the strong effort of the edged wings to unfold had affected him disagreeably, even stirred queasiness, after the sight of the dying man in the bed smiling and nodding like a judge. There was something dreadful to Lucas in the thought of blood pumping through pliant, dilating vessels; he was startled whenever, inadvertently touching fingertips and thumb, he felt the shudder of his own pulse. Living flesh to him felt like food in the act of being eaten by an amorphous, carnivorous creature: life itself. For this reason he disliked touching anyone, or having them touch him. He asked Gregg, "Did you steal the cup?"

Gregg produced it: white china. "Slop it in," he commanded.

Lucas worried off the cap, held in place by a new-fangled set of wires, and, keeping the bottle dressed in the paper bag, poured a bit of liquor into the cup Gregg held, enough to cover the bottom. Before taking a sip Gregg carefully swirled the cup, and like a flexible brass coin the half-inch of liquid swayed in the white cavity. Then with some delicacy of gesture he took his swig. As in the flavor of certain vegetables acres of bland rural landscape are contained, stone houses, fields, and grassy lanes, so this rasping hard taste flowered in Gregg's mouth into high brick blank walls, streets of pocked asphalt bleeding in summer heat, the blue glint on corrugated iron where it is not rusted orange, the sun multiplied down a row of parked cars, tangerines pyramided behind plate glass, manhole covers, filth in gutters, condoms discarded on window sills, and unpainted doorways scratched with wobbly slogans like F. THE POPE.

Gregg coughed and hawked. "Goddam Lucas, this is p. you've bought here."

"Hey, hey," the other men clamored, waving their arms but keeping their chairs.

Gregg darted off the porch into the rain and returned running with two bottles of ginger ale cooled by the rain in the cases Buddy and Ted had stacked. "To kill the rotten taste," he explained, and they drank it this way, at the proportion of 1 to 2, out of the common cup.

"ATHE-ISM," Hook said in answer to Conner's attribution of Deism to Lincoln, "wears as many faces as Satan."

This rejoinder fell among them neglected, for Elizabeth's hopes of Heaven had disjointed their commerce awkwardly. Her own mouth tightened into a sharp, impervious expression unsuited to her, and Conner realized she had expected some sort of praise. He realized as well that Hook was attempting to offer it when he said, "No doubt, Elizabeth, Heaven will be something of what each wants it to be." But this, too, was ignored, and for the moment Conner wondered if Hook, like himself, was not excluded from a certain alliance of affection that existed among these people.

It was Tommy Franklin who at last spoke and was turned to eagerly by the blind woman.

"Well *my* ideas of the next place," he began, and lifted his downcast face to ask, "Did you say you wondered what other people thought?"

"Yes," she said, "please tell, everyone. I'm so interested."

"Well,"—he spoke with difficulty throughout—"I've not given it the thought you have. The last I remember thinking was as a boy of maybe fourteen, that it couldn't be in the sky. It turned out my father thought the same. He said, and he claimed he got this from the Bible, one day we'd be lifted up from our graves and Heaven would begin right here. I liked to hear that because I had always liked the section of country around our place. Then I wondered about the animals, because if we came out of the ground they might too, and I wondered where they'd go. I thought of all the stock I'd seen my folks kill, and even if we got the whole farm back, I didn't see the place for them all. And a lot of wildlife depend on eating each other, foxes and hawks to mention two, and what would they eat? I asked him, my dad, and this time he said there would only be two of each animal, a male and a female, like they came off Noah's ark. It didn't seem to be enough, but I let it go at that, and that's the last thinking I recall doing on the subject." Aware that he had disappointed Elizabeth, he scowled at his knitted fingers, nicked and red from filing peachstones.

"Rafe Beam used to recite," Hook said,

> "The animals came out two by two,
>   The chipmunk, mink, and kangaroo;
> The horse came down, clippety-clop,
>   And Mrs. Noah shook out her mop."

He couldn't help chuckling himself at this, a distant tickled laugh.

"All right, Tommy," Elizabeth said. "Who now? Amy? Bessie dear."

Fuller left the circle to put more logs on the waning fire Conner had built. Conner coveted his chair, for it symbolized inclusion, but he didn't intend to stay; Buddy must be up in the office alone, and the boy's probable petulance tugged at Conner's official side.

"The Book says," Bessie Jamiesson said, "the rich will be poor, and the poor rich. So I've always thought I'd be a beauty, and my mother not; but I won't let on; I'll treat her better than she treated me, when I was her girl. I expect we'll all be about the same age."

"If you lose your long jaw," Amy Mortis said, "that means my goiter goes too. And your bad eyes, Elizabeth. It's your right."

How tiny, Conner thought, this woman's head was without her bonnet. A mere egg and, as she had said, partially bald. He wondered if, technically, she was a dwarf. He wondered what the technical definition of a dwarf was.

"Mr. Conner," Elizabeth appealed, "will I be made to see?"

"I'm not really an expert on eschatology." The coldness of his voice disappointed even him.

"Please, won't you give us your ideas? They say you don't believe, but I think everyone believes, in their heart."

Conner on the contrary believed that in their hearts no one believed, which accounted for the strained, or bluff, expressions on the faces of the few clergy he had met. "I'll try to tell you"—in his earnestness he touched the blind woman on the shoulder, sharp bones at variance with her velvet appearance—"my conception of Heaven. Like Mr. Franklin, I see it placed on this earth. There will be no disease. There will be no oppression, political or economic, because the administration of power will be in the hands of those who have no hunger for power, but who are, rather, dedicated to the cause of all humanity. There will be ample leisure for recreation."

"Naked girls on the seashore," Mrs. Jamiesson interpolated.

"Leisure, and no further waste of natural resources. Cities will be planned, and clean; power will be drawn from the atom, and food from the sea. The land will recover its topsoil. The life span of the human being will be increased to that of the animals, that is, ten times the period of growth to maturity."

"More poorhouses," Mrs. Mortis said.

"There will be no poor."

"All the more reason for poorhouses; the only reason people put up with their old ones now is to get their money."

"Money too may have vanished. The state will receive what is made and give what is needed. Imagine this continent—the great cities things of beauty; squalor gone; the rivers conserved; the beauty of the landscape, conserved. No longer suffering but beauty will be worshipped. Art will mirror no longer struggle but fulfillment. Each man will know himself—without delusions, without muddle, and within the limits of that self-knowledge will construct a sane and useful life. Work and love: parks: orchards. Understand me. The factors which for ages have warped the mind of man and stunted his body will be destroyed; man will grow like a tree in the open. There will be no waste. No pain and above all no *waste*. And this heaven *will* come to *this* earth, and come soon."

Mrs. Mortis asked, "Soon enough for us?"

"Not you personally perhaps. But for your children, and your grandchildren."

"But for us ourselves?"

"No." The word hung huge in the living room, the "o" a hole that let in the cold of the void.

"Well, then," Mrs. Mortis spryly said, "to hell with it."

They all laughed, but it was Hook's laughter, because of the common exclusion from the run of human hearts that minutes before he had imagined as binding them, that wounded Conner and brought on his controlled anger.

"MR. HOOK," he said in an insistent voice, claiming the initiative, "you've laughed several times. What strikes you as amusing?"

"Now I meant no offense."

"Is it the wish to eliminate pain that strikes you as amusing?"

"Indeed not, but it is an error now to believe that the absence of evil will follow from the elimi-nation of pain."

"Pain *is* evil."

"The Roman Empire was very pros-perous, and yet evil."

"There was a good deal of pain in pagan Rome."

"Arti-ficially induced," Hook said, lifting his flattened hand edgewise, like an ax poised to cleave the chair arm. "It need not have been. The Emperor Nero, now, besides ar-ranging exhibitions for the enter-tainment of others, had torments inflicted upon himself, to re-lieve his boredom."

"There can be mental as well as physical pain," Conner said. "I've never encountered anything I considered evil that couldn't be described as pain."

"Well, then, is your vive-section evil? And hurling animals off to perish on the moon?"

"You must understand that there is a distinction—"

"Ah; I am grateful to hear that word. Dis-tinctions, Harry Gorman, my old instructor in debate, used to say, consti-tute the anatomy of discussion. Now there are many sorts of pain. There is that which we undergo gratefully, such as dental work. There is that which we cause ourselves, as in war or automobile accidents. And there is that caused by our body in attempting to warn us of disease. When one reads in the paper that the state has declared war on suf-fering, these distinctions are not mentioned."

"I don't know if they're worth mentioning. All suffering comes upon the individual uninvited, and it all interferes with his fulfillment."

"Why, on the contrary, in most cases even disease is in-vited by trans-gressing the commandments, notably those against gluttony and greed. And far from opposing the exist-tence of virtue, suffering provides the opportunity for its exercise."

Conner smiled regretfully; he saw no great good in de-priving a man of what had comforted him for ninety years, yet more than his immediate authority had been insulted, and he devoutly wished to pin his antagonist against the rock that underlay his own philosophy. "I'm afraid I have little use for a virtue purchased at the price of some of the suffering I've seen."

"I read the papers," Hook said with some indignation. "I have lived in the world. Now in whose shoes would you rather stand, your own as a young man certi-fied to a long career in govern-ment, or in mine, those of an old fella who has buried all his children and idly waits to be struck down any day? You have heard our blind lady speak; did she pro-test of injustice?"

Elizabeth brightened and said, "Oh, no: as I said, I was a very vain and fretful girl, and I tremble to think what I would have become had my sight been cured. Very quarrel-some, I'd imagine, and with *no* insights."

"And Bessie," Hook went on, "are you indig-nant, because you lacked the blessing of beauty?"

"I thank God I do," she responded. "You take my mother; she thought for being a looker the world owed her a living, and she never gave herself or anybody else around her any rest. I've had an easy life and won't be sorry to go. But my mother, the day she died, she was hopping, and gave me a cut I still carry the scar of around."

Conner began too wryly, "I wish—"

"Now in my own life," Hook said, and brought down the edge of his hand upon the chopping-block of the chair arm, "looking back I perceive a mar-velous fitting together of right and wrong, like the joints the old-time carpenters used to make, before everything was manufactured metal and plastic. I was sickly as a child, and could not enjoy the sports the others did. But due to my ill health I learned to care for my body and have outlived those that were stronger by nature. The penalty I've paid for this has been burying all of my kin, until there is none living who remembers me as I was before" —and a disagreeable expression, like a lavender shadow, passed over his face—"I reached this state. But the conso-lation here is, I shall be willing to die, having made the Gentleman's acquaintance before, and having sent so many ahead to welcome me. Ver-y seldom, in my life, did a trans-gression not bring its own punishment, so that in some cases, as drunkenness, I could not tell where the offense left off and the penalty began. And who is to say how the ailments of my childhood may have been the fruit of my father's short-comings or of his before him."

"You believe that too?" Conner was sincerely surprised.

"Indeed and double. The bookkeeping is far more strict than even that of a Boston banker. If the size of a mouth is passed down, why not the burden of wrong-doing? Had the men so busy at tor-menting the atom busied them-selves inspecting the sins of unfortu-nates, we would have books of the balances Providence strikes. Virtue is a solid thing, as firm and workable as wood. Your bitterness"—he looked directly at Conner, his eyes greatly magnified by cataract lenses—"is the wilful work of your own heart."

"VIRTUE," Conner said, his level tone making clear that while willing to take this last, frontal attack, he now felt free to repay in kind. "How do you define virtue?"

"Virtue," Hook said, "I understand as obedience to the commands of God."

"Where do you locate these commands?"

"Why, they locate you."

"We are born with them."

"As we are born with ten fingers; they grow in strength."

"But a baby is essentially virtuous."

"Why, does a baby seem evil to you?"

"A baby seems neutral. A baby is a bundle of appetites that society, for its convenience, teaches certain restrictions. To enforce these it invokes the supernatural as a mother would an absentee father."

"He is not absen-tee."

"No? What makes you think, God exists?" As soon as he pronounced the ominous hollow noun, Conner knew absolutely he could drive the argument down to the core of shame that lay heavily in any believer's heart.

"Why, there are sever-al sorts of evidence," Hook said, as he held up one finger and then added a second, "there is what of Cre-ation I can see, and there are the inner spokesmen."

"Creation. Look at the smoke of your cigar; twisting, expanding, fading. That's the shape of Creation. You've seen, in the newspapers you've just said you read, photographs of nebulae: smears of smoke billions of miles wide. What do you make of their creation?"

"I know little of astronomy. Now a flower's creation—"

"Is also an accident."

"An ac-cident?" Hook smiled softly and he touched the fingertips together, better to give his attention.

"Lightning stirred certain acids present on the raw earth. Eventually the protein molecule occurred, and in another half-billion years the virus, and from then on its evolution. Imagine a blind giant tossing rocks through eternity. At some point he would build a cathedral."

"It seems implaus-ible."

"It's mathematics. The amount of time it takes is the factor that seems implausible. But the universe has endless time."

"Not according to Scripture."

"Not according to Scripture, no."

"I do not quite see how any amount of time can generate something from nothing."

"Presumably there was always something. Though relatively, very little. The chief characteristic of the universe is, I would say, emptiness. There is infinitely more nothing in the universe than anything else."

"Indeed, you propose to extinguish re-ligion by measuring quantities of nothing. Now why should no matter how much nothing be imposing, when my little fingernail, by being something, is of more account?"

"Yes, but there is something. Stars; many of such size that were one placed in the position of the sun we would be engulfed in flame. The issue is, can any sane mind believe that a young carpenter in Syria two thousand years ago *made* those monstrous balls of gas?"

For the first time, Hook was slow in answering. He shifted his position, and the old dry leather audibly protested. "As to being a carpenter, it has often struck me that there is no profession so native to holy and constructive emotions, or so appropriate for God-made flesh to assume."

"The truth is, Mr. Hook, that if the universe was made, it was made by an idiot, and an idiot crueler than Nero. There are no laws. Atoms and animals alike do only what they can't help doing. Natural history is a study of horrible things. You say you read the papers; but have you ever walked around

*remarkable for a
27 yr old novelist!*

the skeleton of a brontosaurus? Or watched microbes in a drop of water gobble each other up?"

"No, but I have seen a lobster being cooked."

"These are our fathers, Mr. Hook. Monsters. *We* are mostly monster. People speak of loving life. Life is a maniac in a closed room."

"Now it has never been claimed," Hook said, "that the Creator's mind is a book open for all to read. This I do know, that that part of the uni-verse which is visible to me, as distinct from that which is related to me, is an unfailing source of consolation. Dumb creatures are more than their skeletons. Even a spider may set us a lesson. As to the stars which so repel you, they are to me points of light arranged at random, to give the night sky adorn-ment. I have sometimes thought, had you and your kind arranged the stars, you would have set them geometrically, or had them spell a thought-provoking sentence."

Conner waved his hand impatiently. "As a student of debate you know how little humor proves. What was your second piece of evidence? Inner spokesmen? The truth here is, there is no door where these spokesman could get in. We've sifted the body in a dozen directions, looking for a soul. Instead we've found what? A dog's bones, an ape's glands, a few quarts of sea water, a rat's nervous system, and a mind that is actually a set of electrical circuits. An experiment that might interest you, Mr. Hook, was conducted several years ago by a team of Latin-American scientists. They took a young Indian girl from the mountains of Peru who had been educated entirely by Catholic nuns. By means of a series of precisely directed electrical shocks, administered while she was under drugs, she was induced to have a vision of Christ as real to her as I am to you."

With this he knew that he had indeed succeeded, had touched the core of shame and shaken Hook. All the old man could say was, "That was a very cruel experi-ment."

"I don't know why. The girl was ecstatic. He spoke to her in Quechua."

"He spoke?"

Conner paused. "I think the report said the appearance told her not to be afraid."

The fire had failed to take Fuller's large logs; and the rain continued more quietly outside, infrequently pattering on the ashes as a few drops found their way down the chimney. Hook was silent a moment, but might have spoken again, had not an interruption occurred. "Mr. Hook," Buddy said sharply, and he stepped forward, lithe and clean in his crisp shirt and his skin quickened by indignation. "I'll tell you my own experience with popular religion." Conner realized that, however long Buddy had been listening by the door, he did not comprehend the situation, that Conner stood among the ruins of a venerable faith; helplessly Conner perceived that in the boy's brain the grotesque idea of a rescue had taken form. "I watched a friend die," Buddy continued quickly, speaking solely to Hook. "It took a long time. His bones were riddled with cancer. Every time he'd turn over in his sleep, he would break a bone; this was toward the end; at first it was just his joints, one by one, stiffening, and not obeying. He and I were very young; we prayed. We prayed for years, yet the pain came on, and in the end we prayed simply that he die now, before the diesase was through playing with him. It would have been such a little thing for God to do, yet it was not done, even that little thing. At last the doctors themselves did it, and killed my twin brother with drugs, on his fifteenth birthday."

"Why Buddy," Fuller asked, "wasn't that your brother on the lawn this morning with the bare arms?"

His manner of asking was so sincere, laughter was general.

Hook had not laughed, however, and now pronounced tiredly, "That is a ver-y terrible tale. Let an old fella say one thing more, and then he'll hold his peace. When you get to be my age—and I shall pray that you never do, I wish it on no one, but if you do—you shall know this: There is no goodness, without belief. There is nothing but busy-ness. And if you have not believed, at the end of your life you shall know you have buried your talent in the ground of this world and have nothing saved, to take into the next."

THOSE on the porch thought they were seeing things. A small red car—foreign no doubt—drove up in the rain and stopped at the break at the wall, blocking the entrance. Black snouts commenced to poke from the little windows. Ends of bulky cases, they stuck out and sneaked back, like the heads of several turtles caught in one shell. Then the doors jumped open, and six men with raincoats with blue pants showing beneath hopped out, slamming each other's doors, and raced up the path, bobbing with the effort of carrying cumbersome shapes.

The foremost and first to reach the shelter of the porch, a little one with hair parted centrally and a sharp nose, asked, "Who's in charge?" Three of the men with him were in their sixties—the biggest, and oldest, with an overbearing pious brow, carried under an orange canvas what had to be a tuba—and the other two were boys, insolent and drowsy.

"He is," August Hay said of Gregg, who quickly hid the bottle beneath the wicker chair.

"Him? In charge of what?"

Furious to have attention thrown on him, Gregg snapped, "Son of a bitch does it look like we're in charge sitting here with tags on our chairs like pigs in a zoo?"

"You're the band," Lucas told them. "Conner's probably up in his office."

"The band!" Hay crowed. "What the hell are you doing here? Look at the mob out there." He threw his hand toward the empty grass beyond the soaked porch rail. "Ice cream, ice cream," he began to call, "getcher red-hot ice cream heeyah."

"Bugs in his head," the leader said to his followers.

"Conner's probably in his office," Lucas repeated.

"Ask inside for the stairs."

"Nobody told us not to come," the leader said, half to the men behind him and half to those in front. Conscious of this remark's weak positioning, he added with unnecessary loudness, "This is the third Wednesday of August." The ensuing silence made him appear foolish.

"Bugs in his head," August Hay explained.

As the six, in file, passed into the poorhouse proper they clicked off glances of disdain with industrial precision. The two boys, bringing up the rear, exchanged a lazy comment with the word "characters" easily audible.

The marriage Lucas had looked forward to, between the pain in his ear and the rye, had proved a mournful disappointment. The liquor dulled the pain less than the pain dulled the uplift of the liquor; in an oval area inches above the back point of his left jaw the sum of his existence, it seemed, was absorbed in the rhythm of a cautiously pulsing sponge. Pain seemed green—the green of old grass—and its absence—the penetration of the liquor—brown. Like infringing watercolors these sensations blurred into one another, one dominant and now the other, and at moments like paint over wax the slow movement brought into relief the exact shape of the small bones of his ear, three white, few-fingered, interlocking hands. His upper lip lifted in self-dislike. Perhaps, if he had obeyed Angelo and kept the matchstick out, the pain would be gone; again, if he had never seen Angelo, the pain would be sharper and not so broad and smothered in quality. Lucas felt uncommonly depressed and careless. Drunkenness, in a man like August Hay, melts the restraints on cheerfulness. On the contrary with Lucas: he kept up courage consciously. Sap his mind, and the lid was lifted from a cesspool of muddy colors.

WHILE upstairs Martha, wakened by a sweep of rain, had discovered the parakeet returned to his cage and had taken this bird onto her shoulder; each time the black-and-yellow head, striped finer than any fabric, dipped to touch its down-turned beak to the blue skin beneath her eye, she sang out, "Aren't you silly? Aren't you silly?"

Such ecstasy for so small a bird to undergo!

.   .   .

"AND why else does anybody these days put up with old people except in the hope of getting their money when they pass on?" Amy Mortis thus concluded explaining why the world of the future would be a world of poorhouses.

Conner stood over them, hardly considering her point—that poverty alone held the generations together. His attempt at intercourse with the inmates was ending less well than it had begun. What had caused the fury of this old woman? They were all furious. Their heads were dark in their chairs, facing away from what light the windows admitted. "Poverty," he said, "isn't a positive thing; it's a lack. The scientific state adds; it takes nothing away." He stood in such an ambiguous relation to these people, between that of a shepherd and that of a captive, and his quarrel with Hook had produced such a darkness, that he spoke blindly, uncertain even of whether he lingered among them in the hope of making himself clear, or merely to avoid the appearance of a retreat. One retreat had taken place: they had withdrawn from him.

"It almost seems," Elizabeth Heinemann sighed aloud to herself, "there's to be no fair."

Like a flicker of a tail a silent stroke of dry light whitened the room, occupying in its moment every corner, even the black mouths of the carven bear heads. "Isn't it a wonder now," Hook offered, "that so few men are struck by lightning now, compared to my day. So many were struck standing on the loaded hay wagons, coming in under a storm. Now in Matthew it speaks of lightning going from east to west, at the end." He cleared his throat and concluded, "At the beginning of the first war with the Germans it seemed the End had come, the portents were so plentiful: Halley's Comet, and the men in the trenches saw the angels overhead. Lucy had such terrible dreams." Lucy had been his second daughter, the child that had died most recently.

Buddy came whispering up to Conner, who repeated "The band?" involuntarily.

The elderly men and under their direction the two youths had removed their raincoats and hung them in a closet Buddy had showed them. Now they stood forth in creased cerulean uniforms. With double rows of chased silver buttons and brilliant braid looping and running along every seam, they glinted like seraphim in the dull light.

The shortest, whom Conner remembered from the two previous years, stepped up and said, "You should have called before this if you didn't want us to come."

"You didn't want to come?"

"It's not the point what I want. If there wasn't to be an affair because of the weather, you were obliged to notify. In all the years we've come here before there's never been rain."

"As a matter of fact," Conner said, smiling, "I did call your home around noon, but your daughter said you were gone."

"Sure, I was gone. There's more to this job than putting on blue pants and combing my hair and getting into the car. There's a lot of managing in connection here. Rain or shine we fulfil our obligations to the letter, is the way we do it. It's always worked before."

"I respect you for it," Conner said. "I'm glad you're here," he added, seeing that this wasn't assumed.

In ones and twos more inmates were drifting from spots around the Home into the room, shuffling amusedly through the screen of uniforms drawn up like a guard. It was as if the world had been holding its breath while Hook and Conner debated its condition, and now resumed bumping onward.

The leader persisted in making himself clear. "That half of the fee given in advance, you can't get back now. We can't return it. What kind of business would that be, if we came all the way out here and then handed back your money?"

"Is this the whole band?"

"Wind ensemble. We use the term 'wind ensemble.' There's no call for marching bands any more. The parades they have now are all floats with whores on 'em advertising some soap."

"Last year, weren't there more of you?"

"Yes and twenty years ago there were twenty more. Times change, if you haven't heard. If there's a half-dozen bands like this left south of Trenton I'll be surprised. If you're

worried about your money you won't have to pay for per-
sonnel you don't get. But this is the third Wednesday of
August and rain or shine we expect to play and get paid.
There's two more cars should be here now, if they'd listen
to their orders. Young ones driving; they'll show up I guess
when the mood hits 'em. What's the humor?"

Conner too did not know why he laughed, except that the
wooden fixity wrought by economic concern on the other's
face challenged his own to keep impossibly stiff. "Young
people in cars coming," he repeated.

"That's what I said. I got 'em dressed and wiped their noses
and I guess they'll turn up. Between sixteen and sixty it seems
nobody can carry a tune, that's the impression you get if you
try to keep a band going."

"A wind ensemble," Conner said. "I can believe it." He
laughed, and laughed again when he felt Buddy beside
him flinch. Buddy's mechanical generation had never learned
how to laugh; Conner's own was the last that knew how.
"Well, make yourselves comfortable," Conner continued.
"You can dry out by the fire. Oh. The fire's gone out. Well,
have some chairs. You can talk or play—" He was going to
say "cards."

"Play? You want us to play our instruments?"

The idea struck Conner as remarkable. "Why not?" he said
quickly. "You came here to play and get paid."

"We're short two-thirds of the parts," the leader protested.

It seemed, as Elizabeth had said, that there was to be no fair;
a gust of irresponsibility had swept into the room, as if the
fair were, rather than an awaited holiday, an annual humilia-
tion from which they were this year to be delivered. The
six musicians were egged on. Chairs were arranged. The instruments were unsheathed: flute, cornet, trombone, tuba,
French horn, parade drum. This last was a gay thing, painted
with long lozenges. Sheets of yellow music were unfolded
and clipped to the instruments. Mrs. Mortis remarked to
Hook how much the fella on trumpet resembled Truman,
who gave away China to the Russians. Without his customary

spark he countered that the tuba man was the image of
Hoover, who plunged the common man into the Great Depression for the benefit of the Wall Street bears. The musicians
made their instruments speak haltingly, and twisted mouth-
pieces and shook out moisture. Then they commenced definite
tunes: marches that colored the air, dimly at first, with the
colors of the flag. The weave of the orchestration was tattered and torn on the fewness of the instruments, but here
the cornet placed a white star, and there the flute and drum
together spread a broad red stripe, and above the heads of
the men, moving minimally, a phantom banner beat. They
rendered, with rising spirit, *Fairest of the Fair*, then *Hands
Across the Sea*, then *On the Mall*, by E. F. Goldman, in
which the teen-age flautist strangely excelled.

LUCAS had sunk into an apathy so profound that even his
earache seemed a stranger. He had held no hopes, really, for
his alcohol party. Gregg, who had held some, was generating
a savage temper, and had established a monopoly of rye. The
rain was letting up, and it seemed to Gregg that as the rain
slackened his revenge on Conner was being taken from him.
As a pearly light infiltrated between the upright rods of rain,
which was more like a harp now and less like a massive sail
filling and sagging as the wind came and went, Conner seemed
to lord it over them again.

"Son of a f.ing bitch," Gregg began, "be putting tags on
our necks next, and balls and chains on our feet. Fairy doesn't
even have the sense of half a man. Where's that cat I sneaked
in? What I'm going to do is pry every stinking tag off these
f.ing chairs and make a f.ing collar and throw that cat right
in Conner's puked-up face. Pale turd." He jumped from his
chair and whirled to peer in the windows. "Now what the s.
is that music? Who the s. says we have to have music when his
goddam fair is washed out? Son of a bitch; birdbrain noise."
Heedless of the diminished rain, he raced off the porch to go
out back and find the cat, who must be keeping dry in one
of the barns.

Like many humanists, Conner was deeply responsive to music. In the language of melody speeches about man's aspirations and eventual victory could be made that explicit language would embarrass. He could not hear a dozen chords without crystals building in his head, images: naked limbs, the exact curve of the great muscle of a male thigh, cities, colored spires soaring. Man was good. There was a destination. Health could be bought. A remark of Amy Mortis's exerted a subconcious effect: he envisioned grown men and women, lightly clad, playing, on the brilliant sand of a seashore, children's games. A man threw a golden ball, his tunic slowly swirling with the exertion; a girl caught it. No fear here, no dread of time. Another man caught the girl by the waist. She had a wide belt. He held her above his head; she bent way back, her throat curved against the sky above the distant domes. The man was Conner. Then there was Conner again, at his desk, speaking to grateful delegates, calm, flexible, humorous; the listeners laughed, admiringly. Conner shunned admiration, and gained it doublefold; the world was under his wing. Yet in visualizing this world which worshipped him, he returned to the triangles and rhomboids flashingly formed by the intersection of legs and torsos scissoring in sport, and the modulated angles of nude thoracic regions, brown breasts leaning one against another, among scarves of everlasting cloth, beneath the sun.

Hook, less imaginative, tapped his toe out of respect for the patriotic content of Sousa's songs—he had witnessed many a parade to these tunes—and swiftly grew restive. Music affected him as women's talking did, when there was no interceding in it. He was an instructor, not a listener. Further he had been closeted within for three hours—he judged it was shortly after three—and now that he had been absent from him for such a time he missed his final pupil, Gregg.

He stood, whispering his intention to "give his knees a bending," words no one quite heard, though the sound drew some attention to himself, tall and stiff from his long sitting, trying to focus in the narrow beams of his sight the way out, as he made uncertain protestations with his elegant tan hands. "Let me disoblige no one; I want no more than room to die," his manner of exit declared.

"Hookie looks bad," Mrs. Mortis said to Bessie Jamiesson, under cover of the martial music. "Conner ought to be shot, going after the old man that way."

"What did Conner want down here with us anyway?" Mrs. Jamiesson asked. "Mendelssohn never made himself common like that."

"We won't see another Mendelssohn, not in our little time."

Hook did feel slightly shaken; his discussion with the prefect had sent his blood pumping with unaccustomed force. He wished again, contemplating the distances visible from the porch, that the poor home were in sight of water. The rain was lifting; the far hills bearing the orchards glistened, existing in a washed atmosphere. Though he had thought he had noticed his piercing voice through the windows, Gregg was absent from the porch. Lucas sat in a near chair; further down the line three of the disreputable element had established themselves. "Isn't it peculiar now," he said to Lucas, "but I remember, after such a storm, how the Dela-ware would show blue before there was any blue in the sky to reflect. Now look how heavy the drops are, as their number lessens."

"It just seems so," Lucas said, covering both remarks, and unable to say more, though he bore the old man no hard feeling.

"Did you in-quire about the tags?"

"I asked this morning. He had a good reason, I forget what."

"He is a re-markably earnest man," Hook stated generously, after which he added, "I believe a demon drives him."

Gregg, damp and beside himself with shock and fury, came onto the far end of the porch and, advancing, cried, "The goddam rotten cat, they've killed the dumb son of a bitch and let the body lie in the rain, they just let it lie! The f.heads shot it and let it lie out there, the cat I brought over the wall, they killed for no reason."

"That animal that was so sick?"

"No sicker than Conner will be when I get to him."

Hook recognized in the small man's melting eyes signs of a madness that created a hazard for them all, and the old disciplinarian showed as he said, "Why, it was better to put it out of its misery than let it linger."

"I'll kill the c.sucker. I have rights."

"No, now," Hook said, "you don't, if truth be known."

THE DAY'S RAIN lifted; the high yellow house hove clear of spray; the many gray connections between below and above were snapped. The unpainted wood of the tables was soaked black. Drop by drop the colored bulbs slipped their thin jackets of water. A few of the women ventured into the open, treading distastefully the drenched lawn in which the circular cobwebs of the grass spiders showed like mirrors left lying in the grass. The song of the birds was especially strident. Hook from the porch heard what he rarely heard, a bobolink. Mrs. Lucas came down from her room, her legs better. The musicians laid their instruments aside. The inmates of the home, already united in expectation of the holiday, had passed as a group through two turns of fortune: the rain, and the rain's abatement, which last joined them together in a mood of raucous, cruel exhilaration quite unlike the sweet and moderate expectation of the morning. Boxed within the house three hours, they retained the nature of a mob. They spoke loudly; old people who seldom conversed, being of different types, cackled together. They were like school children whose vacillating principal at last grants them an excursion which he had threatened to withhold as discipline and which he believes is a greater treat for them than it truly is.

Conner was immediately concerned with the broken wall. The litter must be removed, before any townspeople came. He hated waste and liked things clean. He was so anxious that the stones be taken from the lawn that he dared use, he hoped tactfully, his authority as prefect to assemble some of the inmates before they became involved in other tasks, or ran away. He marshalled the men in the living-room, who had witnessed his argument with Hook, and, passing the porch with this troop, also enlisted the five men loitering there. He exempted Hook, who was also present, as being too old for even light labor, but Hook, inquisitive, as were some of the women, came along, thereby laying the foundation for a later misunderstanding.

III

ON CONNER'S INSTRUCTIONS Lucas brought the wheelbarrow from a shed behind the west wing. The rest straggled around Conner, rather too closely, a sizeable group of men. "Whose car is this parked across the entrance?" Conner asked aloud.

"The band's," Gregg answered.

"They'll have to move it."

When Lucas came up with the wheelbarrow, Conner had him put it at the far end of the field of fallen stones, beside one of the biggest. This stone, a rough brown egg so soaked by the downpour grains of red sand rubbed off on their palms, Conner and Gregg together lifted into the metal pan of the wheelbarrow, setting it forward, where the wheel would take its weight. It was agreeable for Conner to find Gregg's shoulders beside his; he remembered chatting with him in the morning. This was the man who had been good enough to try to feed the cat. The rock settled resoundingly. Conner's fingers were nearly pinched in his inexperience. Nevertheless it gave him unexpected satisfaction, handling

stones in this wet, freshened world. Stones were man's oldest
companions; handling them, the first civilized act. The sub-
conscious commemoration roused by the abrasion on his
hands and the pull on his forearm muscles made Conner feel
brisk, purged, central; there was a widespread anthropolatry
in things of which he was the focus. Above, the sky seemed a
mammoth negative which, printed, might prove a Michel-
angelesque mural; like the long hair of persons fleeing tendrils
of vapor unwinding slid sideways across blue patches vivid as
paint. Silver rivers lay between clouds.

"Two more such ones," Hook observed, "and you'll have a
load."

Resentfully Conner saw this truth. He had been stupid to
picture the barrow heaped high with rocks; such a load
would break two men's strength. Further it was an error to
load the big rocks at all. When the masons came in a few days,
he assumed they would want the large rocks that had been
already worked. And it was the pebbles that made the look of
litter.

"My mistake," he called. "Let's roll the big ones to the wall,
and just clean up the rubble. You and I," he said to Gregg,
"had better lift this one out again. I'm sorry."

Before he could protest the small wiry man had seized
the ends of the stone in his own two hands with an angry
sound and carried it to the wall. Showing off. Most of the
male inmates had been laboring men. With surprising effi-
ciency the old men rolled the big stones against the wall. This
done, they stood facing him, their arms hanging long, and he,
an amateur foreman pursing his lips to repress a self-depre-
catory smile, demonstrated the next stage by bending and
dropping some fieldstones into the wheelbarrow. Gregg, and
Tommy Fuller, and a man from the porch, came and consumed with steady clatter the area of loose stuff around and
near the wheelbarrow, and the others brought handfuls
from further away. Conner, not needed, stood idle, ready to
pick up any rocks that missed the target. The distance between the wheelbarrow and the stones to be removed from

the grass had increased; the men—several women were also helping now—had taken to tossing them a yard or two. Conner, dully watching the stones accumulate, stones of tints from milk to dung, ranging through lilac, cream, and pencil-gray, many speckled, infrequent ones stratified, did not think to move the wheelbarrow closer. To this extent he was at fault.

Deliberately Gregg flipped one too far. It struck Conner on the left thigh as he stood, his eyes downcast, between the handles. Unhurt and expecting such errors from these feeble people, he automatically bent to retrieve it, and Gregg threw another one, overhand, which stung him on the back, an inch to one side of the spine, thrust up in knobs by his bending. Puzzled, Conner straightened; the abrupt act tipped his brain a second, so that to the off-balance chemicals there the people standing upright at some distance from him seemed weirdly opaque, their presence magical and menacing.

Without his knowledge his white face plainly expressed this moment of fear. His flash of bewildered cowardice jarred loose the last pin restraining Gregg. Half-hidden in the midst of the other old people, Gregg loosed a cry, shaking full of spittle, that stirred them. His wrist whipped where they could see, and a stone dug the grass to Conner's left. Conner turned his back and strode rapidly away, without quite running, and at this retreating target all—Hay and his two friends, Lucas, Tommy Franklin, even Fuller and the women and others who had come freshly to the group—flung small stones, most of them falling short.

One stone of medium size hit Conner on the back of the head, where the skull is thinnest. Stunned and quickly sickened, Conner felt as a revelation dropped from a red heaven the word *unjust*. He wheeled for a moment under the hail of pebbles and glimpsed Hook, the tallest, standing there as if presiding.

Hook had been studying the clouds above the west horizon, where numerous types were superimposed—a bank of indigo making a false sky behind crumbling nimbus suds, bars of high cirrus and faint true sky behind it all—and Gregg's outcry had slowly recalled his mind; stiffly, shifting his gaze but not lowering it, he had his narrow field of vision crossed by a flow of arrowing stones, speeding through the air in swift flocks, and before he considered, he had the thought that here was something glorious. Battles of old had swayed beneath such a canopy of missiles.

It was unjust, but Conner was too much a man of reason to be propelled by an impulse back, blinking, through the onslaught to choke the source. Attempting to assert control, he steadied his gaze on them, even as they threw, while he took a few casual steps backwards; then he decided on disdain, and turned on his heels and kept walking.

As if at the end of a side tunnel Amy Mortis saw in her mind the tiny black figure of Mendelssohn, his heavy head nodding, and, encouraged, she clawed rocks from the ground, flinging one even as she stooped for another; scrabbling and hilariously cawing, she worked her way to the forefront of the pack, and led the second stage, where the ones throwing laughed at the realization of what they were doing. More laughter came from people scattered about the lawn, who at the distance could appreciate the comedy of Conner's pudgy figure stubbornly striding with a vestige of composure beneath the harmless pepper of tiny black objects. Gregg had ceased to throw, and spouted sarcastic obscenities forward.

Buddy came to view the tag end, when Conner was nearly out of their range, and the stones were tossed without seriousness. Amazed as he was, and alarmed for his superior, while his feet raced across the lawn his aloof boy's mind indifferently pictured a newspaper story, himself being interviewed as witness.

"What is this?" Hook asked deliberately, at last conceiving the situation.

"Son of a bitch of a cat-killer, brave bastard run your a.h. off," Gregg called.

Fifteen yards away Conner turned. His cheeks were red, but only at the moment of turning and glimpsing Hook had he moved irrationally. He had known the game would turn within seconds. He stared at the cluster of inmates; two stones fell well before his feet, and then no more.

Buddy stormed right up to them. "You're insane! Do you know what you've done? You'll all go to Fryeton—they'll put you in padded cells!" Fryeton was the insane asylum of the county.

They all seemed to look through him, toward Conner, who softly rubbed his occiput, where the one stone had caught him. "Go away," he said huskily, cleared his throat, and repeated, "Go away." Then, the least expected thing, he stooped and collected a double handful of the stones that had fallen around him, and brought them forward to the wheel-barrow. As he advanced toward them the old people, save Hook, turned and walked away, into the crowd that had gathered. "I know you all," he called to their backs.

Since Conner seemed interested in nothing but gathering the stones, Buddy helped him. No one strayed near them. "How did it start?" Buddy asked.

"I have no idea."

"What are you going to do?"

"Forgive them."

"Forgive them? Just that?"

"All of that. It's a great deal. I'm quite hurt; I had no idea of that much hate."

"But at least you could punish their leader."

"I'm their leader."

Buddy decided this wasn't a joke, for his superior's red hands were trembling so much he had difficulty holding pebbles. Buddy took his master's forbearance as a lesson learned. One of the obscurer lessons, but true to the man, whom Buddy, melodramatically moved, observed passionately: the pores of the wall of his cheek astounding pits, and the curve of his upper lip a marvelous bulge assaulting space. Filled by the forward movement of Buddy's love, the wrinkles at the corners of Conner's eye seemed to mark off significant intervals.

But Conner was feeling that perhaps it was not quite enough, merely to forgive them. The ache on the back of his head dilated and contracted like a living parasitic cap. After depositing the last handful in the wheelbarrow, he came close to Hook, who had held his post and lit another cigar. Conner was convinced that this man had been the cause.

"Mr. Hook," he said, "in your wide experience have you ever seen anything like that madness?"

"Ah," Hook said, "when I was teaching at Furlowe, the children trapped a flying squirrel, and broke its bones with sticks. Bore-dom is a ter-rible force."

"Doesn't there have to be one man to release the force?"

"Now the little fella," Hook said, who had been waiting to make this explanation, "had been sipping alcohol, and had not expected that the cat would be put out of the way." For he had imagined himself, after the other retreated, as staying, as an innocent onlooker, to allay Conner's wrath against Gregg. Hook conceived of himself as a politician and arbiter.

Conner did not know who the "little fella" was. He did not suspect Gregg at all of being the instigator, and his case against Hook as a schemer was strengthened. "What made them do it?" he asked.

"Yes, what? Idleness. Idle hands make devil's work," Hook said, suddenly tired and not very interested. The irregularity of the afternoon had worn him. He wished only now to take a stroll, in solitude, around the exterior of the wall.

"Don't they realize what this man has done for them?" Buddy asked, unable to hold his tongue longer, Conner's circumspection again making him impatient.

"I repeat," Hook said, "he was taken aback, and not in his right mind."

"My patience," Conner said, "is not limitless. Any repetition of mass defiance, and there will be measures taken. I promise that. In the meantime I suggest, Mr. Hook, that you yourself stop endangering your own health and the safety of the wooden buildings with cigars and matches. I more than suggest it, I order it."

Not fully understanding, Hook stated, "There is little danger, for a man above ninety. The poor fear no thief."

"He said you're for*bid*den," Buddy said shrilly off the roof of his mouth, and snatched the cigar from Hook's softly posed hand and threw it onto the ground and vengefully stamped on it, though in the deep damp grass the ash continued to smoke.

The expression on Hook's face scarcely changed, and Conner felt, looking up toward the dark womanish lips of the disapproving mouth, a wince of grief, as he had when, in connection with some negligible venture, he had balked his own father, a generation ago.

But there was nothing which could be done now which would improve what had been done.

ALIKE FORBIDDEN the dark hours, the old and young came first to the fair, the old for talk and the young for candy. Fred Kegerise, once burgess of Andrews, brought his daughter's son, who was eight. This boy's fresh face ignited anxiety in the heart of his grandfather, who felt the hot flexible hand he held grow slippery and, as they proceeded on their walk, more and more frankly try to pull away. Yet fear of his daughter's disappointment if anything, even skinned knees, happened to the boy kept his grip firm.

As soon as the weather cleared they had set out from their common home in Andrews, Fred's old manse, where his daughter had been reared. When she yearned to marry a boy from Chicago—college had exposed her to all sorts—Fred, enjoying the afternoon of his powerful day, had preyed upon her own timidity and that of his wife, alive then, and between menacing and pathetically wheedling the two women had brought the affair to nothing. Then Annabelle had married a town boy, not the man he would have picked either, but, guilty about the first one, he had let this one go. A dentist, his son-in-law came to live in his great house. Fred had wanted this but not his old sun room turned into an anteroom and his living-room partitioned to hold two dental chairs hidden

from each other. But by the time this step was taken his day
of authority had set. The son-in-law took to sly complaining about supporting the old man and his great house, never
letting a fuel bill pass without lament, yet not being man
enough to state his thought bluntly: that men who had
built for themselves such massive shells must have been crazy
with pride. When Fred had built the house solely to let his
two women hold their heads as high as any. Esther had
needed dignity. His two women's shyness, fitting in the
home, had not suited his pretensions in the town. Now Annabelle, her mother gone, sided with her husband against her
father. Yet the two of them made no secret, in fact seemed
proud, of the grandson's strong resemblance to him. To their
shame they were giving the child no religious instruction.
His son-in-law had been bold enough to say it did more
harm than good in the last analysis.

His grandfather's dry grip enveloping the end of his arm,
David had walked up Wilson Avenue, where men were digging for the cloverleaf, past the house of the woman who
teased, along the wall where fearless bad boys dared run
along the top, when a fall would probably break their necks.
At all points the poorhouse wall was taller than David, a high
brown thing to keep the poorhouse people in, though a few
sometimes got out and wandered into town and waggled a
claw at children coming back to the grade school after lunch.
David also knew, from older children, that in the field on the
other side of the road, way behind, boys from the high school
and girls took off their clothes and walked in the car headlights. David was in process of subduing the town to memory.
Finally there would be no intersection or lot where something had not happened to him, and every crack of pavement
would have experienced the tread of his foot in some season
of the year. Already he had been to the fair, twice before,
and remembered the candy.

Coconut strips, peanut butter eggs, vanilla fudge squares,
wax jugs of green syrup you drank then chewed the wax,

gingery horehound sticks, penuche in chunks, thick coins of white and pink mint, licorice belts you punched the silhouettes of animals and birds out of, little vegetables of sugar, gum drops in the shape of trademarks, tacky cups of amber, licorice that burned your throat and gave you bad breath, Turkish delight you couldn't touch without spilling powdered sugar, licorice pipes with red dots sprinkled to imitate burning, all loose and unwrapped, jumbled in jars and cardboard boxes.

Mrs. Johnson, the lady who annually managed the extensive candy stand, took pride in the old-fashioned, by-bulk look. Coughdrops that came in boxes she spilled into a tray and sold three for a penny. The boxes cost seven cents each; there was no profit. Most of her candies she ordered from a small firm in Trenton, managed by a man himself old, whose death would be the company's finish.

Under his grandfather's eye David with difficulty selected five sorts, which he received in his hands as his guardian paid out a nickel, saying, "In town this wouldn't buy the boy a lick of salt."

"With the prices now I wonder that modern people aren't all driven out of their heads," Mrs. Johnson said. "Penny candy used to make a profit of sorts. Now I believe there's a loss. They don't let me keep the accounts any more."

"Not? After you've done this so many years?"

"Yes, these are new times."

David ate licorice without great happiness. Their being among the first to arrive embarrassed him; he had the fear that only they would come. He hated worse than even fur in darkness going to empty places. He saw one boy he knew in the second grade at school.

"The people running the country today," Fred Kegerise protested, "are trying to do all God's work instead of their own."

"Well we're all in His hands one way or another," Mrs. Johnson said, resigned.

God: to David the word was a vast empty place, yet personified with a mouth and long eyes, always steadily watching him, from the air above the top of a house. "They have whips over there," he said.

"What, son?"

His grandfather bent. The great eroded face, with the inner lips coated brown, frightened him. "I saw a boy I know," he mumbled, limply pointing with his free hand.

"Whips eh?" His grandfather winked at the old woman and in going for his pocket let David's other hand drop free; it felt cold as the moisture on it evaporated in the air. "Your mom and dad gave me this to spend on you," he said, and gave an old quarter. "And here's something from your mother's daddy to add to it." He offered, delicately pinched in his two fingers so the circular flash of it was plain, a slick half-dollar, one of the new kind, with President Lowenstein's face molded on it.

Not deaf to the hate in his home, where his parents, at night in bed, whispered bitterly of the old man's self-important ways, and proudly conscious that his grandfather's status there was lower than his own, David accepted the large coin sadly, afraid to turn his eyes to his grandfather's lest the old man see through their clear substance into a well of pity. Then he abruptly trotted off to flaunt his money before the acquaintance he had seen.

Hurt that the boy had made no show of gratitude, Fred called after him, "Mind and stay within the wall," and turned to find Mrs. Johnson busy with other customers.

"They want us home by six or I guess they'll call the fire department," he said, regardless.

THOSE PERSONS, a dozen or so, who had stoned Conner had swiftly drifted apart, each seeking separate refuge in the company of the guiltless. Tommy Franklin and the women had their stands to attend to. Lucas went to his wife. The three men Gregg had collected on the porch to share Lucas's rye clung together for some minutes, laughing at their own imitations of Conner's posture and expression at different points of the incident—when the second pebble struck him on the back; when, puzzled, he decided to turn and run; when, after the stone (which both August Hay and another claimed to have thrown) hit his head, he wheeled like a bird with a foot in a trap, his arms spread winglike and his mouth open like he wanted a worm put in it. Hay, with crossed arms and protruding rump, burlesqued the dignified way Conner had stood when the rain of pebbles ceased. "I know you all," another squeaked. Attracted by their muster, Fuller joined them for safety, swelling their laughter. To his perplexity, the brave group dissolved the instant it gained the house; from the vestibule each man took a separate corridor.

They did not know they had been forgiven. And they would have known no more than Buddy knew what Conner meant, "forgiving" them. However, apart from the three with criminal consciences, accustomed as boys to despise and dread the police, the culprits were disposed to forget. Lucas put the case bluntly to his wife: "What can he do? This is no jail or a school. We don't have property he can take from us. He can't take a paddle to us." The exertion of throwing had sobered him and brought his ear back to its customary pitch—a feathery, almost flirtatious, hint of pain. Mrs. Mortis's thoughts were: she had led a common life, no worse than most. Here Conner came tramping in on the heels of Mendelssohn's funeral with a lot of needless improvements, and then he comes down full force on Hook, who from boyhood up had been attended to and ought to be allowed to keep saying his piece now that he was half in the grave. As for herself, anything Conner did to get even was better than the same thing day in and day out; if he killed her tomorrow it would be a blessing.

AS HE had intended Hook circumambulated the wall. Buddy's display put him in mind of high-strung competitive students he had had. In Conner he recognized the type of dutiful good boy who had no defense but forbearance against teasing, and the knowledge that in the end he would succeed. As Hook made his way cautiously over the uneven ground on the other side of the wall, reaching out now and then to touch its damp stones, his angel wrestled with the gloom that overcame him customarily in the late afternoon, when the sun's rays, growing oblique, commenced to turn golden. The grounds were bathed in broad intense sun, a single mammoth shaft down which heaven like a negligent janitor sought to pump into the little remainder of the day sufficient heat to last the night through. At the edges of two boards laid on the wall steam curled as if several hidden cigarettes were smoking beneath them. The trees, tousled by the storm, showed the undersides of some leaves. A flicker cried *kee-yew, yik yik*. Birdsong on all sides seemed quick condensations in the barely less dense matter of pleased air. Hook's breath worked up and down dry pipes; the labor of his heart, a faithful servant as old as himself, he noticed now, and consciously appreciated. The walk of his life—across easy and firm meadows into the doubtful terrain of stony foothills, or from another aspect down a long smooth gallery hung with the portraits of presidents of the United States— seemed to have its end near. He felt his death—whom he had called previously that day in jest, the Gentleman—waiting for him like a woman at the end of a path; and blinking under the breath of her near presence he wondered what task she had waiting for him in the house. He was tired after his day and only wished to rest. Even listening to her voice would be a job. Her tasks would have to wait a moment, while he sat in a chair, and indeed it seemed forever would not be too long, for him to regain his breath. He could picture no job he would ever be ready again to do. His lips wrinkled as if a bad taste had wormed into his mouth. Walking weighed on him. The deep landscape off to his right called to an appetite he no longer possessed. The feel of the rocks, which he touched, issued a protest his spirit for this moment could not rise at. His legs seemed of a material as insubstantial as that of the daytime moon, which, shot with blue, had come prematurely to the northern sky. Hook's farsighted eyes picked out, jagged and bristling, the houses of Andrews visible from the corner where he paused. Along the town side of the western wall lettered wrappers of candy bars and cigarettes littered the beaten grass. Andrews himself had planted outside the wall a hedge of horsechestnut saplings. Slowly Hook proceeded down the nave of the cathedral that had resulted, whose high roof released spatterings of water coagulate as wax and admitted, in the gaps between shifting leaves, bits of light, cool yet unquiet, like the flames of clustered candles. Between the trunks, the painted houses of the town lunged forward, some not a hundred feet away. Voices led Hook to direct his eyes forward; at the far end, unified by sunshine, townspeople were streaming past, some going in at the southwest gate and others continuing on the long way around. His forebodings lifted at the sight of their gay-making clothes, the round limbs of the children, the young women holding their bodies so upright. It seemed a resurrection of his students, and he sensed that he would never leave them, never be abandoned by this parade.

GREGG had gone like an animal with his kill to the most secret place he could reach rapidly; the open area out back, by the west wing, hemmed in with an irregular outlay of sheds. Buddy had taken the body of the cat away and buried it. Gregg was insanely proud and happy. In all his years he had never dared do such a thing as hurl rocks at the head of another man. His wildness had all been in his mouth, rabid saliva. His entire life, the entire black mass of the great city of Newark, had been funnelled into this one feat. He had shown pastyfaced Conner; he had shown Hay who led laughter against him; he had shown the women he never dared speak to but who had followed him with their stones to add to the pile crushing fat-assed pansyvoiced Conner. He had shown there were rights. Unable to keep his feet still, he danced over the plaza of dirt, kicking chips of wood and poking his fist against the deteriorating wooden walls of sheds. Sons of screwed-up f.faced white-faced bitches. Gregg was happy, proud, happy; he had never before dreamed that such intense innocent pleasure existed anywhere in old age. He cried out, so a few patients in the west wing were startled to hear, "Horse's ass!"

HOOK'S "sharper" had arrived from Trenton to purchase Mrs. Mortis's quaint and beautiful quilts. This year he wanted to buy them all, he had had such success with the four he had got last year. A slight man with large ears and a red cleft chin that looked as though it had once been burnt, he had discovered that in this age there existed a hungry market for anything—trivets, samplers, whalebone swifts, buttonhooks, dragware, Staffordshire hens, bleeding knives, mechanical apple parers, ferrotypes, weather vanes—savouring of an older America. There was a keen subversive need, at least in the cities, for objects that showed the trace of a hand, whether in an irregular seam, the crescent cuts of a chisel, or the dents of a forge hammer.

"No," Mrs. Mortis said. "Last year you bought what I had and there was nothing left for me but to go to bed."

"Missus, I don't ask that you go to bed, only let me purchase what you are offering for sale. Shall we say at half again the asking price?"

"What would you do with them all?"

"Do, Missus? Admire them. Such as this one—look at this lovely little Palladian temple! Where do you find the cloth?"

"It's not easy," she said. "I doubt if next year I'll be able to find any, but I'll be dead then anyway, with luck."

"Twice the asking price," he bid. "Six at twenty dollars, that would be one hundred and twenty dollars."

"What's money to me? You can't give me enough to buy my way out of the poorhouse?" A tilt of her bonnet (itself, he thought, a treasure) strengthened his impression that this was a serious question.

"No . . . no, I suppose not. But tell me, missus, when you work, do you use what they call a 'sewing bird,' a clip in the shape usually of a bird that holds the cloth in its beak? Do you have a wicker sewing basket? Or one of the early Sing-ers, with all that beautiful foliate relief on the pedal? Or pin-cushions? Pincushions bearing political slogans, or portraits of presidents worked in colored thread, or actual wildflowers?"

"Oh, well," said Mrs. Mortis, who loved to have men in conversation with her, "I haven't looked in Mother's chest in years."

"Butter molds?" he inquired rapidly. "Shoe lasts or boot-jacks? Once in a great while, you know, you still find boot-jacks in the shape of a beetle or frog. Is the chest painted? With birds dipping their beaks into their throats? That's a very interesting motif. Do you remember your mother using Phoebe lamps? Or pofferje pans? Porringers? Stoneware, creamware? Pewter? Anything, really, I'd be extremely inter-ested."

"Well, I'll maybe look. If you want to give me your ad-dress. . . ."

He gave her his card. She said, "So it's like they said, you run a shop and sell what I do for a profit to yourself."

"Profit? Very little. Shop, yes, but as to profit, you'd be the one to make the profit. Modern people don't care for old things; they all want the newest of whatever it is. Gadgets, glass furniture. My shop runs on one part money to three parts love."

"I guess that's so, all the young want new things. There's no reverence, as there used to be. Well, why should there be? What'd we do for them? Here we all sit, outliving our time, a drain on their pockets."

"One hundred dollars, Missus, for the lot. How long has it been since you have had a hundred dollars? And these quilts will be going to someone who appreciates them. This marvel-ous linen of roses. . . . There must be a dozen colors of thread here."

"Yes, well. You wait a bit and let me have my fun; I spent all day setting this up. Go down there, a man makes little baskets out of peachstones." She half-turned her head, her face completely shielded by the side of the bonnet.

He promised sincerely, "I'll be back shortly. I've enjoyed

talking with you, Missus—?" Though she did not answer, he was well pleased with the conversation. Her mother's chest, and she must be eighty herself!

ELIZABETH HEINEMANN sat beside Tommy Franklin at his stand and was saying, "much nicer than I had been led to expect he would be. He was at such a disadvantage, being our prefect yet so much younger; didn't his voice seem boy-ish?"

Tommy made agreeing sounds. No one had told her of the stoning. She would learn in time. His miniature baskets and animals were selling slowly, at a quarter to adults and a dime to children. Children were better customers. To adults the small objects, at a distance looking like pebbles and when examined seen to be neither toys nor paperweights nor ornaments, were indistinguishable from those badges and tags given for subscribing to a charity. Having subscribed in previous years they did not wish to do so again and again. Children however recognized the objects as what they were, charms. Children sensed in them the childlike emotion Tommy Franklin had felt making them, in the odd hours, usually at dusk, of the days of the previous year. They were especially pleased by just that place, the hole gingerly widened to make an actual handle free in space, where Franklin in working had himself experienced most satisfaction. Placed in a box or drawer these artifacts would exhale an innocent air like a square of lavender whose scent is never exhausted.

"Are the people coming?" Elizabeth asked.

"Pretty well. The bulk will wait till after supper now that it's rained."

"Perhaps I should go to the house. Does my being here disturb you?"

"No, not at all," he answered. In fact the curious eyes of passersby, shifting from himself to Elizabeth, did affect his tongue, so he was unable to talk fluently enough to keep her mind occupied.

Her lips wavered as she saw herself on the brink of the

gulf between here and the security of the house, with no guarantee of soft hands reaching to guide her through the crowds
and tables. That she had a need for the bathroom further complicated her worry. For what she wanted in her heart was to
remain, in the warm sun, on the edge of this pretty lake of
noise.

"Oh the music!" she cried when this broke forth. "I'll stay,"
she firmly said, as a beautiful girl would whose any decision
gives pleasure, because it comes from her.

THE LEADER of the band had gone down and moved his
foreign car, placing it among the shipshape American models
parked diagonally on the band of untended grass along the
outside of the wall, their bumpers jutting into the road. Dazzling distortions of the sun—oblong, parabolic, linear—occurred wherever the curving metal of a car chassis entered a
certain angle, burning whitely here regardless of the color of
the paint. As he left his car, the two cars he was expecting
pulled up in tandem. "There's Jack; hey, Jack!" these youngsters called at him, smoke of cigarettes issuing from their windows. "Were you worried, Jack?"

"Hell, it's no worry of mine what happens to you; go
drive in a ditch for all I care," the old leader said back, and
the kids howled within their cars, and Jack himself smiled a
little, because the kids' familiarity with him was to some extent heartening. As the boys got out, a few old men, the difference muted by the uniforms they all wore, got out also,
and had been scrunched in there.

Men of the poorhouse meanwhile had dragged from the
barn a great dais of lumber, a table for giants, and, having
sledded it over the slippery lawn, inverted it next to the
porch, which was the same height. As many of the wicker
porch chairs as could be were arranged by the band on this
rickety platform, the gray boards giving beneath their black
shoes. There were nineteen musicians and the platform ac-
commodated a dozen chairs; the remaining seven, including
the parade drum, the tuba, and the cymbals, were seated on a

row brought next to the porch rail. The chairs, with their metal tags, remained scrambled ever after. Goaded by their leader, the musicians took positions, each stepping over the bannister in turn, even while women were tacking Old Glory bunting to the front and sides of the platform. Before the hammers subsided they unfolded small music-sheets as tattered and yellowed as the bunting and began to play *March Carillon, Op. 19, No. 2,* by Howard Hanson, and then, their faces wooden as they sought for perfect time, went into *The U.S. Field Artillery,* by Sousa. The music was more than a feature of the fair, it was its atmosphere, a ponderable medium through which the celebrants moved.

Hook, wandering through the crowd with a presiding beneficent air, his high head rigidly held and his nostrils slightly flaring, had located Fred Kegerise, with whom he had conversed on occasion before. Like two chieftains meeting upon the ridge that separates their armies, the two men spoke face to face in the exact center of the main path. The mob streamed around them. "Now Cleveland had the mettle," Hook affirmed, repeating himself so the other (whose will to domineer was declared by the sheen of his jaw, remarkably clean-shaven considering that the skin had fallen into an old man's folds, and by a harsh haircut that made him bald as a boy above the ears) would not seize space in which to interrupt, "Cleveland had the mettle. He was no Tilden, to let the carpet-baggers steal the office from him. Not that Tilden failed to do battle out of cowardice, but for the good of the country as he con-ceived it, for the Re-publicans were willing to have another Civil War, now that the profits from the first had drifted through their pockets, to the European wines and fancy women, such as the old Commodore kept. But with all respect for Tilden's for-bearance, a war might have been the lesser evil over Hayes with Vanderbilt managing him, and then the nonentity Garfield and Conkling's man Arthur. Isn't it significant, now, that of the three presidents assassinated, all were Re-publican?" He paused more for breath than for an answer.

"Public office is all changed," Fred Kegerise said. "All these examinations and boards of professors and cities managed by schoolboys they never heard of or asked for—there's not an elective office left, except the highest, and there there's but one party."

"Public office," Hook quoted, "is a Public Trust. Cleveland had that mettle needed to turn the muckrakers out, for a time, though McKinley followed, sinking Spanish ships for show. Why, did you know, in his second term—and the one in between, when the old fella Harrison took over, Cleveland had won the vote but juggling the electorate kept him out—in his second term Cleveland had a tumor of the throat, and rather than make the fuss to get the public's sympathy, like that Eisenhower who won on the strength of his de-terio-rated heart, Cleveland went upon a boat in the Hudson, and while sitting there on the deck after enjoying a cigar, had a surgeon cut it out, without any anesthetic but a sip of whiskey, and returned to his duties and it was never known till after his death?"

"A long ways from the boys in power today. Between them and the Russians there's little to choose for my money. Even when I was burgess, so many directives so-called and surveys and poll-sheets came spilling from above, it was like running a department store instead of a town. And that was ten years ago."

"This last decade," Hook claimed, not clear what it meant but feeling the words, momentous and rounded, yearning to be said, "has witnessed the end of the world, if the people would but wake to it."

"They vomited paper on me," Kegerise said with pride, re-envisioning those days when he went to a desk every day, a man responsible for public safety and welfare and permit-ted, when he chose to inspect street works, to ride the steam-roller. "I finally told my councilmen, this isn't a town, it's a wastebasket. Let's go home to our wives and let the state run it itself if it's so anxious."

"I wonder, now, if the lightning Matthew mentioned, as

running from east to west, might have referred to the a-tomic bombs."

"Paper diarrhoea," Kegerise insisted, glancing around through the growing crowd for his grandson; the time was nearing, as the shadow of the high house approached the east wall, glinting in the declining sunshine like a rim of pink frosting, when he had promised his daughter to bring the boy and himself home. He had not been deaf to Hook's last saying. But it was a recent rule of his to avoid religious discussion. Though a Christian, a few assaults from his dentist son-in-law had given him a dread of the subject in any form, as a disciplined dog will flatten its ears at the mere sight of a folded newspaper.

The boy Mark was in an ecstasy of suavity. Two years before, when he was six, he had created a neighborhood byword by confiding in his piano teacher's girlish mother, beside him on her porch swing, that he liked to be "where the people are." The dawn of evening, the bright trousers and luminous skirts brushing past him, the weight of silver in his pocket, the smell of crushed grass beneath him, and the net of conversation spread above his head seemed to make good the fantastic promise that someday he would inherit the delights of adulthood. He had purchased a cardboard packet of hollow licorice cigarettes. Tipping two or three outward as in the advertisements, he offered the pack to his friend, who took two and gobbled them roughly, as if they had been any candy. Mark smoked his, placing each nicely between his lips, off-center, and, without using his hands, taking tiny bites, as finely as a rabbit, until the cigarette was down to a butt; the butt he flipped away, sacrificing good licorice to the grown-up world which he felt great enough to reach out and touch, right through the tough intervening mass of future time. He inaugurated each new cigarette by tapping one end, in an inaccurate imitation of a gesture of his father's, on the flat place above his belly; the chest of the white T-shirt had begun to show gray traces. These did not worry him enough to make him doubt the rite. The older brother of his friend came to collect him. He was four grades older, of grown-up height, with a sick skin. He watched Mark show off and laughed and said, "Not on your stomach, good God. On your *thumbnail*." From this instant Mark hated the older boy and did the thing correctly. Stupid because his thumbnail was no bigger around than the cigarette. How to hit it? The mottled face of the older boy hung like a moon where he had stood, after he had gone.

Her working day ending on alternate weeks at five-thirty, Grace the nurse by six was down on the lawn to meet Joe and another couple. They planned to go elsewhere soon, for a dinner, then a night. Grace wore a flowered sheath, reds and browns, and a brief white top, Spanish in inspiration, trimmed in narrow lace, that looked put on backwards: closely set buttons ran down her spine and in front the cloth fell straight and stiffly from her breasts. Joe kept dropping a step behind her, for the flowered cloth tightened across her buttocks, making one plane slanting up into the narrow soft waist. This stretch of cloth, steady and smooth above the vibration of the wrinkles charged with the action of her walking, dizzied him with desire. Beneath the cloth he had imagined the triangular plate, hard between pads of fat, where, had she been an animal, her tail would have been attached. Cloth taut over rises— the straight lines of her bolero, boxing her chest—made the cave of Joe's mouth a little dry, knowing it was Grace there.

The band played in the soldierly fashion of gallants who maintain parade formation though between the dimishing numbers new gaps are constantly opened by the enemy's fire. At the place in the arrangement where squadrons of trumpets once chorused, the single high instrument of the jut-jawed man sang out from the unstable platform festooned with antique bunting. When in old days the glockenspiel had been scored for a solo bar, the men simply took their instruments from their lips for these measures and let drums of the imagination supply *Va rum. va rum. va dum de umpity rum de um. va rum. va rum.*

The music dimly penetrated to the cupola. Conner, while

in his corner Buddy touch-typed for a third time a budgetary report of great complexity, studied the scene. The grounds were filling up. From this height the people in the crowds appeared to bumble like brainless insects, bumping into one another, taking random hurried courses across the grass. Another successful fair. The deepening blue of the eastern sky was clear, except for a few sweepings of strato-cirrus and for the crooked pale face of the premature moon. He was grateful that the old people would have their entertainment after all. His anxiety on that score was another dead issue.

As he looked the colored lights came on, far-reaching strings of them. It was not quite dark enough for them to make a brilliant effect.

The shock of the incident this afternoon had ebbed enough for him to dare open the door which he had slammed on the fresh memory. A monster of embarrassment, all membrane, sprang out and embraced him. The emotion clung to him in disgusting glutinous webs, as if he were being born and fully conscious. He tried in vain to close the door again on the memory—the little stones flying, the animal cries of the old people, his own necessarily absurd appearance.

The muddled bumping world below would certainly hear of it. In the eyes of the town he would be a fool.

In the eyes of the inmates—their opinion would be less vigorous. There was security for him in their shallowness; their memory was frail, and grasped at ancient things. Present time to them must appear weightless, a thin edge of paper. Further he imagined their judgments of him would be clement; the past seasons had inevitably bred some degree of affection and tolerance. This thought entailed momentarily forgetting who had stoned him. He realized, suddenly and clearly, that the dozen guilty had acted for all; any would have leaped for stones at Hook's signal (which he had not seen). Why? Because, Conner supposed, he was better than they.

At any rate there was nothing to do but persevere in his work. He would not, unlike Mendelssohn, be a poorhouse prefect forever. In another year or two, if his progress here

continued to look impressive on paper—the two most important statistics were the yield from the farm and the longevity
of the inmates—he would be moved up, perhaps into a State
Health Service Council. He expected association with scientists to be pleasanter, more suited to his gifts and to the quality of his dedication. Still, he prized a useful over a pleasant
life. Wherever I can serve, he told himself. At the same time
his mind ran off a film. He was sitting at a table of dignitaries,
not in the center but with becoming modesty at one end. He
rose, papers in hand. "My department is pleased to report the
possession of evidence which would indicate," he said, and
paused, "that the cure for cancer has been found." The turn
of his thoughts to medicine recalled, with an ache, the wound
on his own skull, and embarrassment surged over him again,
with a rushing murmur like that in a seashell. He said aloud,
to say something to hide the noise, "A good crowd. It's funny
that the town always turns out in strength for such a tame
affair."

"The age-old appeal of the freak show," Buddy replied,
speaking floridly now that Conner was safely closeted with
him. "See the fat lady, who suffers from a thyroid condition;
see the alligator man, a victim of psoriasis. See the hermaphro-
dite, deified in ancient Greece."

"Do they still have those? Freak shows? Jesus as a kid they
used to give me the holy horrors."

"I must confess I've never been to one in person. Weren't
they attached to circuses?"

"You're too young," Conner said. "You didn't miss a thing."

He was tempted, in his need for consolation, to let his
tongue run on before this boy, but sensed that silence now
was in order. There was a danger of over-encouraging fondness. Buddy's love, or that of any one soul, was not to Conner's purpose.

Cars were parked the full length of the wall; more came
slowly up the road. Buddy's white hands resumed their quick
tapping. On the grounds below, the broad shadow of the
house muted distinctions; tables, heads, cartons, white arms.

flashes of cloth and patches of grass seemed cells of one living conglomerate, through whose sprawling body veins of traffic with effort circulated: a beast more monstrous than any he had told Hook of. For the third time a wave of embarrassment swept over him—he had been mocked—but within he stubbornly retained, like the spark of life in the shattered cat, the conviction that he was the hope of the world.

HEART had gone out of these people; health was the principal thing about the faces of the Americans that came crowding through the broken wall to the poorhouse fair. They were just people, members of the race of white animals that had cast its herd over the land of six continents. Highly neural, brachycephalic, uniquely able to oppose their thumbs to the four other digits, they bred within elegant settlements, and both burned and interred their dead. History had passed on beyond them. They remembered its moment and came to the fair to be freshened in the recollection of an older America, the America of Dan Patch and of Senator Beveridge exhorting the Anglo-Saxons to march across the Pacific and save the beautiful weak-minded islands there, an America of stained-glass lampshades, hardshell evangelists, Flag Days, ice men, plug tobacco, China trade, oval windows marking on the exterior of a house a stair landing within, pungent nostrums for catarrhal complaints, opportunism, churchgoing, and well-worded orations in the glare of a cemetery on summer days. The London Pacts with the Eurasian Soviet had been new in the experience of America, who had never fought a war that was not a holy war, and never lost one once begun. There was to be no war; we were to be allowed to decay of ourselves. And the population soared like diffident India's, and the economy swelled, and iron became increasingly dilute, and houses more niggardly built, and everywhere was sufferance, good sense, wealth, irreligion, and peace. The nation became one of pleasure-seekers; the people continued to live as cells of a body do in the coffin, for the conception "America" had died in their skulls. "Why, in Nero's day," Hook was saying in their midst, "they had peace a-plenty. And such an odor was e-mitted his name even today is recalled as easily as that of Lincoln. Now, the officials express surprise that so many of the high-schoolers have taken to homosexuality. Per-version is the most natural thing in the world, once pleasure is conceived of as something for more than evening hours."

The man—middle-aged, sunburned—he was addressing nodded appreciatively; he had come to hear such talk as this. Every sentiment of Hook's was as precious to him as a piece of creamware or a sewing bird to the antique dealer from Trenton. "You don't mean," the man protested, "your God don't want us to have a happy minute."

"Ah, yes,"—Hook lifted a brown forefinger to within half an inch of his trimmed mustache—"but minutes given as a present, while the hands are busy with serious matters."

"You can't think we ought to be at war all the time. I fought in a war, you know."

"There is a war we can wage without blood. Now Nero murdered his mother as the logical out-come of his philosophy. What surprises me in this day and age is that everyone doesn't do the same. Make no mis-take. There is little store of virtue left."

Thus pronouncing, Hook had a very clear inner apprehension of what virtue was: An austerity of the hunt, a manliness from which comes all life, so that it can be written that the woman takes her life from the man. As the Indian once served the elusive deer he hunted, men once served invisible goals, and grew hard in such services and pursuit, and lent their society an indispensable temper. Impotent to provide this tempering salt, men would sink lower than women, as indeed they had. Women are the heroes of dead lands.

Hook felt the gall of this intuition as unique within him; but perhaps, less harshly, it existed in many of the hearts around him. Andrews was a small town, a backwater: most of its inhabitants were only a few generations removed from farm owners. They passed among the handmade quilts, loose candies, pyramids of sweet corn, and the sage misshapen faces of the inmates as in certain industrial processes a liquid to be purified passes, bubbling, through a bed of mineral fragments.

"I said not to do that."

"Well, we don't know. We hope but we don't know for sure."

"So I asked him why, because I wondered, and he wouldn't tell me."

"*Don't.*"

"You're probably the last person on the street to know, so I see no harm in telling you what's common knowledge anyway."

"My poor sicklies," Grace said. "Up there all alone."

"He came home pale as a sheet and went upstairs to wash his face by himself, which he never does, and after the longest time told me about this man he had met."

"You know how when she comes home at night she crosses the Leonards' back yard to get into her own. I guess she doesn't dare in her condition to walk the full way around."

"You want to really? *I'd* like to, but I don't see why any of you . . . Joe? All right?"

"Didn't you hear me? I said *don't do that.*"

"Yes, you have to have hope."

"I love you all."

"The principal says he has an idea who the man was. Respectable, is all he'd say. You'd think we'd have a right to know, wouldn't you?"

"So Leonard leans from the window and shouts, so you could hear it six houses down, Get off my flowers, you— well if he said it I suppose I must—whore. Get off my flowers, you whore."

"Must Daddy spank you?"

They felt the poorhouse would always be there, exempt from time. That some residents died, and others came, did not occur to them; a few believed that the name of the prefect was still Mendelssohn. In a sense the poorhouse would indeed outlast their homes. The old continue to be old-fashioned, though their youths were modern. We grow backward, aging into our father's opinions and even into those of our grandfathers.

WHILE the festivities in front were flattened in the plane of shadow, the west wing received the benefit of the declining sun, which hung behind the smoked glass of the lower atmosphere, orange, oblate, and distended. More color than light, it was bearable to look at. Eyes whose pupils like its image had enlarged in growing darkness studied without squinting this blank medallion. Angelo had gone home. Except for the echo of band music the room was quiet. All the energy used for moans and talk was consumed in the reception, by tiny discs of sensitive plate embedded in faces in turn embedded in pillows, of the horizontal rays of the daily omen. Orange bars streamed parallel to the beds; from the peaks on the sheets conic shadows fell upward, toward heads and shoulders, slashing linen which was, in the contrast, faint green-blue. Sunset in the summer was framed between two horsechestnut trees; in winter one tree obscured it, fretting its unpredictable colors with a system of twigs that never changed. Tonight, a bank of gray, like washed slate upon which the schoolchild's sun had been pasted, sloped upward into purple, and changed to soft cloth, undulating in long even folds as if crimped for display. At the horizon stood the thunderheads of the storm that had passed. Diminished by distance and pierced by light, they seemed transparent. The air was unmarked except by their blue outlines, dividing a gray that was cool from one within that was (heightened in the sky's superior scale of luminiscence) the same dull lilac Hook had observed shining through the ears of the rabbit on the grass beyond the wall.

Grace and her three companions entered the room softly. For all of them—even Grace, whose pity, foreknowing its object, was most moved—it was something of a prank. Ascending the stairs they had talked in whispers. "Night Nurse look in yet, Mrs. Dice?"

"Why Grace," this woman murmured, whose kidneys would never let her rest. "Aren't you off?"

"Yes, honey. See how I'm dressed." She lifted her round arms and moved backward, so it could be seen that beneath the white bolero jacket a street dress flowered.

"Oh. Pretty."

"These are my friends. We've come to see how you're enjoying the fair."

Mrs. Dice turned her head and said to Joe, "She's an angel to us. We wouldn't last without her." Her eyes fastened on the paper bags in his hands.

"We've brought some things they're selling," Grace explained. "Which would you like, Mrs. Dice? Apples or candy?"

"Oh, dear. I can't refuse candy." She took a piece of chocolate and, since Joe did not immediately snatch the bag from under her hovering hand, another. "No one but you would have thought of us, Grace," she said, with an expression of pathetic daughterly gratitude slowed and made solid by complacence, to which Grace's too-fleeting and tentative expression of maternal serenity exactly corresponded. For Grace, here in her love dress, felt queer, whereas Mrs. Dice lay on a bed drenched with her existence and inseparable from it, and was more hostess than guest.

Aware, through the eyes of the immobile patients, of their health's splendor, the young people drifted, with a patter of shoes, through the beams of red sunshine that scored the room like a sheet of music-paper. Grace did not introduce her friends by name. Made timid by the thought that their presence might be a breach of regulations, she communicated stealth to the expedition. To some bewildered eyes the rays of sunshine seemed visible through these visitant bodies, a bar persisting now through a waist, now a set of shoulders.

The girl who was not Grace took an apple for herself and

bit into it sharply; the moisture of her lips glistened around the white crescent she had opened in the skin. She was rapidly growing at ease in this ward, which upon her entering it had given her a choking feeling, shocked as she was by the absence of oranges and flowers. She moved away from the group, visiting beds independently, asking, "How are you feeling? Don't you see lovely sunsets here? Wouldn't you like your pillow plumped? Let me." As the young people moved from bed to bed, emptying their paper bags, hilarity swelled in the ward. Old people leaned their heads toward one another and compared candies. As a joke Grace left a licorice pipe on Angelo's desk. The tide of conversation, dry laughter of surprise, exclamations—"Wasn't that charitable?" "Gum drops and I have no teeth." "Who would have thought?" "Winesap, this one." "When she straightened my pillow I thought I'd scream with the pain." "Such a pert blouse." "Did you notice how Grace's boy kept his eyes on her behind?" —continued in the great room (Mrs. Andrews's foolish ballroom) for minutes after the young people had left, then gradually subsided into silence before the new and tragic spectacle the wide windows were offering.

The disc of the sun was no longer seen. Opaque air had descended to the horizon, hills beyond the housetops of the town. On one side, the northern, a slab of blue-black, the mantle of purple altered, reared upward; on the other, inky rivers tinged with pink fled in one diagonal direction. Between these two masses glowed a long throat, a gap flooded with a lucent yellow whiter than gold, that seemed to mark the place where, trailing blue clouds, a sublime creature had plunged to death. The titanic yellow furrow dimmed into blue as it approached the zenith, now capped by night, and was rounded like a comet head nearest the horizon, where the color was most intense, the color of an unnatural element, transuranic, created atom by atom in the scientist's laboratory, at inestimable expense. Off to the south the rivulets of dark vapor left in the wake of the catastrophe broadened into horizontals pale by contrast to the deepening sky behind

them. Upon the terraces of these ranged clouds blackish em-
bryos of cumulus stood on their tails like sea horses or cen-
taurs performing. As the patients watched, the golden chasm
shaded, through faint turquoise, into blue, and clouds propelled by evening winds trespassed its margins.

WEARY of his wife's chatter—always about Joan, Joan who
was always on the move, never in one place a week, who
wished this parakeet on them, always wishing things on them
yet not writing two letters a year, her husband not steady,
always on the move, why can't they have a nice home like we
gave her? why can't they make roots?: all this when Martha
should know that the world had changed and Joan was moving with it—Lucas left the porch and went out back to see the
hogs. In crossing the open space between the outbuildings he
stepped on the spot where, throughout the storm, the cat's
body had lain. Lucas rested his forearms on the rough
breadth of the top rail. His ear hurt slightly. Within the pen
the swine drifted in small families, sucking and snorting; rippling lips slapped wet teeth and exhalations poured whistling
through contracted nostrils. One huge Hampshire hog, a king,
groaned rhapsodically as he staggered up from pit of mud.
Lucas minded the stench of the pen no more than the smells
of his own body. Between his teeth he crooned, "Sooey.
Sooey. Sow sow sow." Dignified by dark into silver zeppelins,
the sleepy swine drifted toward him, their sharp feet sucked
by the soft ground, their voices raised to a pitch of expectation. Embarrassed at the misunderstanding—had had nothing
to give them; morning was their time—Lucas said, "Look at
your trough. Half-full." A few carrots and grapefruit rinds
remained in the trough; the pigs disdained these.

The lights in the west wing came on. Night Nurse had entered. The squares of artificial light cast this distance touched
with yellow the notched ears, made a brown eye shine, caught
the innocent faces in something of their pinkness, and turned
the shell of half a lime vivid green. As at the approach of day
the pigs squealed gaily; the tits of a great sow stood out erect.

The Hampshire hog collapsed on his side with a brilliant peal, and a single tide of fat swung across his body. Then Night Nurse cut back the electricity, letting a few bulbs guide her. As the general body of pigs withdrew into the darker reaches of the pen, a few flung back, across their haunches, looks of distrust at the silhouette of the spy leaning on the fence. One baby, paralyzed on rigid legs, abruptly rooted at the lime rind, and wheeled and fled, crying.

What could Conner do to them? A man with a family was always more vulnerable than one who had none. It had been he who had brought the bottle of rye onto the property. Conner had said, *I know you all.* Buddy would uncover everything. He sensed that Buddy hated him, because he treated Conner like a human and got him dirty that way. Tomorrow he had better see Conner in his office. Were anything to happen the shock would crumple Martha's legs. The bottle, was it still on the porch? Better find it, throw it on the trash.

By an unexpected tension beneath his eyes he learned that he was smiling. He had remembered a domestic incident of thirty years ago. Joan was just two. Poor Eddy was a new baby. Martha had been lying upstairs, trying for an afternoon nap, and Joan, wakened from hers, came downstairs to her father. Lucas from where he sat on the sofa had heard Joan and Martha talking. The child's forehead was bumpy with a frown. "Don't," he had said, reaching out to smooth the skin.

"Whez ahm?"

"Where's what? Did you have a good nap?"

"Whez *ahm?*" Her eyes widened. "In, in *bakket*, with boko bottle."

"Martha," he had shouted, "what is she saying?"

There had been no reply but the sound of Martha's laughter.

"Martha, what did you tell Joan?"

Her laughter, louder, tumbled down the stairs. The child had gone into the kitchen, and Lucas found her at the waste-basket, taking out boxes and scraps. "Burn bottles," she explained earnestly, knowing this was naughty. "Whez mommy *ahm?*"

This much he understood: a few days before, Martha had let the water boil away under two bottles she was sterilizing for Eddy, and the sight of these cracked and blackened bottles had worried Joan considerably. "The bottles aren't there any more," he told her.

Then Martha came down, small-eyed from her nap and laughing, and hugged the child and showed her her left arm and said, "Here's Mommy's arm. See: two arms. You can't take an arm off and put it in the wastebasket. It was Mommy's joke. It's all right, sweet. Oh, sweetie. Little girl." She explained to Lucas that Joan had crawled up on the bed while she was napping on her side, and had asked where was the other arm. Yielding in her drowsy state to a silly impulse, she had answered that Mommy had grown tired of her arm, it was no good, and she had thrown it away, with the burnt bottles.

They laughed together and consoled with embraces the puzzled girl, who for the next days continued to poke in the wastebasket. It had moved them close to tears to discover that the child, whose vocabulary and cunning daily fattened, could still be deceived so outrageously, her trust in her parents so far exceeding her knowledge of things.

"WHORE? she says. Is that what I am? So that's what you call me? And calm as you please she pulls out every one of his tulips and gladiola, and tosses them into his birdbath. This about two A.M. in the morning, mind you."

"Come on, Maryann. Why not? Just tell me why not."

"Isn't she beautiful? I think the blind are always so calm, as if, you know, they see things we don't."

"No now," Hook said, "the people nowadays have it so good, they are unable to con-ceive of a better place awaiting them."

"Yes, the blue of her eyes."

"Well, I slept through everything, but Jack says it was Leonard's bellow woke him up. And nobody sleeps sounder than Jack, usually; I'm the one who's awake at the drop of a pin, usually."

"Anybody else would, if they liked a person. Come *on*. We promise nobody'll touch you."

"I suppose," Kegerise admitted, "I should be heading home myself. I told them I'd have the boy home by six."

"We promise on a stack of telephone directories nobody'll touch you."

"Yes, as innocent as a baby's. Do you suppose she really is? She moves them just like anybody else."

"It was awfully sweet of you all. I really feel like having a good time now."

"The time is ap-proaching when us old fellas should be climbing the wooden hill. Rafe Beam, my father's hired man, used to recite,

'Late in bed,
Soon dead.
Up by dawn,
Never gone.' "

A young couple was interested in one of Mrs. Mortis's quilts. The boy was saying, "No ma'am, I don't want to let you do that. Your price is fair, it's just that, Honest to God, we don't have the M-O-N-E-Y."

The girl said, "Here's a patch exactly like the wallpaper we want for the living room."

"Honey, we can't ask the lady to let us pay a dollar a week or anything like that."

"Jack says he heard Leonard shout he was calling the police. You know how you can hear a pin drop on that street since all the lovely elms died. Jack said she said, and I couldn't re-peat the exact words, that he could take the police and push them up his pants and furthermore she hopes they do come, because what he said to her was slander. Which I suppose is true. She never takes money."

"All we want to do is *see*. Dotty's agreed."

"I have *not*."

"What would it hurt? Just tell me one thing it would hurt."

"When she bit that apple I thought I'd crawl under a bed."

"Look how she touches the sleeve of the man. They must be in love."

"Isn't *he* a horror though? What *are* those things he's selling?"

"I guess we *do* have seven dollars. But—"

"We'll let you see *us*."

Conner from above wished they would disperse; the quicker they dispersed, the less chance there was of the story of to-day's incident spreading among them. Thinking of the incident made his stomach tremble with nervousness. Buddy came over and stood beside him, placing a hand on Conner's shoulder, then dropping it to his waist. Conner pulled away, amazed and annoyed. Buddy flushed, pardoned himself, and went downstairs, leaving the office divided between Conner and the unused piano.

"Now I think I *will* spank you."

"But where should we go? *Not* Lorry's again. Anything but Lorry's."

"How could it hurt you? What are you ashamed of? Huh? What are you ashamed of?"

"He went around in his pajamas to their front porch, and the only thing there of course was their rubber welcome mat, so he tried to tear it with his bare hands and couldn't. He actually had the presence of mind, while she had let herself into her half by the kitchen door and was weeping and waking up her girl—the husband of course was off at work; his working nights is ninety-nine per cent of her trouble if you ask me— Leonard actually had the coolness to go back into his house, get his gardening shears, and cut the rubber welcome mat into tiny bits while she's in her front parlor shouting at him through the window. She was scared to come out and I don't blame her, he's so big."

"Oh, I'm too old for shopkeeper's hours," Mrs. Mortis said aloud to herself. "Where's that chair I begged?"

"What do you mean, not nice? If your own body's not nice, what is? Why not shoot yourself if you don't want a body?"

"Ken boy! I missed you at Lions. Kay here? I wanted to ask her how did *she* enjoy Florida? I know *you* enjoyed it."

"Your body's yours, isn't it? It's not your mother's or any-body's."

Buddy had found someone he knew, a young man who worked in Town Hall, where Buddy sometimes went on business. To him and his companions he said immediately, "Do any of you know what the hell happened here this after-noon? The ancients in residence in this pleasure-palace seized rocks the size of suckling pigs and brained their shepherd, the reverend Mr. Conner. Seriously."

"I think living in a double house like that, with just the partition between families, must build up tensions. I'm so thankful we have grass on all four sides of us, even if it's not much as yards go."

"Indeed it is not wise, to dis-obey one's daughter. The warmer the love, the harder the tem-per bites."

Hook made these words his farewell to Kegerise, who, certain of being more than an hour late, was beginning to perspire unhealthily. His eye caught his grandson, himself tired and queasy, coming to be taken home. Hook went on to the porch, at the end farthest from the band, which was taking a rest, and lit a cigar, his day's last. Conner's childish prohibition had quite faded from his mind. His mind vaulted far over it. The level farm land beyond the merrymakers might well have been, in the darkness, water, steadily flow-ing beneath its unbroken black skin. Near at hand Mrs. John-son waited behind her display of candies. Hook remembered an incident of twenty years before, when he had been an old man, as now. He had retired from schoolteaching and lived with the family of his daughter, then alive, in a rural house several miles outside of the town beside the Delaware. They rented the land to a combine. At the bend of a nearby high-way Harry Petree operated a modest store, a shack of two rooms. In one there was a wood stove and the papers of several Sundays ago; in the other a case of candy, and shelves of cigarettes, cigars, lighter fluid, scotch tape, ballpoint pens, and other oddments for which there was small demand. In the summer months Harry kept a tank of soft-drink; the old flavors, lime, sarsaparilla, birch. Outside two gasoline pumps stood, the outmoded bubble-head style. Because the shack was at a bend of the road, the high-powered cars came upon it too late to brake, and indeed they may have thought, from the look of the place, that it was deserted. Whatever the cause, few stopped. Perhaps Harry did three or four dollars' worth of business a day, on the cigars and candy occasionally purchased by the old men—Hook alone still living—who loitered out the afternoons in the room with the wood stove. Harry was an uncouth, almost savage man, very short in stature, never without a great wad of tobacco plug in his mouth, a stain dribbling from the corner of his gray lips. He spoke in a growl, garbled by the piece of plug, which it took a considerable period of acquaintance to understand. He and his sister owned the land; she did housework around the neighborhood, and he had a small pension, as a veteran of the first world war. They lived in their father's sandstone house, by the light of kerosene, well back from the road. With their truck garden, they survived, but never had the money for improvements, at the house or at the store. In the seven years Hook had his acquaintance, Harry grew blacker in the face, and growled more and more obscurely. The children of the countryside around were frightened of him, and seldom came into the dark shack, where the candies waited beneath the curved case. One day in the spring, the gasoline company, of its own accord, changed the two rusted pumps to squat, square, red, new pumps, visible for a mile, and hung a new sign on the pole. That week a young man in an expensive car stopped and had Harry fill up the tank. It was a powerful car, with a big tank, and it came to sixteen gallons and over four dollars. Holding a creased twenty-dollar bill between his fingers, the young man asked Harry if he would fetch him a pack of cigarettes, and while Harry was within pulled away and disappeared down the road. Harry lingered at the store a few more days, his eyes no darker than the skin around them and the juice spilling unrestrainedly from his lips, telling the story to whoever would listen. Then the store was shut, which had stayed open often as late as ten, while the wags loitering there completed their conversations. The screen door was padlocked and Harry never came down from the sandstone house. In a short while, nursed by his sister, he died, of liver and heart. Then all the neighbors, who had never patronized the store except for odd gallons of gasoline to get them into town, sent fifteen-dollar bouquets to the funeral, and the recollected sting of those fragrant banked blooms, or perhaps it was the smoke of his cigar, caused Hook's eyes to water behind their shields of glass.

At the time his daughter had scolded him, "Yes, now you can grieve; but did you ever buy ten pennies' worth from the old man, instead of sitting there rollicking at all hours, when he wanted to be in bed?" He had explained, he had never thought, and how much money did he have to spend? But now, as he stood there on the porch, it seemed that in the whole vast tract of his life this was the one offense, the one sin against God sharp enough to make a film of regret mount in his eyes.

He opened his mouth idly, as if again to offer his explanation to his daughter.

He cast his mind ahead, to the trip up the stairs, the "wooden hill," and the hard chair and firm bed, and the Bible, its spine in shreds, from which he would read a chapter of the Gospels, those springs of no certain bottom, which you never find dry. But these doings seemed to lie far distant in the future, more distant even than the backward horizon of his life, and for the present his old man's thin tears, magnified by his spectacles' strong lenses, sank, one great transparent membrane, over the entire gay scene.

"Because your father and I *said* so."

"Well, come with us and watch Dotty do it. You can't mind that."

"Then the good man simply states, 'I forgive them.' And the doddering assassins disappear into the crowd. And that's the high tone of the management we have down here."

"Then in fifteen minutes the police car was going up the street. The green light on top was winking but the siren wasn't blowing, not at two A.M. From my window I just saw that it was Benny Young driving, sober for one night of the week. The way he carries on at the fire hall I don't know what he dared tell them, but there wasn't any more noise from that end of the street, and the next morning her daughter walked past on the way to school, her books in her arms, as normal as you please. She's such a nice girl. You can't get her to say a word against her mother."

"I won't if Maryann won't. I won't anyway."

"You can see the headlines," Buddy said, spacing the bars with his fingers in the air,

"POOR PELT PREFECT
CONNER STONED
ON DAY OF FAIR."

"The first day we made Raleigh, and the next we really pushed ourselves and stopped just this side of Jacksonville, at a very fine motel, to give ourselves leeway next day, so we could get there in time for a swim before supper. Man that sea felt like a million dollars."

"Oh, we're not worried yet."

"Tell him I asked after him."

"I told him: brother, you're psychological."

"Now see what you've done, Maryann. Proud of yourself? I bet you are. I'm going to tell everybody you're frigid."

"Have you heard about any trouble they had with the inmates this afternoon? I guess they didn't want to go on with the fair."

"Her eye was swollen so you couldn't see the lashes."

"Well," Mrs. Mortis said to the dealer from Trenton, "I sold one by giving it away. You can have the rest I guess." She was lapsed into her chair, her little head, in its stiff bonnet, sunk on her goiter.

"This is wonderful news, missus. Look, I bought from your friend down the line some of these trinkets." He showed a handful of Tommy Franklin's carved peachpits. "In my profession, you never know what people will buy. Now let us see. I said a hundred dollars for six, so for five that would be, oh, eighty-five dollars."

"Whatever is fair. These are my last. I won't do any more."

"It kills me to hear you say that. Suppose I sent you cloth?"

"Send it care of my casket."

Upstairs Conner was rereading, for the tenth time, the letter that had preyed on him since morning. It was a kind of sickness, to run his eye through it again and again:

Stephen Conner—

Who do you think you are a Big shot? Yr duty is to help not hinder these old people on there way to there final Reward. I myself have heard bitter complant from these old people when they come into town where I live. They call you Pieface you and that moran Buddy. The nature of there complants I will disclose latter, and will write the U.S. gov.ment depending. Things have not gone so far these old people have no rights no pale peeny-notchin basterd can take away.

A "Town's person"

A woman, certainly. Conner remembered from textbook cases the resources of obscenity to be found in spinsters. The handwriting was painfully, jerkily formed, on five and dime notepaper with the kind of blue ballpoint Conner associated with post offices. The capitals had all the superstructure of the orthodox Spenserian hand that had been taught in public schools forty years ago. Each "r" was an anvil. The two abbreviations hinted at some acquaintance with making out bills and invoices. The townsperson had become very real to him, with her swinging strings of black beads and wideset, flat, dim, hysteric eyes, the eyes of Christian Science. Like his old music teacher, when he lived in Wilmington. He moved to the piano, lifted the varnished lid, and beat out several harsh chords in her memory. This chased the sad phantom. He was grateful that tomorrow would be a normal day. Ever since he could remember, he hated holidays.

"Before we got there we wondered if the people at this hotel wouldn't, you know, act above us. From what we were paying it seemed they might. But not at all, they were common as dirt—real people. Kay had a wonderful time. This one woman from St. Louis and she struck up a real friendship. While me and her husband—he sold parts to the knitting industry and cleared over twenty thousand a year, but he was humble, a hell of a good egg—while we were down on the beach Kay and the wife sat on the porch yakkity yakkity yak. Kay didn't go into the sun six times all the time we were down there. Her skin stayed just as white—I said to her, here we are, paying thirty dollars a day for this sunshine, and you sit up there yakking away all day. But then what the hell, on a vacation you should do what you want, is the way I look at it. Her skin just as white as that moon up there."

"At first they thought it was an allergy but now they've decided it's an infection. The doctor said, penicillin, and I told him, you don't know my daughter. She will *not* take medicine. He said, she'll take this and want more. You know what it was?"

"Ken, this is interesting. I'm as happy you had a good time as if I had it myself. You convinced me the people that say Wildwood is just as good are full of crap. Say, speaking of nothing, I glanced in at your house when you were off, and it looks to me that with a fresh coat *now*, it would do you for five more years."

"Banana penicillin!"

"Maryann," the boy whispered to the girl he wanted to walk naked in front of his headlights, "I love you, can't you understand? Look." He took out his switchknife and holding the blade at an angle pressed it deeply into the white of his forearm, so deeply that in the crook of the arrow-shaped purple bruise one drop of dark blood appeared.

"Am I impressed," Dotty said.

"I'll do more if you don't," he said to Maryann, ignoring Dotty, who was safe, "deeper this time." He began.

Maryann said, "You dope; don't."

He said urgently in her ear, "I love you that much, is what I'm trying to say. I'd cut off an arm to prove it. I'd eat s. for you; I mean it: *anything.* I love you, love love love *you, every*thing about you; can't I see what I love? I'd do anything for *you.*"

"Fred, I know you're sincere, and you wouldn't tell me just to drum up business, but to be frank, after this vacation I'm strapped for spare cash. You know how I am; if I can't pay on the nail, I don't buy. That's the way I've operated, and it's a method that's stood by me."

"Now we're going home and you're going to get a spanking."

"It doesn't surprise me. You need to have an older man in a drab job like this. The state just loves these younger men, but you sometimes need a man with a look of authority. Nothing ever happened I'm sure when that one was here who was in the tavern so often. With the big head."

Indeed Mrs. Mortis was thinking, as she walked across the grass, her apron pockets full of dollar bills, *Not like in Mendelssohn's day* . . .

Mendelssohn, Mendelssohn in his beautiful knobbed casket, a carnation in his lapel, legs pillowed in satin, can we believe that he will never rise? Grass returns. Perfectly preserved his blind lids stretch above the crumbled smile. The skin that life has fled is calm as marble. Can we believe, who have seen his vital nostrils flare expressively, revealing in lifting the flaming septum, the secret wall red with pride within, that there is no resurrection? That bright bit of flesh; where would such a thing have gone?

"Well," Maryann said, "let's get away from here anyway. Everybody's going home." The four children went to the one boy's car, and while he anxiously coaxed the old motor— the glow from the dash catching the orange arcs of the girl's clipped, tossed hairdo and glazing the flat of her cheeks—the radio warmed and sang:

> "Bajo de la peña nace
> la rosa que no quema el aire."

In the silence of the band, which had stopped to smoke and wipe the instruments, the snatch of tune drifted over the wall into the crowd.

It was not true that everyone was going home. It was not yet eight o'clock; the adults, disposed in groups of three and four, were just warming to each other. Only a few children, the offspring of irresponsible homes, raced between their legs and wrestled on the trampled grass, which was starting to exhale dampness as the dew set in. The pyramids of sweet corn were diminished to a few bruised ears. The women on hot dogs wondered if they should send to the kitchen for another pack; the buying seemed to be over. Tommy Franklin had led Elizabeth Heinemann to the porch. Under the colored lights Mrs. Johnson scolded two giggling boys who had attempted, under cover of a penny purchase, to steal some cough drops. They constantly edged one behind the other, like a deck of two cards shuffling itself.

"He was absolutely right. She loved it. I gave myself a spoonful, and it was delicious. It *was*. The druggist said you can get it in peach and cherry and orange flavors too."

"The thing is this, Ken. Your paint now is in good shape. Another summer of this heat and it will start to flake. Now it would be to my advantage, if I was solely concerned in making work for myself, to let you let it go until it really needed it, then the scraping down would add, say, three hundred to your bill. Slap it on *now*, and the whole house could be done for, well, if you want an estimate I'll be glad to come over."

"I'll talk it over with Kay."

"At first it seemed to make it go up more. Well, John said, another ten dollars down the drain, and poor Popeye's worse than ever. When she had this condition, he called her Popeye. I said, wait a minute. You can't go around saying all doctors are crooks. You have to believe somebody."

"I'll say this. A big outfit would charge you fourteen hundred for one coat. That's a fair-sized house you have there, and all that trim is what makes a job long. We used to figure eighty dollars for a twelve-pane window. But if you were, and I'm just saying this so when you talk it over with Kay you will have something concrete to go on, if you were to let me do it between now and Labor day, when I still have my summer boys, I'd say, oh—" He squinted.

"The next day a little splinter of blue showed."

"Oh, eleven fifty, at a very rough guess. Without the grape arbor."

"Hey wait for me."

"Kay loves that place, I can tell you that much. On the way back, did I mention it, past Baltimore, I was doing, hell, I was doing eighty, and she steps on my foot and floors the accelerator and keeps it there. Don't poke, she says, I want to get home. I didn't think going eighty miles an hour was poking, but I said, You're the doctor. We'll die happy."

"Now it's just a little droopy, but *he* says we don't know what caused it, and what's to prevent it from coming back and us being in hock to the doctors for the rest of our life? I told him, Relax. Have a little faith."

"Wa-it, for Chrissake!"

"That's just like the Kay I knew: the original live wire. When I knew her at school, Ken, there wasn't exactly grass growing under her feet. She's every inch a woman, as of course you'd know."

"I kind of hope, really, it doesn't clear up for another few days, so I can try the peach flavor."

"I'll level with you Fred. I don't think I can swing it after this wonderful vacation. The house looks good to me."

"Don't laugh. The banana was really yummy; I pity you, having such healthy brats."

"Hey wai-it *up*."

The north horizon glowed at the place where, deep in a field behind a rise, the two girls stiffly basked in the headlights, wondering what emotion they should feel, and what eyes might be in the trees. The boys, staring, were hidden beyond the opaque windshield, the girls' clothes lying neatly in their laps. Above, the stars were not specks but needles of light suspended point downward in a black depth of stiff jelly. The band resumed its sheaf of Sousa with *American Patrol*, played *dolce*, then *forte*. The effect created was that of a band coming toward you from far down the street. A disturbed sparrow dipped under the string of burning colored bulbs, taking crimson on its back for an instant. The people who had come to the fair talked more slowly, tending toward affectionate gossip about the past they had in common as citizens of the town, and about roads and schools and old houses sold. Coarsened hands of still handsome women nervously tucked back stray stands of hair; young mothers pouted under the weight of sleeping babies. Above them in the cupola Conner worked unseen, checking Buddy's typed reports. Except for Gregg and a few weary biddies keeping their stands going, the old people had vanished from this crowd, having gone to bed, for they had to rise early, to guard the gates of the deserted kingdom.

THE MAN of flesh, the man of passion, the man of thought. Lucas slept. His body, stripped to underclothes and half-covered with a sheet, submitted in oblivion to a harmony of forms. Gregg hopped and chirruped on the lawn, dazzling himself with the illumination and talking aloud in his self-delight, though tomorrow he would be as cross as ever. Hook sat up with a start. The pillow and his horizontal position had been smothering him, and the phlegm in his throat could not be rasped away. His heart doubled its speed of beating; and gradually slowed. He moved his legs, blue bones in the cold light, to the floor and stood up in his nightshirt and walked about in his tiny room aimlessly. The moon so feeble previously now cast shadows through the window and rendered shapes: the bent boards of the little thick Bible, the open mouths of his shoes, the hang of his vest on the hook, the ribs of caning on the seat of his one chair. He opened his door and saw the blank bright green corridor wall across the way and closed it. His encounter with Conner had commenced to trouble him. The young man had been grievously stricken. The weakness on his face after his henchman had stolen the cigar was troubling to recall; an intimacy had been there Hook must reward with help. A small word would perhaps set things right. As a teacher, Hook's flaw had been over-conscientiousness; there was nowhere he would not meddle. He stood motionless, half in moonlight, groping after the fitful shadow of the advice he must impart to Conner, as a bond between them and a testament to endure his dying in the world. What was it?

RABBIT, RUN

The motions of Grace, the hardness of the heart;
external circumstances.

PASCAL, Pensée 507

BOYS are playing basketball around a telephone pole with a backboard bolted to it. Legs, shouts. The scrape and snap of Keds on loose alley pebbles seems to cata-- pult their voices high into the moist March air blue above the wires. Rabbit Angstrom, coming up the alley in a business suit, stops and watches, though he's twenty-six and six three. So tall, he seems an unlikely rabbit, but the breadth of white face, the pallor of his blue irises, and a nervous flutter under his brief nose as he stabs a cigarette into his mouth partially explain the nickname, which was given to him when he too was a boy. He stands there thinking. The kids keep coming, they keep crowding you up.

His standing there makes the real boys feel strange. Eye-balls slide. They're doing this for themselves, not as a show for some adult walking around town in a double-breasted cocoa suit. It seems funny to them, an adult walking up the alley at all. Where's his car? The cigarette makes it more sin-ister still. Is this one of those going to offer them cigarettes or money to go out in back of the ice plant with him? They've heard of such things but are not too frightened; there are six of them and one of him.

The ball, rocketing off the crotch of the rim, leaps over the heads of the six and lands at the feet of the one. He catches it on the short bounce with a quickness that startles them. As they stare hushed he sights squinting through blue clouds of weed smoke, a suddenly dark silhouette like a smokestack against the afternoon spring sky, setting his feet with care, wiggling the ball with nervousness in front of his chest, one widespread white hand on top of the ball and the other underneath, jiggling it patiently to get some adjustment in air itself. The cuticle moons on his fingernails are big. Then the ball seems to ride up the right lapel of his coat and comes off his shoulder as his knees dip down, and it appears the ball will miss because though he shot from an angle the ball is not going toward the backboard. It was not aimed there. It drops into the circle of the rim, whipping the net with a ladylike whisper. "Hey!" he shouts in pride.

"Luck," one of the kids says.

"Skill," he answers, and asks, "Hey. O.K. if I play?"

There is no response, just puzzled silly looks swapped. Rabbit takes off his coat, folds it nicely, and rests it on a clean ashcan lid. Behind him the dungarees begin to scuffle again. He goes into the scrimmaging thick of them for the ball, flips it from two weak grubby-knuckled child's hands, has it in his own. That old stretched-leather feeling makes his whole body go taut, gives his arms wings. It feels like he's reaching down through years to touch this tautness. His arms lift of their own and the rubber ball floats toward the basket from the top of his head. It feels so right he blinks when the ball drops short, and for a second wonders if it went through the hoop without riffling the net. He asks, "Hey whose side am I on?"

In a wordless shuffle two boys are delegated to be his. They stand the other four. Though from the start Rabbit handicaps himself by staying ten feet out from the basket, it is still unfair. Nobody bothers to keep score. The surly silence bothers him. The kids call monosyllables to each other but to him they don't dare a word. As the game goes on he can feel them at his legs, getting hot and mad, trying to trip him, but their tongues are still held. He doesn't want this respect, he wants to tell them there's nothing to getting old, it takes nothing. In ten minutes another boy goes to the other side, so it's just Rabbit Angstrom and one kid standing five. This boy, still midget but already diffident with a kind of rangy ease, is the best of the six; he wears a knitted cap with a green pompon well down over his ears and level with his eyebrows, giving his head a cretinous look. He's a natural. The way he moves sideways without taking any steps, gliding on a blessing: you can tell. The way he waits before he moves. With luck he'll become in time a crack athlete in the high school; Rabbit knows the way. You climb up through the little grades and then get to the top and everybody cheers; with the sweat in your eyebrows you can't see very well and the noise swirls around you and lifts you up, and then you're out, not forgotten at first, just out, and it feels good and cool and free. You're out, and sort of melt, and keep lifting, until you become like to these kids just one more piece of the sky of adults that hangs over them in the town, a piece that for some queer reason has clouded and visited them. They've not forgotten him: worse, they never heard of him. Yet in his time Rabbit was famous through the county; in basketball in his junior year he set a B-league scoring record that in his senior year he broke with a record that was not broken until four years later, that is, four years ago.

He sinks shots one-handed, two-handed, underhanded, flat-footed, and out of the pivot, jump, and set. Flat and soft the ball lifts. That his touch still lives in his hands elates him. He feels liberated from long gloom. But his body is weighty and his breath grows short. It annoys him, that he gets winded. When the five kids not on his side begin to groan and act lazy, and a kid he accidentally knocks down gets up with a blurred face and walks away, Rabbit quits readily. "O.K.," he says. "The old man's going. Three cheers."

To the boy on his side, the pompon, he adds, "So long,

ace." He feels grateful to the boy, who continued to watch
him with disinterested admiration after the others grew sullen.
Naturals know.

Rabbit picks up his folded coat and carries it in one hand
like a letter as he runs. Up the alley. Past the deserted ice
plant with its rotting wooden skids on the fallen loading
porch. Ashcans, garage doors, fences of chicken-wire caging
crisscrossing stalks of dead flowers. The month is March.
Love makes the air light. Things start anew; Rabbit tastes
through sour aftersmoke the fresh chance in the air, plucks
the pack of cigarettes from his bobbling shirt pocket, and
without breaking stride cans it in somebody's open barrel. His
upper lip nibbles back from his teeth in self-pleasure. His big
suede shoes skim in thumps above the skittering litter of alley
gravel.

Running. At the end of this block of the alley he turns up a
street, Wilbur Street in the town of Mt. Judge, suburb of the
city of Brewer, fifth largest city in Pennsylvania. Running
uphill. Past a block of big homes, small fortresses of cement
and brick inset with doorways of stained and beveled glass
and windows of potted plants; and then half-way up another
block, which holds a development built all at once in the
thirties. The frame homes climb the hill like a single staircase.
The space of six feet or so that each double house rises above
its neighbor contains two wan windows, wide-spaced like the
eyes of an animal, and is covered with composition shingling
varying in color from bruise to dung. The fronts are scabby
clapboards, once white. There are a dozen three-story homes,
and each has two doors. The seventh door is his. The wood
steps up to it are worn; under them there is a cubbyhole of
dirt where a lost toy molders. A plastic clown. He's seen it
there all winter but he always thought some kid would be
coming back for it.

Rabbit pauses in the sunless vestibule, panting. Overhead,
a daytime bulb burns dustily. Three tin mailboxes hang empty
above a brown radiator. His downstairs neighbor's door
across the hall is shut like a hurt face. There is that smell

which is always the same but that he can never identify; sometimes it seems cabbage cooking, sometimes the furnace's
rusty breath, sometimes something soft decaying in the walls.
He climbs the stairs to his home, the top floor.

The door is locked. In fitting the little key into the lock his
hand trembles, pulsing with unusual exertion, and the metal
scratches. But when he opens the door he sees his wife sitting
in an armchair with an Old-fashioned, watching television
turned down low.

"You're *here*," he says. "What's the door locked for?"

She looks to one side of him with vague dark eyes red-
dened by the friction of watching. "It just locked itself."

"Just locked itself," he repeats, but bends down to kiss her
glossy forehead nevertheless. She is a small woman whose
skin tends toward olive and looks tight, as if something swelling inside is straining against her littleness. Just yesterday, it
seems to him, she stopped being pretty. With the addition of
two short wrinkles at the corners, her mouth has become
greedy; and her hair has thinned, so he keeps thinking of her
skull under it. These tiny advances into age have occurred im-
perceptibly, so it seems just possible that tomorrow they'll
be gone and she'll be his girl again. He makes a stab at kidding her into it. "Whaddeya afraid of? Whodeya think's
gonna come in that door? Errol Flynn?"

She doesn't answer. Carefully he unfolds his coat and goes
to the closet with it and takes out a wire hanger. The closet is
in the living-room and the door only opens half-way, since
the television set is in front of it. He is careful not to kick the
wire, which is plugged into a socket on the other side of the
door. One time Janice, who is especially clumsy when pregnant or drunk, got the wire wrapped around her foot and
nearly pulled the set, a hundred and forty-nine dollars, down
smash on the floor. Luckily he got to it while it was still rocking in the metal cradle and before Janice began kicking out in
one of her panics. What made her get that way? What was
she afraid of? An order-loving man, he deftly inserts the corners of the hanger into the armholes of the coat and with

his long reach hangs it on the painted pipe with his other clothes. He wonders if he should remove the Demonstrator badge from the lapel but decides he will wear the same suit tomorrow. He has only two, not counting a dark blue that is too hot for this time of year. He presses the door shut and it clicks but then swings open again an inch or two. Locked doors. It rankles: his hand trembling in the lock like some old wreck and her sitting in here listening to the scratching.

He turns and asks her, "If you're home where's the car? It's not out front."

"It's in front of my mother's. You're in my way."

"In front of your mother's? That's terrific. That's just the frigging place for it."

"What's brought this on?"

"Brought what on?" He moves out of her line of vision and stands to one side.

She is watching a group of children called Mouseketeers perform a musical number in which Darlene is a flower girl in Paris and Cubby is a cop and that smirky squeaky tall kid is a romantic artist. He and Darlene and Cubby and Karen (dressed as an old French lady whom Cubby as a cop helps across the street) dance. Then the commercial shows the seven segments of a Tootsie Roll coming out of the wrapper and turning into the seven letters of "Tootsie." They, too, sing and dance. Still singing, they climb back into the wrapper. It echoes like an echo chamber. Son of a bitch: cute. He's seen it fifty times and this time it turns his stomach. His heart is still throbbing; his throat feels narrow.

Janice asks, "Harry, do you have a cigarette? I'm out."

"Huh? On the way home I threw my pack into a garbage can. I'm giving it up." He wonders how anybody could think of smoking, with his stomach on edge the way it is.

Janice looks at him at last. "You threw it into a garbage can! Holy Mo. You don't drink, now you don't smoke. What are you doing, becoming a saint?"

"Shh."

The big Mouseketeer has appeared, Jimmy, a grown man

who wears circular black ears. Rabbit watches him attentively; he respects him. He expects to learn something from him helpful in his own line of work, which is demonstrating a kitchen gadget in several five-and-dime stores around Brewer. He's had the job for four weeks. "Proverbs, proverbs, they're so true," Jimmy sings, strumming his Mouseguitar, "proverbs tell us what to do; proverbs help us all to *bee*—better—Mouse-ke-teers."

Jimmy sets aside his smile and guitar and says straight out through the glass, "Know Thyself, a wise old Greek once said. Know Thyself. Now what does this mean, boys and girls? It means, be what you are. Don't try to be Sally or Johnny or Fred next door; be yourself. God doesn't want a tree to be a waterfall, or a flower to be a stone. God gives to each one of us a special talent." Janice and Rabbit become un-naturally still; both are Christians. God's name makes them feel guilty. "God wants some of us to become scientists, some of us to become artists, some of us to become firemen and doctors and trapeze artists. And He gives to each of us the special talents to become these things, *provided we work to develop them.* We must *work,* boys and girls. So: Know Thyself. Learn to understand your talents, and then work to develop them. That's the way to be happy." He pinches his mouth together and winks.

That was good. Rabbit tries it, pinching the mouth together and then the wink, getting the audience out front with you against some enemy behind, Walt Disney or the MagiPeel Peeler Company, admitting it's all pretending but, what the hell, making it likable. We're all in it together. Pretending makes the world go round. The base of our economy. Vita-conomy, the modern housewife's password, the one-word expression for economizing vitamins by the MagiPeel Method.

Janice gets up and turns off the set when the six-o'clock news tries to come on. The little hard star left by the current slowly dies.

Rabbit asks, "Where's the kid?"

"At your mother's."

"At *my* mother's? The car's at your mother's and the kid's at my mother's. Jesus. You're a mess."

She stands up and her pregnancy infuriates him with its look of stubborn lumpiness. She wears one of those maternity skirts with a U cut in the belly. A white crescent of slip shines under the hem of her blouse. "I was tired."

"No wonder," he says. "How many of those have you had?" He gestures at the Old-fashioned glass. Sugar has stained the side she drank from.

She tries to explain. "I left Nelson at your mother's on my way to my mother's to go into town with her. We went in in her car and walked around looking at the spring clothes in the windows and she bought a nice Liberty scarf at Kroll's at a sale. Purply Paisley." She falters; her little narrow tongue pokes between her parted rows of dim teeth.

He feels frightened. When confused, Janice is a frightening person. Her eyes dwindle in their frowning sockets and her little mouth hangs open in a dumb slot. Since her hair has be-gun to thin back from her shiny forehead, he keeps getting the feeling of her being brittle, and immovable, of her only going one way, toward deeper wrinkles and skimpier hair. He married relatively late, when he was twenty-four and she was two years out of high school, still scarcely adult, with shy small breasts that when she lay down flattened against her chest so that they were only there as a tipped softness. Nelson was born seven months after the Episcopal service, in pro-longed labor: Rabbit's fright then mixes with his fright now and turns it tender. "What did you buy?"

"A bathing suit."

"A bathing suit! Chh. In March?"

She closes her eyes for a moment; he can feel the undertow of liquor sweep over her and is disgusted. "It made it seem closer to when I could fit into it."

"What the hell ails you? Other women *like* being pregnant. What's so damn fancy about you? Just tell me. What *is* so frigging fancy?"

She opens her brown eyes, brown and stirred like dissolving

coffee, and tears fill them and break over the lower lids and drop down her cheeks, pink with injury, while she looks at him and says "You bastard" very thoughtfully.

Rabbit goes to his wife and, putting his arms around her, has a vivid experience of her, her tear-hot breath, the blood-tinged whites of her eyes. In an affectionate reflex he dips his knees to bring his loins against hers, but her solid belly prevents him. He straightens to his full height above her and says, "O.K. You bought a bathing suit."

Sheltered by his chest and arms she blurts with an earnestness he didn't know she still could hold, "Don't run from me, Harry. I love you."

"I love *you*. Now come on, you bought a bathing suit."

"Red," she says, rocking sadly against him. But her body when tipsy has a brittleness, an unconnectedness, that feels disagreeable in his arms. "With a strap that ties behind your neck and a pleated skirt you can take off in the water. Then my varicose veins hurt so much Mother and I went into the basement of Kroll's and had chocolate sodas. They've redone the whole luncheonette section, the counter isn't there any more. But my legs still hurt so Mother brought me home and said you could pick up the car and Nelson."

"Your legs hell, they were probably her legs."

"I thought you'd be home before now. Where were you?"

"Oh, clowning around. I played ball with some kids down the alley." They have parted.

"I tried to take a nap but I couldn't. Mother said I looked tired."

"You're supposed to look tired. You're a modern housewife."

"And meanwhile you're off in the alley playing like a twelve-year-old?"

It gripes him that she didn't see his crack about being a housewife, based on the "image" the MagiPeel people tried to have their salesmen sell to, as ironical and at bottom pitying and fond. There seems no escaping it: she is dumb. He says, "Well what's the difference if you're sitting here watching a program for kids under two?"

"Who was *shush*ing a while ago?"

"Ah, Janice." He sighs. "Screw you. Just screw you."

She looks at him clearly a long moment. "I'll get supper," she at last decides.

He is all repentance. "I'll run over and get the car and bring the kid back. The poor kid must think he has no home. What the hell makes your mother think my mother has nothing better to do than take care of other people's kids?" Indignation rises in him again at her missing the point of why he wanted to watch Jimmy, for professional reasons, to earn a living to buy sugar for her to put into her rotten Old-fashioneds.

She moves into the kitchen, angry but not angry enough. She should be really sore, or not sore at all, since all he had said was what he had done a couple hundred times. Maybe a thousand times. Say, on the average once every three days since 1956. What's that? Three hundred. That often? Then why is it always an effort? She used to make it easier before they got married. She could be sudden then. Just a girl. Nerves like new thread. Skin smelled like fresh cotton. Her girl friend at work had an apartment in Brewer they used. Pipe-frame bed, silver medallions in the wallpaper; a view westward of the great blue gas tanks by the edge of the river. After work, working both at Kroll's then, she selling candy and cashews in a white smock with "Jan" stitched on her pocket and he lugging easy chairs and maple end tables around on the floor above, hammering apart packing crates from nine to five, the itch of the packing excelsior getting into his nose and eyes and making them burn. That filthy black crescent of bins behind the elevators, the floor covered with bent nails, his palms black and Chandler the fairy mincing in every hour on the hour telling him to wash his hands so he wouldn't foul the furniture. Lava soap. Its lather was gray. His hands grew yellow calluses from using the crowbar. After 5:30, the dirty day done, they would meet by the doors, chained to keep customers out, a green-glass-paved chamber of silence between the two sets of doors, in the shallow side windows the bodiless mannequin heads in their feathered hats and necklaces of pink pearls eavesdropping on the echoing farewell gossip. Every employee hated Kroll's; yet they left it slow as swimming. Janice and Rabbit would meet in this chamber, with the dim light and green floor like something underwater, and push at the one unchained door, push up into the light, and walk, never admitting they were going there, toward the silver medallions, hand in hand tired walking gently against the current of homegoing traffic, and make love with the late daylight coming level in the window. She was shy about him seeing her. She made him keep his eyes shut. And then with a shiver come as soon as he was in, her inside softly grainy, like a silk slipper. Lying side by side on this other girl's bed, feeling lost, having done the final thing; the wall's silver and the fading day's gold.

The kitchen is a narrow room off the living-room, a tight aisle between machines that were modern five years ago. She drops something metal, a pan or cup. "Think you can make it without burning yourself?" he calls in.

"Are you still here?" is the answer.

He goes to the closet and takes out the coat he hung up so neatly. It seems to him he's the only person around here who cares about neatness. The clutter behind him in the room— the Old-fashioned glass with its corrupt dregs, the choked ashtray balanced on the easy-chair arm, the rumpled rug, the floppy stacks of slippery newspapers, the kid's toys here and there broken and stuck and jammed, a leg off a doll and a piece of bent cardboard that went with some breakfast-box cutout, the rolls of fuzz under the radiators, the continual crisscrossing mess—clings to his back like a tightening net. He tries to sort out picking up his car and then his kid. Or should he pick up the kid first? He wants more to see the kid. It would be quicker to walk over to Mrs. Springer's, she lived closer. But suppose she was watching out the window for him to come so she could pop out and tell him how tired Janice looked? *Who wouldn't be tired after tramping around trying to buy something with you you miserable nickel-*

hugger? You fat hag. You old gypsy. If he had the kid along this might not happen. Rabbit likes the idea of walking up from his mother's place with his boy. Two-and-a-half, Nelson walks like a trooper, with choppy stubborn steps. They'd walk along in the day's last light under the trees and then like magic there would be Daddy's car at a curb. But it will take longer this way, what with his own mother talking slyly and roundabout about how incompetent Janice is. It ruined him when his mother went on like that; maybe she did it just to kid him, but he couldn't take her lightly, she was somehow too powerful, at least with him. He had better go for the car first and pick the kid up with it. But he doesn't want to do it this way. He just doesn't. The problem knits in front of him and he feels sickened by the intricacy.

Janice calls from the kitchen, "And honey pick up a pack of cigarettes, could you?" in a normal voice that says everything is forgiven, everything is the same.

Rabbit freezes, standing looking at his faint yellow shadow on the white door that leads to the hall, and senses he is in a trap. It seems certain. He goes out.

Outdoors it is growing dark and cool. The Norway maples exhale the smell of their sticky new buds and the broad living-room windows along Wilbur Street show beyond the silver patch of a television set the warm bulbs burning in kitchens, like fires at the backs of caves. He walks downhill. The day is gathering itself in. He now and then touches with his hand the rough bark of a tree or the dry twigs of a hedge, to give himself the small answer of a texture. At the corner, where Wilbur Street meets Potter Avenue, a mailbox stands leaning in twilight on its concrete post. Tall two-petaled street sign, the cleat-gouged trunk of the telephone pole holding its insulators against the sky, fire hydrant like a golden bush: a grove. He used to love to climb the poles. To shinny up from a friend's shoulders until the ladder of spikes came to your hands, to get up to where you could hear the wires sing. Their song was a terrifying motionless whisper. It always tempted you to fall, to let the hard spikes in your palms go and feel the space on your back, feel it take your feet and ride up your spine as you fell. He remembers how hot your hands felt at the top, rubbed full of splinters from getting up to where the spikes began. Listening to the wires as if you could hear what people were saying, what all that secret adult world was about. The insulators giant blue eggs in a windy nest.

As he walks along Potter Avenue the wires at their silent height strike into and through the crowns of the breathing maples. At the next corner, where the water from the ice plant used to come down, sob into a drain, and reappear on the other side of the street, Rabbit crosses over and walks beside the gutter where the water used to run, coating the shallow side of its course with ribbons of green slime waving and waiting to slip under your feet and dunk you if you dared walk on them. He can remember falling in but not why he was walking along this slippery edge in the first place. Then he remembers. To impress the girls—Lotty Bingaman, Margaret Schoelkopf, sometimes June Cobb and Mary Hoyer —he walked home from grade school with. Margaret's nose would often start bleeding, for no reason. She had had so much life. Her father was a drunk and her parents had made her wear high-laced shoes long after everybody else had stopped.

He turns down Kegerise Street, a narrow gravel alley curving past the blank back side of a small box factory where mostly middle-aged women work, the cement-block face of a wholesale beer outlet, and a truly old stone farmhouse, now boarded up, one of the oldest buildings in town, thick crude masonry of Indianskin sandstone. This building, which once commanded half of the acreage the town is now built on, still retains, behind a shattered and vandalized fence, its yard, a junkheap of brown stalks and eroded timber that will in the summer bloom with an unwanted wealth of weeds, waxy green wands and milky pods of silk seeds and airy yellow heads almost liquid with pollen.

So there is some space between the old farmhouse and the Sunshine Athletic Association, a tall thin brick building like a city tenement misplaced in this disordered alley of backsides and leftovers. The entrance is made ominous by a strange sheathing, the size of an outhouse, erected each winter on the stone steps, to protect the bar from the weather. Rabbit has several times entered the club. There was no sunshine in it. The first floor was a bar and the second was full of card tables where the old bucks of the town sat muttering strategically. Alcohol and cards Rabbit both associates with a depressing kind of sin, sin with bad breath, and he was further depressed by the political air of the place. His old basketball coach, Marty Tothero, who before scandal had ousted him from the high school had a certain grip on local affairs, lived in this building supposedly and still, they said, manipulated. Rabbit dislikes manipulation but he had liked Tothero. Next to his mother Tothero had had the most *force*.

The thought of his old coach crouching in there frightens him. He walks on, past a body shop and an unused chicken house. His progress is always down, for the town of Mt. Judge is built on the east side of the mountain Mt. Judge, whose west face overlooks the city of Brewer. Though the town and the city meet along the highway that skirts the mountain on the south on the way to Philadelphia fifty miles away, they will never merge, for between them the mountain lifts a broad green spine, two miles long north to south, assaulted by gravel pits and cemeteries and new developments but above a line preserved, hundreds of acres of forest Mt. Judge boys can never wholly explore. Much of it is penetrated by the sound of cars climbing the scenic drives in second gear. But in long patches of forgotten pine plantation the needle-hushed floor of land glides up and up, on and on, under endless tunnels of dead green and you seem to have passed through silence into something worse. And then, coming upon a patch of sunlight the branches neglect to keep out or upon a softened stone-filled cellar pit dug by some brave and monstrous settler centuries ago, you become vividly frightened, as if this other sign of life will call attention to yourself, and the menace of the trees will become

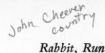
active. Your fear trills like an alarm bell you cannot shut off,
the louder the faster you run, hunchbacked, until distinctly, with a gasp of the clutch, a near car shifts gears, and
the stumpy white posts of the guard fence dawn behind the
pine trunks. Then, safe on the firm blacktop, you decide
whether to walk back down home or to hike up to the
Pinnacle Hotel for a candy bar and a view of Brewer spread
out below like a carpet, a red city, where they paint wood,
tin, even red bricks red, an orange rose flowerpot red that is
unlike the color of any other city in the world yet to the
children of the county is the only color of cities, the color all
cities are.

The mountain brings dusk early to the town. Now, just
a few minutes after six a day before the vernal equinox, all
the houses and gravel-roofed factories and diagonal hillside
streets are in the shadow that washes deep into the valley of
farmland east of the mountain. Huts on the shadow's shore,
twin rows of ranch-houses blare from their picture windows
the reflection of the setting sun. One by one, as suddenly as
lamps, these windows dim as the sunlight ebbs, drawing across
the development and across the tan fenced land waiting for
planting and a golf course that at the distance could be a long
pasture except for the yellow beans of sand: traps; drawing
upward into the opposing hills on whose westward slopes it
still burns with afternoon pride. Rabbit pauses at the end of
the alley, where he has an open view. He used to caddy over
there.

Pricked by an indefinite urgency, he turns away, going left
on Jackson Road, where he lived for twenty years. His
parents' home is in a two-family brick house on the corner;
but it is their neighbors, the Bolgers, who had the corner
half, with a narrow side yard Mrs. Angstrom had always
envied. *The Bolgers' windows getting all that light and here
we sit wedged in.*

Rabbit stealthily approaches his old home on the grass,
hopping the little barberry hedge and the wire meant to
keep kids on the pavement. He sneaks down the strip of grass

between the two cement walks that go with the two brick walls; he used to live behind the one and the Zims behind the other. All day long Mrs. Zim, who was plain, with big thyroid eyes and bluish, slack skin, screamed at her daughter Carolyn, who was prettier than a five-year-old girl had a right to be. Mr. Zim was a thick-lipped redhead, and in Carolyn thick and thin, red and blue, health and high-strungness had blended just right; her precocious beauty was like something that had happened elsewhere, in France or Persia or Heaven. Even Harry, six years older and blind to girls, could see this. All day long Mrs. Zim screamed to her and when Mr. Zim came home from work the two of them would shout together for hours. It would begin with Mr. defending the little girl, and then as the neighbors listened old wounds opened like complicated flowers in the night. Sometimes Mom said that Mr. would murder Mrs., sometimes she said that the little girl would murder them both, as they lay asleep. It was true there was something cold-blooded about Carolyn; when she reached school age, she never left the house without a smile on her little heart-face, swinging herself along like she owned the world, though the Angstroms had just heard her mother throw hysterics at her all through breakfast, the kitchen windows not six feet apart. *How does that poor man endure? If Carolyn and her mother don't settle their differences they're going to wake up some fair morning without a protector.* But Mom was never proved right in any of her predictions. When the Zims left, it was together, Mr. and Mrs. and Carolyn, vanishing in a station wagon while half their furniture still stood on the sidewalk beside the mover's truck. He had a new job in Cleveland, Ohio. Poor souls, they won't be missed. But they were. They had sold their half-house to an old couple, strict Methodists, and the old man refused to cut the strip of grass between his house and the Angstroms'. Mr. Zim, who worked outdoors rain or shine on weekends, *as if it's his only pleasure in life and I don't wonder,* had always cut it. The old Methodist cut exactly his half, one swath of a lawnmower, and then pushed his lawnmower back inverted on his own walk, when it would have been just as easy to push it back along the other half of the strip and not leave such a ridiculous job. *When I hear that old fool's wheels rattle along his walk so self-righteously, my blood pressure goes up so I hear my ears pop.* Mother refused to let him or his father mow their half for one whole summer, and the grass grew knee-high in that little sunless space and stalks of like wheat came up and one or two goldenrod until a man from the town came around in August and said they must cut it on account of an ordinance; he was sorry. Harry had gone to the door and was saying, Sure, O.K., when Mother came up behind him saying, What did he mean? That was her flowerbed. She had no intention of letting it be destroyed. As her son, Rabbit felt terribly embarrassed. The man just looked at her and got a little thumbed book out of his hip pocket and showed her the ordinance. She still said it was her flowerbed. The man read to her what the fine was and went off the porch. That Saturday when she was in Brewer shopping, Pop got the sickle out of the garage and chopped all the weeds down and Harry pushed the lawnmower back and forth across the stubble until it looked as trim as the Methodist's half, though browner. He felt guilty doing it, and was frightened of the fight his parents would have when Mother came back. He dreaded their quarrels: when their faces went angry and flat and words flew, it was as if a pane of glass were put in front of him, cutting off air; his strength drained away and he had to go to a far corner of the house. This time there was no fight. His father shocked him by simply lying, and doubled the shock by winking as he did it. He told her the Methodist had at last broken down and cut the strip of grass himself. Mother believed it but wasn't pleased; she talked all the rest of the day and off and on all week about suing the old holy-roller. In a way she had come to think it *was* her flowerbed. From cement to cement the strip is not much more than a foot across. Walking along it feels slightly precarious to Harry, like treading the top of a wall.

He walks back as far as the lit kitchen window and steps onto the cement without the sole of his shoe scraping and on tiptoe looks in one bright corner. He sees himself sitting in a high chair, and a quick strange jealousy comes and passes. It is his son. The boy's little neck gleams like one more clean object in the kitchen among the cups and plates and chromium knobs and aluminum cake-making receptacles on shelves scalloped with glossy oilcloth. His mother's glasses glitter as she leans in from her place at the table with a spoon of smoking beans at the end of her fat curved arm. Her face shows none of the worry she must be feeling about why nobody comes for the boy and instead is narrowed, her nose a faceted beak, into one wish: that the boy eat. Her mouth is focused into white crinkles. They smooth in a smile; Nelson's lips, hidden from Rabbit's angle, must have taken the beans. The others around the table express praise, blurred syllables from his father, piercing from his sister, something thin about both voices. Rabbit, with the intervening glass and the rustle of blood in his head, can't hear what they say. His father, fresh from work, is in an ink-smeared blue shirt and, when his face lapses from applauding his grandson, looks old: tired and grizzled. His throat a loose bundle of cords. The new teeth he got a year ago have changed his face, collapsed it a fraction of an inch. Miriam, dolled up in gold and jet for Friday night, picks at her food indifferently and offers a spoonful to the kid; the reach of her slender white braceleted arm across the steaming table rings a barbaric chord into the scene. She makes up too much; at nineteen she would be good enough without green eyelids. Because she has buck teeth she tries not to smile. Nelson's big whorly head dips on its bright neck and his fore-shortened hand, dots of pink, dabbles toward the spoon, wants to take it from her. Pop's face lurches into laughter above his plate, and Mim's lips leap in a grin that cracks her cautious wised-up squint and breaks through to the little girl Rabbit used to ride on his handlebars, her streaming hair tickling his eyes as they coasted down the steep Mt. Judge streets. She lets Nelson take her spoon and he drops it. The kid cries

"Peel! Peel!": this Rabbit can hear, and understand. It means "spill." Pop and Mim smile and make remarks but Mom, mouth set, comes in grimly with her spoon. Harry's boy is being fed, this home is happier than his, he glides a pace backward over the cement and rewalks the silent strip of grass.

His acts take on decisive haste. In darkness he goes down another block of Jackson. He cuts up Joseph Street, runs a block, strides another, and comes within sight of his car, its grid grinning at him, parked the wrong way on this side of the street. He taps his pocket and fear hits him. He doesn't have the key. Everything depends, the whole pure idea, on which way Janice was sloppy. Either she forgot to give him the key when he went out or she never bothered to take it out of the ignition. He tries to imagine which is more likely and can't. He doesn't know her that well. He never knows what the hell she'll do. She doesn't know herself. Dumb.

The back but not the front of the big Springer house is lit up. He moves cautiously in the sweet-smelling shadows under the trees in case the old lady is waiting inside the darkened living-room to tell him what she thinks. He crosses around in front of the car, the '55 Ford that old man Springer with his little sandy Hitler mustache sold him for an even thousand in 1957 because the scared bastard was ashamed, cars being his business he was ashamed of his daughter marrying somebody who had nothing but a '36 Buick he bought for $125 in the Army in Texas in 1953. Made him cough up a thousand he didn't have when the Buick had just had eighty dollars' worth of work. That was the kind of thing. They deserve everything they get. He opens the car from the passenger side, wincing at the *pung* of the brittle door spring and quickly ducking his head into the car. Thank God. Beneath the knobs for lights and wipers the octagon of the ignition key tells in silhouette. Bless that dope. Rabbit slithers in, closing the side door until metal touches metal but not slamming it. The front of the stucco Springer house is still unlit. It reminds him for some reason of an abandoned ice-cream stand. He turns the key through On into Start and the motor churns and catches. In his anxiety to be secret he is delicate on the accelerator and the motor, idle for hours in the air of an early spring day, is cold, sticks, and stalls. Rabbit's heart rises and a taste of straw comes into his throat. But of course what the hell if she *does* come out? The only thing suspicious is that he doesn't have the kid and he can say he's on his way to pick him up. That would have been the logical way to do it anyway. Nevertheless he doesn't want to be put to the inconvenience of lying, however plausibly. He pulls the hand choke out a fraction, just enough to pinch his finger-tips, and starts the motor again. He pumps once, and glances aside to see the Springers' living-room light flash on, and lets the clutch out, and the Ford bucks away from the curb.

He drives too fast down Joseph Street, and turns left, ignoring the sign saying STOP. He heads down Jackson to where it runs obliquely into Central, which is also 422 to Philadelphia. STOP. He doesn't want to go to Philadelphia but the road broadens on the edge of town beyond the electric-power station and the only other choice is to go back through Mt. Judge around the mountain into the thick of Brewer and the supper-time traffic. He doesn't intend ever to see Brewer again, that flowerpot city. The highway turns from three-lane to four-lane and there is no danger of hitting another car; they all run along together like sticks on a stream. Rabbit turns on the radio. After a hum a beautiful Negress sings, "Without a song, the dahay would nehever end, without a song." Rabbit wishes for a cigarette to go with the washed feeling inside and remembers he gave up smoking and feels cleaner still. He slumps down and puts one arm up on the back of the seat and glides down the twilight pike left-handed. "A field of corn" the Negress's voice bending dark and warm like the inside of a cello "the grasses grow" the countryside dipping around the road like a continuous dark bird "it makes no mind no how" his scalp contracts ecstat-ically "wihithout a." The smell of parched rubber says the heater has come on and he turns the little lever to MOD.

"Secret Love," "Autumn Leaves," and something whose title he missed. Supper music. Music to cook by. His mind nervously shifts away from the involuntary vision of Janice's meal sizzling in the pan, chops probably, the grease-tinted water bubbling disconsolately, the unfrozen peas steaming away their vitamins. He tries to think of something pleasant. He imagines himself about to shoot a long one-hander; but he feels he's on a cliff, there is an abyss he will fall into when the ball leaves his hands. He tries to repicture his mother and sister feeding his son, but the boy is crying in backward vision, his forehead red and his mouth stretched wide and his helpless breath hot. There must be something: the water from the ice plant running in the gutter, yellowish, the way it curled on stones and ran in diagonal wrinkles, waving the fragile threads of slime attached to its edges. Suddenly Janice shivers in memory on the other girl's bed in declining daylight. He tries to blot out the sensation with Miriam, Mim on his handlebars, Mim on a sled in dark snowfall being pulled up Jackson Street by him, the little kid laughing in her hood, himself the big brother, the red lights in snowfall marking the trestles the town crew have used to block off the street for sledding, down, down, the runners whistling on the dark packed slick, *Hold me Harry*, the sparks as the runners hit the cinders spread at the bottom for safety, the scraping stop like the thump of a great heart in the dark. *Once more Harry, then we'll go home, I promise Harry, please, oh I love you*, little Mim only seven or so, in her dark hood, the street waxy with snow still falling. Poor Janice would probably have the wind up now, on the phone to her mother or his mother, somebody, wondering why her supper was getting cold. So dumb. Forgive me.

He accelerates. The growing complexity of lights threatens him. He is being drawn into Philadelphia. He hates Philadelphia. Dirtiest city in the world, they live on poisoned water, you can taste the chemicals. He wants to go south, down, down the map into orange groves and smoking rivers and barefoot women. It seems simple enough, drive all night through the dawn through the morning through the noon park on a beach take off your shoes and fall asleep by the Gulf of Mexico. Wake up with the stars above perfectly spaced in perfect health. But he is going east, the worst direction, into unhealth, soot, and stink, a smothering hole where you can't move without killing somebody. Yet the highway sucks him on, and a sign says POTTSTOWN 2. He almost brakes. But then he thinks.

If he is heading east, south is on his right. And then, as if the world were just standing around waiting to serve his thoughts, a broad road to the right is advertised, ROUTE 100 WEST CHESTER WILMINGTON. Route 100 has a fine ultimate sound. He doesn't want to go to Wilmington but it's the right direction. He's never been to Wilmington. The Du Ponts own it. He wonders what it's like to make it to a Du Pont.

He doesn't drive five miles before this road begins to feel like a part of the same trap. The first road offered him he turns right on. A keystone marker in the headlights says 23. A good number. The first varsity game he played in he made 23 points. A sophomore and a virgin. Trees overshadow this narrower road.

A barefoot Du Pont. Brown legs probably, bitty birdy breasts. Beside a swimming pool in France. Something like money in a naked woman, deep, millions. You think of millions as being white. Sink all the way in softly still lots left. Rich girls frigid? Nymphomaniacs? Must vary. Just women after all, descended from some old Indian-cheater luckier than the rest, inherit the same stuff if they lived in a slum. Glow all the whiter there, on drab mattresses. That wonderful way they have of coming forward around you when they want it. Otherwise just fat weight. Funny how the passionate ones are often tight and dry and the slow ones wet. They want you up and hard on their little ledge. The thing is play them until just a touch. You can tell: their skin under the fur gets all loose like a puppy's neck.

Route 23 works west through little tame country towns, Coventryville, Elverson, Morgantown. Rabbit likes these.

Square high farmhouses nuzzle the road. Soft chalk sides. In one town a tavern blazes and he stops at a hardware store opposite with two gasoline pumps outside. He knows from the radio it's about seven-thirty, but the hardware store is still open, shovels and seeders and post-hole diggers and axes blue and orange and yellow in the window, along with some fishing rods and a string of fielder's gloves. A middle-aged man comes out in boots, baggy suntans, and two shirts. "Yes *sir*," he says, coming down on the second word with forced weight, like a lame man stepping.

"Couldya fill it up with regular?"

The man starts to pump it in and Rabbit gets out of the car and goes around to the back and asks, "How far am I from Brewer?"

The farmer looks up with a look of curt distrust from listening to the gas gurgle. He lifts a finger. "Back up and take that road and it's sixteen miles to the bridge."

Sixteen. He had driven forty miles to get sixteen miles away. But it was far enough, this was another world. It smells differently, smells older, of nooks and pockets in the ground that nobody's poked into yet. "Suppose I go straight?"

"That'll take you to Churchtown."

"What's after Churchtown?"

"New Holland. Lancaster."

"Do you have any maps?"

"Son, where do you want to go?"

"Huh? I don't know exactly."

"Where are you headed?" The man is patient. His face at the same time seems fatherly and crafty and stupid.

For the first time, Harry realizes he is a criminal. He hears the gasoline rise in the neck of the tank and notices with what care the farmer squeezes every drop he can into the tank without letting it slosh over the lip insolently the way a city garageman would. Out here a drop of gas isn't supposed to escape and he's in the middle of it at night. Laws aren't ghosts in this country, they walk around with the smell of earth on them. Senseless fear cakes over Rabbit's body.

"Check the oil?" the man asks after hanging up the hose on the side of the rusty pump, one of the old style, with the painted bubble head.

"No. Wait. Yeah. You better had. Thanks." Simmer down. All he'd done was ask for a map. Damn dirtdigger so stingy, what was suspicious about that? Somebody was always going somewhere. He better get the oil checked because he wasn't going to stop again until he was halfway to Georgia. "Hey, how far is Lancaster south of here?"

"Due south? Don't know. It's about twenty-five miles on the road. Your oil's all right. You think you're going to Lancaster now?"

"Yeah, I might."

"Check your water?"

"No. It's O.K."

"Batteries?"

"They're fine. Let's go."

The man lets the hood slam down and smiles over at Harry. "That's three-ninety on the gas, young fella": the words are pronounced in that same heavy cautious crippled way.

Rabbit puts four ones in his hand, which is stiff and crusted and has fingernails that remind you of those old shovels you see worn into weird shapes. The farmer disappears into the hardware store; maybe he's phoning the state cops. He acts like he knows something, but how could he? Rabbit itches to duck into the car and drive off. To steady himself he counts the money left in his wallet. Seventy-three. Today was pay-day. Fingering so much lettuce strengthens his nerves. Switching off the lights in the hardware store as he comes, the farmer comes back with the dime and no map. Harry cups his hand for the dime and the man pushes it in with his broad thumb and says, "Looked around inside and the only road map is New York State. You don't want to go that way, do you now?"

"No," Rabbit answers, and walks to his car door. He feels through the hairs on the back of his neck the man following him. He gets into the car and slams the door and the farmer is right there, the meat of his face hung in the open door window. He bends down and nearly sticks his face in. His cracked thin lips with a scar tilting toward his nose move thoughtfully. He's wearing glasses, a scholar. "The only way to get somewhere, you know, is to figure out where you're going before you go there."

Rabbit catches a whiff of whisky. He says in a level way, "I don't think so." The lips and spectacles and black hairs poking out of the man's tear-shaped nostrils show no surprise. Rabbit pulls out, going straight. Everybody who tells you how to act has whisky on their breath.

He drives to Lancaster and all the way his good airy feeling inside is spoiled. That that guy didn't know a thing but was just half-crocked makes the whole region sinister. Outside of Churchtown he passes an Amish buggy in the dark and catches a glimpse of a bearded man and a woman in black in this horsedrawn shadow glaring like devils. The beard inside the buggy like hairs in a nostril. He tries to think of the good life these people lead, of the way they keep clear of all this phony business, this twentieth-century vitamin racket, but in his head they stay devils, risking getting killed trotting along with one dim pink reflector behind, hating Rabbit and his kind, with their big furry tail lights. Who they think they were? He can't shake them, mentally. They never appeared in his rearview mirror. He passed them and there was nothing. It was just that one sideways glance; the woman's face a hatchet of smoke in the square shadow. Tall coffin lined with hair clopping along to the tune of a dying horse. Amish overworked their animals, he knew. Fanatics. Hump their women standing up, out in the fields, wearing clothes, just hoist black skirts and there it was, nothing underneath. No underpants. Fanatics. Worship manure.

The rich earth seems to cast its darkness upward into the air. The farm country is somber at night. He is grateful when the lights of Lancaster merge with his dim beams. He stops at a diner whose clock says 8:04. He hadn't intended to eat until he got out of the state. He takes a map from the rack by the door and while eating three hamburgers at the counter studies his position. He is in Lancaster, surrounded by funny names, Bird in Hand, Paradise, Intercourse, Mt. Airy, Mascot. They probably didn't seem funny if you lived in them. Like Mt. Judge; you get used. A town has to be called something.

Bird in Hand, Paradise: his eyes keep going back to this dainty lettering on the map. He has an impulse, amid the oil-filmed shimmer of this synthetic and desultory diner, to drive there. Little plump women, toy dogs in the street, candy houses in lemon sunshine.

But no, his goal is the white sun of the south like a great big pillow in the sky. And from the map he's been traveling more west than south; if the dirtdigger back there had had a map he could have gone due south on 10. Now the only thing to do is go into the heart of Lancaster and take 222 out and take it all the way down into Maryland and then catch 1. He remembers reading in the *Saturday Evening Post* how 1 goes from Florida to Maine through the most beautiful scenery in the world. He asks for a glass of milk and to go with it a piece of apple pie; the crust is crisp and bubbled and they've had the sense to use cinnamon. His mother's pies always had cinnamon. He pays by cracking a ten and goes out into the parking lot feeling pleased. The hamburgers had been fatter and warmer than the ones you get in Brewer, and the buns had seemed steamed. Things are improving already.

It takes him a half-hour to pick his way through Lancaster. On 222 he drives south through Refton, Hessdale, New Providence, and Quarryville, through Mechanics Grove and Unicorn and then a long stretch so dull and unmarked he doesn't know he's entered Maryland until he hits Oakwood. On the radio he hears "No Other Arms, No Other Lips," "Stagger Lee," a commercial for Rayco Clear Plastic Seat Covers, "If I Didn't Care" by Connie Francis, a commercial for Radio-Controlled Garage Door Operators, "I Ran All the Way Home Just to Say I'm Sorry," "That Old Feeling" by Mel Torme, a commercial for Big Screen Westinghouse TV Set with One-Finger Automatic Tuning, "needle-sharp pictures a nose away from the screen," "The Italian Cowboy Song," "Yep" by Duane Eddy, a commercial for Papermate Pens, "Almost Grown," a commercial for Tame Cream Rinse, "Let's Stroll," news (President Eisenhower and Prime Minister Harold Macmillan began a series of talks in Gettysburg, Tibetans battle Chinese Communists in Lhasa, the whereabouts of the Dalai Lama, spiritual ruler of this remote and backward land, are unknown, a $250,000 trust fund has been left to a Park Avenue maid, Spring scheduled to arrive tomorrow), sports news (Yanks over Braves in Miami, somebody tied with somebody in St. Petersburg Open, scores in a local basketball tournament), weather (fair and seasonably warm), "The Happy Organ," "Turn Me Loose," a commercial for Savings Bank Life Insurance, "Rocksville, P-A" (Rabbit loves it), "A Picture No Artist Could Paint," a commercial for New Formula Barbasol Presto-Lather, the daily cleansing action tends to prevent skin blemishes and emulsifies something, "Pink Shoe Laces" by Dody Stevens, a letter about a little boy called Billy Tessman who was hit by a car and would appreciate cards or letters, "Petit Fleur," "Fungo" (great), a commercial for Wool-Tex All-Wool Suits, "Fall Out" by Henry Mancini, "Everybody Likes to Cha Cha Cha," a commercial for Lord's Grace Table Napkins and the gorgeous Last Supper Tablecloth, "The Beat of My Heart," a commercial for Speed-Shine Wax and Lanolin Clay, "Venus," and then the same news again. Where is the Dalai Lama?

Shortly after Oakwood he comes to Route 1, which with its hot-dog stands and Calso signs and roadside taverns aping log cabins is unexpectedly discouraging. The further he drives the more he feels some great confused system, Baltimore now instead of Philadelphia, reaching for him. He stops at a gas station for two dollars' worth of regular. What he really wants is another map. He unfolds it standing by a Coke machine and reads it in the light coming through a window stained green by stacked cans of liquid wax.

His problem is to get west and free of Baltimore—Washington, which like a two-headed dog guards the coastal route to the south. He doesn't want to go down along the water anyway; his image is of himself going right down the middle, right into the broad soft belly of the land, surprising the dawn cottonfields with his northern plates.

Now he is somewhere here. Further on, then, a road numbered 23 will go off to his left—no, his right. That goes up and over and back into Pennsylvania but at this place, Shawsville, he can take a little narrow blue road without a number. Then go down a little and over again on 137. There is a ragged curve then that this road makes with 482 and then 31. Rabbit can feel himself swinging up and through that curve into the red line numbered 26 and down that into another numbered 340. Red, too; he is really gliding and suddenly sees where he wants to go. Over on the left three red roads stream parallel northeast to southwest; Rabbit can just feel them sliding down through the valleys of the Appalachians. Get on one of them it would be a chute dumping you into sweet low cottonland in the morning. Yes. Once he gets on that he can shake all thoughts of the mess behind him.

He gives two dollars for gas to the attendant, a young but tall colored boy whose limber lazy body slumping inside his baggy Amoco coveralls Rabbit has a weird impulse to hug. This far south the air already feels warmed. Warmth vibrates in brown and purple arcs between the lights of the service station and the moon. The clock in the window above the green cans of liquid wax says 9:10. The thin red second hand sweeps the numbers calmly and makes Rabbit's way seem smooth. He ducks into the Ford and in that fusty hot interior starts to murmur, "Ev, reebody loves the, cha cha cha."

He drives bravely at first. Over blacktop and whitetop, through towns and fields, past false intersections with siren voices, keeping the map on the seat beside him, keeping the numbers straight and resisting the impulse to turn blindly south. Something animal in him knows he is going west.

The land grows wilder. The road evades great lakes and tunnels through pines. In the top of the windshield the telephone wires continually whip the stars. The music on the radio slowly freezes; the rock and roll for kids cools into old standards and show tunes and comforting songs from the Forties. Rabbit pictures married couples driving home to babysitters after a meal out and a movie. Then these melodies turn to ice as real night music takes over, pianos and vibes erecting clusters in the high brittle octaves and a clarinet wandering across like a crack on a pond. Saxes doing the same figure 8 over and over again. He drives through Westminster. It takes forever to reach Frederick. He picks up 340 and crosses the Potomac.

Growing sleepy, Rabbit stops before midnight at a roadside café for coffee. Somehow, though he can't put his finger on the difference, he is unlike the other customers. They sense it too, and look at him with hard eyes, eyes like little metal studs pinned into the white faces of young men sitting in zippered jackets in booths three to a girl, the girls with orange hair hanging like seaweed or loosely bound with gold barrettes like pirate treasure. At the counter middle-aged couples in overcoats bunch their faces forward into the straws of gray ice-cream sodas. In the hush his entrance induces, the excessive courtesy the weary woman behind the counter shows him amplifies his strangeness. He orders coffee quietly and studies the rim of the cup to steady the sliding in his stomach. He had thought, he had read, that from shore to shore all America was the same. He wonders, Is it just these people I'm outside, or is it all America?

Outside in the sharp air, he flinches when footsteps pound behind him. But it is just two lovers, holding hands and in a hurry to reach their car, their locked hands a starfish leaping through the dark. Their license plate says West Virginia. All the plates do except his. On the other side of the road the wooded land dips down so he can look over the tops of trees at the side of a mountain like a cutout of stiff paper mounted on a slightly faded blue sheet. He climbs into his Ford distastefully, but its stale air is his only haven.

He drives through a thickening night. The road unravels with infuriating slowness, its black wall wearilessly rising in

front of his headlights no matter how they twist. The tar
sucks his tires. He realizes that the heat on his cheeks is anger;
he has been angry ever since he left that diner full of mer-
maids. So angry his cheeks feel parched inside his mouth and
his nostrils water. He grinds his foot down as if to squash
this snake of a road, and nearly loses the car on a curve, as
the two right wheels fall captive to the dirt shoulder. He
brings them back but keeps the speedometer needle leaning to
the right of the legal limit.

He turns off the radio; its music no longer seems a river he
is riding down but instead speaks with the voice of the cities
and brushes his head with slippery hands. Yet into the silence
that results he refuses to let thoughts come. He doesn't want
to think, he wants to fall asleep and wake up pillowed by
sand. How stupid, how frigging, fucking stupid he was, not
to be further than this. At midnight, the night half gone.

The land refuses to change. The more he drives the more
the region resembles the country around Mt. Judge. The
same scruff on the embankments, the same weathered bill-
boards for the same products you wondered anybody would
ever want to buy. At the upper edge of his headlight beams
the naked tree-twigs make the same net. Indeed the net
√ seems thicker now.

The animal in him swells its protest that he is going west.
His mind stubbornly resists. The only way to get somewhere
is to decide where you're going and go. His plan calls for him
to bear left 28 miles after Frederick and that 28 miles is used
up now and, though his instincts cry out against it, when a
broad road leads off to the left, though it's unmarked, he
takes it. It is unlikely that the road *would* be marked, from its
thickness on the map. But it is a short cut, he knows. He remembers that when Marty Tothero began to coach him he
didn't want to shoot fouls underhand but that it turned out in
the end to be the way. There is this quality, in things, of the
right way seeming wrong at first.

The road is broad and confident for miles, but there is a
sudden patched stretch, and after that it climbs and narrows.

Narrows not so much by plan as naturally, the edges crumbling in and the woods on either side crowding down. The road twists more and more wildly in its struggle to gain height and then without warning sheds its skin of asphalt and worms on in dirt. By now Rabbit knows this is not the road but he is afraid to stop the car to turn it around. He has left the last light of a house miles behind. When he strays from straddling the mane of weeds, brambles rake his painted sides. Tree-trunks and low limbs are all his headlights pick up; the scrabbling shadows spider backward through the web of wilderness into a black core where he fears his probe of light will stir some beast or ghost. He supports speed with prayer, praying that the road not stop, remembering how on Mt. Judge even the shaggiest most forgotten logging lane eventually sloped to the valley. His ears itch; his height presses on them.

The prayer's answer is blinding. The trees at a far bend leap like flame and a car comes around and flies at him with its beams tilted high. Rabbit slithers over into the ditch and, faceless as death, the bright car rips by at a speed twice his own. For more than a minute Rabbit drives through this bastard's insulting dust. Yet the good news makes him meek, the news that this road goes two ways. And shortly he seems to be in a park. His lights pick up green little barrels stenciled PLEASE and the trees are thinned on both sides and in among them picnic tables and pavilions and outhouses show their straight edges. The curves of cars show too, and a few are parked close to the road, their passengers down out of sight. So the road of horror is a lovers' lane. In a hundred yards it ends.

It meets at right angles a smooth broad highway overhung by the dark cloud of a mountain ridge. One car zips north. Another zips south. There are no signs. Rabbit puts the shift in neutral and pulls out the emergency brake and turns on the roof light and studies his map. His hands and shins are trembling. His brain flutters with fatigue behind sandy eyelids; the time must be 12:30 or later. The highway in front of him is empty. He has forgotten the numbers of the routes he has taken and the names of the towns he has passed through. He remembers Frederick but can't find it and in time realizes he is searching in a section due west of Washington where he has never been. There are so many red lines and blue lines, long names, little towns, squares and circles and stars. He moves his eyes north but the only line he recognizes is the straight dotted line of the Pennsylvania—Maryland border. The Mason—Dixon Line. The schoolroom in which he learned this recurs to him, the rooted desk rows, the scarred varnish, the milky black of the blackboard, the packed pieces of ass all up and down the aisles in alphabetical order. His eyes blankly founder. Rabbit hears a clock in his head beat, monstrously slow, the soft ticks as far apart as the sound of waves on the shore he had wanted to reach. He burns his attention through the film fogging his eyes down into the map again. At once "Frederick" pops into sight, but in trying to steady its position he loses it, and fury makes the bridge of his nose ache. The names melt away and he sees the map whole, a net, all those red lines and blue lines and stars, a net he is somewhere caught in. He claws at it and tears it; with a gasp of exasperation he rips away a great triangular piece and tears the large remnant in half and, more calmly, lays these three pieces on top of each other and tears them in half, and then those six pieces and so on until he has a wad he can squeeze in his hand like a ball. He rolls down the window and throws the ball out; it explodes, and the bent scraps like disembodied wings flicker back over the top of the car. He cranks up the window. He blames everything on that farmer with glasses and two shirts. Funny how the man sticks in his throat. He can't think past him, his smugness, his *solidity*, somehow. He stumbled over him back there and is stumbling still, can't get him away from his feet, like shoelaces too long or a stiff stick between his feet. The man mocked, whether out of his mouth or in the paced motions of his work-worn hands or through his hairy ears, somewhere out of his body he mocked the furtive wordless hopes that at moments make the ground

firm for Harry. *Figure out where you're going before you go* *·/X̄*
there: it misses the whole point and yet there is always the
chance that, little as it says, it says it. At any rate if he'd
trusted to instinct he'd be in South Carolina now. He wishes
he had a cigarette, to help him decide what his instinct is.
He decides to go to sleep in the car for a few hours.

But a car starts up in the petting grove behind him and the
headlights wheel around and press on Rabbit's neck. He
stopped his car right in the middle of the road to look at the
map. Now he must move. He feels unreasoning fear of being
overtaken; the other headlights swell in the rear-view mirror
and fill it like a burning cup. He stamps the clutch, puts the
shift in first, and releases the handbrake. Hopping onto the
highway, he turns instinctively right, north.

The trip home is easier. Though he has no map and hardly
any gas, an all-night Mobilgas appears near Hagerstown like
a wizard waved a wand and green signs begin to point to
the Pennsylvania Turnpike. The music on the radio is soothing now, lyrical and unadvertised, and, coming first from
Harrisburg and then from Philadelphia, makes a beam he
infallibly flies in on. He has broken through the barrier of
fatigue and come into a calm flat world where nothing matters
much. The last quarter of a basketball game used to carry
him into this world; you ran not as the crowd thought for
the sake of the score but for yourself, in a kind of idleness.
There was you and sometimes the ball and then the hole, the
high perfect hole with its pretty skirt of net. It was you, just
you and that fringed ring, and sometimes it came down right
to your lips it seemed and sometimes it stayed away, hard
and remote and small. It seemed silly for the crowd to applaud
or groan over what you had already felt in your fingers or
even in your arms as you braced to shoot or for that matter in
your eyes: when he was hot he could see the separate threads
wound into the strings looping the hoop. Yet at the start of
the night when you came out for warm-up and could see all
the town clunkers sitting in the back of bleachers elbowing
each other and the cheerleaders wisecracking with the racier

male teachers, the crowd then seemed right inside you, your liver and lungs and stomach. There was one fat guy used to come who'd get on the floor of Rabbit's stomach and really make it shake. *Hey, Gunner! Hey, Showboat, shoot! Shoot!* Rabbit remembers him fondly now; to that guy he had been a hero of sorts.

Throughout the early morning, those little hours that are so black, the music keeps coming and the signs keep pointing. His brain feels like a frail but alert invalid with messengers bringing down long corridors all this music and geographical news. At the same time he feels abnormally sensitive on the surface, as if his skin is thinking. The steering wheel is thin as a whip in his hands. As he turns it lightly he can feel the shaft stiffly pivot, and the differential gears part, and the bearings rotate in their sealed tunnels of grease. The phosphorescent winkers at the side of the road beguile him into thinking of young Du Pont women: strings of them winding through huge glassy parties, potentially naked in their sequined sheath gowns. Are rich girls frigid? He'll never know.

He wonders why there are so many signs coming back and so few going down. Of course he didn't know what he was going toward going down. He takes the Brewer turnoff off the Pike and the road takes him through the town where he first bought gas. As he takes the road marked BREWER 16 he can see cattycornered across the main street the dirtdigger's pumps and his dark window full of glinting shovels and fishing rods. The window looks pleased. There is just a lavender touch of light in the air. The radio's long floe of music is breaking up in warm-weather reports and farm prices.

He comes into Brewer from the south, seeing it in the smoky shadow before dawn as a gradual multiplication of houses among the trees beside the road and then as a treeless waste of industry, shoe factories and bottling plants and company parking lots and knitting mills converted to electronics parts and elephantine gas tanks lifting above trash-filled swampland yet lower than the blue edge of the mountain from whose crest Brewer was a warm carpet woven around a single shade of brick. Above the mountain, stars are fading.

He crosses the Running Horse Bridge and is among streets he knows. He takes Warren Avenue through the south side of town and comes out on 422 near City Park. He drives around the mountain in company with a few hissing trailer trucks. Sunrise, an orange strip crushed against a far hill, flares between their wheels. As he turns left from Central into Jackson he nearly sideswipes a milk truck idling yards out from the curb. He continues up Jackson, past his parents' house, and turns into Kegerise Alley. Suddenly cool pink pallor tinges the buildings. He glides past the old chicken house, past the silent body shop, and parks the car in front of the Sunshine Athletic Association, a few steps from the boxed-in entrance, where anyone coming out would have to notice. Rabbit glances up hopefully at the third-story windows but no light shows. Tothero, if he is in there, is still asleep.

Rabbit settles himself to sleep. He takes off his suit coat and lays it over his chest like a blanket. But the daylight is growing, and the front seat is far too short, and the steering wheel crowds his shoulders. He doesn't move to the back seat because that would make him vulnerable; he wants to be able to drive away in a second if he must. Further, he doesn't want to sleep so heavily he will miss Tothero when he comes out.

So there he lies, his long legs doubled and no place for his feet, gazing up with crusty vision across the steering wheel and through the windshield into the sky's renewed flat fresh blue. Today is Saturday, and the sky has that broad bright blunt Saturday quality Rabbit remembers from boyhood, when the sky of a Saturday morning was the blank scoreboard of a long game about to begin. Roofball, box hockey, tether ball, darts . . .

A car goes by up the alley, and Rabbit closes his eyes, and the darkness vibrates with the incessant automobile noises of the night past. He sees again the woods, the narrow road, the dark grove full of cars each containing a silent couple. He thinks again of his goal, lying down at dawn in sand by the Gulf of Mexico, and it seems in a way that the gritty seat of his car *is* that sand, and the rustling of the waking town the rustling of the sea.

He must not miss Tothero. He opens his eyes and tries to rise from his stiff shroud. He wonders if he has missed any time. The sky is the same.

He becomes anxious about the car windows. He hoists his chest up on one elbow and checks them all. The window above his head is open a crack and he cranks it tight and pushes down all the lock buttons. This security relaxes him hopelessly. He turns his face into the crack between seat and back. This twisting pushes his knees into the tense upright cushion, an annoyance that for the moment makes him more wakeful. He wonders where his son slept, what Janice has done, where his parents and her parents hunted. Whether the police know. The thought of police for a second paints his mind blue. He feels the faded night he left behind in this place as a net of telephone calls and hasty trips, trails of tears and strings of words, white worried threads shuttled through the night and now faded but still existent, an invisible net overlaying the steep streets and in whose center he lies secure in his locked hollow hutch.

Cotton and gulls in half-light and the way she'd come on the other girl's bed, never as good on their own. But there were good things: Janice so shy about showing her body even in the first weeks of wedding yet one night coming into the bathroom expecting nothing he found the mirror clouded with steam and Janice just out of the shower standing there doped and pleased with a little blue towel lazily and un-ashamed her bottom bright pink with hot water the way a woman was of two halves bending over and turning and laughing at his expression whatever it was and putting her arms up to kiss him, a blush of steam on her body and the back of her neck slippery. Rabbit adjusts his position and re-turns his mind to its dark socket; the back of her neck slip-pery, the pit of her back pliant, both on their knees together, contortions that never were. His shin knocks the door handle, the pain becoming oddly mixed with the knocks of metal on metal down in the body shop. Work had begun. Eight o'clock? He recognizes elapsed time in the parched puffiness on his lips. He writhes and sits up, the covering coat falling to the car floor, and indeed through the splotched windshield there *is* Tothero's figure, walking away down the alley. He is up beyond the very old farmhouse; Rabbit jumps from the car, puts on his coat, and runs after him. "Mr. Tothero! Hey Mr. Tothero!" His voice sounds flaked and rusty after hours of disuse.

The man turns, looking stranger than Rabbit had expected. He looks like a big tired dwarf. He seems foreshortened: a balding big head and a massively checkered sports coat and then stubby legs in blue trousers that are too long, so the crease buckles and zigzags above the shoes. As he brakes his run, and walks the last strides, Rabbit fears he's made a mistake.

But Tothero says the perfect thing. "Harry," he says, "the great Harry Angstrom." He puts out his hand for Harry to seize and with the other squeezes the boy's arm in a clasp of rigor. It comes back to Rabbit how he always had his hands on you. Tothero just stands there holding on and looking at him, smiling crookedly, the nose bent, one eye wide open and the other heavy-lidded. His face has grown more lopsided with the years. He is not going bald evenly; brushed strands of gray and pale brown streak the top of his skull.

"I need your advice," Rabbit says, and corrects himself. "What I really need is a place to sleep."

Tothero is silent before replying. His great strength is in these silences; he has the disciplinarian's trick of waiting a moment while his words gather weight. At last he asks, "What's happened to your home?"

"Well, it kind of went."

"How do you mean?"

"It was no good. I've run out. I really have."

Another pause. Rabbit narrows his eyes against the sunlight that rebounds off the asphalt. His left ear aches. His
teeth on that side feel as if they might start hurting.

"That doesn't sound like very mature behavior," Tothero
says.

"It was a mess as it was."

"What sort of mess?"

"I don't know. My wife's an alcoholic."

"And have you tried to help her?"

"Sure. How?"

"Did you drink with her?"

"No sir, never. I can't stand the stuff, I just don't like the
taste." He says this readily, proud to be able to report to his
old coach that he has not abused his body.

"Perhaps you should have," Tothero offers after a moment.
"Perhaps if you had shared this pleasure with her, she could
have controlled it."

Rabbit, dazed by the sun, numb through weariness, can't
follow this thought.

"It's Janice Springer, isn't it?" Tothero asks.

"Yeah. God she's dumb. She really is."

"Harry, that's a harsh thing to say. Of any human soul."

Rabbit nods because Tothero himself seems certain of
this. He is beginning to feel weak under the weight of the
man's pauses. These pauses seem longer than he remembered
them, as if Tothero too feels their weight. Fear touches Rabbit again; he suspects his old coach is addled, and begins all
over. "I thought maybe I could sleep a couple hours somewhere in the Sunshine. Otherwise I might as well go home.
I've had it."

To his relief Tothero becomes all bustling action, taking
his elbow, steering him back along the alley, saying, "Yes of
course, Harry, you look terrible, Harry. Terrible." His hand
holds Rabbit's arm with metallic inflexibility and as he pushes
him along Rabbit's bones jolt, pinned at this point. Something
frantic in so tight a grip diminishes the comfort of its firmness. Tothero's voice, too, having turned precise, hasty, and

gay, cuts into Rabbit's woolly state too sharply. "You asked me for two things," he says. "Two things. A place to sleep, and advice. Now, Harry, I'll give you the place to sleep provided, provided, Harry, that when you wake up the two of us have a serious, a long and serious talk about this crisis in your marriage. I'll tell you this now, it's not so much you I'm worried about, I know you well enough to know you always land on your feet, Harry; it's not so much you as Janice. She doesn't have your coordination. Do you promise?"

"Sure. Promise what?"

"Promise, Harry, we'll thrash out a way between us to help her."

"Yeah, but I don't think I can. I mean I'm not that interested in her. I was, but I'm not."

They reach the cement steps and the wood weather-box of the entrance. Tothero opens the door with a key he has. The place is empty, the silent bar shadowy and the small round tables looking rickety and weak without men sitting at them. The electrical advertisements behind the bar, tubing and tinsel, are unplugged and dead. Tothero says, in a voice too loud, "I don't believe it. I don't believe that my greatest boy would grow into such a monster."

Monster: the word seems to clatter after them as they climb the stairs to the second floor. Rabbit apologizes: "I'll try to think when I get some sleep."

"Good boy. That's all we want." What does he mean, we? All these tables are empty. Sunlight strikes blond squares into the drawn tan shades above a low radiator dyed black with dust. Men's steps have worn paths in the narrow bare floorboards.

Tothero leads him to a door he has never entered; they go up a steep flight of attic stairs, a kind of nailed-down ladder between whose steps he sees sections of insulated wire and ragged gaps of carpentry. They climb into light. "Here's my mansion," Tothero says, and fidgets with his coat pocket flaps.

The tiny room faces east. A slash in a window shade throws a long knife of sun on a side wall, above an unmade

Army cot. The other shade is up. Between the windows stands a bureau cleverly made of six beer cases wired together, three high and two wide. In the six boxes are arranged shirts in their laundry cellophane, folded undershirts and shorts, socks balled in pairs, handkerchiefs, shined shoes, and a leather-backed brush with a comb stuck in the bristles. From two thick nails some sport coats, jarringly gay in pattern, are hung on hangers. Tothero's housekeeping stops at caring for his clothes. The floor is dotted with rolls of fluff. Newspapers and all kinds of magazines, from the *National Geographic* to teen-age crime confessions and comic books, are stacked around. The space where Tothero lives merges easily with the rest of the attic, which is storage space, containing old pinochle tournament charts and pool tables and some lumber and metal barrels and broken chairs with cane bottoms and a roll of chicken wire and a rack of softball uniforms, hung on a pipe fixed between two slanting beams and blocking out the light from the window at the far end.

"Is there a men's?" Rabbit asks.

"Downstairs, Harry." Tothero's enthusiasm has died; he seems embarrassed. While Rabbit uses the toilet he can hear the old man fussing around upstairs, but when he returns he can see nothing changed. The bed is still unmade.

Tothero waits and Rabbit waits and then realizes Tothero wants to see him undress and undresses, sliding into the rumpled lukewarm bed in his T-shirt and Jockey shorts. Though the idea is distasteful, getting into the old man's hollow, the sensations are good, being able to stretch out at last and feeling the solid cool wall close to him and hearing cars moving maybe hunting him far below. He twists his neck to say something to Tothero and is surprised by solitude. The door at the foot of the attic steps has closed and footsteps diminish down one, two flights of stairs, and a key scratches in the outside door and a bird cries by the window and the clangor of the body shop comes up softly. The old man's standing there was disturbing but Rabbit is sure that's not his problem. Tothero was always known as a lech but never

queer. Why watch? Suddenly Rabbit knows. It takes Tothero
back in time. Because of all the times he had stood in locker
rooms watching his boys change clothes. Solving this problem
relaxes Rabbit's muscles. He remembers the couple with
linked hands running on the parking lot outside the diner in
West Virginia and it seems a great loss that it hadn't been him
about to nail her, her seaweed hair sprawling. Red hair?
There? He imagines West Virginia girls as coarse hard-bod-
ied laughers, like the young whores in Texas. Their sugar
drawls always seemed to be poking fun but then he was nineteen. Coming down the street with Hanley and Jarzylo and
Shamberger the tight khaki making him feel nervous and the
plains breaking away on all sides the horizon no higher than
his knees it seemed and the houses showing families sitting on
sofas inside like chickens at roost facing TV's. Jarzylo a maniac, cackling. Rabbit couldn't believe this house was right. It
had flowers in the window, actual living flowers innocent in
the window and he was tempted to turn and run. Sure enough
the woman who came to the door could have been on television selling cake mix. But she said, "Come on in boys, don't
be shaaeh, come on in and heyiv a good taam," said it so
motherly, and there they were, not as many as he had pictured,
in the parlor on old-fashioned-looking furniture with scrolls
and knobs. That they were pretty homely made him less
timid, just ordinary factory-looking women, you wouldn't
even call them girls, with a glaze on their faces like under fluorescent lights. They pelted the soldiers with remarks like
balls of dust and the men sneezed into laughter and huddled
together surprised and numb. The one he took, but she took
him, came up and touched him, hadn't buttoned her blouse
more than one button from the last one and upstairs asked
him in her gritty sugar voice if he wanted the light on or off
and when out of a choked throat he answered "Off" laughed,
and then now and then smiled under him, working around to
get him right, and even speaking kindly: "You're all right,
honey. You're gone along all right. Oh yeaas. You've had lessons." So that when it was over he was hurt to learn, from

the creases of completion at the sides of her lips and the hard
way she wouldn't keep lying beside him but got up and sat
on the edge of the metal-frame bed looking out the dark window at the green night sky of Texas, that she had faked her
half. Her mute back showing in yellow-white the bar of a
swimming-suit bra angered him; he took the ball of her shoulder in his hand and turned her roughly. The weighted shadows of her front hung so careless and undefended he looked
away. She said down into his ear, "Honey, you didn't pay to
be no two-timer." Sweet woman, *she* was money. The clangor
of the body shop comes up softly. Its noise comforts him,
tells him he is hidden and safe, that while he hides men are
busy nailing the world down, and toward the disembodied
sounds his heart makes in darkness a motion of love.

His dreams are shallow, furtive things. His legs switch. His
lips move a little against the pillow. The skin of his eyelids
shudders as his eyeballs turn, surveying the inner wall of vision. Otherwise he is as dead, beyond harm. The slash of sun
on the wall above him slowly knifes down, cuts across his
chest, becomes a coin on the floor, and vanishes. In shadow he
suddenly awakes, his ghostly blue irises searching the unfamiliar planes for the source of men's voices. These voices
are downstairs, and a rumble suggests that they are moving the
furniture, tramping in circles, hunting him. But a familiar bul-
bous basso rings out, it is Tothero, and around this firm center
the noises downstairs crystallize as the sounds of card-playing,
drinking, horseplay, companionship. Rabbit rolls in his hot
hollow and turns his face to his cool companion, the wall, and
through a red cone of consciousness falls asleep again.

"Harry! Harry!" The voice is plucking at his shoulder,
rumpling his hair. He rolls away from the wall, squinting upward into vanished sunshine. Tothero sits in the shadows, a
hulk of darkness dense with some anxiousness. His dirty-milk
face leans forward, scarred by a lopsided smile. There is a
smell of whisky. "Harry, I've got a girl for you!"

"Great. Bring her in."

The old man laughs, uneasily? What does he mean?

"You mean Janice?"

"It's after six o'clock. Get up, get up, Harry; you've slept like a beautiful baby. We're going out."

"Why?" Rabbit meant to ask "Where?"

"To eat, Harry, to dine. D-I-N-E. Rise, my boy. Aren't you hungry? Hunger. Hunger." He's a madman. "Oh Harry, you can't understand an old man's hunger, you eat and eat and it's never the right food. You can't understand that." He walks to the window and looks down into the alley, his lumpy profile leaden in the dull light.

Rabbit slides back the covers, angles his naked legs over the edge, and holds himself in a sitting position. The sight of his thighs, parallel, pure, aligns his groggy brain. The hair on his legs, once a thin blond fur, is getting dark and whiskery. The odor of his sleep-soaked body rises to him. "Whatsis girl business?" he asks.

"What is it, yes, what is it? Cunt," Tothero exclaims in a stream, and in the gray light by the window his face falls; he seems amazed to hear himself say such an abrupt ugly thing. Yet he's also watching, as if this was some sort of test. The result determined, he corrects himself, "No. I have an acquaintance, an acquaintance in Brewer, a lady-love perhaps; whom I stand to a meal once in a blue moon. But it's nothing more than that, little more than that. Harry, you're so innocent."

Rabbit begins to be afraid of Tothero, these phrases don't follow. He stands up in his underclothes. "I think I just better run along." The floor-fluff sticks to the soles of his bare feet.

"Oh Harry, Harry," Tothero cries in a rich voice mixed of pain and affection, and comes forward and hugs him with one arm. "You and I are two of a kind." The big lopsided face looks up into his with eager confidence, but Rabbit doesn't understand. Yet his memory of the man as his coach still disposes him to listen. "You and I know what the score is, we know—" And right here, arriving at the kernel of his lesson, Tothero is balked, and becomes befuddled. He repeats, "We know," and removes his arm.

Rabbit says, "I thought we were going to talk about Janice when I woke up." He retrieves his trousers from the floor and puts them on. Their being rumpled disturbs him, reminds him that he has taken a giant step, and makes nervous wrinkles in his stomach and throat.

"We will, we will," Tothero says, "the moment our social obligations are satisfied." A pause. "Do you want to go back now? You must tell me if you do."

Rabbit remembers the dumb slot of her mouth, the way the closet door bumps against the television set. "No. God."

Tothero is overjoyed; it is happiness making him talk so much. "Well then, well then; get dressed. We can't go to Brewer undressed. Do you need a fresh shirt?"

"Yours wouldn't fit me, would it?"

"No, Harry, no? What's your size?"

"Fifteen three."

"Mine! Mine exactly. You have short arms for your height. Oh, this is wonderful, Harry. I can't tell you how much it means to me that you came to me when you needed help. All those years," he says, taking a shirt from the bureau made of beer cases and stripping off the cellophane, "all those years, all those boys, they pass through your hands and into the blue. And never come back, Harry; they never come back."

Rabbit is startled to feel and to see in Tothero's wavy mirror that the shirt fits. Their difference must be all in their legs. With the rattling tongue of a proud mother Tothero watches him dress. His talk makes more sense, now that the embarrassment of explaining what they're going to do is past. "It does my heart good," he says. "Youth before the mirror. How long has it been, Harry, now tell me truly, since you had a good time? A long time?"

"I had a good time last night," Rabbit says. "I drove to West Virginia and back."

"You'll like my lady, I know you will, a city flower," Tothero goes on. "The girl she's bringing I've never met. She says she's fat. All the world looks fat to my lady—how she eats, Harry: the appetite of the young. That's a fascinating knot, you young people have so many tricks I never learned."

"It's just a Windsor." Dressed, Rabbit feels a return of calm. Waking up had in a way returned him to the world he deserted. He had missed Janice's crowding presence, the kid and his shrill needs, his own walls. He had wondered what he was doing. But now these reflexes, shallowly scratched, are spent, and deeper instincts flood forward, telling him he is right. He feels freedom like oxygen everywhere around him; Tothero is an eddy of air, and the building he is in, the streets of the town, are mere stairways and alleyways in space. So perfect, so consistent is the freedom into which the clutter of the world has been vaporized by the simple trigger of his decision, that all ways seem equally good, all movements will put the same caressing pressure on his skin, and not an atom of his happiness would be altered if Tothero told him they were not going to meet two girls but two goats, and they were going not to Brewer but to Tibet. He adjusts his necktie with infinite attention, as if the little lines of this juncture of the Windsor knot, the collar of Tothero's shirt, and the base of his own throat were the arms of a star that will, when he is finished, extend outward to the rim of the universe. *He* is the Dalai Lama. Like a cloud breaking in the corner of his vision Tothero drifts to the window. "Is my car still there?" Rabbit asks.

"Your car is blue. Yes. Put on your shoes."

"I wonder if anybody saw it there. While I was asleep, did you hear anything around town?" For in the vast blank of his freedom Rabbit has remembered a few imperfections, his home, his wife's, their apartment, clots of concern. It seems impossible that the passage of time should have so soon dissolved them, but Tothero's answer implies it.

"No," he says. He adds, "But then of course I didn't go where there would have been talk of you."

It annoys Rabbit that Tothero shows no interest in him except as a partner on a joyride. "I should have gone to work today," he says in a pointed voice, as if blaming the old man. "Saturday's my big day."

"What do you do?"

"I demonstrate a kitchen gadget called the MagiPeel Peeler in five-and-dime stores."

"A noble calling," Tothero says, and turns from the window. "Splendid, Harry. You're dressed at last."

"Is there a comb anywhere, Mr. Tothero? I ought to use the can."

Under their feet the men in the Sunshine Athletic Association laugh and catcall at some foolishness. Rabbit pictures passing among them and asks, "Say, should everybody see me?"

Tothero becomes indignant, as he used to now and then at practice, when everybody was just fooling around the basket and not going into the drills. "What are you afraid of, Harry? That poor little Janice Springer? You overestimate people. Nobody cares what you do. Now we'll just go down there and don't be too long in the toilet. And I haven't heard any thanks from you for all I've done for you, and all I *am* doing." He takes the comb stuck in the brush bristles and gives it to Harry.

A dread of marring his freedom blocks the easy gesture of expressing gratitude. Rabbit pronounces "Thanks" thin-lipped.

They go downstairs. Contrary to what Tothero had promised, all of the men—old men, mostly, but not very old, so their misshapen bodies are weirdly quick—look up with interest at him. Insanely, Tothero introduces him repeatedly: "Fred, this is my finest boy, a wonderful basketball player, Harry Angstrom, you probably remember his name from the papers, he twice set a county record, in 1950 and then he broke it in 1951, a wonderful accomplishment."

"Is that right, Marty?"

"Harry, an honor to meet you."

Their alert colorless eyes, little dark smears like their mouths, feed on the strange sight of him and send acid impressions down to be digested in their disgusting big beer-tough stomachs. Rabbit sees that Tothero is a fool to them, and is ashamed of his friend and of himself. He hides in the lavatory. The paint is worn off the toilet seat and the washbasin is stained by the hot-water faucet's rusty tears; the walls are oily and the towel-rack empty. There is something terrible in the height of the tiny ceiling: a square yard of a dainty metal pattern covered with cobwebs in which a few white husks of insects are suspended. His depression deepens, becomes a kind of paralysis; he walks out and rejoins Tothero limping and stiffly grimacing, and they leave the place in a dream. He feels affronted, vaguely invaded, when Tothero gets into his car. But, just as in a dream, he never stops to question, Rabbit slides in behind the wheel and, in the renewed relation of his arms and legs to the switches and pedals, puts on again the mantle of power. His wet-combed hair feels stiff on his head.

He says sharply, "So you think I should've drunk with Janice."

"Do what the heart commands," Tothero says. "The heart is our only guide." He sounds weary and far away.

"Into Brewer?"

There is no answer.

Rabbit drives up the alley, coming to Potter Avenue, where the water from the ice plant used to run down. He goes right, away from Wilbur Street, where his apartment is, and two more turns bring him into Central Street heading around the mountain to Brewer. On the left, land drops away into a chasm floored by the slick still width of the Running Horse River; on the right, gasoline stations glow, twirlers flicker on strings, spotlights protest.

As the town thins, Tothero's tongue loosens. "The ladies we're going to meet, now Harry, I have no conception of what the other one will be like, but I know you'll be a gentleman. And I guarantee you'll like my friend. She is a remarkable girl, Harry, with seven strikes against her from birth, but she's done a remarkable thing."

"What?"

"She's come to grips. Isn't that the whole secret, Harry; to come to grips? It makes me happy, happy and humble, to have, as I do, this very tenuous association with her. Harry?"

"Yeah?"

"Do you realize, Harry, that a young woman has hair on every part of her body?"

"I hadn't thought about it." Distaste stains his throat.

"Do," Tothero says. "Do think about it. They are monkeys, Harry. Women are monkeys."

He says it so solemn, Rabbit has to laugh.

Tothero laughs too, and comes closer on the seat. "Yet we love them, Harry, don't we? Harry, why do we love them? Answer that, and you'll answer the riddle of life." He is squirming around, crossing and uncrossing his legs, leaning over and tapping Rabbit's shoulder and jerking back and glancing out the side window and turning and tapping again. "I am a hideous person, Harry. A person to be abhorred. Harry, let me tell you something." As a coach he was always telling you something. "My wife calls me a person to be abhorred. But do you know when it began? It began with her skin. One day in the spring, in nineteen forty-three or four, it was during the war, without warning it was hideous. It was like the hides of a thousand lizards stitched together. Stitched together *clumsily*. Can you picture that? That sense of it being *in pieces* horrified me, Harry. Are you listening? You're not listening. You're wondering why you came to me."

"What you said about Janice this morning kind of worries me."

"Janice! Let's not talk about little mutts like Janice Springer, Harry boy. This is the night. This is no time for pity. The real women are dropping down out of the trees." With his hands he imitates things falling out of trees. "Plippity, plippity."

Even discounting the man as a maniac, Rabbit becomes expectant. They park the car off Weiser Avenue and meet the girls in front of a Chinese restaurant.

The girls waiting under crimson neon have a floral delicacy; like a touch of wilt the red light rims their fluffy hair. Rabbit's heart thumps ahead of him down the pavement. They all come together and Tothero introduces Margaret, "Margaret Kosko, Harry Angstrom, my finest athlete, it's a pleasure for me to be able to introduce two such wonderful young people to one another." The old man's manner is queerly shy; his voice has a cough waiting in it.

After Tothero's build-up Rabbit is amazed that Margaret is just another Janice—that same sallow density, that stubborn smallness. Scarcely moving her lips, she says, "This is Ruth Leonard. Marty Tothero, and you, whatever your name is."

"Harry," Rabbit says. "Or Rabbit."

"That's right!" Tothero cries. "The other boys used to call you Rabbit. I had forgotten." He coughs.

"Well you're a big bunny," Ruth remarks. She is fat alongside Margaret, but not *that* fat. Chunky, more. But tall. She has flat blue eyes in square-cut sockets. Her thighs fill the front of her dress so that even standing up she has a lap. Her hair, kind of a dirty ginger color, is bundled in a roll at the back of her head. Beyond her the parking meters with their red tongues recede along the curb, and at her feet, pinched in lavender straps, four sidewalk squares meet in an x.

"Just big outside," he said.

"That's me too," she says.

"God I'm hungry," Rabbit tells them all, just to say something. From somewhere he's got the jitters.

"Hunger, hunger," Tothero says, as if grateful for the cue. "Where shall my little ones go?"

"Here?" Harry asks. He sees from the way the two girls look at him that he is expected to take charge. Tothero is moving back and forth like a crab sideways and bumps into a middle-aged couple strolling along. His face shows such surprise at the collision, and he is so elaborately apologetic, that Ruth laughs; her laugh rings on the street like a handful of change thrown down. At the sound Rabbit begins to loosen up; the space between the muscles of his chest feels padded with warm air. Tothero pushes into the glass door first, Margaret follows, and Ruth takes his arm and says, "I know you. I went to West Brewer High and got out in fifty-one."

"That's *my* class." Like the touch of her hand on his arm,

her being his age pleases him, as if, even in high schools on opposite sides of the city, they have learned the same things and
gained the same view of life. The Class of '51 view.

"You beat us," she says.

"You had a lousy team."

"No we didn't. I went with three of the players."

"Three at once?"

"In a way."

"Well. They looked tired."

She laughs again, the coins thrown down, though he feels
ashamed of what he has said, she is so good-natured and maybe
was pretty then. Her complexion isn't good now. But her hair
is thick, and that's the sign.

A young Chinaman in a drab linen coat blocks their way
past the glass counter where an American girl in a kimono sits
counting threadbare bills. "Please, how many?"

"Four," Rabbit says, when Tothero is silent.

Unexpected, generous gesture, Ruth slips off her short
white coat and gives it to Rabbit; soft, bunched cloth. The
motion stirs up a smell of perfume on her.

"Four, yes please, this way," and the waiter leads them to a
red booth. The place has just recently reopened as Chinese;
pink paintings of Paris are still on the wall. Ruth staggers a
little; Rabbit sees from behind that her heels, yellow with
strain, tend to slip sideways in the net of lavender straps that
pin her feet to the spikes of her shoes. But under the shiny
green stretch of her dress her broad bottom packs the cloth
with a certain composure. Her waist tucks in trimly, squarely,
like the lines of her face. The cut of the dress bares a big V-
shaped piece of fat fair back. In arriving at the booth, he
bumps against her; the top of her head comes to his nose. The
prickly smell of her hair stitches the store-bought scent behind her ears. They bump because Tothero is ushering Margaret into her seat so ceremoniously, a gnome at the mouth of
his cave. Standing there waiting, Rabbit is elated to think that
a stranger passing outside the restaurant window, like himself
last night outside that West Virginia diner, would see him

with a woman. He seems to be that stranger, staring in, envying himself his body and his woman's body. Ruth bends down and slides over. The skin of her shoulders gleams and then dims in the shadow of the booth. Rabbit sits down too and feels her rustle beside him, settling in, the way women do, fussily, as if making a nest.

He discovers he has held on to her coat. Pale limp pelt, it sleeps in his lap. Without rising he reaches up and hangs it on the coatpole hook above him.

"Nice to have a long arm," she says, and looks in her purse and takes out a pack of Newports.

"Tothero says I have short arms."

"Where'd you meet that old bum?" This so Tothero can hear if he cares.

"He's not a bum, he's my old coach."

"Want one?" A cigarette.

He wavers. "I've stopped."

"So that old bum was your coach," she sighs. She draws a cigarette from the turquoise pack of Newports and hangs it between her orange lips and frowns at the sulphur tip as she strikes a match, with curious feminine clumsiness, away from her, holding the paper match sideways and thus bending it. It flares on the third scratch.

Margaret says, "*Ruth.*"

"Bum?" Tothero says, and his heavy face looks unwell and lopsided in cagey mirth, as if he's started to melt. "I am, I am. A vile old bum fallen among princesses."

Margaret sees nothing against her in this and puts her hand on top of his on the table and in a solemn dead voice insists, "You're nothing like a bum."

"Where is our young Confucian?" Tothero asks and looks around with his free arm uplifted. When the boy comes he asks, "Can we be served alcoholic beverages here?"

"We bring in from next door," the boy says. Funny the way the eyebrows of Chinese people look embedded in the skin instead of sticking out from it.

"Double Scotch whisky," Tothero says. "My dear?"

"Daiquiri," Margaret says; it sounds like a wisecrack.
"Children?"

Rabbit looks at Ruth. Her face is caked with orange dust.
Her hair, her hair which seemed at first glance dirty blonde or
faded brown, is in fact many colors, red and yellow and
brown and black, each hair passing in the light through a series of tints, like the hair of a dog. "Hell," she says. "I guess a
Daiquiri."

"Three," Rabbit tells the boy, thinking a Daiquiri will be
like a limeade.

The waiter recites, "Three Daiquiri, one double whisky
Scotch on the rocks," and goes.

Rabbit asks Ruth, "When's your birthday?"

"August. Why?"

"Mine's April," he says. "I win."

"You win." As if she knows how this makes him feel
warmer; you can't feel master, quite, of a woman who's
older.

"If you recognized me," he asks, "why didn't you recognize
Mr. Tothero? He was coach of that team."

"Who looks at coaches? They don't do any good, do
they?"

"Don't do any good? A high-school team is all coach; isn't
it?"

Tothero answers, "It's all boy, Harry. You can't make gold
out of lead. You can't make gold out of lead."

"Sure you can," Rabbit says. "When I came out in my fresh-
man year I didn't know my head from my elbow."

"Yes you did, Harry, yes you did. I had nothing to teach
you; I just let you run." He keeps looking around. "You
were a young deer," he continues, "with big feet."

Ruth asks, "How big?"

Rabbit tells her, "Twelve D. How big are yours?"

"They're tiny," she says. "Teeny weeny little."

"It looked to me like they were falling out of your shoes."
He pulls his head back and slumps slightly, to look down past
the table edge, into the submarine twilight where her fore-

shortened calves hang like tan fish. They dart back under the seat.

"Don't look too hard, you'll fall out of the booth," she says, ruffled, which is good. Women like being mussed. They never say they do, but they do.

The waiter comes with the drinks and begins laying their places with paper placemats and lusterless silver. He does Margaret and is halfway done on Tothero when Tothero takes the whisky glass away from his lips and says in a freshened, tougher voice, "Cutlery? For Oriental dishes? Don't you have chopsticks?"

"Chopsticks, yes."

"Chopsticks all around," Tothero says positively. "When in Rome."

"Don't take mine!" Margaret cries, slapping her hand with a clatter across her spoon and fork when the waiter reaches. "I don't want any sticks."

"Harry and Ruth?" Tothero asks. "Your preference?"

The Daiquiri does have the taste of limeade, riding like oil on the top of a raw transparent taste. "Sticks," Rabbit says in a deep voice, delighted to annoy Margaret. "In Texas we never touched metal to chicken hoo phooey."

"Ruth?" Tothero's facial attitude toward her is timid and forced.

"Oh I guess. If this dope can I can." She grinds out her cigarette and fishes for another.

The waiter goes away like a bridesmaid with his bouquet of unwanted silver. Margaret is alone in her choice, and this preys on her. Rabbit is glad; she is a shadow on his happiness.

"You ate Chinese food in Texas?" Ruth asks.

"All the time. Give me a cigarette."

"You've stopped."

"I've started. Give me a dime."

"A dime! The hell I will."

The needless urgency of her refusal offends him, it sounds as if she wants a profit. Why does she think he'd steal from her? What would he steal? He dips into his coat pocket and comes up with coins and takes a dime and puts it into the little ivory tune-selector that burns mildly on the wall by their table. Leaning over, close to her face, he turns the leaves listing titles and finally punches the buttons, B and 7, for "Rocksville, P-A." "Chinese food in Texas is the best Chinese food in the United States except Boston," he says.

"Listen to the big traveler," Ruth says. She gives him a cigarette. He forgives her about the dime.

"So you think," Tothero says steadily, "that coaches don't do anything."

"They're worthless," Ruth says.

"Hey come on," Rabbit says.

The waiter comes back with their chopsticks and two menus. Rabbit is disappointed in the chopsticks; they feel like plastic instead of wood. The cigarette tastes rough, a noseful of straw. He puts it out. Never again.

"We'll each order a dish and then share it," Tothero tells them. "Now who has favorites?"

"Sweet and sour pork," Margaret says. One thing about her, she is very definite.

"Harry?"

"I don't know."

"Where's the big Chinese-food specialist?" Ruth asks.

"This is in English. I'm used to ordering from a Chinese menu."

"Come on, come on, tell me what's good."

"Hey cut it out; you're getting me rattled."

"You were never in Texas," she says.

He remembers the house on that strange treeless residential street, the green night growing up from the prairie, the flowers in the window, and says, "Absolutely I was."

"Doing what?"

"Serving Uncle."

"Oh, in the Army; well that doesn't count. Everybody's been to Texas with the Army."

"You order whatever you think is good," Rabbit tells Tothero. He is irritated by all these Army veterans Ruth seems to know, and strains to hear the final bars of the song he spent a dime to play. In this Chinese place he can just make out a hint, coming it seems from the kitchen, of the jangling melody that lifted him up last night in the car.

Tothero gives the waiter the order and when he goes away tries to give Ruth the word. The old man's thin lips are wet with whisky. "The coach," he says, "the coach is concerned with developing the three tools we are given in life; the head, the body, and the heart."

"And the crotch," Ruth says. Margaret, of all people, laughs. She really gives Rabbit the creeps.

"Young woman, you've challenged me, and I deserve the respect of your attention." He speaks with grave weight.

"Shit," she says softly, and looks down. "Don't bleed on *me*." He has hurt her. The wings of her nostrils whiten; her coarse make-up darkens.

"One. The head. Strategy. Most boys come to a basketball coach from alley games and have no conception of the, of the *elegance* of the game played on a court with two baskets. Won't you bear me out, Harry?"

"Yea, sure. Just yesterday—"

"Second—let me finish, Harry, and then you can talk—second, the body. Work the boys into condition. Make their legs hard." He clenches his fist on the slick table. "Hard. Run, run, run. Run every minute their feet are on the floor. You can't run enough. Thirdly"—he puts the index finger and thumb of one hand to the corners of his mouth and flicks away the moisture—"the heart. And here the good coach, which I, young lady, certainly tried to be and some say *was*, has his most solemn opportunity. Give the boys the will to achieve. I've always liked that better than the will to win, for there can be achievement even in defeat. Make them feel the, yes, I think the word is good, the *sacredness* of achievement, in the form of giving our best." He dares a pause now, and wins through it, glancing at each of them in turn to freeze their tongues. "A boy who has had his heart enlarged by an inspiring coach," he concludes, "can never become, in the

deepest sense, a failure in the greater game of life. And now
may the peace of God, et cetera . . ." He draws on his glass,
which is mostly ice cubes. As he tilts it up they ride forward
and rattle against his lips.

Ruth turns to Rabbit and asks quietly, as if to change the
subject, "What do you do?"

He laughs. "Well I'm not sure I do anything any more. I
should have gone to work this morning. I uh, it's kind of
hard to describe, I demonstrate something called the Magi-
Peel Kitchen Peeler."

"And I'm sure he does it well," Tothero says. "I'm sure
that when the MagiPeel Corporation board sits down at their
annual meeting, and ask themselves 'Now who has done the
most to further our cause with the American public?' the
name of Harry Rabbit Angstrom leads the list."

"What do you do?" Rabbit asks her in turn.

"Nothing," Ruth answers. "Nothing." And her eyelids
make a greasy blue curtain as she sips her Daiquiri. Her chin
takes something of the liquid's green light.

The Chinese food arrives. Delicious saliva fills his mouth.
He really hasn't had any since Texas. He loves this food that
contains no disgusting proofs of slain animals, a bloody slab
of cow haunch, a hen's sinewy skeleton; these ghosts have been
minced and destroyed and painlessly merged with the shapes
of insensate vegetables, plump green bodies that invite his appetite's innocent gusto. Candy. Heaped on a smoking breast of
rice. Each is given such a tidy hot breast, and Margaret is in a
special hurry to muddle hers with glazed chunks; all eat well.
Their faces take color and strength from the oval plates of
dark pork, sugar peas, chicken, stiff sweet sauce, shrimp, water
chestnuts, who knows what else. Their talk grows hearty.

"He was terrific," Rabbit says of Tothero. "He was the
greatest coach in the county. I would've been nothing without
him."

"No, Harry, no. You did more for me than I did for you.
Girls, the first game he played he scored twenty points."

"Twenty-three," Harry says.

"Twenty-three points! Think of it." The girls eat on. "Remember, Harry, the state tournaments in Harrisburg; Dennistown and their little set-shot artist."

"He was tiny," Harry tells Ruth. "About five two and ugly as a monkey. Really a dirty player too."

"Ah, but he knew his trade," Tothero says, "he knew his trade. Harry had met his match."

"Then he tripped me, remember?"

"So he did," Tothero says. "I'd forgotten."

"This runt trips me, and over I go, bonk, against the mat. If the walls hadn't been padded I'd'a been killed."

"Then what happened, Harry? Did you cream him? I've forgotten this whole incident." Tothero's mouth is full of food and his hunger for revenge is ugly.

"Why, no," Rabbit says slowly. "I never fouled. The ref saw it and it was his fifth foul and he was out. Then we smothered 'em."

Something fades in Tothero's expression; his face goes slack. "That's right, you never fouled. Harry was always the idealist."

Rabbit shrugs. "I didn't have to."

"The other strange thing about Harry," Tothero tells the two women. "He was never hurt."

"No, I once sprained my wrist," Rabbit corrects. "The thing you said that really helped me—"

"What happened next in the tournaments? I'm frightened at how I've forgotten this."

"Next? Pennoak, I think. Nothing happened. They beat us."

"They won? Didn't we beat them?"

"Oh hell no. They were good. They had five good players. What'd we have? Just me, really. We had Harrison, who was O.K., but after that football injury he never had the touch, really."

"*Ronnie* Harrison?" Ruth asks.

Rabbit is startled. "You *know* him?" Harrison had been a notorious bedbug.

"I'm not sure," she says, complacently enough.

"Shortish guy with kinky hair. A little bitty limp."

"No, I don't know," she says. "I don't think so." She is pleasingly dexterous with the chopsticks, and keeps one hand lying palm up on her lap. He loves when she ducks her head, that thick simple neck moving forward making the broad tendons on her shoulder jump up, to get her lips around a piece of something. Pinched with just the right pressure between the sticks; funny how plump women have that delicate touch. Margaret shovels it in with her dull bent silver.

"We didn't win," Tothero repeats, and calls, "Waiter." When the boy comes Tothero asks for another round of the same drinks.

"No, not for me, thanks," Rabbit says. "I'm high enough on this as it is."

"You're just a big clean-living kid, aren't you, you," Margaret says. She doesn't even know his name yet. God, he hates her.

"The thing, I started to say, the thing you said that really helped me," Rabbit says to Tothero, "is that business about almost touching your thumbs on the two-handers. That's the whole secret, really, getting the ball in front of your hands, where you get that nice lifty feeling. Just zwoops off." His hands show how.

"Oh, Harry," Tothero says sadly, "you could shoot when you came to me. All I gave you was the will to win. The will to achievement."

"You know my best night," Rabbit says, "my best night wasn't that forty-pointer that time against Allenville, it was in my junior year, we went down to end of the county real early in the season to play, a funny little hick school, about a hundred in all six grades; what was its name? Bird's Nest? Something like that. You'll remember."

"Bird's Nest," Tothero says. "No."

"It was the only time I think we ever scheduled them. Funny little square gymnasium where the crowd sat up on the stage. Some name that meant something."

"Bird's Nest," Tothero says. He is bothered. He keeps touching his ear.

"Oriole!" Rabbit exclaims, perfect in joy. "Oriole High. This little kind of spread-out town, and it was early in the season, so it was kind of warm still, and going down in the bus you could see the things of corn like wigwams out in the fields. And the school itself kind of smelled of cider; I remember you made some joke about it. You told me to take it easy, we were down there for practice, and we weren't supposed to try, you know, to *smother* 'em."

"Your memory is better than mine," Tothero says. The waiter comes back and Tothero takes his drink right off the tray, before the boy has a chance to give it to him.

"So," Rabbit says. "We go out there and there are these five farmers clumping up and down, and we get about fifteen points up right away and I just take it easy. And there are just a couple dozen people sitting up on the stage and the game isn't a league game so nothing matters much, and I get this funny feeling I can do anything, just drifting around, passing the ball, and all of a sudden I know, you see, I *know* I can do anything. The second half I take maybe just ten shots, and every one goes right in, not just bounces in, but doesn't touch the rim, like I'm dropping stones down a well. And these farmers running up and down getting up a sweat, they didn't have more than two substitutes, but we're not in their league either, so it doesn't matter much to them, and the one ref just leans over against the edge of the stage talking to their coach. Oriole High. Yeah, and then afterwards their coach comes down into the locker room where both teams are changing and gets a jug of cider out of a locker and we all passed it around. Don't you remember?" It puzzles him, yet makes him want to laugh, that he can't make the others feel what was so special. He resumes eating. The others are done and on their second drinks.

"Yes, sir, Whosie, you're a real sweet kid," Margaret tells him.

"Pay no attention, Harry," Tothero says, "that's the way tramps talk."

Margaret hits him: her hand flies up from the table and across her body into his mouth, flat, but without a slapping noise.

"Touché," Ruth says. Her voice is indifferent. The whole thing is so quiet that the Chinaman, clearing their dishes away, doesn't look up, and seems to hear nothing.

"We're going," Tothero announces, and tries to stand up, but the edge of the table hits his thighs, and he can stand no higher than a hunchback. The slap has left a little twist in his mouth that Rabbit can't bear to look at, it's so ambiguous and blurred, such a sickly mixture of bravado and shame and, worst, pride or less than pride, conceit. This deathly smirk emits the words, "Are you coming, my dear?"

"Son of a bitch," Margaret says, yet her little hard nut of a body slides over, and she glances behind her to see if she is leaving anything, cigarettes or a purse. "Son of a bitch," she repeats, and there is something pretty in the level way she says it. Both she and Tothero seem calmer now, determined and kind of rigid.

Rabbit starts to push up from the table, but Tothero sets a rigid urgent hand on his shoulder, the coach's touch, that Rabbit had so often felt on the bench, just before the pat on the bottom that sent him into the game. "No no, Harry. You stay. One apiece. Don't let our vulgarity distract you. I couldn't borrow your car, could I?"

"Huh? How would I get anywhere?"

"Quite right, you're quite right. Forgive my asking."

"No, I mean, you can if you want—" In fact he feels deeply reluctant to part with a car that is only half his.

Tothero sees this. "No no. It was an insane thought. Good night."

"You bloated old bastard," Margaret says to him. He glances toward her, then down fuzzily. She is right, Harry realizes, he is bloated; his face is lopsided like a tired balloon. Yet this

balloon peers down at him as if there was some message bulging it, heavy and vague like water.

"Where will you go?" Tothero asks.

"I'll be fine. I have money. I'll get a hotel," Rabbit tells him.
He wishes, now that he has refused him a favor, that Tothero
would go.

"The door of my mansion is open," Tothero says. "There's
the one cot only, but we can make a mattress—"

"No, look," Rabbit says severely. "You've saved my life,
but I don't want to saddle you. I'll be fine. I can't thank you
enough anyway."

"We'll talk sometime," Tothero promises. His hand
twitches, and accidentally taps Margaret's thigh.

"I could kill you," Margaret says at his side, and they go off,
looking from the back like father and daughter, past the
counter where the waiter whispers with the American girl,
and out the glass door, Margaret first. The whole thing seems
so *settled:* like little wooden figures going in and out of a ba-
rometer.

"God, he's in sad shape."

"Who isn't?" Ruth asks.

"You don't seem to be."

"I eat, is what you mean."

"No, listen, you have some kind of complex about being
big. You're not fat. You're right in proportion."

She laughs, catches herself, looks at him, laughs again and
squeezes his arm and says, "Rabbit, you're a Christian gentleman." Her using his own name enters his ears with unsettling
warmth.

"What she hit him for?" he asks, giggling in fear that her
hands, resting on his forearm, will playfully poke his side. He
feels in her grip the tension of this possibility.

"She likes to hit people. She once hit me."

"Yeah, but you probably asked for it."

She replaces her hands on the table. "So did he. He likes
being hit."

He asks, "You know him?"

"I've heard her talk about him."

"Well, that's not knowing him. That girl is dumb."

"Isn't she. She's dumber than you can know."

"Look, I know. I'm married to her twin."

"Ohhh. Married."

"Hey, what's this about Ronnie Harrison? Do you know him?"

"What's this about you being married?"

"Well, I was. Still am." He regrets that they have started talking about it. A big bubble, the enormity of it, crowds his heart. It's like when he was a kid and suddenly thought, coming back from somewhere at the end of a Saturday afternoon, that this—these trees, this pavement—was life, the real and only thing.

"Where is she?"

This makes it worse, picturing Janice, where would she go? "Probably with her parents. I just left her last night."

"Oh. Then this is just a holiday. You haven't left her."

"I think I have."

The waiter brings them a plate of sesame cakes. Rabbit takes one tentatively, thinking they will be hard, and is delighted to have it become in his mouth mild elastic jelly, through the shell of bland seeds. The waiter asks, "Gone for good, your friends?"

"It's O.K., I'll pay," Rabbit says.

The Chinaman lifts his sunken eyebrows in a smile and retreats.

"You're rich?" Ruth asks.

"No, poor."

"Are you really going to a hotel?" They both take several sesame cakes. There are perhaps twenty on the plate.

"I guess. I'll tell you about Janice. I never thought of leaving her until the minute I did; all of a sudden it seemed obvious. She's about five-six, sort of dark-complected—"

"I don't want to hear about it." Her voice is positive; her many-colored hair, as she tilts back her head and squints at a ceiling light, settles into one grave shade. The light was more flattering to her hair than it is to her face; on this side of her nose there are some spots in her skin, blemishes that make bumps through her powder.

"You don't," he says. The bubble rolls off his chest. If it doesn't worry anybody else why should it worry him? "O.K. What shall we talk about? What's your weight?"

"One-fifty."

"Ruth, you're tiny. You're just a welterweight. No kidding. Nobody wants you to be all bones. Every pound you have on is priceless."

He's talking just for happiness, but something he says makes her tense up. "You're pretty wise, aren't you?" she asks, tilting her empty glass toward her eyes. The glass is a shallow cup on a short stem, like an ice-cream dish at a fancy birthday party. It sends pale arcs of reflection swimming across her face.

"You don't want to talk about your weight, either. Huh." He pops another sesame cake into his mouth, and waits until the first pang, the first taste of jelly, subsides. "Let's try this. What you need, Mrs. America, is the MagiPeel Kitchen Peeler. Preserve those vitamins. Shave off fatty excess. A simple adjustment of the plastic turn screw, and you can grate carrots and sharpen your husband's pencils. A host of uses."

"Don't. Don't be so funny."

"O.K."

"Let's be nice."

"O.K. You start."

She plops a cake in and looks at him with a funny full-mouth smile, the corners turned down tight, and a frantic look of agreeableness strains her features while she chews. She swallows, her blue eyes widened round, and gives a little gasp before launching into what he thinks will be a remark but turns out to be a laugh, right in his face. "Wait," she begs. "I'm trying." And returns to looking into the shell of her glass, thinking, and the best she can do, after all that, is to say, "Don't live in a hotel."

"I got to. Tell me a good one." He instinctively thinks she knows about hotels. At the side of her neck where it shades into her shoulder there is a shallow white hollow where his attention curls and rests.

"They're all expensive," she said. "Everything is. Just my little apartment is expensive."

"Where do you have an apartment?"

"Oh a few blocks from here. On Summer Street. It's one flight up, above a doctor."

"It's yours alone?"

"Yeah. My girl friend got married."

"So you're stuck with all the rent and you don't do anything."

"Which means what?"

"Nothing. You just said you did nothing. How expensive is it?"

She looks at him curiously, with that alertness he had noticed right off, out by the parking meters.

"The apartment," he says.

"A hundred-ten a month. Then they make you pay for light and gas."

"And you don't do anything."

She gazes into her glass, making reflected light run around the rim with a rocking motion of her hands.

"Whaddeya thinking?" he asks.

"Just wondering."

"Wondering what?"

"How wise you are."

Right here, without moving his head, he feels the wind blow. So this is the drift; he hadn't been sure. He says, "Well I'll tell ya. Why don't you let me give you something toward your rent?"

"Why should you do that?"

"Big heart," he says. "Ten?"

"I need fifteen."

"For the light and gas. O.K. O.K." He is uncertain what to do now. They sit looking at the empty plate that had held a pyramid of sesame cakes. They have eaten them all. The waiter, when he comes, is surprised to see this; his eyes go from the plate to Rabbit to Ruth, all in a second. The check amounts to $9.60. Rabbit puts a ten and a one on top of it, and beside these bills he puts a ten and a five. He counts what's left in his wallet; three tens and four ones. When he looks up, Ruth's money has vanished from the slick table. He stands up and takes her little soft coat and holds it for her, and like a great green fish, his prize, she heaves across and up out of the booth and coldly lets herself be fitted into it. He calculates, Ten cents a pound.

And that's not counting the restaurant bill. He takes the bill to the counter and gives the girl a ten. She makes change with a frown; the frightening vacancy of her eyes is methodically ringed with mascara. The purple simplicity of her kimono does not go with her frizzly permed hair and rouged, concave, sour-American face. When she puts his coins on the pink cleats of the change pad, he flicks his hand in the air above the silver, adds the dollar to it, and nods at the young Chinese waiter, who is perched attentively beside her. "Tank you vewy much, sir. Tank you vewy much," the boy says to him. But his gratitude does not even last until they are out of sight. As they move toward the glass door he turns to the cashier and in a reedy, perfectly inflected voice completes his story: "—and then this other cat says, 'But man, mine was *he*lium!' "

With this Ruth, Rabbit enters the street. On his right, away from the mountain, the heart of the city shines: a shuffle of lights, a neon outline of a boot, of a peanut, of a top hat, of an enormous sunflower erected, the stem of green neon six stories high, along one building to symbolize Sunflower Beer, the yellow center a second moon. One block down, a monotone bell tolls hurriedly, and as long as knives the red-tipped railroad-crossing gates descend, slicing through the soft mass of neon, and the traffic slows, halts.

Ruth turns left, toward the shadow of Mt. Judge, and Rabbit follows; they walk uphill on the rasping pavement. The slope of cement is a buried assertion, an unexpected echo, of the land that had been here before the city. For Rabbit the pavement is a shadow of the Daiquiri's luminous transparence; he is gay, and skips once, to get in step with this girl he loves. Her eyes are turned up, toward where the Pinnacle Hotel adds its coarse constellation to the stars above Mt. Judge. They walk together in silence while behind them a freight train chuffs and screaks through the crossing.

He recognizes his problem; she dislikes him now, like that whore in Texas. "Hey," he says. "Have you ever been up to the top there?"

"Sure. In a car."

"When I was a kid," he says, "we used to walk up from the other side. There's a sort of gloomy forest, and I remember once I came across an old house, just a hole in the ground with some stones, where I guess a pioneer had had a farm."

"The only time I ever got up there was in a car with some eager beaver."

"Well, congratulations," he says, annoyed by the self-pity hiding in her toughness.

She bites at being uncovered. "What do you think I care about your pioneer?" she asks.

"I don't know. Why shouldn't you? You're an American."

"How? I could just as easy be a Mexican."

"You never could be, you're not little enough."

"You know, you're a pig really."

"Oh now baby," he says, and puts his arm around the substance of her waist, "I think I'm sort of neat."

"Don't tell me."

She turns left, off Weiser, out of his arm. This street is Summer. Faces of brick run together to make a single dark face. The house numbers are set in fanlights of stained glass above the doors. The apple-and-orange-colored light of a small grocery store shows the silhouettes of some kids hanging around the corner. The supermarkets are driving these little stores out of business, make them stay open all night.

He puts his arm around her and begs, "Come on now, be a pleasant piece." He wants to show her that her talking tough won't keep him off. She wants him to be content with just her heavy body, but he wants whole women, light as feathers. To his surprise her arm mirrors his, comes around his waist. Thus locked, they find it awkward to walk, and part at the traffic light.

"Didn't you kind of like me in the restaurant?" he asks. "The way I tried to make old Tothero feel good? Telling him how great he was?"

"All I heard was you telling how great *you* were."

"I *was* great. It's the fact. I mean, I'm not much good for anything now, but I really was good at that."

"You know what I was good at?"

"What?"

"Cooking."

"That's more than my wife is. Poor kid."

"Remember how in Sunday school they'd tell you everybody God made was good at something? Well, that was my thing, cooking. I thought, Jesus, now I'll really be a great cook."

"Well aren't you?"

"I don't know. All I do is eat out."

"Well, stop it."

"It's in the trade," she says, and this really stops him. He doesn't think of her this bluntly. It frightens him to think of her this way. It makes her seem, in terms of love, so vast.

"Here I am," she says. Her building is brick like all the others on the west side of the street. Across the way a big limestone church hangs like a gray curtain under the streetlamp. They go in, passing beneath stained glass. The vestibule has a row of doorbells under brass mailboxes and a varnished umbrella rack and a rubber mat on the marble floor and two doors, one to the right with frosted glass and another in front of them of wire-reinforced glass through which he sees rubber-treaded stairs. While Ruth fits a key in this door he reads the gold lettering on the other: F. X. PELLIGRINI, M.D. "Old fox," Ruth says, and leads him up the stairs.

She lives one flight up. Her door is the one at the far end of a linoleum hall, nearest the street. He stands behind her as she scratches her key at the lock. Abruptly, in the cold light of the streetlamp which comes through the four flawed panes of the window by his side, blue panes so thin-seeming the touch of one finger might crack them, he begins to tremble, first his legs, and then the skin of his sides. The key fits and her door opens.

Once inside, as she reaches for the light switch, he knocks her arm down, pulls her around, and kisses her. It's insanity, he wants to crush her, a little gauge inside his ribs doubles and redoubles his need for pressure, just pure pressure, there is no love in it, love that glances and glides along the skin, he is unconscious of their skins, it is her her heart he wants to grind into his own, to comfort her completely. By nature in such an embrace she grows rigid. The small moist cushion of slack willingness with which her lips had greeted his dries up and turns hard, and when she can get her head back and her hand free she fits her palm against his jaw and pushes as if she wanted to throw his skull back into the hall. Her fingers curl and a long nail scrapes the tender skin below one eye. He lets her go. The nearly scratched eye squints and a tendon in his neck aches.

"Get out," she says, her chunky mussed face ugly in the light from the hall.

He kicks the door shut with a backward flip of his leg. "Don't," he says. "I had to hug you." He sees in the dark she is frightened; her big black shape has that pocket in it, that his instinct feels like a tongue probing a pulled tooth. The air tells him he must be motionless; for no reason he wants to laugh. Her fear and his inner knowledge are so incongruous; he knows there is no harm in him.

"Hug," she says. "Kill felt more like it."

"I've been loving you so much all night," he says. "I had to get it out of my system."

"I know all about your systems. One squirt and done."

"It won't be," he promises.

"It better be. I want you out of here."

"No you don't."

"You all think you're such lovers."

"I am," he assures her. "I am a lover." And on a tide of alcohol and stirred semen he steps forward, in a kind of swoon. Though she backs away, it is not so quickly that he cannot feel her socket of fear healing. The room they are in, he sees by streetlight, is small, and two armchairs and a sofa-bed and a table furnish it. She walks to the next room, a little larger, holding a double bed. The shade is half drawn, and low light gives each nubbin of the bedspread a shadow.

"All right," she says, "You can get into that."

"Where are you going?" Her hand is on a doorknob.

"In here."

"You're going to undress in there?"

"Yeah."

"Don't. Let me undress you. Please." In his concern he has come to stand beside her, and touches her arm now.

She moves her arm from under his touch. "You're pretty bossy."

"Please. Please."

Her voice grates with exasperation: "I have to go to the *john*."

"But come out dressed."

"I have to do something else, too."

"Don't do it. I know what it is. I hate them."

"You don't even feel it."

"But I know it's there. Like a rubber kidney or something."

Ruth laughs. "Well aren't you choice? Do you have the answer then?"

"No. I hate them even worse."

"Look. I don't know what you think your fifteen dollars entitles you to, but I got to protect myself."

"If you're going to put a lot of gadgets in this, give me the fifteen back."

She tries to twist away, but now he holds the arm he touched. She says, "Say, do you think we're married or something the way you boss me around?"

The transparent wave moves over him again and he calls to her in a voice that is almost inaudible, "Yes; let's be." So quickly her arms don't move from hanging at her sides, he kneels at her feet and kisses the place on her fingers where a ring would have been. Now that he is down there, he begins to undo the straps of her shoes. "Why do you women wear heels?" he asks, and yanks her one foot up, so she has to grab the hair on his head for support. "Don't they hurt you?" He heaves the shoe, sticky web, through the doorway into the next room, and does the same to the other. Her feet being flat on the floor gives her legs firmness all the way up. He puts his hands around her ankles and pumps them up and down briskly, between the boxy ankle bones and the circular solid fat of her calves. He has a nervous habit of massage.

"Come on," Ruth says, in a voice slightly tense with the fear of falling, his weight pinning her legs. "Get into bed."

He senses the trap. "No," he says, and stands up. "You'll put on a flying saucer."

"No, I won't. Listen, you won't know if I do or don't."

"Sure I will. I'm very sensitive."

"Oh Lord. Well anyway I got to take a leak."

"Go ahead, I don't care," he says, and won't let her close the bathroom door. She sits, like women do, primly, her back straight and her chin tucked in. Her knees linked by stretched underpants, Ruth waits above a whispering gush. At home he and Janice had been trying to toilet-train Nelson, so leaning in the doorway tall as a parent he feels a ridiculous impulse to praise her. She is so tidy, reaching under her dress with a piece of lemon-colored paper; she tugs herself together and for a sweet split second the whole intimate vulnerable patchwork of stocking tops and straps and silk and fur and soft flesh is exposed.

"Good girl," he says, and leads her into the bedroom. Behind them, the plumbing vibrates and murmurs. She moves with shy stiffness, puzzled by his will. Trembling again, shy himself, he brings her to a stop by the foot of the bed and searches for the catch of her dress. He finds buttons on the back and can't undo them easily; his hands come at them reversed.

"Let me do it."

"Don't be in such a hurry; I'll do it. You're supposed to enjoy this. This is our wedding night."

"Say, I think you're sick."

He turns her roughly, and falls again into a deep wish to give comfort. He touches her caked cheeks; she seems small as he looks down into the frowning planes of her set, shadowed face. He moves his lips into one eye socket, gently, trying to say this night has no urgency in it, trying to listen through his lips to the timid pulse beating in the bulge of her lid. With a careful impartiality he fears she will find comic, he kisses also her other eye; then, excited by the thought of his own tenderness, his urgency spills; his mouth races across her face, nibbling, licking, so that she does laugh, tickled, and pushes away. He locks her against him, crouches, and presses his parted teeth into the fat hot hollow at the side of her throat. Ruth tenses at his threat to bite, and her hands shove at his shoulders, but he clings there, his teeth bared in a silent exclamation, crying out against her smothering throat that it is not her body he wants, not the machine, but her, her.

Though there are no words she hears this, and says, "Don't try to prove you're a lover on me. Just come and go."

"You're *so* smart," he says, and starts to hit her, checks his arm, and offers instead, "Hit me. Come on. You want to, don't you? Really pound me."

"My Lord," she says, "this'll take all night." He plucks her limp arm from her side and swings it up toward him, but she manages her hand so that five bent fingers bump against his cheek painlessly. "That's what poor Maggie has to do for your old bastard friend."

He begs, "Don't talk about them."

"Damn men," she continues, "either want to hurt somebody or be hurt."

"I don't, honest. Either one."

"Well then undress me and stop farting around."

He sighs through his nose. "You have a sweet tongue," he says.

"I'm sorry if I shock you." Yet in her voice is a small metallic withdrawal, as if she really is.

"You don't," he says and, business-like, stoops and takes the hem of her dress in his hands. His eyes are enough accustomed to the dark now to see the cloth as green. He peels it up her body, and she lifts her arms, and her head gets caught for a moment in the neck-hole. She shakes her head crossly, like a dog with a scrap, and the dress comes free, skims off her arms into his hands floppy and faintly warm. He sails it into a chair hulking in a corner. "God," he says, "you're pretty." She is a ghost in her silver slip. Dragging the dress over her head has loosened her hair. Her solemn face tilts as she quickly lifts out the pins. Her hair falls out of heavy loops. Women all look like brides in their slips.

"Yeah," she says. "Pretty plump."

"No," he says, "you are," and in the space of a breath goes to her and picks her up, great glistening sugar in her sifty-grained slip, and carries her to the bed, and lays her on it. "So pretty."

"You lifted me," she says. "That'll put you out of action."

Harsh direct light falls on her face; the creases on her neck show black. He asks, "Shall I pull the shade?"

"Please. It's a dismal view."

He goes to the window and bends to see what she means. There is only the church across the way, gray, grave, confident. Lights behind its rose window are left burning, and this circle of red and purple and gold seems in the city night a hole punched in reality to show the abstract brilliance burning underneath. He feels gratitude to the builders of this ornament, and lowers the shade on it guiltily. He turns quickly, and

Ruth's eyes watch him out of shadows that also seem gaps in a surface. The curve of her hip supports a crescent of silver; his sense of her weight seems to make an aroma.

"What's next?" He takes off his coat and throws it; he loves this throwing things, the way the flying cloth puts him at the center of a gathering nakedness. "Stockings?"

"They're tricky," she says. "I don't want a run."

"You do it then."

In a sitting position, with the soft-pawed irritable deftness of a cat, she extricates herself from a web of elastic and silk and cotton. When she has peeled off the stockings and tucked them, tidily rolled, into the crevice by the footboard of the bed, she unexpectedly lies down and arches her back to push off the garter belt and pants. As unexpectedly, he bends his face into a small forest smelling of spice. He is out of all dimension, and in a dark land, and a tender entire woman seems an inch away around a kind of corner. When he straightens up on his knees, kneeling as he is by the bed, Ruth under his eyes is an incredible continent, the pushed-up slip a north of snow.

"So much," he says.

"Too much."

"No, listen. You're good." Cupping a hand behind her hot sheltered neck, he pulls her up, and slides her slip over her head. It comes off with liquid ease; clothes just fall from a woman who wants to be stripped. The cool hollow his hand finds in the small of her back mixes in his mind with the shallow shadows of the stretch of skin that slopes from the bones of her shoulders. He kisses this expanse. Where her skin is whiter it is cooler. The hardness of his chin hits the hardness of her bra. He whispers "Hey let me" when Ruth's one arm crooks back to unfasten it. He gets behind her. She sits upright with her fat legs jackknifed sideways and her back symmetrical as a great vase. The tiny dingy catches are hard to undo; she draws her shoulder blades together. With a pang the tough strap parts. Her back broadens and turns convex as she shrugs the straps down off her shoulders. As one arm tosses her brassière over the edge of the bed the other, on his side, presses against her breast, so he won't see. But he does see; a quick glimmer of tipped weight. He moves away and sits on the corner of the bed and drinks in the pure sight of her. She keeps her arm tight against the one breast and brings up her hand to cover the other; a ring glints. Her modesty praises him; it shows she is feeling. The straight arm props her weight. Her belly is a pond of shadow deepening to a black eclipsed by the inner swell of her thighs. Light seizes her right side as her body turns in its stillness; rigidity is her one defense against his eyes. She holds the pose until his eyes smart with echoes of white. When her voice breaks from her frozen form, he is startled: "What about you?"

He is still dressed, even to his necktie. While he is draping his trousers over a chair, arranging them to keep the crease, she slips beneath the covers. He stands over her in his underclothes and asks, "Now you really don't have anything on?"

"You wouldn't let me."

He remembers the glint. "Give me your ring."

She brings her right hand out from under the covers and he carefully works a thick brass ring, like a class ring, past her bunching knuckle. In letting her hand drop she grazes the distorted front of his Jockey shorts.

He looks down at her, thinking. The covers come up to her throat and the pale arm lying on top of the bedspread has a slight serpent's twist. "There's nothing else?"

"I'm all skin," she says. "Come on. Get in."

"You want me?"

"Don't flatter yourself. I want it over with."

"You have all that crust on your face."

"God, you're insulting!"

"I just love you too much. Where's a washrag?"

"I don't want my God-damned face washed!"

He goes into the bathroom and turns on the light and finds a facecloth and holds it under the hot faucet. He wrings it out and turns off the light. As he comes back across the room Ruth laughs from the bed. He asks, "What's the joke?"

"In those damn underclothes you *do* look kind of like a rabbit. I thought only kids wore those elastic kind of pants."

He looks down at his T-shirt and snug underpants, pleased and further stirred. His name in her mouth feels like a physical touch. She sees him as special. When he puts the rough cloth to her face, it goes tense and writhes with a resistance like Nelson's, and he counters it with a father's practiced method. He sweeps her forehead, pinches her nostrils, abrades her cheeks and, finally, while her whole body is squirming in protest, scrubs her lips, her words shattered and smothered. When at last he lets her hands win, and lifts the washrag, she stares at him, says nothing, and closes her eyes.

In kneeling by the bed to grip her face he presses the sensitive core of his love against the edge of the mattress and now without his will a little spills, like cream forced over the neck of the bottle by the milk's freezing. He backs away from contact; the shy series of hops, puzzled, throbs to a slow halt. He stands and presses the cloth against his own face, like a man sobbing. He goes to the foot of the bed, throws the rag toward the bathroom, peels out of his underclothes, bobs, and hurries to hide in the bed. The long dark space between the sheets buries him.

He makes love to her as he would to his wife. After their marriage, and her nerves lost that fineness, Janice needed coaxing; he would begin by rubbing her back. Ruth submits warily when he tells her to lie on her stomach. To lend his hands strength he sits up on her buttocks and leans his weight down through stiff arms into his thumbs and palms as they work the broad muscles and insistent bones of the spine's terrain. She sighs and shifts her head on the pillow. "You should be in the Turkish-bath business," she says. He goes for her neck, and advances his fingers around to her throat, where the columns of blood give like reeds, and massages her shoulders with the balls of his thumbs, and his fingertips just find the glazed upper edges of her pillowing breasts. He returns to her back, until his wrists ache, and flops from astride his mermaid truly weary, as if under a sea-spell to sleep. He pulls the covers up over them, to the middle of their faces.

Janice was shy of his eyes so Ruth heats in his darkness. His lids flutter shut though she arches anxiously against him. Her hand seeks him, and angles him earnestly for a touch his sealed lids feel as red. He sees blue when with one deliberate hand she pries open his jaw and bows his head to her burdened chest. Lovely wobbly bubbles, heavy: perfume between. Taste, salt and sour, swirls back with his own saliva. She rolls away, on to her back, the precious red touch breaking, twists, giving him cool new skin. Rough with herself, she forces the dry other breast into his face, coated with a pollen that dissolves. He opens his eyes, seeking her, and sees her face a soft mask gazing downward calmly, caring for him, and closes his eyes on the food of her again; his hand abandoned on the breadth of her body finds at arm's length a split pod, an open fold, shapeless and simple. She rolls further, turning her back, cradling her bottom in his stomach and thighs. They enter a lazy space. He wants the time to stretch long, to great length and thinness. Between her legs she strokes him with fingertips. She brings back her foot and he holds her heel. As they deepen together he feels impatience that through all their twists they remain separate flesh; he cannot dare enough, now that she is so much his friend in this search; everywhere they meet a wall. The body lacks voice to sing its own song. Impatience tapers; she floats through his blood as under his eyelids a salt smell, damp pressure, the sense of her smallness as her body hurries everywhere into his hands, her breathing, bedsprings' creak, accidental slaps, and the ache at the parched root of his tongue each register their colors.

Nudge enters his softness, "Now?" Her voice croaky. He kneels in a kind of sickness between her spread legs. With her help their blind loins fit. Something sad in the capture. It grows. He braces himself on his arms above her, afraid, for it is here he most often failed Janice, by coming too soon. Yet, what with the alcohol drifting in his system, or his coming a little before, his love is slow to burst in her warmth. He hides his face beside her throat, in the mint of her hair. With thin, thin arms she hugs him and presses him down and rises above him. From her high smooth shoulders down she is one long underbelly erect in light above him; he says in praise softly, "Hey."

She answers, "Hey."

"You're pretty."

"Come on. Work."

Galled, he shoves up through her and in addition sets his hand under her jaw and shoves her face so his fingers slip into her mouth and her slippery throat strains. As if unstrung by this anger, she tumbles and carries him over and he lies on top of her again, the skin of their chests sticking together; she reaches her hand down and touches their mixed fur and her breathing snags on something sharp. Her thighs throw open wide and clamp his sides and throw open again so wide it frightens him, she wants, impossible, to turn inside out; the muscles and lips and bones of her expanded underside press against him as a new anatomy, of another animal. She feels transparent; he sees her heart. She suspends him, subsides, and in the folds of her withering, his love and pride revive. So she is first, and waits for him while at a trembling extremity of tenderness he traces again and again the arc of her eyebrow with his thumb. His sea of seed buckles, and sobs into a still channel. At each shudder her mouth smiles in his and her legs, locked at his back, bear down.

She asks in time, "O.K.?"

"You're pretty."

Ruth takes her legs from around him and spills him off her body like a pile of sand. He looks in her face and seems to read in its shadows a sad expression of forgiveness, as if she knows that at the moment of release, the root of love, he betrayed her by feeling despair. Nature leads you up like a mother and as soon as she gets her little price leaves you with nothing. The sweat on his skin is cold in the air; he brings the blankets up from her feet.

"You were a beautiful piece," he says from the pillow listlessly, and touches her soft side. Her flesh still soaks in the act; it ebbs slower in her.

"I had forgotten," she says.

"Forgot what?"

"That I could have it too."

"What's it like?"

"Oh. It's like falling through."

"Where do you fall to?"

"Nowhere. I can't talk about it."

He kisses her lips; she's not to blame. She lazily accepts, then in an afterflurry of affection flutters her tongue against his chin.

He loops his arm around her waist and composes himself against her body for sleep.

"Hey. I got to get up."

"Stay."

"I got to go into the bathroom."

"No." He tightens his hold.

"Boy, you better let me up."

He murmurs, "Don't scare me," and snuggles more securely against her side. His thigh slides over hers, weight on warmth. Best bedfriend, fucked woman. Gentle ebb. Oh, how! when she got up on him like the bell of a big blue lily slipped down on his slow head. He could have hurt her shoving her jaw. He reawakens enough to feel his dry breath drag through sagged lips as she rolls from under his leg and arm. "Hey get me a glass of water," he says.

She stands by the edge of the bed, baggy in nakedness, and goes off into the bathroom to do her duty. There's that in women repels him; handle themselves like an old envelope. Tubes into tubes, wash away men's dirt, insulting, really. Faucets cry. The more awake he gets the more depressed he is. From deep in the pillow he stares at the horizontal strip of stained-glass church window that shows under the window shade. Its childish brightness seems the one kind of comfort left to him.

Light from behind the closed bathroom door tints the air in

the bedroom. The splashing sounds are like the sounds his parents would make when as a child Rabbit would waken to realize they had come upstairs, that the whole house would soon be dark, and the sight of morning would be his next sensation. He is asleep when like a faun in moonlight Ruth, washed, creeps back to his side, holding a glass of water.

During this sleep he has an intense dream. He and his mother and father and some others are sitting around their kitchen table. It's the old kitchen. A girl at the table reaches with a very long arm weighted with a bracelet and turns a handle of the wood icebox and cold air sweeps over Rabbit. She has opened the door of the square cave where the cake of ice sits; and there it is, inches from Harry's eyes, lopsided from melting but still big, holding within its metal-black bulk the white partition that the cakes have when they come bumping down the chute at the ice plant. He leans closer into the cold breath of the ice, a tin-smelling coldness he associates with the metal that makes up the walls of the cave and the ribs of its floor, delicate rhinoceros gray, mottled with the same disease the linoleum has. Having leaned closer he sees that under the watery skin are hundreds of clear white veins like the capillaries on a leaf, as if ice too were built up of living cells. And further inside, so ghostly it comes to him last, hangs a jagged cloud, the star of an explosion, whose center is uncertain in refraction but whose arms fly from the core of pallor as straight as long eraser-marks diagonally into all planes of the cube. The rusted ribs the cake rests on wobble through to his eyes like the teeth of a grin. Fear probes him; the cold lump is alive.

His mother speaks to him. "Close the door."

"I didn't open it."

"I know."

"She did."

"I know. My good boy wouldn't hurt anyone." The girl at the table fumbles a piece of food and with terrible weight Mother turns and scolds her. The scolding keeps on and on, senselessly, the same thing over and over again, a continuous pumping of words like a deep inner bleeding. It is himself bleeding; his grief for the girl distends his face until it feels like a huge white dish. "Tart can't eat decently as a baby," Mother says.

"Hey, hey, hey," Rabbit cries, and stands up to defend his sister. Mother rears away, scoffing. They are in the narrow place between the two houses; only himself and the girl; it is Janice Springer. He tries to explain about his mother. Janice's head meekly stares at his shoulder; when he puts his arms around her he is conscious of her eyes being bloodshot. Though their faces are not close he feels her breath, hot with tears. They are out behind the Mt. Judge Recreation Hall, out in back with the weeds and tramped-down bare ground and embedded broken bottles; through the wall they hear music on loudspeakers, Janice has a pink dance dress on, and is crying. He repeats, numb at heart, about his mother, that she was just getting at *him* but the girl keeps crying, and to his horror her face begins to slide, the skin to slip slowly from the bone, but there is no bone, just more melting stuff underneath; he cups his hands with the idea of catching it and patting it back; as it drips in loops into his palms the air turns white with what is his own scream.

The white is light; the pillow glows against his eyes and sunlight projects the flaws of the window panes onto the drawn shade. This woman is curled up under the blankets between him and the window. Her hair in sunlight sprays red, brown, gold, white, and black across her pillow. Smiling with relief, he gets up on an elbow and kisses her solid slack cheek, admires its tough texture of pores. He sees by faint rose streaks how imperfectly he scrubbed her face in the dark. He returns to the position in which he slept, but he has slept too much in recent hours. As if to seek the entrance to another dream he reaches for her naked body across the little distance and wanders up and down broad slopes, warm like freshly baked cake. Her back is toward him; he cannot see her eyes.

Not until she sighs heavily and stretches and turns toward him does he know she is awake.

Again, then, they make love, in morning light with cloudy mouths, her breasts floating shallow on her ridged rib cage. Her nipples are sunken brown buds, her bush a froth of tinted metal. It is almost too naked; his climax seems petty in relation to the wealth of brilliant skin, and he wonders if she pretends. She says not; no, it was different but all right. Really all right. He goes back under the covers while she pads around on bare feet getting dressed. Funny how she puts on her bra before her underpants. Her putting on her underpants makes him conscious of her legs as separate things: thick pink liquid twists diminishing downward into her ankles. They take pink light from the reflection of each other as she moves. Her accepting his watching her flatters him, shelters him. They have become domestic.

Church bells ring loudly. He moves to her side of the bed to watch the crisply dressed people go into the limestone church across the street, whose lit window had lulled him to sleep. He reaches and pulls up the shade a few feet. The rose window is dark now, and above the church, above Mt. Judge, the sun glares in a façade of blue. It strikes a shadow down from the church steeple, a cool stumpy negative in which a few men with flowers in their lapels stand and gossip while the common sheep of the flock stream in, heads down. The thought of these people having the bold idea of leaving their homes to come here and pray pleases and reassures Rabbit, and moves him to close his own eyes and bow his head with a movement so tiny Ruth won't notice. *Help me, Christ. Forgive me. Take me down the way. Bless Ruth, Janice, Nelson, my mother and father, Mr. and Mrs. Springer, and the unborn baby. Forgive Tothero and all the others. Amen.*

He opens his eyes to the day and says, "That's a pretty big congregation."

"Sunday morning," she says. "I could throw up every Sunday morning."

"Why?"

She just says, "Fuh," as if he knows the answer. After thinking a bit, and seeing him lie there looking out the window seriously, she says, "I once had a guy in here who woke me up at
eight o'clock because he had to teach Sunday school at nine-
thirty."

"You don't believe anything?"

"No. You mean you do?"

"Well, yeah. I think so." Her rasp, her sureness, makes him
wince; he wonders if he's lying. If he is, he is hung in the middle of nowhere, and the thought hollows him, makes his heart
tremble. Across the street a few people in their best clothes
walk on the pavement past the row of worn brick homes; are
they walking on air? Their clothes, they put on their best
clothes: he clings to the thought giddily; it seems a visual
proof of the unseen world.

"Well, if you do what are you doing here?" she asks.

"Why not? You think you're Satan or somebody?"

This stops her a moment, standing there with her comb, before she laughs. "Well you go right ahead if it makes you
happy."

He presses her. "Why don't you believe anything?"

"You're kidding."

"No. Doesn't it ever, at least for a second, seem obvious to
you?"

"God, you mean? No. It seems obvious just the other way.
All the time."

"Well now if God doesn't exist, why does anything?"

"Why? There's no why to it. Things just are." She stands
before the mirror, and her comb pulling back on her hair
pulls her upper lip up; women are always looking that way
in the movies.

"That's not the way I feel about you," he says, "that you
just are."

"Hey, why don't you get some clothes on instead of just
lying there giving me the Word?"

This, and her turning, hair swirling, to say it, stir him.

"Come here," he asks. The idea of making it while the churches are full excites him.

"No," Ruth says. She is really a little sore. His believing in God grates against her.

"You don't like me now?"

"What does it matter to you?"

"You know it does."

"Get out of my bed."

"I guess I owe you fifteen more dollars."

"All you owe me is getting the hell out."

"What! Leave you all alone?" He says this as with comical speed, while she stands there startled rigid, he jumps from bed and gathers up some of his clothes and ducks into the bathroom and closes the door. When he comes out, in underclothes, he says, still clowning, "You don't like me any more," and moves sadly to where his trousers are neatly laid on the chair. While he was out of the room she made the bed.

"I like you enough," she says in a preoccupied voice, tugging the bedspread smooth.

"Enough for what?"

"Enough."

"Why do you like me?"

" 'Cause you're bigger than I am." She moves to the next corner and tugs. "Boy that used to gripe hell out of me, the way these little women everybody thinks are so cute grab all the big men."

"They have something," he tells her. "They seem easier to get to."

She laughs and says, "I guess that's right."

He pulls up his trousers and buckles the belt. "Why else do you like me?"

She looks at him. "Shall I tell you?"

"Tell me."

" 'Cause you haven't given up. In your stupid way you're still fighting."

He loves hearing this; pleasure spins along his nerves, mak-

ing him feel immense, and he grins. But the American protest
of modesty is instinctive with him, and "the will to achievement" glides out of his mouth, which he tries to make look
lopsided. She gets it.

"That poor old bastard," she says. "He really is a bastard
too."

"Hey, I'll tell you what," Rabbit says. "I'll run out and get
some stuff at that grocery store you can cook for our lunch."

"Say, you settle right in, don't you?"

"Why? Were you going to meet somebody?"

"No, I don't have anybody."

"Well, then. You said last night you liked to cook."

"I said I used to."

"Well, if you used to you still do. What shall I get?"

"How do you know the store's open?"

"Isn't it? Sure it is. Those little stores make all their money
on Sundays, what with the supermarkets." He goes to the
window and looks up at the corner. Sure, the door of the store
opens and a man comes out with a newspaper.

"Your shirt's filthy," she says behind him.

"I know." He moves away from the windowlight. "It's
Tothero's shirt. I got to get some clothes. But let me get
food now. What shall I get?"

"What do you like?" she asks.

He leaves pleased. The thing about her is, she's good-natured. He knew it the second he saw her standing by the parking meters. He could just tell from the soft way her belly
looked. With women, you keep bumping against them, because they want different things, they're a different race.
Either they give, like a plant, or scrape, like a stone. In all the
green world nothing feels as good as a woman's good nature.
The pavement kicks under his feet as he runs to the grocery
store in his dirty shirt. *What do you like?* He has her. He
knows he has her.

He brings back eight hot dogs in cellophane, a package of
frozen lima beans, a package of frozen French fries, a quart of
milk, a jar of relish, a loaf of raisin bread, a ball of cheese

wrapped in red cellophane, and, on top of the bag, a Ma Sweitzer's shoo-fly pie. It all costs $2.43. As she brings the things out of the bag in her tiny stained kitchen, Ruth says, "You're kind of a bland eater."

"I wanted lamb chops but he only had hot dogs and salami and hash in cans."

While she cooks he wanders around her living-room and finds a row of pocketbook mysteries on a shelf under a table beside a chair. The guy in the bunk beside his at Fort Hood used to read those all the time. Ruth has opened the windows, and the cool March air is sharpened by this memory of baking Texas. Ruth's curtains of dingy dotted Swiss blow; their gauze skin gently fills and they lean in toward him as he stands paralyzed by a more beautiful memory: his home, when he was a child, the Sunday papers rattling on the floor, stirred by the afternoon draft, and his mother rattling the dishes in the kitchen; when she is done, she will organize them all, Pop and him and baby Miriam, to go for a walk. Because of the baby, they will not go far, just a few blocks maybe to the old gravel quarry, where the ice pond of winter, melted into a lake a few inches deep, doubles the height of the quarry cliff by throwing its rocks upside down into a pit of reflection. But it is only water; they take a few steps farther along the edge and from this new angle the pond mirrors the sun, the illusion of inverted cliffs is wiped out, and the water is as solid as ice with light. Rabbit holds little Mim hard by the hand. "Hey," he calls to Ruth. "I got a terrific idea. Let's go for a walk this afternoon."

"Walk! I walk all the time."

"Let's walk up to the top of Mt. Judge from here." He can't remember having ever gone up the mountain from the Brewer side; gusts of anticipation sweep over him, and as he turns, exalted, away from the curtains stiff and leaning with the breeze, huge church bells ring. "Yeah let's," he calls into the kitchen. "Please." Out on the street people leave church carrying wands of green absentmindedly at their sides.

When Ruth serves lunch he sees she is a better cook than

Janice; she has boiled the hot dogs somehow without splitting them. With Janice, they always arrived at the table torn and twisted and tortured-looking. He and Ruth eat at a small porcelain table in the kitchen. As he touches his fork to his plate he remembers the cold feel in his dream of Janice's face dropping into his hands, and the memory spoils his first bite, makes it itself a kind of horror. Nevertheless he says, "Terrific," and gamely goes ahead and eats, and does regain some appetite.

Ruth's face across from him takes some of the pale glare of the table-top; the skin of her broad forehead shines and the two blemishes beside her nose are like spots something spilled has left. She seems to sense that she has become unattractive, and eats obsequiously, with quick little self-effacing bites.

"Hey," he says.

"What?"

"You know I still have that car parked over on Cherry Street."

"You're O.K. The meters don't matter on Sunday."

"Yeah, but they will tomorrow."

"Sell it."

"Huh?"

"Sell the car. Simplify your life. Get rich quick."

"No, I mean— Oh. You mean for you. Look, I still have thirty dollars, why don't you let me give it to you now?" He reaches toward his hip pocket.

"No, no, I did *not* mean that. I didn't mean anything. It just popped into my fat head." She is embarrassed; her neck goes splotchy and his pity is roused, to think how pretty she appeared last night.

He explains. "You see, my wife's old man is a used-car dealer and when we got married he sold us this car at a pretty big discount. So in a way it's really my wife's car and anyway since she has the kid I think she ought to have it. And then as you say my shirt's dirty and I ought to get my clothes if I can. So what I thought was, after lunch why don't I sneak over to my place and leave the car and pick up my clothes?"

"Suppose she's there?"

"She won't be. She'll be at her mother's."

"I think you'd like it if she was there," Ruth says.

He wonders; imagines opening the door and finding Janice sitting there in the armchair with an empty glass watching television, and feels, like a small collapse within him, like a piece of food stuck in his throat at last going down, his relief at finding her face still firm, still its old dumb tense self of a face. "No, I wouldn't," he tells Ruth. "I'm scared of her."

"Obviously," Ruth says.

"There's something about her," he insists. "She's a menace."

"This poor wife you left? *You're* the menace, I'd say."

"No."

"Oh that's right. You think you're a rabbit." Her tone in saying this is faintly jeering and irritable, he doesn't know why.

She asks, "What do you think you're going to do with these clothes?" That's it; she feels him moving in.

He admits, "Bring them here."

She takes in the breath but comes out with nothing.

"Just for tonight," he pleads. "You're not doing anything are you?"

"Maybe. I don't know. Probably not."

"Well then, great. Hey. I love you."

She rises to clear away the plates and stands there, thumb on china, staring at the center of the white table. She shakes her head heavily and says, "You're bad news."

Across from him her broad pelvis, snug in a nubbly brown skirt, is solid and symmetrical as the base of a powerful column. His heart rises through that strong column and, enraptured to feel his love for her founded anew yet not daring to lift his eyes to the test of her face, he says, "I can't help it. You're such good news."

He eats three pieces of shoo-fly pie and a crumb in the corner of his lips comes off on her sweater when he kisses her breasts good-by in the kitchen. He leaves her with the dishes. His car is waiting for him on Cherry Street in the cool spring noon mysteriously; it is as if a room of a house he owned had been detached and scuttled by this curb and now that the tide of night was out stood up glistening in the sand, slightly tilting but unharmed, ready to sail at the turn of a key. Under his rumpled dirty clothes his body feels clean, narrow, hollow. He is loved. The car smells secure: rubber and dust and painted metal hot in the sun. A sheath for the knife of himself. He cuts through the Sunday-stunned town, the soft rows of domestic brick, the banistered porches of calm wood. He drives around the great flank of Mt. Judge; its slope by the highway is dusted the yellow-green of new leaves; higher up, the evergreens make a black horizon with the sky. The view has changed since the last time he came this way. Yesterday morning the sky was ribbed with thin-stretched dawn clouds, and he was exhausted, heading into the center of the net, where alone there seemed a chance of rest. Now the noon of another day has burned away the clouds, and the sky in the windshield is blank and cold, and he feels nothing ahead of him, Ruth's blue-eyed nothing, the nothing she told him she did, the nothing she believes in. Your heart lifts forever through that blank sky.

His mood of poise crumbles as he descends into the familiar houses of Mt. Judge. He becomes cautious, nervous. He turns up Jackson, up Potter, up Wilbur, and tries to make out from some external sign if there is anyone in his apartment. No telltale light would show; it is the height of day. No car is out front. He circles the block twice, straining his neck to see a face at the window. The panes are high and opaque. Ruth was wrong; he doesn't want to see Janice.

The bare possibility makes him so faint that when he gets out of the car the bright sun hits him like a pillow. As he climbs the stairs, the steps seem to calibrate, to restrain by notches, a helpless tendency in his fear-puffed body to rise. He raps on the door, braced to run. Nothing answers on the other side. He taps again, listens, and takes the key out of his pocket.

Though the apartment is empty, it is yet so full of Janice he begins to tremble; the sight of that easy chair turned to face the television attacks his knees. Nelson's broken toys on the floor derange his head; all the things inside his skull, the gray matter, the bones of his ears, the apparatus of his eyes, seem clutter clogging the tube of his self; his sinuses choke, with a sneeze or tears, he doesn't know. The living-room has the feel of dust. The shades are still drawn. Janice drew them in the afternoons to keep glare off the television screen. Someone has made gestures of cleaning up; her ashtrays and her empty glass have been taken away. Rabbit puts the door key and the car keys on top of the television case, metal painted brown in imitation of wood grain. As he opens the closet door the knob bumps against the edge of the set. Some of her clothes are gone.

He means to reach for his clothes but instead turns and wanders toward the kitchen, trying to gather up the essence of what he has done. Their bed sags in the filtered sunlight. Never a good bed. Her parents had given it to them. On the bureau sit a few of her bottles and a pair of fingernail scissors and a spool of white thread and a needle and some brass hair-pins and a telephone book and a Baby Ben with luminous numbers and a recipe she never used torn from a magazine and a necklace made of wood beads carved in Java he got her for Christmas. Insecurely tilted against the wall is the big oval mirror they took away when her parents had a new bathroom put in; he always meant to attach it to the plaster above her bureau for her but never got around to buying molly bolts. A glass on the windowsill, half full of stale, bubbled water, throws a curved patch of diluted sun onto the bare place where the mirror should have been fixed. Three long nicks, here, scratched in the wall, parallel; what ever made them, when? Beyond the edge of the made bed a white triangle of bathroom floor shows; the time after her shower, her bottom blushing with steam, lifting her arms gladly to kiss him, soaked licks of hair in her armpits. What gladness had seized her, and then him, unasked?

In the kitchen he discovers an odd oversight: the pork

chops never taken from the pan, cold as death, riding congealed grease. He dumps them out in the paper bag under the sink and with a spatula scrapes crumbs of the stiff speckled fat after them. The bag, stained dark brown at the bottom, smells of something sweetly rotting. He puzzles. The garbage can is downstairs out back, he doesn't want to make two trips. He decides to forget it. He draws scalding water into the sink and puts the pan in to soak. The breath of steam is like a whisper in a tomb.

In frightened haste he takes clean Jockey pants, T-shirts, and socks from a drawer, three shirts in cellophane and blue cardboard from another, a pair of laundered suntans from a third, draws his two suits and a sports shirt from the closet, and wraps the smaller clothing in the suits to form a bundle he can carry. The job makes him sweat. Clutching his clothes between two arms and a lifted thigh, he surveys the apartment once more, and the furniture, carpeting, wallpaper all seem darkly glazed with the murk filming his own face; the rooms are filled with the flavor of an awkward job, and he is glad to get out. The door snaps shut behind him irrevocably. His key is inside.

Toothbrush. Razor. Cuff links. Shoes. At each step down he remembers something he forgot. He hurries, his feet patter. He jumps. His head almost hits the naked bulb burning at the end of a black cord in the vestibule. His name on the mailbox seems to call at him as he sweeps past; its letters of blue ink crowd the air like a cry. He feels ridiculous, ducking into the sunlight like one of those weird thieves you read about in the back pages of newspapers who instead of stealing money and silver carry away a porcelain washbasin, twenty rolls of wallpaper, or a bundle of old clothes.

"Good afternoon, Mr. Angstrom."

A neighbor is passing, Miss Arndt, in a lavender church hat, carrying a palm frond in clutched hands. "Oh. Hello. How are you?" She lives three houses up; they think she has cancer.

"I am just splendid," she says. "Just splendid." And stands there in sunshine, bewildered by splendor, flatfooted, leaning unconsciously against the slope of the pavement. A green car goes by too slowly. Miss Arndt sticks in his way, amiably confused, grateful for something, her simple adherence to the pavement it seems, like a fly who stops walking on the ceiling to marvel at itself.

"How do you like the weather?" he asks.

"I love it, I love it; Palm Sunday is always blue. It makes the sap rise in my legs." She laughs and he follows; she stands rooted to the hot cement between the feathery shade of two young maples. She knows nothing, he becomes certain.

"Yes," he says, for her eyes have fixed on his arms. "I seem to be doing spring cleaning." He shrugs the bundle to clarify.

"Good," she says, with a surprising sarcastic snarl. "You young husbands, you certainly take the bit in your teeth." Then she twists, and exclaims, "Why, there's a clergyman in there!"

The green car has come back, even more slowly, down the center of the street. With a dismay that makes the bundle of clothes double its weight in his arms, Rabbit realizes he is pinned. He lurches from the porch and strides past Miss Arndt saying, "I got to run," right on top of her considered remark, "It's not Reverend Kruppenbach."

No, of course not Kruppenbach; Rabbit knows who it is, though he doesn't know his name. The Episcopalian. The Springers were Episcopalians, more of the old phony's social climbing, they were originally Reformeds. Rabbit doesn't quite run. The downward pavement jars his heels at every stride. He can't see the cement under the bundle he carries. If he can just make the alley. His one hope is the minister can't be sure it's him. He feels the green car crawling behind him; he thinks of throwing the clothes away and really running. If he could get into the old ice plant. But it's a block away. He feels Ruth, the dishes done, waiting on the other side of the mountain. Blue beyond blue under blue.

As a shark nudges silent creases of water ahead of it, the green fender makes ripples of air that break against the back of Rabbit's knees. The faster he walks the harder these ripples break. Behind his ear a childishly twanging voice pipes, "I beg your pardon. Are you Harry Angstrom?"

With a falling sensation of telling a lie Rabbit turns and half-whispers, "Yes."

The fair young man with his throat manacled in white lets his car glide diagonally against the curb, yanks on the hand-brake, and shuts off the motor, thus parking on the wrong side of the street, cockeyed. Funny how ministers ignore small laws. Rabbit remembers how Kruppenbach's son used to tear around town on a motorcycle. It seemed somehow blasphemous. "Well, I'm Jack Eccles," this minister says, and inconsequently laughs a syllable. The white stripe of an unlit cigarette hanging from his lips makes with the echoing collar a comic picture in the car window. He gets out of his car, a '58 olive Buick four-door, and offers his hand. To accept it Rabbit has to put his big ball of clothes down in the strip of grass between the pavement and curb.

Eccles' handshake, eager and practiced and hard, seems to symbolize for him an embrace. For an instant Rabbit fears he will never let go. He feels caught, foresees explanations, embarrassments, prayers, reconciliations rising up like dank walls; his skin prickles in desperation. He feels tenacity in his captor.

The minister is about his age or a little older and a good bit shorter. But not small; a sort of needless muscularity runs under his black coat. He stands edgily, with his chest faintly cupped. He has long reddish eyebrows that push a worried wrinkle around above the bridge of his nose, and a little pale pointed knob of a chin tucked under his mouth. Despite his looking vexed there is something friendly and silly about him.

"Where are you going?" he asks.

"Huh? Nowhere." Rabbit is distracted by the man's suit; it only feigns black. It is really blue, a sober but elegant, light-weight, midnight blue. While his little vest or bib or whatever is black as a stove. The effort of keeping the cigarette between his lips twists Eccles' laugh into a snort. He slaps the breasts of his coat. "Do you have a match by any chance?"

"Gee I'm sorry, no. I quit smoking."

"You're a better man than I am." He pauses and thinks, then looks at Harry with startled, arched eyebrows. The distention makes his gray eyes seem round and as pale as glass. "Can I give you a lift?"

"No. Hell. Don't bother."

"I'd like to talk to you."

"No; you don't really want to, do you?"

"I do, yes. Very much."

"Yeah. O.K." Rabbit picks up his clothes and walks around the front of the Buick and gets in. The interior has that sweet tangy plastic new-car smell; he takes a deep breath of it and it cools his fear. "This is about Janice?"

Eccles nods, staring out the rear window as he backs away from the curb. His upper lip overhangs his lower; there are scoops of weary violet below his eyes. Sunday must be his heavy day.

"How is she? What did she do?"

"She seems much saner today. She and her father came to church this morning." They drive down the street. Eccles adds nothing, just gazes through the windshield, blinking. He pokes the lighter in on the dashboard.

"I *thought* she'd be with them," Rabbit says. He is getting slightly annoyed at the way the minister isn't bawling him out or something; he doesn't seem to know his job.

The lighter pops. Eccles puts it to his cigarette, inhales, and seems to come back into focus. "Evidently," he says, "when you didn't come back in half an hour she called your parents and had your father bring your boy over to your apartment. Your father, I gather, was very reassuring and told her you had probably been sidetracked somewhere. She remembered you had been late getting home because of some street game and thought you might have gone back to it. I believe your father even walked around town looking for the game."

"Where was old man Springer?"

"She didn't call them. She didn't call them until two o'clock that morning, when I suppose the poor thing had given up all hope." "Poor thing" is one word on his lips, worn smooth.

Harry asks, "Not until two?" Pity grips him; his hands tighten on the bundle, as if comforting Janice.

"Around then. By then she was in such a state, alcoholic and otherwise, that her mother called me."

"Why you?"

"I don't know. People do." Eccles laughs. "They're supposed to; it's comforting. To me at least. I always thought Mrs. Springer hated me. She hadn't been to church in months." As he turns to face Rabbit, to follow up this joke, a little quizzical pang lifts his eyebrows and forces his broad mouth open.

"This was around two in the morning?"

"Between two and three."

"Gee, I'm sorry. I didn't mean to get you out of bed."

The minister shakes his head irritably. "That's not to be considered."

"Well I feel terrible about this."

"Do you? That's hopeful. Uh, what, exactly, is your plan?"

"I don't really have a plan. I'm sort of playing it by ear."

Eccles' laughter surprises him; it occurs to Rabbit that the minister is an expert on affairs like this, broken homes, fleeing husbands, and that "playing it by ear" has struck a fresh note. He feels flattered; Eccles has this knack.

"Your mother has an interesting viewpoint," Eccles says. "She thinks it's all an illusion your wife and I have, that you've deserted. She says you're much too good a boy to do anything of the sort."

"You've been busy on this, haven't you?"

"This, and a death yesterday."

"Gee, I'm sorry."

They have been driving idly, at low speed, through the familiar streets; once they passed the ice plant, and at another point rounded a corner from which you can see across the valley. "Say, if you really want to give me a lift," Rabbit says, "you could drive over into Brewer."

"You don't want me to take you to your wife?"

"No. Good grief. I mean I don't think it would do any good, do you?"

For a long time it seems that the other man didn't hear him; his tidy, tired profile stares through the windshield as the big car hums forward steadily. Harry has taken the breath to repeat himself when Eccles says, "Not if you don't want good to come of it."

The matter seems ended this simply. They drive down Potter Avenue toward the highway. The sunny streets have just children on them, some of them still in their Sunday-school clothes. Little girls wear pink bell dresses that stick straight out from their waists. Their ribbons match their socks.

Eccles asks, "What did she do that made you leave?"

"She asked me to buy her a pack of cigarettes."

Eccles doesn't laugh as he had hoped; he seems to dismiss the remark as impudence, a little over the line. But it was the truth. "It's the truth. It just felt like the whole business was fetching and hauling, all the time trying to hold this mess together she was making all the time. I don't know, it seemed like I was glued in with a lot of busted toys and empty glasses and television going and meals late and no way of getting out. Then all of a sudden it hit me how easy it was to get out, just walk out, and by damn it *was* easy."

"For less than two days, it's been."

"Oh. There's the law I suppose—"

"I wasn't thinking of that so much. Your mother-in-law thought of it immediately, but your wife and Mr. Springer are dead against it. I imagine for different reasons. Your wife seems almost paralyzed; she doesn't want anyone to do anything."

"Poor kid. She's such a mutt."

"Why are you here?"

" 'Cause you caught me."

"I mean why were you in front of your home?"

"I came back to get clean clothes."

"Do clean clothes mean so much to you? Why cling to that decency if trampling on the others is so easy?"

Rabbit feels now the danger of talking; his words are coming back to him, little hooks and snares are being fashioned. "Also I was leaving her the car."

"Why? Don't you need it, to escape?"

"I just thought she should have it. Her father sold it to us cheap. Anyway it didn't do me any good."

"No?" Eccles stubs his cigarette out in the car ashtray and goes to his coat pocket for another. They are rounding the mountain, at the highest stretch of road, where the hill rises too steeply on one side and falls too steeply on the other to give space to a house or gasoline station. The river darkly shines down below. "Now if *I* were to leave *my* wife," he says, "I'd get into a car and drive a thousand miles." It almost seems like advice, coming calmly from above the white collar.

"That's what I did!" Rabbit cries, delighted by how much they have in common. "I drove as far as West Virginia. Then I thought the hell with it and came back." He must try to stop swearing; he wonders why he's doing it. To keep them apart, maybe; he feels a dangerous tug drawing him toward this man in black.

"Should I ask why?"

"Oh I don't know. A combination of things. It seemed safer to be in a place I know."

"You didn't come back to protect your wife?"

Rabbit is wordless at the idea.

Eccles continues, "You speak of this feeling of muddle. What do you think it's like for other young couples? In what way do you think you're exceptional?"

"You don't think there's any answer to that but there is. I once did something right. I played first-rate basketball. I really did. And after you're first-rate at something, no matter what, it kind of takes the kick out of being second-rate. And that little thing Janice and I had going, boy, it was really second-rate."

The dashboard lighter pops. Eccles uses it and quickly returns his eyes to his driving. They've come down into the outskirts of Brewer. He asks, "Do you believe in God?"

Having rehearsed that this morning, Rabbit answers promptly, "Yes."

Eccles blinks in surprise. The furry lid in his one-eyed profile shutters, but his face does not turn. "Do you think, then, that God wants you to make your wife suffer?"

"Let me ask you. Do you think God wants a waterfall to be a tree?" This question of Jimmy's sounds, Rabbit realizes, ridiculous; he is annoyed that Eccles simply takes it in, with a sad drag of smoke. He realizes that no matter what he says, Eccles will take it in with the same weary smoke; he is a listener by trade. His big fair head seems stuffed with a gray mash of everybody's precious secrets and passionate questions, a mash that nothing, young as he is, can color. For the first time, Rabbit dislikes him.

"No," Eccles says after thought. "But I think He wants a little tree to become a big tree."

"If you're telling me I'm not mature, that's one thing I don't cry over since as far as I can make out it's the same thing as being dead."

"I'm immature myself," Eccles offers.

It's not enough of an offering. Rabbit tells him off. "Well, I'm not going back to that little fatal dope no matter how sorry you feel for her. I don't know what she feels. I haven't known for years. All I know is what's inside *me*. That's all I have. Do you know what I was doing to support that bunch? I was demonstrating a penny's worth of tin called a frigging MagiPeeler in five-and-dime stores!"

Eccles looks at him and laughs, his eyebrows all surprise now. "Well that explains your oratorical gifts," he says.

This aristocratic sneer rings true; puts them both in place. Rabbit feels less at sea. "Hey, I wish you'd let me out," he

says. They're on Weiser Street, heading toward the great sunflower, dead in day.

"Won't you let me take you to where you're staying?"

"I'm not staying anywhere."

"All right." With a trace of boyish bad temper Eccles pulls
over and stops in front of a fire hydrant. As he brakes racily,
something clatters in the trunk.

"You're coming apart," Rabbit tells him.

"Just my golf clubs."

"You play?"

"Badly. Do you?" He seems animated; the cigarette burns
forgotten in his fingers.

"I used to caddy."

"Could I invite you for a game?" Ah. Here's the hook.

Rabbit gets out hugging his great ball of clothes and stands
on the curb and sidesteps, clowning in his freedom. "I don't
have clubs."

"They're easy to rent. Please. I mean it." Eccles leans far
over, to speak through the door. "It's hard for me to find
partners. Everybody works except me." He laughs.

Rabbit knows he should run, but the thought of a game,
and his idea that it's safest to see the hunter, make resistance.

Eccles presses. "I'm afraid you'll go back to demonstrating
peelers if I don't catch you soon. Tuesday? Tuesday at two?
Shall I pick you up?"

"No; I'll come to your house."

"Promise?"

"Yeah. But don't trust a promise from me."

"I have to." Eccles names an address in Mt. Judge and they
call good-by at the curb. An old cop walks with a wise
squint along the pavement beside the shut, stunned Sunday
store-fronts. To him it must look like a priest parting from
the president of his Youth Group, who is carrying a bundle
of clothes for the poor. Harry grins at this cop, and walks
along the sparkling pavement with his stomach singing.
Funny, the world just can't touch you.

Ruth lets him in, a pocket mystery in one hand. Her eyes

look sleepy from reading. She has changed into another sweater. Her hair seems darker. He dumps the clothes on her bed. "Do you have hangers?"

"Say. You really think you have it made."

"I made you," he says. "I made you and the sun and the stars." Squeezing her in his arms it seems that he did. She is tepid and solid in his embrace, not friendly, not not. The filmy smell of soap lifts into his nostrils while dampness touches his jaw. She has washed her hair. It pulls back from her forehead in darker straighter strands evenly harrowed by the comb. Clean, she is clean, a big clean woman; he puts his nose against her skull to drink in the demure sharp scent. He thinks of her naked in the shower, her hair hanging oozy with lather, her neck bowed to the whipping water. "I made you bloom," he says.

"Oh you're a wonder," she answers, and pushes away from his chest. As he hangs up his suits tidily, Ruth asks, "You give your wife the car?"

"There was nobody there. I snuck in and out. I left the key inside."

"And nobody caught you?"

"As a matter of fact somebody did. The Episcopal minister gave me a ride back into Brewer."

"Say; you *are* religious, aren't you?"

"*I* didn't ask him."

"What did he say?"

"Nothing much."

"What was he like?"

"Kind of creepy. Giggled a lot."

"Maybe just *you* make him giggle."

"I'm supposed to play golf with him on Tuesday."

"You're kidding."

"No, really. I told him I don't know how."

She laughs, on and on, in that prolonged way women use when they're excited by you and ashamed of it. "Oh, my Rabbit," she exclaims in a fond final breath. "You just wander, don't you?"

"He got hold of *me*," he insists, knowing his attempts to explain will amuse her, for shapeless reasons. "I didn't do anything."

"You poor soul," she says. "You're just irresistible."

With keen secret relief, he at last takes off his dirty clothes and changes into clean underwear, fresh socks, and suntans. He left his razor at home but Ruth has a little curved female one for armpits that he uses. He chooses a wool sports shirt, for these afternoons in spring cool off sharply, and puts his suede shoes back on. He forgot to steal any other shoes. "Let's go for that walk," he announces, dressed.

"I'm reading," Ruth says from a chair. The book is open to near the end. She reads books nicely, without cracking their backs, though they cost only 35 cents.

"Come on. Get out in the weather." He goes over and tries to tug the mystery from her hand. The title is *The Deaths at Oxford*. Now what should she care about deaths at Oxford? When she has him here, the great Harry Angstrom.

"Wait," she pleads, and turns a page, and reads some sentences as the book is pulled slowly up, her eyes shuttling, and then suddenly lets him take it. "God, you're a bully."

He marks her place with a burnt match and looks at her bare feet. "Do you have sneakers or anything? You can't wear heels."

"No. Hey I'm sleepy."

"We'll go to bed early."

Her eyeballs turn on him at this, her lips pursed a little. There is this vulgarity in her, that just couldn't let that just go by.

"Come on," he says. "Put on flat shoes and we'll dry your hair."

"I'll have to wear heels." As she bows her head to pinch them on, the white line of her parting makes him smile, it's so straight. Like a little birthday girl's parting.

They approach the mountain through the city park. The trash baskets and movable metal benches have not been set out yet. On the concrete-and-plank benches fluffy old men sun like greater pigeons, dressed in patches of gray multiple as feathers. The trees in small leaf dust the half-bare ground with shadow. Sticks and strings protect the newly seeded margins of the unraked gravel walks. The breeze, flowing steadily down the slope from the empty bandshell, is cool out of the sun. The wool shirt was right. Pigeons with mechanical heads flee on pink legs from their shoetips and re-settle, chuffling, behind them. A derelict stretches an arm along the back of a bench to dry, and out of a gouged face daintily sneezes like a cat. A few toughs, fourteen or younger, smoke and jab near the locked equipment shed of a play pavilion on whose yellow boards someone has painted in red TEX & JOSIE, RITA & JAY. Where would they get red paint? He takes her hand. The ornamental pool in front of the band-shell is drained and scum-stained; they move along a path parallel to the curve of its cold lip, which echoes back the bandshell's silence. A World War II tank, made a monu-ment, points its empty guns at far-off tennis courts. The nets are not up, the lines unlimed.

Trees darken; pavilions slide downhill. They walk through the upper region of the park, which delinquents haunt at night, scattering strippers and candy-bar wrappers. The be-ginning of the steps is almost hidden in an overgrowth of great bushes tinted dull amber with the first buds. Long ago, when hiking was customary entertainment, the city built stairs up the Brewer side of the mountain. They are made of six-foot tarred logs with dirt filled in flat behind them. Iron pipes have since been driven, to hold these tough round risers in place, and fine blue gravel scattered over the packed dirt they dam. The footing is difficult for Ruth; Rabbit watches her body struggle to propel her weight on the digging points of her heels. They catch and buckle. Her backside lurches, her arms swim for balance.

He tells her, "Take off your shoes."

"And kill my feet? You're a thoughtful bastard."

"Well then, let's go back down."

"No, no," she says. "We must be halfway."

"We're nowhere near half up. Take off your shoes. These blue stones are stopping; it'll just be mashed-down dirt."

"With chunks of glass in it."

But further on she does take off her shoes. Bare of stockings, her white feet lift lightly under his eyes; the yellow skin of her heels flickers. Under the swell of calf her ankles are thin. In a gesture of gratitude he takes off his shoes, to share whatever pain there is. The dirt is trod smooth, but embedded pebbles stab his skin, with the force of his weight. Also the ground is cold. "Ouch," he says. "*Owitch.*"

"Come on, soldier," she says, "be brave."

They learn to walk on the grass at the ends of the logs. Tree branches overhang part of the way, making it an upward tunnel. At other spots the air is clear behind them, and they can look over the rooftops of Brewer into the twentieth story of the courthouse, the city's one skyscraper. Concrete eagles stand in relief, wings flared, between its top windows. Two middle-aged couples in plaid scarves, bird-watchers, pass them on the way down; as soon as this couple has descended out of sight behind the gnarled arm of an oak, Rabbit hops up to Ruth's step and kisses her, hugs her hot bulk, tastes the salt in the sweat on her face, which is unresponsive. She thinks this is a silly time; her one-eyed woman's mind is intent on getting up the hill. But the thought of her city girl's paper-pale feet bare on the stones for his sake makes his heart, fevered with exertion, sob, and he clings to her tough body with the weakness of grief. An airplane goes over, rapidly rattling the air.

"My queen," he says, "my good horse."

"Your what?"

"Horse."

Near the top, the mountain rises sheer in a cliff, and here modern men have built concrete stairs with an iron railing that in a Z of three flights reach the macadam parking lot of the Pinnacle Hotel. They put their shoes back on and climb the stairs and watch the city slowly flatten under them.

Rails guard the cliff edge. He grips one white beam,

warmed by the sun now sinking steeply away from the zenith, and looks straight down, into the exploding heads of trees. A frightening view, remembered from boyhood, when he used to wonder if you jumped would you die or be cushioned on those green heads as on the clouds of a dream? In the lower part of his vision the stone-walled cliff rises to his feet foreshortened to the narrowness of a knife; in the upper part the hillside slopes down, faint paths revealed and random clearings and the steps they have climbed.

Ruth's gaze, her lids half-closed as if she were reading a book, rests on the city. The hard silhouette of her cheekbone in the high vigilant air is still. Is she feeling like an Indian? She said she might be Mexican.

O.K. He brought them up here. To see what? The city stretches from dollhouse rows at the base of the park through a broad blurred belly of flowerpot red patched with tar roofs and twinkling cars and ends as a rose tint in the mist that hangs above the distant river. Gas tanks glimmer in this smoke. Suburbs lie like scarves in it. But the city is huge in the middle view, and he opens his lips as if to force the lips of his soul to receive the taste of the truth about it, as if truth were a secret in such low solution that only immensity can give us a sensible taste. Air dries his mouth.

His day has been bothered by God: Ruth mocking, Eccles blinking—why did they teach you such things if no one believed them? It seems plain, standing here, that if there is this floor there is a ceiling, that the true space in which we live is upward space. Someone is dying. In this great stretch of brick someone is dying. The thought comes from nowhere: simple percentages. Someone in some house along these streets, if not this minute then the next, dies; and in that suddenly stone chest the heart of this flat prostrate rose seems to him to be. He moves his eyes to find the spot; perhaps he can see the cancer-blackened soul of an old man mount through the blue like a monkey on a string. He strains his ears to hear the pang of release as this ruddy illusion at his feet gives up this reality. Silence blasts him. Chains of cars creep without noise; a dot comes out of a door. What is he doing here, standing on air? Why isn't he home? He becomes frightened and begs Ruth, "Put your arm around me."

She carelessly obliges, taking a step and swinging her haunch against his. He clasps her tighter and feels better. Brewer at their feet seems to warm in the sloping sunlight; its vast red cloth seems to lift from the valley in which it is sunk concavely, to fill like a breast with a breath, Brewer the mother of a hundred thousand, shelter of love, ingenious and luminous artifact. So it is in an access of security that he asks, voicing like a loved child a teasing doubt, "Were you really a whore?"

To his surprise she turns hard under his arm and twists away and stands beside the railing menacingly. Her eyes narrow; her chin changes shape. In his nervousness he notices three Boy Scouts grinning at them across the asphalt. She asks, "Are you really a rat?"

He feels the need of care in his answer. "In a way."

"All right then."

They take a bus down.

Tuesday afternoon, overcast, he takes a bus to Mt. Judge. Eccles' address is at the north end of town; he rides past his own neighborhood in safety, gets off at Spruce, and walks along singing in a high voice to himself the phrase, "Oh *I'm* just *wild* about Har-ry"—not the beginning of the song, but the place at the end where the girl, repeating, goes way up on "I'm."

He feels on even keel. For two days he and Ruth have lived on his money and he still has fourteen dollars left. Furthermore he has discovered, poking through her bureau this morning while she was out shopping, that she has an enormous checking account, with over five hundred dollars in it at the end of February. They have gone bowling once and have seen four movies—*Gigi; Bell, Book and Candle; The Inn of the Sixth Happiness;* and *The Shaggy Dog.* He saw so many snippets from *The Shaggy Dog* on the Mickey Mouse Club

that he was curious to see the whole thing. It was like looking through a photograph album with about half familiar
faces. The scene where the rocket goes through the roof
and Fred MacMurray runs out with the coffee pot he knew
as well as his own face.

Ruth was funny. Her bowling was awful; she just sort of
paddled up to the line and dropped the ball. *Plok*. Every
time, in *Gigi*, the stereophonic-sound loudspeaker behind
them in the theater would blare out she turned around and
said "Shh" as if it were somebody in the theater talking too
loud. In *The Inn of the Sixth Happiness* every time Ingrid
Bergman's face appeared on the screen she leaned over to
Rabbit and asked him in a whisper, "Is she really a whore?"
He was upset by Robert Donat; he looked awful. He knew
he was dying. Imagine knowing you're dying and going ahead
pretending you're a mandarin. Ruth's comment about *Bell,
Book and Candle* last night was, "Why don't you ever see any
bongo drums around here?" He vowed secretly to get some.
A half-hour ago, waiting for the bus on Weiser Street, he
priced a set in the window of the Chords 'n' Records music
store. $19.95. All the way out on the bus he beat bongo pat-
terns on his knees.

"For *I'm* just *wild* about Harrr-ree—"

Number 61 is a big brick place with white wood trim, a
little porch imitating a Greek temple, and a slate roof that
shines under the clouds' sullen luster. Out back a wire fence
encloses a yellow swing frame and a sandbox. A puppy yaps
in this pen as Harry goes up the walk. The grass wears that intense greasy green that promises rain, the color of grass in
color snapshots. The place looks too cheerful to be right;
Rabbit thinks of ministers as living in black shingled castles.
But a small plate above the fish-shaped door-knocker says in
engraved script *The Rectory*. He bangs the fish twice and,
after waiting, twice again.

A crisp little number with speckled green eyes opens the
door. "What is it?" Her voice as good as says, "How dare
you?" As she adjusts her face to his height her eyes enlarge,

displaying more of the vividly clear whites to which her moss-colored irises are buttoned.

At once, absurdly, he feels in control of her, feels she likes him. Freckles dot her little bumpy nose, kind of a pinched nose, narrow and pale under the dots of tan. Her skin is fair, and fine-grained as a child's. She is wearing orange shorts. With a pleasantness that amounts to arrogance he says, "Hi."

"Hello."

"Say, is Reverend Eccles in?"

"He's asleep."

"In the middle of the day?"

"He was up much of the night."

"Oh gosh. The poor guy."

"Do you want to come in?"

"Well gee, I don't know. He told me to be here. He really did."

"He might well have. Please come in."

She leads him past a hall and staircase into a cool room with a high ceiling and silver wallpaper, a piano, watercolors of scenery, a lot of sets of books in a recessed bookcase, a fireplace whose mantel supports one of those clocks with a pendulum of four gold balls that are supposed to run practically for ever. Photographs in frames all around. Furniture heavy green and red except for a long sofa with a scrolling back and arms whose cushions are cream white. The room smells coldly kept. From far off comes the warmer odor of cake baking. She stops in the center of the rug and says, "Listen."

He stops. The faint bump that he also heard is not repeated. She explains, "I thought that brat was asleep."

"Are you the babysitter?"

"I'm the wife," she says, and sits down in the center of the white sofa, to prove it.

He takes a padded wing chair opposite. The plum fabric feels softly gritty against his naked forearms. He is wearing a checked sports shirt, with the sleeves turned back to his elbows. "Oh, I'm sorry." Of course. Her bare legs, crossed, show the blue dabs of varicose veins. Her face, when she sits, is not as young as at the door. Double chin when she relaxes, head tucked back. Smug little cookie. Firm little knockers. He asks, "How old is your child?"

"Two children. Two girls, one and three."

"I have a boy who's two."

"I'd like a boy," she says. "The girls and I have personality problems; we're too much alike. We know exactly what the other's thinking."

Dislikes her own children! Rabbit is shocked, this from a minister's wife. "Does your husband notice this?"

"Oh, it's wonderful for Jack. He loves to have women fighting over him. It's his little harem. I think a boy would threaten him. Do you feel threatened?"

"Not by the kid, no. He's only two."

"It starts earlier than two, believe me. Sexual antagonism begins practically at birth."

"I hadn't noticed."

"Good for you. I expect you're a primitive father. I think Freud is like God; you make it true."

Rabbit smiles, supposing that Freud has some connection with the silver wallpaper and the watercolor of a palace and a canal above her head. Class. She brings her fingertips to her temples, pushes her head back, shuts her lids, and through plump open lips sighs. He is struck; she seems at this moment a fine-grained Ruth.

Eccles' thin voice, oddly amplified in his home, cries down the stairs, "Lucy! Joyce is getting into bed with me!"

Lucy opens her eyes and says to Rabbit proudly, "See?"

"She says you told her it's all right," the voice whines on, piercing banisters, walls, and layers of wallpaper.

Mrs. Eccles gets up and goes to the archway. The seat of her orange shorts is wrinkled from sitting; the hitched-up legs expose most of the oval backs of her thighs. Whiter than the sofa; the blush of pink from the pressure of sitting fades from her skin. "I told her no such thing!" she calls upward while one fair hand tugs the shorts down and smooths the cloth around her mussed but smug rump, a pocket stitched with black thread to the right half. "Jack," she goes on, "you have a visitor! A very tall young man who says you invited him!"

At the mention of himself Rabbit has risen and right behind her says, "To play golf."

"To play golf!" she echoes in a yell.

"Oh, dear," the voice upstairs says to itself, then shouts, "Hello, Harry! I'll be right down."

A child up there is crying, "Mommy did too! Mommy did too!"

Rabbit shouts in answer, "Hello!"

Mrs. Eccles turns her head with an inviting twist. "Harry—?"

"Angstrom."

"What do you do, Mr. Angstrom?"

"Well. I'm kind of out of work."

"Angstrom. Of course. Aren't you the one who disappeared? The Springers' son-in-law?"

"Right," he says smartly and, in the mindless follow-through, a kind of flower of coördination, she having on the drop of his answer turned with prim dismissal away from him again, slaps! her sassy ass. Not hard; a cupping hit, rebuke and fond pat both, well-placed on the pocket.

She swiftly pivots, swinging her backside to safety behind her. Her freckles dart sharp as pinpricks from her shocked face. Her leaping blood bleaches her skin, and her rigidly cold stare is so incongruous with the lazy condescending warmth he feels toward her, that he pushes his upper lip over his lower in a burlesque expression of penitence.

A chaotic tumble on the stairs shakes the wall. Eccles jolts to a stop in front of them, off-balance, tucking a dirty white shirt into rumpled suntans. His shadowed eyes weep between his furry lids. "I'm sorry," he says. "I hadn't really forgotten."

"It's kind of cloudy anyway," Rabbit says, and smiles involuntarily. Her backside had felt so good, just right, dense yet springy, kind of smacked back. He supposes she'll tell, which will finish him here. Just as well. He doesn't know why he's here anyway.

Maybe she would have told, but her husband starts annoying her immediately. "Oh, I'm sure we can get nine in before it rains," he tells Rabbit.

"Jack, you aren't *really* going to play golf again. You said you had all those calls to make this afternoon."

"I made calls this morning."

"Two. You made two. On Freddy Davis and Mrs. Landis. The same old safe ones. What about the Ferrys? You've been talking about the Ferrys for six months."

"What's so sacred about the Ferrys? They never do anything for the church. She came on Christmas Sunday and went out by the choir door so she wouldn't have to speak to me."

"Of course they don't do anything for the church and that's why you should call as you know perfectly well. I don't think anything's sacred about the Ferrys except that you've been brooding about her going out the side door and making everybody's life miserable for months. Now if she comes on Easter it'll be the same thing. To tell you my honest opinion you and Mrs. Ferry would hit it off splendidly, you're both equally childish."

"Lucy, just because Mr. Ferry owns a shoe factory doesn't make them more important Christians than somebody who works in a shoe factory."

"Oh Jack, you're too tiresome. You're just afraid of being snubbed and don't quote Scripture to justify yourself. I don't care if the Ferrys come to church or stay away or become Jehovah's Witnesses."

"At least the Jehovah's Witnesses put into practice what they say they believe." When Eccles turns to Harry to guffaw conspiratorially after this dig, bitterness cripples his laugh, turns his lips in tightly, so his small-jawed head shows its teeth like a skull.

"I don't know what that's supposed to mean," Lucy says,

"but when you asked me to marry you I told you what I felt and you said all right fine."

"I said as long as your heart remained open for *Grace*." Eccles pours these words on her in a high strained blast that burns his broad forehead, soils it with a blush.

"Mommy I had a *rest*." The little voice, shyly penetrating, surprises them from above. At the head of the carpeted stairs a small brown girl in underpants hangs in suspense. She seems to Rabbit too dark for her parents, too somber in the shadows, braced on silhouetted legs of baby fat knotted on longer stalks. Her hands rub and pluck her naked chest in exasperation. She hears her mother's answer before it comes.

"Joyce. You go right back into your own bed and have a *nap*."

"I can't. There's too many noises."

"We've been screaming right under her head," Eccles tells his wife.

"*You've* been screaming. About Grace."

"I had a scary dream," Joyce says, and thumpingly descends two steps.

"You did not. You were never asleep." Mrs. Eccles walks to the foot of the stairs, holding her throat as if to keep some emotion down.

"What was the dream about?" Eccles asks his child.

"A lion ate a boy."

"That's not a dream at all," the woman snaps, and turns on her husband: "It's those hateful Belloc poems you insist on reading her."

"She asks for them."

"They're hateful. They give her traumas."

"Joyce and I think they're funny."

"Well you *both* have perverted senses of humor. Every night she asks me about that damn pony Tom and what does 'die' mean?"

"Tell her what it means. If you had Belloc's and my faith in the supernatural these perfectly natural questions wouldn't upset you."

"Don't harp, Jack. You're awful when you harp."

"I'm awful when I take myself seriously, you mean."

"Hey. I smell cake burning," Rabbit says.

She looks at him and recognition frosts her eyes. That there is some kind of cold call in her glance, a faint shout from the midst of her enemies, he feels but ignores, letting his gaze go limp on the top of her head, showing her the sensitive nostrils that sniffed the cake.

"If only you *would* take yourself seriously," she says to Eccles, and on glimpsey bare legs flies down the sullen hall of the rectory.

Eccles calls, "Joyce, go back to your room and put on a shirt and you can come down."

The child instead thumps down three more steps.

"Joyce, did you hear me?"

"You get it, Dayud-dee."

"Why should I get it? Daddy's all the way downstairs."

"I don't know where it is."

"You do too. Right on your bureau."

"I don't know where my bruro is."

"In your room, sweet. Of course you know where it is. You get your shirt and I'll let you downstairs."

But she is already halfway down.

"I'm frightened of the li-un," she signs with a little smile that betrays consciousness of her own impudence. Her voice has a spaced, testing quality; Rabbit heard this note of care in her mother's voice too, when she was teasing the same man.

"There's no lion up there. There's nobody up there but Bonnie sleeping. Bonnie's not afraid."

"Please, Daddy. Please please please please *please*." She has reached the foot of the stairs and seizes and squeezes her father's knees.

Eccles laughs, bracing his unbalanced weight on the child's head, which is rather broad and flat-topped, like his own. "All right," he says. "You wait here and talk to this funny man." And bounds up the stairs with that unexpected athleticism.

Rabbit says, "Joyce, are you a good girl?"

She waggles her stomach and pulls her head into her shoulders. The motion forces a little gutteral noise, "cukk," out of her throat. She shakes her head; he has the impression she is trying to hide behind a screen of dimples. But then she says with unexpectedly firm enunciation, "Yes."

"And is your mommy good?"

"Yes."

"What makes her so good?" He hopes Mrs. Eccles hears this in the kitchen. The hurried oven sounds have stopped.

Joyce looks up at him and like a sheet being rippled fear tugs a corner of the surface of her face. Really tears seem close. She scampers from him down the hall, the way her mother went. Fled from, Rabbit wanders uneasily in the hall, trying to attach his excited heart to the pictures hanging there. Surfaces of foreign capitals, a woman in white beneath a tree whose every leaf is rimmed in gold, a laborious pen rendering, brick by brick, of the St. John's Episcopal Church, dated 1927 and signed large by Mildred L. Kramer. Above a small table halfway down the hall hangs a studio photograph of some old rock with white hair above his ears and a clerical collar staring over your shoulder as if square into the heart of Things; stuck into the frame is a yellowed photo clipped from a newspaper showing in coarse dots the same old gent gripping a cigar and laughing like a madman with three others in robes. He looks a little like Jack but fatter and stronger. He holds the cigar in a fist. Further on is a colored print of a painted scene in a workshop where the carpenter works in the light given off by his Helper's head: the glass this print is protected by gives back to Rabbit the shadow of his own head. There is a tangy scent in the hallway of, spot cleaner? new varnish? mothballs? old wallpaper? He hovers among these possibilities, "the man who disappeared." *Sexual antagonism begins practically at birth*—what a bitch, really. Yet with a nice low flame in her, lighting up her legs. Those bright white legs. She'd have an anxious little edge and want her own. Cookie. A sharp vanilla cookie. In spite of herself he loves her.

There must be a back stairs, because he next hears Eccles'
voice in the kitchen, arguing Joyce into her sweater, asking
Lucy if the cake was ruined, explaining, not knowing Rabbit's
ears were around the corner, "Don't think this is pleasure for
me. It's work."

"There's no other way to talk to him?"

"He's frightened."

"Sweetie, everybody's frightened to you."

"But he's even frightened *of* me."

"Well he came through that door cocky enough."

This was the place for, *And he slapped my sweet ass, that's
yours to defend.*

*What! Your sweet ass! I'll murder the rogue. I'll call the
police.*

In reality Lucy's voice stopped at "enough," and Eccles is
talking about if so-and-so called, where are those new golf
balls?, Joyce you *had* a cookie ten minutes ago, and at last
calling, in a voice that has healed too smooth over the
scratches of their quarrel, "Good-by." Rabbit pads up the hall
and is leaning on the front radiator when Eccles, looking like
a young owl, awkward, cross, pops out of the kitchen.

They go to his car. Under the threat of rain the green skin
of the Buick has a tropical waxiness. Eccles lights a cigarette
and they go down, across Route 422, into the valley toward
the golf course. Eccles says, after getting several deep drags
settled in his chest, "So your trouble isn't really lack of religion."

"Huh?"

"I was remembering our other conversation. About the
waterfall and the tree."

"Yeah well: I stole that from Mickey Mouse."

Eccles laughs, puzzled; Rabbit notices how his mouth stays
open after he laughs, the little inturned rows of teeth waiting
a moment while his eyebrows go up and down expectantly.
"It stopped me short," he admits, closing this flirtatious cave.
"Then you said you know what's inside you. I've been wondering all weekend what that was. Can you tell me?"

Rabbit doesn't want to tell him anything. The more he tells, the more he loses. He's safe inside his own skin, he doesn't want to come out. This guy's whole game is to get him out into the open where he can be manipulated. But the fierce convention of courtesy pries open Rabbit's lips. "Hell, it's nothing much," he says. "It's just that, well, it's all there is. Don't you think?"

Eccles nods and blinks and drives without saying a word. In this way he's very sure of himself.

"How's Janice now?" Rabbit asks.

Eccles is startled to feel him veer off. "I dropped by Monday morning to tell them you were in the county. Your wife was in the back yard with your boy and what I took to be an old girl friend, a Mrs.—Foster? Fogleman?"

"What did she look like?"

"I don't really know. I was distracted by her sunglasses. They were the mirror kind, with very wide sidepieces."

"Oh Peggy Gring. That moron. She married that hick Morris Fosnacht."

"Fosnacht. That's right. Like the doughnut. I knew there was something very local about the name."

"You'd never heard of Fosnacht Day before you came here?"

"Never. Not in Norwalk."

"The thing I remember about it, when I was, oh I must have been six or seven, because he died in 1940, my grandfather would wait upstairs until I came down so I wouldn't be the Fosnacht. He lived with us then." Rabbit hasn't thought or spoken of his grandfather in years, it seems; a mild dry taste comes into his mouth.

"What was the penalty for being a Fosnacht?"

"I forget. It was just something you didn't want to be. Wait. I remember, one year I was the last downstairs and my parents or somebody teased me and I didn't like it and I guess I cried, I don't know. Anyway that's why the old man stayed up."

"He was your father's father?"

"My mother's. He lived with us."

"I remember my father's father," Eccles says. "He used to come to Connecticut and have dreadful arguments with my father. My grandfather was the Bishop of Providence, and had kept his church from going under to the Unitarians by becoming almost Unitarian himself. He used to call himself a Darwinian Deist. My father, in reaction I suppose, became very orthodox; almost Anglo-Catholic. He loved Belloc and Chesterton. In fact he used to read to us those poems you heard my wife objecting to."

"About the lion?"

"Yes. Belloc has this bitter mocking streak my wife can't appreciate. He mocks children, which she can't forgive. It's her psychology. Children are very sacred in psychology. Where was I? Yes; along with his watered-down theology my grandfather had kept in his religious *practice* a certain color and a, a *rigor* that my father had lost. Grandpa felt Daddy was *extremely* remiss in not having a family worship service every night. My father would say he didn't want to bore his children the way he had been bored with God and anyway what was the good of worshiping a jungle god in the living-room? 'You don't think God is in the woods?' my grandfather would say. 'Just behind stained glass?' And so on. My brothers and I used to tremble, because it put Daddy in a terrible depression, ultimately, to argue with him. You know how it is with fathers, you never escape the idea that maybe after all they're *right*. A little dried-up old man with a Yankee accent who was really awfully dear. I remember he used to grab us by the knee at mealtimes with this brown bony hand and croak, 'Has he made you believe in Hell?'"

Harry laughs; Eccles' imitation is good; being an old man fits him. "Did he? Do you?"

"Yes, I think so. Hell as Jesus described it. As separation from God."

"Well then we're all more or less in it."

"I don't think so. I don't think so at all. I don't think even the blackest atheist has an idea of what real separation will be.

Outer darkness. What we live in you might call"—he looks
at Harry and laughs—"inner darkness."

Eccles' volunteering all this melts Rabbit's caution. He
wants to bring something of himself into the space between
them. The excitement of friendship, a competitive excitement that makes him lift his hands and jiggle them as if
thoughts were basketballs, presses him to say, "Well I don't
know all this about theology, but I'll tell you. I *do* feel, I
guess, that somewhere behind all this"—he gestures outward
at the scenery; they are passing the housing development
this side of the golf course, half-wood half-brick one-and-a-
half-stories in little flat bulldozed yards with tricycles and
spindly three-year-old trees, the un-grandest landscape in the
world—"there's something that wants me to find it."

Eccles tamps out his cigarette carefully in the tiny cross-
notched cup in the car ashtray. "Of course, all vagrants
think they're on a quest. At least at first."

Rabbit doesn't see, after trying to *give* the man something,
that he deserved this slap. He supposes this is what ministers
need, to cut everybody down to the same miserable size. He
says, "Well I guess that makes your friend Jesus look pretty
foolish."

Mention of the holy name incites pink spots high on Eccles'
cheeks. "He *did* say," the minister says, "that saints shouldn't
marry."

They turn off the road and go up the winding drive to the
clubhouse, a big cinder-block building fronted with a long
sign that has CHESTNUT GROVE GOLF COURSE lettered between
two Coca-Cola insignia. When Harry caddied here it was just
a clapboard shack holding a wood-burning stove and charts
of old tournaments and two armchairs and a counter for
candy bars and golf balls you fished out of the swamp and
that Mrs. Wenrich resold. He supposes Mrs. Wenrich is
dead. She was a delicate old rouged window like a doll with
white hair and it always seemed funny to hear talk about
greens and divots and tourneys and par come out of her

mouth. Eccles parks the Buick on the asphalt lot and says, "Before I forget."

Rabbit's hand is on the door handle. "What?"

"Do you want a job?"

"What kind?"

"A parishioner of mine, a Mrs. Horace Smith, has about eight acres of garden around her home, toward Appleboro. Her husband was an incredible rhododendron enthusiast. I shouldn't say incredible; he was a terribly dear old man."

"I don't know anything about gardening."

"Nobody does, that's what Mrs. Smith says. There are no gardeners left. For forty dollars a week, I believe her."

"A buck an hour. That's pretty poor."

"It wouldn't be forty hours. Flexible time. That's what you want, isn't it? Flexibility? So you can be free to preach to the multitudes."

Eccles really does have a mean streak. Him and Belloc. Without the collar around his throat, he kind of lets go. Rabbit gets out of the car. Eccles does the same, and his head across the top of the car looks like a head on a platter. The wide mouth moves. "Please consider it."

"I can't. I may not even stay in the county."

"Is the girl going to kick you out?"

"What girl?"

"What is her name? Leonard. Ruth Leonard."

"Well. Aren't you smart?" Who could have told him? Peggy Gring? By way of Tothero? More likely Tothero's girl Whatsername. She looked like Janice. It doesn't matter; the world's such a web anyway, things just trickle through. "I never heard of her," Rabbit says.

The head on the platter grins weirdly in the sunglare off the metal.

They walk side by side to the cement-block clubhouse. On the way Eccles remarks, "It's the strange thing about you mystics, how often your little ecstasies wear a skirt."

"Say. I didn't have to show up today, you know."

"I know. Forgive me. I'm in a very depressed mood."

There's nothing exactly wrong with his saying this, but it rubs Harry's inner hair the wrong way. It kind of clings. It says, *Pity me. Love me.* The prickly sensation makes his lips sticky; he is unable to open them to respond. When Eccles pays his way, he can scarcely negotiate thanking him. When they pick out a set of clubs for him to rent, he is so indifferent and silent the freckled kid in charge stares at him as if he's a moron. The thought flits through his brain that Eccles is known as a fag and he has become the new boy. As he and Eccles walk together toward the first tee he feels partially destroyed, like a good horse yoked to a pulpy-hoofed nag. Eccles' presence drags at him so decidedly he has to fight leaning toward that side.

And the ball feels it too, the ball he hits after a little advice from Eccles. It sputters away to one side, crippled by a perverse topspin that makes it fall from flight as dumpily as a blob of clay.

Eccles laughs. "That's the best first drive I ever saw."

"It's not a first drive. I used to hit the ball around when I was a caddy. I should do better than that."

"You expect too much of yourself. Watch me, that'll make you feel better."

Rabbit stands back and is surprised to see Eccles, who has a certain spring in his unconscious movements, swing with a quaint fifty-year-old stiffness. As if he has a pot to keep out of the way. He punches the ball with a cramped backswing. It goes straight, though high and weak, and he seems delighted with it. He fairly prances into the fairway. Harry trails after him heavily. The soggy turf, raw and wet from recently thawing, sinks beneath his big suede shoes. They're on a seesaw; Eccles goes up, he comes down.

Down in the pagan groves and green alleys of the course Eccles is transformed. Brainless gaiety animates him. He laughs and swings and clucks and calls. Harry stops hating him, he himself is so awful. Ineptitude seems to coat him like a scabrous disease; he is grateful to Eccles for not fleeing from him. Often Eccles, fifty yards further on—he has an excited gleeful habit of running ahead—comes all the way back to find a ball Harry has lost. Somehow Rabbit can't tear his attention from where the ball *should* have gone, the little ideal napkin of clipped green pinked with a pretty flag. His eyes can't keep with where it *did* go. "Here it is," Eccles says. "Behind a root. You're having terrible luck."

"This must be a nightmare for you."

"Not at all, not at all. You're extremely promising. You've never played and yet you haven't once missed the ball completely."

This does it; he aims and in the murderous strength of his desire to knock it out in spite of the root he misses the ball completely.

"Your only mistake is trying to use your height," Eccles says. "You have a beautiful natural swing." Rabbit whacks again and the ball flops out and wobbles a few yards.

"Bend to the ball," Eccles says. "Imagine you're about to sit down."

"I'm about to lie down," Harry says. He feels sick, giddily sick, sucked deeper into a vortex whose upper rim is marked by the tranquil tips of the leafing trees. He seems to remember having been up there once. He skids into puddles, is swallowed by trees, infallibly sinks into the mangy scruff at the sides of the fairways.

Nightmare is the word. In waking life only animate things slither and jerk for him this way. He's always had a touch with objects. His unreal hacking dazes his brain; half-hypnotized, it plays tricks whose strangeness dawns on him slowly. In his head he is talking to the clubs as if they're women. The irons, light and thin yet somehow treacherous in his hands, are Janice. *Come on, you dope, be calm; here we go, easy.* When the slotted club face gouges the dirt behind the ball and the shock jolts up his arms to his shoulders his thought is that Janice has struck him. *Oh, dumb, really dumb. Screw her. Just screw her.* Anger turns his skin rotten, so the outside seeps through; his insides go jagged with the tiny dry forks of bitter scratching brambles, where words hang like caterpillar nests that can't be burned away. *She stubs stubs fat she stubs the dirt* torn open in a rough brown mouth *dirt stubs fat:* with the woods the "she" is Ruth. Holding a three wood, absorbed in its heavy reddish head and grass-stained face and white stripe prettily along the edge, he thinks *O.K. if you're so smart* and clenches and swirls. Ahg: when she tumbled so easily, to balk this! The mouth of torn grass and the ball runs, hops and hops, hides in a bush; white tail. And when he walks there, the bush is damn somebody, his mother; he lifts the huffy branches like skirts, in a fury of shame but with care not to break any, and these branches bother his legs while he tries to pour his will down into the hard irreducible pellet that is not really himself yet in a way is; just the way it sits there in the center of everything. As the seven iron chops down *please Janice just once* awkwardness spiders at his elbows and the ball as he stares with bitten elbows hooks with dismal slowness into more sad scruff further on, the khaki color of Texas. *Oh you moron go home.* Home is the hole, and above, in the scheme of the unhappy vision that frets his conscious attention with an almost optical overlay of presences, the mild gray rain sky is his grandfather waiting upstairs so that young Harry will not be a Fosnacht.

And, now at the corners, now at the center of this striving dream, Eccles flits in his grubby shirt like a white flag of forgiveness, crying encouragement, fluttering from the green to guide him home.

The greens, still dead from the winter, are salted with a dry dirt; fertilizer? The ball slips along making bits of grit jump. "Don't stab your putts," Eccles says. "A little easy swing, arms stiff. Distance is more important than aim on the first putt. Try again." He kicks the ball back. It took Harry about twelve to get up here on the fourth green, but this smug assumption that his strokes are past counting irritates him. *Come on, sweet,* he pleads with his wife, *there's the hole, big as a bucket. Everything is all right.*

But no, she has to stab in a panicked way; what was she

afraid of? Too much, the ball goes maybe five feet past. Walking toward Eccles, he says, "You never did tell me how Janice is."

"Janice?" Eccles with an effort drags his attention up from the game. He is absolutely in love with winning; *he is eating me up*, Harry thinks. "She seemed in good spirits on Monday. She was out in the back yard with this other woman, and they were both giggling when I came. You must realize that for a little while, now that she's adjusted somewhat, she'll probably enjoy being back with her parents. It's her own version of your irresponsibility."

"Actually," Harry says gratingly, squatting to line up the putt, the way they do it on television, "she can't stand her parents any more than I can. She probably wouldn't've married me if she hadn't been in such a hurry to get away from um." His putt slides past on the down side and goes two or three fucking feet too far. Four feet. Fuck.

Eccles sinks his. The ball wobbles up and with a glottal rattle bobbles in. The minister looks up with the light of triumph in his eyes. "Harry," he asks, sweetly yet boldly, "why have you left her? You're obviously deeply involved with her."

"I *told* ja. There was this thing that wasn't there."

"What thing? Have you ever seen it? Are you sure it exists?"

Harry's two-foot putt dribbles short and he picks up the ball with trembling fingers. "Well if you're not sure it exists don't ask me. It's right up your alley. If you don't know nobody does."

"No," Eccles cries in the same strained voice in which he told his wife to keep her heart open for Grace. "Christianity isn't looking for a rainbow. If it were what you think it is we'd pass out opium at services. We're trying to *serve* God, not *be* God."

They pick up their bags and walk the way a wooden arrow tells them.

Eccles goes on, explanatorily, "This was all settled centuries ago, in the heresies of the early Church."

"I tell you, I know what it is."

"What is it? What *is* it? Is it hard or soft? Harry. Is it blue? Is it red? Does it have polka dots?"

It hits Rabbit depressingly that he really wants to be told. Underneath all this I-know-more-about-it-than-you heresies-of-the-early-Church business he really wants to be told about it, wants to be told that it is there, that he's not lying to all those people every Sunday. As if it's not enough to be trying to get some sense out of this crazy game you have to carry around this madman trying to swallow your soul. The hot strap of the bag gnaws his shoulder.

"The truth is," Eccles tells him with womanish excitement, in a voice agonized by embarrassment, "you're monstrously selfish. You're a coward. You don't care about right or wrong; you worship nothing except your own worst instincts."

They reach the tee, a platform of turf beside a hunch-backed fruit tree offering fists of taut pale buds. "I better go first," Rabbit says. 'Til you calm down." His heart is hushed, held in mid-beat, by anger. He doesn't care about anything except getting out of this mess. He wishes it would rain. In avoiding looking at Eccles he looks at the ball, which sits high on the tee and already seems free of the ground. Very simply he brings the clubhead around his shoulder into it. The sound has a hollowness, a singleness he hasn't heard before. His arms force his head up and his ball is hung way out, lunarly pale against the beautiful black blue of storm clouds, his grandfather's color stretched dense across the east. It recedes along a line straight as a ruler-edge. Stricken; sphere, star, speck. It hesitates, and Rabbit thinks it will die, but he's fooled, for the ball makes his hesitation the ground of a final leap: with a kind of visible sob takes a last bite of space before vanishing in falling, "That's *it!*" he cries and, turning to Eccles with a smile of aggrandizement, repeats, "That's it."

SUN and moon, sun and moon, time goes. In Mrs. Smith's acres, crocuses break the crust. Daffodils and narcissi unpack their trumpets. The reviving grass harbors violets, and the lawn is suddenly coarse with dandelions and broad-leaved weeds. Invisible rivulets running brokenly make the low land of the estate sing. The flowerbeds, bordered with bricks buried diagonally, are pierced by dull red spikes that will be peonies, and the earth itself, scumbled, stone-flecked, raggedly patched with damp and dry, looks like the oldest and smells like the newest thing under Heaven. The shaggy golden suds of blooming forsythia glow through the smoke that fogs the garden while Rabbit burns rakings of crumpled stalks, perished grass, oak leaves shed in the dark privacy of winter, and rosebush prunings that cling together in infuriating ankle-clawing clumps. These brush piles, ignited soon after he arrives, crusty-eyed and tasting coffee, in the midst of the webs of dew, are still damply smoldering when he leaves, making ghosts in the night behind him as his footsteps crunch on the spalls of the Smith driveway. All the way back to Brewer in the bus he smells the warm ashes.

Funny, for these two months he never has to cut his finger-nails. He lops, lifts, digs. He plants annuals, packets the old lady gives him—nasturtiums, poppies, sweet peas, petunias. He loves folding the hoed ridge of crumbs of soil over the seeds. Sealed, they cease to be his. The simplicity. Getting rid of something by giving it. God Himself folded into the tiny adamant structure, Self-destined to a succession of explosions, the great slow gathering out of water and air and silicon: felt without words in the turn of the round hoe-handle in his palms.

Now, after the magnolias have lost their grip but before any but the leaves of the maple have the breadth to cast deep shade, the cherry trees and crabapples and, in a remote corner of the grounds, a solitary plum tree ball with bloom, a white-ness the black limbs seem to gather from the blowing clouds and after a moment hurl away, so the reviving grass is bleached by an astonishing storm of confetti. Fragrant of gasoline, the power mower chews the petals; the lawn digests them. The lilac bushes bloom by the fallen tennis-court fences. Birds come to the birdbath. Busy one morning with a crescent-shaped edger, Harry is caught in a tide of perfume, for be-hind him the breeze has turned and washes down through a thick sloping bank of acrid lily-of-the-valley leaves in which on that warm night a thousand bells have ripened, the high ones on the stem still the bitter sherbet green of cantaloupe rind. Apple trees and pear trees. Tulips. Those ugly purple tatters the iris. And at last, prefaced by azaleas, the rhododen-drons themselves, with a profusion increasing through the last week of May. Rabbit had waited all spring for this crown-ing. The bushes had puzzled him, they were so big, almost trees, some twice his height, and there seemed so many. They were planted all along the edges of the towering droop-limbed spruces that sheltered the place, and in the acres shel-tered there were dozens of great rectangular clumps like loaves of porous green bread. The bushes were evergreen.

With their zigzag branches and long leaves fingering in every direction they seemed to belong to a different climate, to a different land, whose gravity pulled softer than this one. When the first blooms came they were like the single big flower Oriental prostitutes wear on the sides of their heads, on the covers of the paperback spy stories Ruth reads. But when the hemispheres of blossom appear in crowds they remind him of nothing so much as the hats worn by cheap girls to church on Easter. Harry has often wanted and never had a girl like that, a little Catholic from a shabby house, dressed in flashy bargain clothes; in the swarthy leaves under the pert soft cap of five-petaled flowers he can imagine her face; he can almost smell her perfume as she passes him on the concrete cathedral steps. On inspection, each flower wears on the roof of its mouth two fans of freckles where the anthers tap.

At this climax of her late husband's garden, Mrs. Smith comes out of the house and on Rabbit's arm walks deep into the rhododendron plantation. A woman once of some height, she is bent small, and the lingering strands of black look dirty in her white hair. She carries a cane, but in forgetfulness, perhaps, hangs it over her forearm and totters along with it dangling loose like an outlandish bracelet. Her method of gripping her gardener is this: he crooks his right arm, pointing his elbow toward her shoulder, and she shakily brings her left forearm up within his and bears down heavily on his wrist with her lumpish and freckled fingers. Her hold is like that of a vine to a wall; one good pull will destroy it, but otherwise it will survive all weathers. He feels her body jolt with every step, and every word twitches her head. Not that the effort of speaking is so great; it is the excitement of communication that seizes her, wrinkling the arch of her nose fiercely, making her lips snarl above her snaggle-teeth with a comic overexpressiveness that is self-conscious, like the funny faces made by a thirteen-year-old girl in constant confession of the fact that she is not beautiful. She sharply tips her head to look up at Harry, and in tiny brown sockets afflicted by creases like so many drawstrings, her cracked blue eyes bulge frantically with captive life as she speaks: "Oh, I *don't* like Mrs. R. S. Holford; she always looks so washed-out and flossy to me. Harry loved those salmon colors so; I'd say to him, 'If I want red, give me red; a fat red rose. And if I want white, give me white, a tall white lily; and don't bother me with all these in-betweens and would-be-pinks and almost-purples that don't know what their mind is. Rhody's a mealymouthed plant,' I'd say to Harry, 'she doesn't have a brain, so she gives you some of everything,' just to tease him. But in truth I meant it." The thought seems to strike her. She stops dead on the path of grass and her eyes, the irises a kind of broken-glass white within rings of persisting blue, roll nervously, looking from one side of him to the other. "In truth I meant every word of it. I'm a farmer's daughter, Mr. Angstrom, and I would have rather seen this land gone under to alfalfa. I'd say to him, 'Why don't you plant buckwheat if you must fuss in the ground? Now there's a real crop. You raise the wheat, I'll bake the bread.' I would have, too. 'What do we want with all these corsages that after they're gone we have to look at their ugly leaves all the year round?' I'd say to him, 'What pretty girl are you growing these for?' He was younger than I, that's why I took advantage of my right to tease him. I won't say by how much. What are we standing here for? Old body like mine, stand still in one place you'll stick fast." She jabs the cane into the grass, the signal for him to extend his arm. They move on down the alley of bloom. "Never thought I'd outlive him. That was his weakness. Come in out of the garden he'd be forever sitting. A farmer's daughter never learns the meaning of sit."

Her unsteady touch on his wrist bobs like the swaying tops of the giant spruces. He associates these trees with forbidden estates; it gives him pleasure to be within their protection. "Ah. Now here is a *plant.*" They stop at a corner and she lifts her dangling cane toward a small rhododendron clothed in a pink of penetrating purity. "Harry's Bianchi," Mrs. Smith says. "The only rhody except some of the whites, I forget their names, silly names anyway, that says what it means. It's the only true pink there is. When Harry first got it, he set it among the other so-called pinks and it showed them up as just so muddy he tore them out and backed the Bianchi with crimsons. The crimsons are by, aren't they? Is today June?" Her wild eyes fix him crazily and her grip tightens.

"I don't know. No. Memorial Day's next Saturday."

"Oh, I remember so well the day we got that silly plant. Hot! We drove to New York City to take it off the boat and put it in the back seat of the Packard like a favorite aunt or some such thing. It came in a big blue wooden tub of earth. There was only one nursery in England that carried the stock and it cost two hundred dollars to ship. A man came down to the hold to water it every day. Hot, and all that vile traffic through Jersey City and Trenton and this scrawny bush sitting in its blue tub in the back seat like a prince of the realm! There weren't any of these turnpikes then so it was a good six-hour trip to New York. The middle of the Depression and it looked like everybody in the world owned an automobile. You came over the Delaware at Burlington. This was before the war. I don't suppose when I say 'the war' you know which one I mean. You probably think of that Korean thing as the war."

"No, I think of the war as World War Two."

"So do I! So do I! Do you really remember it?"

"Sure. I mean I was pretty old. I flattened tin cans and bought War Stamps and we got awards at grade school."

"Our son was killed."

"Gee. I'm sorry."

"Oh he was old, he was old. He was almost forty. They made him an officer right off."

"Still—"

"I know. You think of only young men being killed."

"Yeah, you do."

"It was a good war. It wasn't like the first. It was ours to win, and we won it. All wars are hateful things, but that one was satisfying to win." She gestures with her cane again at the pink plant. "The day we came over from the boat docks it of course wasn't in flower that late in the summer so it looked just like foolishness to me, to have it riding in the back seat like a"—she realizes she is repeating herself, falters, but goes on—"like a prince of the realm." In her almost transparent blue eyes there is pinned this little sharpness watching his face to see if he smiles at her addlement. Seeing nothing, she snaps roughly, "It's the only one."

"The only Bianchi?"

"Yes! Right! There's not another in the United States. There's not another good pink from the Golden Gate to— wherever. The Brooklyn Bridge, I suppose they say. All the truly *good* pink in the nation is right here under our eyes. A florist from Lancaster took some cuttings but they died. Probably smothered them in lime. Stupid man. A Greek."

She claws at his arm and moves on more heavily and rapidly. The sun is high and she probably feels a need for the house. Bees swim in the foliage; hidden birds scold. The tide of leaf has overtaken the tide of blossom, and a furtively bitter smell breathes from the fresh walls of green. Maples, birches, oaks, elms, and horsechestnut trees compose a thin forest that runs, at a varying depth, along the far property-line. In the damp shaded fringe between the lawn and this copse, the rhododendrons are still putting forth, but the unsheltered clumps in the center of the lawn have already dropped petals, in oddly neat rows, along the edge of the grass paths. "I don't like it, I don't like it," Mrs. Smith says, hobbling with Rabbit down such a trench of overblown brilliance. "I appreciate the beauty but I'd rather see alfalfa. A woman—I don't know why it should vex me so—Horace used to encourage the neighbors to come in and see the place in blooming time, he was like a child in many ways. This woman, Mrs. Foster, from down the hill in a little orange shack with a metal cat climbing up the shutters, used to *inva*riably say, turn to me with lipstick halfway up to her nose and say"—she mimics a too-sweet voice with a spirited spite that shakes her frame—" 'My, Mrs. Smith, this must be what Heaven is like!' One year I said to her, I couldn't hold my tongue any longer, I said, 'Well if I'm driving six miles back and forth to St. John's Episcopal Church every Sunday just to get into another splash of rhodies, I might as well save the mileage because I don't want to *go*.' Now wasn't that a dreadful thing for an old sinner to say?"

"Oh, I don't know—"

"To this poor woman who was only trying to be civil? Hadn't a bean of a brain in her head, of course; painting her face like a young fool. She's passed on now, poor soul; Alma Foster passed on two or three winters back. Now she knows the truth and I don't."

"Well, maybe what looks like rhododendrons to her will look like alfalfa to you."

"*Heh!* Eh-HA! Exactly! Exactly! You know, Mr. Angstrom, it's *such* a pleasure—" She stops them in the walk and caresses his forearm awkwardly; in the sunshine the tiny tan landscape of her face tips up toward his, and in her gaze, beneath the fumbling girlish flirtatiousness and the watery wander, there glitters the edge of an old acuteness, so that Rabbit uneasily standing there feels a stab of the unkind force that drove Mr. Smith out to the brainless flowers. "You and I, we think alike. Don't we? Now *don't we?*"

"You have it pretty good, don't you?" Ruth asks him. They have gone on the afternoon of this Memorial Day to the public swimming pool in West Brewer. She was self-conscious about getting into a bathing suit but in fact when she came out of the bath-house she looked great, her head made small by the bathing cap and her shoulders stately. Standing in the water she looked great, cut off at the thighs like a statue. She swam easily, her big legs kicking slowly and her clean arms lifting and her back and bottom shimmering black under the jiggled green. Once she stopped and floated, putting her face down in the water in a motion that quickened his heart with its slight danger. Her bottom of its own buoyance floated up and broke the surface, a round black island glistening there, a clear image suddenly in the water wavering like a blooey television set: the solid sight swelled his heart with pride, made him harden all over with a chill clench of ownership. His, she was his, he knew her as well as the water, like the water has been everywhere on her body. When she did the backstroke the water bubbled and broke and poured down her front into her breastcups, flooding her breasts with touch; the arch of her submerged body tightened; she closed her eyes and moved blindly. Two skinny boys dabbling at the shallow end of the pool splashed away from her headfirst approach. She brushed one with a backsweep of her arm, awoke, and squatted smiling in the water; her arms waved bonelessly to keep her balance in the nervous tides of the crowded pool. The air sparkled with the scent of chlorine. Clean, clean: it came to him what clean was. It was nothing touching you that is not yourself. Her in water, him in grass and air. Her head, bobbing like a hollow ball, made a face at him. Himself, he was not a water animal. Wet was cold to him. Having dunked, he preferred to sit on the tile edge dipping his feet and imagining that high-school girls behind him were admiring the muscle-play of his broad back; he revolved his shoulders and felt the blades stretch his skin in the sun. Ruth waded to the end, through water so shallow the checker pattern of the pool floor was refracted to its surface. She climbed the little ladder, shedding water in great pale-green grape-bunches. He scrambled back to their blanket and lay down so that when she came over he saw her standing above him straddling the sky, the black hair high on the insides of her thighs pasted into swirls by the water. She tore off her cap and shook out her hair and bent over for the towel. Water on her back dripped over her shoulders. As he watched her rub her arms the smell of grass rose through the blanket and shouts made the crystalline air vibrate. She lay down beside him and closed her eyes and submitted to the sun. Her face, seen so close, was built of great flats of skin pressed clean of color by the sun, except for a burnish of yellow that added to their size mineral weight, the weight of some pure ungrained stone carted straight from quarries to temples. Words come from this monumental Ruth in the same scale, as massive wheels rolling to the porches of his ears, as mute coins spinning in the light. "You have it pretty good."

"How so?"

"Oh"—her words seem slightly delayed in passage from her lips; he sees them move, and then hears—"look at all you've got. You've got Eccles to play golf with every week and to keep your wife from doing anything to you. You've got your flowers, and you've got Mrs. Smith in love with you. You've got me."

"You think she really is in love with me? Mrs. Smith."

"All I know is what I get from you. You say she is."

"No, I never actually said that. Did I?"

She doesn't bother to answer him out of her huge face, magnified by his drowsy contentment. Chalk highlights rest on her tanned skin.

He repeats, "Did I?" and pinches her arm, hard. He hadn't meant to do it so hard; something angered him at the touch of her skin. The sullen way it yielded.

"Ow. You son of a bitch."

Still she lies there, paying more attention to the sun than him. He gets up on an elbow and looks across her dead body to the lighter figures of two sixteen-year-olds standing sipping orange crush from cardboard cones. The one in a white strapless peeks up at him from her straw with a brown glance, her skinny legs dark as a Negro's. Her hipbones make gaunt peaks on either side of her slanted flat belly.

"Oh all the *world* loves you," Ruth says suddenly. "What I wonder is why?"

"I'm lovable," he says.

"I mean why the hell *you*. What's so special about *you*?"

"I'm a mystic," he says. "I give people faith." Eccles has told him this. Once, with a laugh, probably meaning it sarcastically. You never knew what Eccles was really meaning; you had to take what you wanted. Rabbit took this to heart. He never would have thought of it himself. He doesn't think much about what he gives other people.

"You give *me* a pain," she says.

"Well I'll be damned." The injustice: after he was so proud of her in the pool, loved her so much.

"What in hell makes you think you don't have to pull your own weight?"

"What's your kick? I support you."

"The hell you do. I have a job." It's true. A little after he went to work for Mrs. Smith she got a job as a stenographer with an insurance company that has a branch in Brewer. He wanted her to; he was nervous about how she'd spend her afternoons with him away. She said she never enjoyed that business; he wasn't so sure. She wasn't exactly suffering when he met her.

"Quit it," he says. "I don't care. Sit around all day reading mysteries. I'll support ja."

"You'll support me. If you're so big why don't you support your wife?"

"Why should I? Her father's rolling in it."

"You're so smug, is what gets me. Don't you ever think you're going to have to pay a price?" She looks at him now, squarely with eyes bloodshot from being in the water. She shades them with her hand. These aren't the eyes he met that night by the parking meters, flat pale discs like a doll might have. The blue of her irises has deepened inward and darkened with a richness that, singing the truth to his instincts, disturbs him.

These eyes sting her and she turns her head away to keep down the tears, thinking, That's one of the signs, crying easily. God, at work she has to get up from the typewriter and rush into the john like she had the runs and sob, sob, sob. Standing there in a booth looking down at a toilet laughing at herself and sobbing till her chest hurts. And sleepy. God, after coming back from lunch it's all she can do to keep from stretching out in the aisle right there on the linoleum floor between Lilly Orff and Rita Fiorvante where slimy-eyed old Honig would have to step over her. And hungry. For lunch an ice-cream soda with the sandwich and then a doughnut with the coffee and still she has to buy a candy bar at the

cash register. After she's been trying to slim down for him
and *had* lost six pounds, at least one scale said. For him, that
was what was rich, changing herself in one direction for him
when in his stupidity he was changing her in the other. He
was a menace, for all his mildness. Still he did have the mildness and was the first man she ever met who did. You felt at
least you were *there* for him instead of being something pasted
on the inside of their dirty heads. God she used to hate them
with their wet mouths and little laughs but when she had it
with Harry she kind of forgave them all, it was only half
their fault, they were a kind of wall she kept battering against
because she knew there was something there and all of a sudden with Harry there it was and it made everything that had
gone before seem pretty unreal. After all nobody had ever
really hurt her, left her scarred or anything, and when she
tries to remember it it sometimes seems it happened to somebody else. They seemed sort of vague, as if she had kept
her eyes shut, vague and pathetic and eager, wanting some
business their wives wouldn't give, a few army words or a
whimper or that business with the mouth. That. What do they
see in it? It can't be as deep, she doesn't know. After all it's
no worse than them at your bees and why not be generous,
the first time it was Harrison and she was drunk as a monkey
anyway but when she woke up the next morning wondered
what the taste in her mouth *was*. But that was just being a
superstitious kid there isn't much taste to it a little like seawater, just harder work than they probably think, women are always working harder than they think. The thing was, they
wanted to be admired there. They really did want that. They
weren't that ugly but they thought they were. That was the
thing that surprised her in high school how ashamed they
were really, how grateful they were if you just touched them
there and how quick word got around that you would. What
did they think, they were monsters? If they'd just thought
they might have known you were curious too, that you could
like that strangeness there like they liked yours, no worse than
women in their way, all red wrinkles, my God, what was it in

the end? No mystery. That was the great thing she discovered, that it was no mystery, just a stuck-on-looking bit that
made them king and if you went along with it could be good
or not so good and anyway put you with them against those
others, those little snips running around her at hockey in gym
like a cow in that blue uniform like a baby suit she wouldn't
wear it in the twelfth grade and took the demerits. God
she hated some of those girls with their contractors and drug-
gists for fathers. But she got it back at night, taking what they
didn't know existed like a queen. Boy, there wasn't any fancy
business then, you didn't even need to take off your clothes,
just a little rubbing through the cloth, your mouths tasting
of the onion on the hamburgers you'd just had at the diner
and the car heater ticking as it cooled, through all the cloth,
everything, off they'd go. They couldn't have felt much it
must have been just the *idea* of you. All their ideas. Sometimes
just French kissing not that she ever really got with that,
sloppy tongues and nobody can breathe, but all of a sudden
you knew from the way their lips went hard and opened and
then eased shut and away that it was over. That there was no
more push for you and you better back off if you wanted to
keep your dress dry. They wrote her name on the lavatory
walls; she became a song in the school. Allie told her about
that, kindly. But she had some sweet things with Allie; once
after school with the sun still up they drove along a country
road and up an old lane and stopped in a leafy place where
they could see Mt. Judge, the town against the mountain both,
dim in the distance, and he put his head in her lap, her sweater
rolled up and her bra undone, and it was like a baby gently,
her bees (who called them her bees? not Allie) firmer and
rounder then, more sensitive; his waiting wet mouth so happy
and blind and the birds making their warm noises overhead
in the sunshine. Allie blabbed. He had to blab. She forgave
him but it made her wiser. She began the older ones; the mistake if there was one but why not? Why not? was the question and still held; wondering if there was a mistake makes her
tired just thinking, lying there wet from swimming and see-

ing red through her eyelids, trying to move back through all that red wondering if she was wrong. She was wise. With them being young did for being pretty, and them being older it wasn't such a rush. Boy some bastards you think *never*, like their little contribution's the greatest thing the world's ever going to see if it ever gets here.

But *this* one. What a nut. She wonders what he has. He's beautiful for a man, soft and uncircumcised lying sideways in his fleece and then like an angel's sword, he fits her tight but it must be more than that, and it isn't just him being so boyish and bringing her bongo drums and saying sweet grateful things because he has a funny power over her too; when they're good together she feels like next to nothing with him and that must be it, that must be what she was looking for. To feel like next to nothing with a man. Boy that first night when he said that so sort of proudly "Hey" she didn't mind so much going under in fact it felt like she should. She forgave them all then, his face all their faces gathered into a scared blur and it felt like she was falling under to something better than she was. But then after all it turns out he's not so different, hanging on you all depressed and lovey and then when he's had it turning his back to think of something else. Men don't live by it the way a woman must. It's getting quicker and quicker more like a habit, he really hurries now when he senses or she tells him she's lost it. Then she can just lie there and in a way listen and it's soothing; but then she can't go to sleep afterwards. Some nights he tries to bring her up but she's just so sleepy and so heavy down there it's nothing; sometimes she just wants to push him off and shake him and shout, I *can't*, you dope, don't you know you're a *father!* But no. She mustn't tell him. Saying a word would make it final; it's just been one period and the next is coming up in a day maybe she'll have it and then she won't have anything. As much of a mess as it is she doesn't know how happy that would make her really. At least this way she's *doing* something, sending those candy bars down. God she isn't even sure she doesn't want it because *he* wants it from the way he acts, with his damn no stripper just a nice clean piece. She isn't even sure she didn't just deliberately bring it on by falling asleep under his arm just to show the smug bastard. For the thing about him he didn't mind her getting up when he was asleep and crawling into the cold bathroom just so long as he didn't have to watch anything or do anything. That was the thing about him, he just lived in his skin and didn't give a thought to the consequences of anything. Tell him about the candy bars and feeling sleepy he'll probably get scared and off he'll go, him and his good clean piece and his cute little God and his cute little minister playing golf every Tuesday. For the damnedest thing about that minister was that, before, Rabbit at least had the idea he was acting wrong but now he's got the idea he's Jesus Christ out to save the world just by doing whatever comes into his head. I'd like to get hold of the bishop or whoever and tell him that minister of his is a menace. Filling poor Rabbit full of something nobody can get at and even now, filling her ear, his soft cocksure voice answers her question with an idle remote smugness that infuriates her so the tears *do* come.

"I'll tell you," he says. "When I ran from Janice I made an interesting discovery." The tears bubble over her lids and the salty taste of the pool-water is sealed into her mouth. "If you have the guts to be yourself," he says, "other people'll pay your price."

Making awkward calls is agony for Eccles; at least anticipation of them is. Usually, the dream is worse than the reality: God rules reality. The actual presences of people are always bearable. Mrs. Springer is a plump, dark, small-boned woman with a gypsy look about her. Both the mother and the daughter have a sinister aura, but in the mother this ability to create uneasiness is a settled gift, thoroughly meshed into the strategies of middle-class life. With the daughter it is a floating thing, useless and as dangerous to herself as to others. Eccles is relieved that Janice is out of the house; he feels guiltiest in her presence. She and Mrs. Fosnacht have gone into Brewer to a matinee of *Some Like It Hot.* Their two sons are in the Springers' back yard. Mrs. Springer takes him through the house to the screened-in porch, where she can keep an eye on the children. Her house is expensively but confusedly furnished; each room seems to contain one more easy chair than necessary. To get from the front door to the back they take a crooked path in the packed rooms. She leads him slowly; both of her ankles are bound in elastic bandages. The pained littleness of her steps reinforces his illusion that her hips are encased in a plaster cast. She gently lowers herself on to the cushions of the porch glider and startles Eccles by kicking up her legs as with a squeak and sharp sway the glider takes her weight. The action seems to express pleasure; her bald pale calves stick out stiff and her saddle shoes are for a moment lifted from the floor. These shoes are cracked and rounded, as if they've been revolved in a damp tub for years. He sits down in a trickily hinged aluminum-and-plastic lawn chair. Through the porch screen at his side, he can see Nelson Angstrom and the slightly older Fosnacht boy play in the sun around a swing-slide-sandbox set. Eccles once bought one of those and when it came, all in pieces in a long cardboard box, was humiliated to find himself unable to put it together. Henry the old deaf sexton finally did it for him.

"It's nice to see you," Mrs. Springer says. "It's been so long since you came last."

"Just three weeks, isn't it?" he says. The chair presses against his back and he hooks his heels around the pipe at the bottom to keep it from folding. "It's been a busy time, with the confirmation classes and the Youth Group deciding to have a softball team this year and a series of deaths in the parish." His previous contacts with this woman have not disposed him to be apologetic. Her having so large a home offends his aristocratic sense of place; he would like her better, and she would be more comfortable, if this were the porch of a shanty.

"Yes I wouldn't want your job for the world."

"I enjoy it most of the time."

"They say you do. They say you're becoming quite an expert golf player."

Oh dear. And he thought she was relaxing. He thought for the moment they were on the porch of a shabby peeling house and she was a long-suffering fat factory wife who had learned to take life as it came. That is what she looked like; that is easily what she might have been. Fred Springer when he married her was probably less likely-looking than Harry Angstrom when her daughter married him. He tries to imagine Harry four years ago, and gets a presentable picture: tall, fair, famous in his school days, clever enough—a son of the morning. His air of confidence must have especially appealed to Janice. David and Michal. *Defraud ye not one the other.* . . . He scratches his forehead and says, "Playing golf with someone is a good way to get to know him. That's what I try to do, you understand—get to know people. I don't think you can lead someone to Christ unless you know him."

"Well now what do you know about my son-in-law that I don't?"

"That he's a good man, for one thing."

"Good for what?"

"Must you be good *for* something?" He tries to think. "Yes, I suppose you must."

"Nelson! Stop that this minute!" She turns rigid in the glider but does not rise to see what is making the boy cry. Eccles, sitting by the screen, can see. The Fosnacht boy stands by the swing, holding two red plastic trucks. Angstrom's son, some inches shorter, is batting with an open hand toward the bigger boy's chest, but does not quite dare to move forward a step and actually strike him. Young Fosnacht stands with the maddening invulnerability of the stupid, looking down at the flailing hand and contorted face of the smaller boy without even a smile of satisfaction, a true scientist, observing without passion the effect of his experiment. Mrs. Springer's voice leaps to a frantic hardness and cuts through the screen: *"Did you hear me I said stop that bawling!"*

Nelson's face turns up toward the porch and he tries to explain, "Pilly have—Pilly—" But just trying to describe the injustice gives it unbearable force, and as if struck from behind he totters forward and slaps the thief's chest and receives a mild shove that makes him sit on the ground. He rolls on his stomach and spins in the grass, revolved by his own incoherent kicking. Eccles' heart seems to twist with the child's body; he knows so well the propulsive power of a wrong, the way the mind batters against it and each futile blow sucks the air emptier until it seems the whole frame of blood and bone must burst in a universe that can be such a vacuum.

"The boy's taken his truck," he tells Mrs. Springer.

"Well let him get it himself," she says. "He must learn. I can't be getting up on these legs and running outside every minute; they've been at it like that all afternoon."

"*Billy.*" The boy looks up in surprise toward Eccles' male voice. "Give it back." Billy considers this new evidence and hesitates indeterminately. "*Now,* please." Convinced, Billy walks over and pedantically drops the toy on his sobbing playmate's head.

The new pain starts fresh grief in Nelson's throat, but seeing the truck on the grass beside his face chokes him. It takes him a moment to realize that the cause of his anguish is removed and another moment to rein the emotion in his body. His great dry gasps as he rounds these corners seem to heave the sheet of trimmed grass and the sunshine itself. A wasp bumping persistently against the screen dips and the aluminum chair under Eccles threatens to buckle; as if the wide world is participating in Nelson's readjustment.

"I don't know why the boy is such a sissy," Mrs. Springer says. "Or maybe I do."

Her sly adding this irks Eccles. "Why?"

The liverish skin under her eyes lifts and the corners of her mouth pull down in an appraising scowl. "Well, he's like his dad: spoiled. He's been made too much of and thinks the world owes him what he wants."

"It was the other boy; Nelson only wanted what was his."

"Yes and I suppose you think with his dad it was all Janice's fault." The way she pronounces "Janice" makes the girl seem more substantial, precious, and important than the pathetic shadow in Eccles' mind. He wonders if she's not, after all, right: if he hasn't gone over to the other side.

"No I don't," he says. "I think his behavior has no justification. This isn't to say, though, that his behavior doesn't have reasons, reasons that in part your daughter could have controlled. With my Church, I believe that we are all responsible beings, responsible for ourselves and for each other." The words, so well turned-out, taste chalky in his mouth. He wishes she'd offer him something to drink. Spring is turning hot.

The old gypsy sees his uncertainty. "Well that's easy to say," she says. "It's not so easy maybe to take such a view if you're nine months expecting and from a respectable home and your husband's running around a few miles away with some bat and everybody thinks it's the funniest thing since I don't know what." The word "bat" darts into the air like one, quick and black.

"Nobody thinks it's funny, Mrs. Springer."

"You don't hear the talk I do. You don't see the smiles. Why, one woman as good as said to me the other day if she can't keep him she has no right to him. She had the gall to grin right in my face. I could have strangled her. I said to her, "A man has duty too. It isn't all one way." It's women like her give men the ideas they have, that the world's just here for their pleasure. From the way you act you half-believe it too. Well if the world is going to be full of Harry Angstroms how much longer do you think they'll need your church?"

She has sat up and her dark eyes are lacquered by tears that do not fall. Her voice has risen in pitch and abrades Eccles' face like a file; he feels covered with cuts. Her talk of the smiling gossip encircling this affair has surrounded him with a dreadful reality, like the reality of those hundred faces when on Sunday mornings at 11:30 he mounts the pulpit and the text flies from his mind and his notes dissolve into nonsense. He fumbles through his memory and manages to bring out, "I feel Harry is in some respects a special case."

"The only thing special about him is he doesn't care who he hurts or how much. Now I mean no offense Reverend Eccles, and I'm sure you've done your best considering how busy you are, but to be honest I wish that first night I had called the police like I wanted to."

He seems to hear that she is going to call the police to arrest *him*. Why not? With his white collar he forges God's name on every word he speaks. He steals belief from the children he is supposed to be teaching. He murders faith in the minds of any who really listen to his babble. He commits fraud with every schooled cadence of the service, mouthing Our Father when his heart knows the real father he is trying to please, has been trying to please all his life, the God who smokes cigars. He asks her, "What can the police do?"

"Well I don't know but more than play golf I expect."

"I'm quite sure he will come back."

"You've been saying that for two months."

"I still believe it." But he doesn't, he doesn't believe anything. There is silence while Mrs. Springer seems to read this fact in his face.

"Could you"—her voice is changed; it beseeches—"bring me over that stool there in the corner? I have to get my legs up."

When he blinks, his eyelids scratch. He rouses from his daze and gets the stool and takes it to her. Her broad shins in their green childlike socks lift meekly, and as he places the stool under the heels, his bending, with its echo of religious-pamphlet paintings of Christ washing the feet of beggars, fits his body to receive a new flow of force. He straightens up and towers above her. She plucks at her skirt at the knees, tugging it down.

"Thank you," she says. "That's a real relief for me."

"I'm afraid it's the only sort of relief I've given you," he confesses with a simplicity that he finds, and mocks himself for finding, admirable.

"Ah," she sighs. "There's not much anybody can do I guess."

"No, there are things to do. Perhaps you're right about the police. The law provides protection for wives; why not use it?"

"Fred's against it."

"Mr. Springer has good reasons. I don't mean merely business reasons. All the law can extract from Harry is financial support; and I don't think, in this case, that money is really the point. In fact I'm not sure money is *ever* really the point."

"That's easy to say if you've always had enough." He doesn't mind. It seemed to slip from her automatically, with less malice than lassitude; he is certain she wants to listen.

"That may be. I don't know. But at any rate my concern—everyone's concern for that matter, I'm sure—is with the general health of the situation. And if there's to be a true healing, it must be Harry and Janice who act. Really, no matter how much we want to help, no matter how much we try to do on the fringes, we're *outside*." In imitation of his father he has clasped his hands behind him and turned his back on his auditor; through the screen he watches the one other who, perhaps, is not outside, Nelson, lead the Fosnacht boy across the lawn in pursuit of a neighbor's dog. Nelson's laughter spills from his head as his clumsy tottering steps jar his body. The dog is old, reddish, small, and slow; the Fosnacht boy is puzzled yet pleased by his friend's cry of "Lion! Lion!" It interests Eccles to see that under conditions of peace Angstrom's boy leads the other. The green air seen through the muzzy screen seems to vibrate with Nelson's noise. Eccles feels the situation: this constant translucent outpour of selfless excitement must naturally now and then dam in the duller boy's narrower passages and produce a sullen backflow, a stubborn bullying act. He pities Nelson, who will be stranded in innocent surprise many times before he locates in himself the source of this strange reverse tide. It seems to Eccles that he himself was this way as a boy, always giving and giving and always being suddenly swamped. The old dog's tail wags

as the boys approach. It stops wagging and droops in an uncertain wary arc when they surround it like hunters, crow-
ing. Nelson reaches out and beats the dog's back with both
hands. Eccles wants to shout; the dog might bite; he can't
bear to watch.

"Yes but he drifts further *away*," Mrs. Springer is whining.
"He's well off. He has no reason to come back if we don't
give him one."

Eccles sits down in the aluminum chair again. "No. He'll
come back for the same reason he left. He's fastidious. He has
to loop the loop. The world he's in now, the world of this girl
in Brewer, won't continue to satisfy his fantasies. Just in seeing him from week to week, I've noticed a change."

"Well not to hear Peggy Fosnacht tell it. She says *she* hears
he's leading the life of Riley. I don't know how many women
he has."

"Just one, I'm sure. The strange thing about Angstrom, he's
by nature a domestic creature. *Oh dear.*"

There is a flurry in the remote group; the boys run one
way and the dog the other. Young Fosnacht halts but Nelson
keeps coming, his face stretched large by fright.

Mrs. Springer hears his sobbing and says angrily, "Did they
get Elsie to snap again? That dog must be sick in the head
the way she keeps coming over here for more."

Eccles jumps up—his chair collapses behind him—and opens
the screen door and runs down to meet Nelson in the sunshine. The boy shies from him. He grabs him. "Did the dog
bite?"

The boy's sobbing is paralyzed by this new fright, the man
in black grabbing him.

"Did Elsie bite you?"

The Fosnacht boy hangs back at a safe distance.

Nelson, unexpectedly solid and damp in Eccles' arms, releases great rippling gasps and begins to find his voice.

Eccles shakes him to choke this threat of wailing and, wild
to make himself understood, with a quick lunge clicks his
teeth at the child's cheek. "Like that? Did the dog do that?"

The boy's face goes rapt at the pantomime. "Like dis," he says, and his fine little lip lifts from his teeth and his nose wrinkles and he jerks his head an inch to one side.

"No bite?" Eccles insists, relaxing the grip of his arms.

The little lip lifts again with that miniature fierceness. Eccles feels mocked by a petite facial alertness that recalls, in tilt and cast, Harry's. Sobbing sweeps over Nelson again and he breaks away and runs up the porch steps to his grandmother. Eccles stands up; in just that little time of squatting the sun has started sweat on his black back.

As he climbs the steps he is troubled by something pathetic, something penetratingly touching, in the memory of those tiny square teeth bared in that play snarl. The harmlessness yet the reality of the instinct: the kitten's instinct to kill the spool with its cotton paws.

He comes onto the porch to find the boy between his grandmother's legs, his face buried in her belly. In worming against her warmth he has pulled her dress up from her knees, and their exposed breadth and pallor, undesired, laid bare defenselessly, superimposed upon the tiny, gamely gritted teeth the boy exposed for him, this old whiteness strained through this fine mesh, make a milk that feels to Eccles like his own blood. Strong—as if pity is, as he has been taught, not a helpless outcry but a powerful tide that could purge the dust and rubble from every corner of the world—he steps forward and promises to the two bowed heads, "If he doesn't come back when she has the baby, then we'll get the law after him. There *are* laws, of course; quite a few."

"Elsie snaps," Mrs. Springer says, "because you and Billy tease her."

"Naughty Elsie," Nelson says.

"Naughty Nelson," Mrs. Springer corrects. She lifts her face to Eccles and continues in the same correcting voice, "Yes well she's a week due now and I don't see him running in."

His moment of fondness for her has passed; he leaves her

on the porch. *Love never ends,* he tells himself, using the Re-
vised Standard Version. The King James has it that it never
fails. Mrs. Springer's voice carries after him into the house,
"Now the next time I catch you teasing Elsie you're going to
get a whipping from your grandmom."

"No, Mom-mom," the child begs coyly, fright gone.

Eccles thought he would find the kitchen and take a drink
of water from the tap but the kitchen slips by him in the
jumbled rooms. He makes a mouth that works up saliva and
swallows it as he leaves the stucco house. He gets into his
Buick and drives down Joseph Street and then a block along
Jackson Road to the Angstroms' address.

Mrs. Angstrom has four-cornered nostrils. Lozenge-shape,
they are set in a nose that is not so much large as extra-ana-
tomical; the little pieces of muscle and cartilage and bone are
individually emphatic and divide the skin into many facets in
the sharp light. Their interview takes place in her kitchen
amid several burning light bulbs. Burning in the middle of
day; their home is the dark side of a two-family brick house.
She came to the door wearing suds on her red forearms and
returns with him to a sink full of bloated shirts and underwear. She plunges at these things vigorously while they talk.
She is a vigorous woman. Mrs. Springer's fat—soft, aching excess—had puffed out from little bones, the bones once of a slip
of a girl like Janice; Mrs. Angstrom's is packed on a great
harsh frame. Harry's size must come from her side. Eccles is
continually conscious of the long faucets, heraldic of cool
water, shielded by her formidable body; but the opportunity
never arises for a request so small.

"I don't know why you come to me," she says. "Harold's
one and twenty. I have no control over him."

"He hasn't been to see you?"

"No sir." She displays her profile above her left shoulder.
"You've made him so ashamed I suppose he's embarrassed
to."

"He *should* be ashamed, don't you think?"

"I wouldn't know why. I never wanted him to go with the girl in the first place. Just to look at her you know she's two-thirds crazy."

"Oh now, that's not true, is it?"

"Not true! Why the first thing that girl said to me was Why don't I get a washing machine? Comes into my kitchen, takes one look around, and starts telling me how to manage my life."

"Surely you don't think she meant anything."

"No, she didn't mean anything. All she meant was, What was I doing living in such a run-down half-house when she came from a great big barn on Joseph Street with the kitchen full of gadgets, and Wasn't I lucky to be fobbing off my boy on such a well-equipped little trick? I never liked that girl's eyes. They never met your face full-on." She turns her face on Eccles and, warned, he returns her stare. Beneath her misted spectacles—an old-fashioned type, circles of steel-rimmed glass in which the bifocal crescents catch a pinker tint of light —her arrogantly tilted nose displays its meaty, intricate underside. Her broad mouth is stretched slightly by a vague expectation. Eccles realizes that this woman is a humorist. The difficulty with humorists is that they will mix what they believe with what they don't; whichever seems likelier to win an effect. The strange thing is how much he likes her, though in a way she is plunging at him as roughly as she plunges the dirty clothes. But that's it, it's the same to her. Unlike Mrs. Springer, she doesn't really see him at all. Her confrontation is with the whole world, and secure under the breadth of her satire, he can say what he pleases.

He bluntly defends Janice. "The girl is shy."

"Shy! She wasn't too shy to get herself pregnant so poor Hassy has to marry her when he could scarcely tuck his shirt-tail in."

"He was one and twenty, as you say."

"Yes, well, years. Some die young; some are born old."

Epigrams, everything. My, she is funny. Eccles laughs out loud. She doesn't acknowledge hearing him, and turns to her wash with furious seriousness. "About as shy as a snake," she says, "that girl. These little women are poison. Mincing around with their sneaky eyes getting everybody's sympathy. Well she doesn't get mine; let the men weep. To hear her father-in-law talk she's the worst martyr since Joan of Arc."

He laughs again; but isn't she? "Well uh, what does Mr. Angstrom think Harry should do?"

"Crawl back. What else? He will, too, poor boy. He's just like his father underneath. All soft heart. I suppose that's why men rule the world. They're all heart."

"That's an unusual view."

"Is it? It's what they keep telling you in church. Men are all heart and women are all body. I don't know who's supposed to have the brains. God, I suppose."

Eccles smiles, wondering if the Lutheran church gives everyone such ideas. Luther himself was a little like this, perhaps—overstating half-truths in a kind of comic wrath. The whole black Protestant paradox-thumping maybe begins there. Deep fundamental hopelessness in such a mind. *Hubris* in shoving the particular aside. Maybe: he's forgotten most of the theology they made him absorb. It occurs to him that he should see Angstrom's pastor.

Mrs. Angstrom picks up a dropped thread. "Now my daughter Miriam is as old as the hills and always was; I've never worried about her. I remember, on Sundays long ago when we'd walk out by the quarry Harold was so afraid—he wasn't more than twelve then—he was so afraid she'd fall over the edge. I knew she wouldn't. You watch her. She won't marry out of pity like poor Hassy and then have all the world jump on him for trying to get out."

"I don't think the world *has* jumped on him. The girl's mother and I were just discussing that it seemed quite the contrary."

"Don't you think it. That girl gets no sympathy from me. She has everybody on her side from Eisenhower down. They'll talk him around. *You'll* talk him around. And there's another."

The front door has opened with a softness she alone hears. Her husband comes into the kitchen wearing a white shirt and a tie but with his fingernails outlined in black; he is a printer. He is as tall as his wife but seems shorter. His mouth works self-deprecatorily over badly fitted false teeth. His nose is Harry's, a neat smooth button. "How do you do, Father," he says; either he was raised as a Catholic or among Catholics.

"Mr. Angstrom, it's very nice to meet you." The man's hand has tough ridges but a soft, dry palm. "We've been discussing your son."

"I feel terrible about that." Eccles believes him. Earl Angstrom has a gray, ragged look. This business has blighted him. He thins his lips over his slipping teeth like a man with stomach trouble biting back gas. He is being nibbled from within. Color has washed from his hair and eyes like cheap ink. A straight man, who has measured his life with the pica-stick and locked the forms tight, he has returned in the morning and found the type scrambled.

"He goes on and on about the girl as if she was the mother of Christ," Mrs. Angstrom says.

"That's not true," Angstrom says mildly, and sits down in his white shirt at the porcelain kitchen table. Four settings, year after year, have worn black blurs through the enamel. "I just don't see how Harry could make such a mess. As a boy he was always so trim. He wasn't like other boys, sloppy. He was a neat worker."

With raw sudsy hands Mrs. Angstrom has set about heating coffee for her husband. This small act of service seems to bring her into harmony with him; they begin, in the sudden way of old couples apparently at odds, to speak as one. "It was the Army," she says. "When he came back from Texas he was a different boy."

"He didn't want to come into the shop," Angstrom says. "He didn't want to get dirty."

"Reverend Eccles, would you like some coffee?" Mrs. Angstrom asks.

At last, his chance. "No, thank you. What I would *love*, though, is a glass of water."

"Just water? With ice?"

"Any way. Any way would be lovely."

"Yes, Earl is right," she says. "People now say how lazy Hassy is, but he's not. He never was. When you'd be proud of his basketball in high school you know, people would say, 'Yes well but he's so tall, it's easy for him.' But they didn't know how he had worked at that. Out back every evening banging the ball way past dark; you wondered how he could see."

"From about twelve years old on," Angstrom says, "he was at that night and day. I put a pole up for him out back; the garage wasn't high enough."

"When he set his mind to something," Mrs. Angstrom says, "there was no stopping him." She yanks powerfully at the lever of the ice-cube tray and with a brilliant multiple crunch that sends chips sparkling the cubes come loose. "He wanted to be best at that and I honestly believe he was."

"I know what you mean," Eccles says. "I play a little golf with him and already he's become better than I am."

She puts the cubes in a glass and holds the glass under a spigot and brings it to him. He tilts it at his lips and Earl Angstrom's palely vehement voice wavers through the liquid. "Then he comes back from the Army and all he cares about is chasing ass. He won't come work in the print shop because it'll get his fingernails dirty." Eccles lowers the glass and Angstrom says full in his face across the table, "He's become the worst kind of Brewer bum. If I could get my hands on him, Father, I'd try to thrash him if he killed me in the process." His ashen face bunches defiantly at the mouth; his colorless eyes swarm with glitter.

"Your language, Earl," his wife says, setting coffee in a flowered cup on the table between his hands.

He looks down into the steam and says, "Excuse me. When I think of what that boy's doing my stomach does somersaults."

Eccles lifts his glass and says "No" into it like a megaphone and then drinks until no more water can be sucked from under the ice cubes that bump his upper lip. He wipes the moisture from his mouth and says, "There's a great deal of goodness in your son. When I'm with him—it's rather unfortunate, really—I feel so cheerful I quite forget what the point of my seeing him is." He laughs, first at Mr., and, failing here to rouse a smile, at Mrs.

"This golf you play," Angstrom says. "What is the point? Why don't the girl's parents get the police after him? In my opinion a good swift kick is what he needs."

Eccles glances toward Mrs. Angstrom and feels the arch of his eyebrows like drying paste on his forehead. He didn't expect, a minute ago, to be looking toward her as an ally and toward this worn-out good man as a rather vulgar and disappointing foe.

"Mrs. Springer wants to," he tells Angstrom. "The girl and her father want to wait."

"Don't talk nonsense, Earl," Mrs. Angstrom says. "What does old Springer want with his name in the papers? The way you talk you'd think poor Harry was your enemy."

"He is my enemy," Angstrom says. He touches the saucer from both sides with his stained fingertips. "That night I spent walking the streets looking for him he became my enemy. You can't talk. You didn't see the girl's face."

"What do I care about her face? You talk about tarts: they don't become ivory-white saints in my book just by having a marriage license. That girl wanted Harry and got him with the only trick she knew and now she's run out of tricks."

"Don't *talk* that way, Mary. It's just words with you. Suppose I had acted the way Harry has."

"Ah," she says, and turns, and Eccles flinches, seeing her face taut to release a special missile. "I didn't want *you;* you wanted *me.* Or wasn't it that way?"

"Yes of course it was that way," Angstrom mutters.

"Well then: there's no comparison."

Angstrom has hunched his shoulders over the coffee, drawn himself in very small, as if she has painted him into a tiny corner. "Oh Mary," he sighs, not daring move with words.

Eccles tries to defend him; he goes to the weaker side of a fight almost automatically. "I don't think you can say," he tells Mrs. Angstrom, "that Janice didn't imagine that her marriage was built on mutual attraction. If the girl was such a clever schemer she wouldn't have let Harry slip away so easily."

Mrs. Angstrom's interest in this discussion, now that she knows she pressed her husband too hard, has waned; she maintains a position—that Janice is in control—so obviously false that it amounts to a concession. "She hasn't let him slip away," she says. "She'll have him back, you watch."

Eccles turns to the man; if he will agree, they will all three be united, and he can leave. "Do you think too that Harry will come around?"

"No," Angstrom says, looking down, "never. He's too far gone. He'll just slide deeper and deeper now until we might as well forget him. If he was twenty, or twenty-two; but at his age . . . In the shop sometimes you see these young Brewer bums. They can't stick it. They're like cripples only they don't limp. Human garbage, they call them. And I sit there at the machine for two months wondering how the hell it could be my Harry, that used to hate a mess so much."

Eccles looks over at Harry's mother and is jarred to see her leaning against the sink with soaked cheeks gleaming under the glasses. He gets up in shock. Is she crying because she thinks her husband is speaking the truth, or because she thinks he is saying this just to hurt her, in revenge for making him admit that he had wanted her? "I hope you're wrong," Eccles says. "I must go now; I thank you both for discussing this with me. I realize it's painful."

Angstrom takes him back through the house and in the dark of the dining room touches his arm. "He liked things just so," he says. "I never saw a boy like him. Any rumpus in the family he'd take hard out of all reason—when Mary and I, you know, would have our fun." Eccles nods, but doubts that "fun" quite describes what he's seen.

In the living-room shadows a girl stands in a bare-armed summer dress. "Mim! Did you just get in?"

"Yeah."

"This is Father—I mean Reverend—"

"Eccles."

"Eccles, he came to talk about Harry. My daughter Miriam."

"Hello, Miriam. I've heard Harry speak very fondly of you."

"Hi."

With that word the big window behind her takes on the intimate glaze of the big window in a luncheonette. Flip greetings seem to trail behind her with wisps of cigarette smoke and drugstore perfume. Mrs. Angstrom's nose has delicacy on the girl's face, a sharpness Saracen or even more ancient, barbaric. Taken with the prominent nose her height at first glance seems her mother's, but when her father stands beside her, Eccles sees that it is his height; their bodies, the beautiful girl's and the weary man's, are the same. They have the same narrowness; a durable edge that, Eccles knows after seeing the wounds open under Mrs. Angstrom's spectacles, can cut. That narrowness, and a manageable vulgarity that offends him. They'll get through. They know what they're doing. It's a weakness of his, to prefer people who don't know what they're doing. The helpless: these, and the people on top, beyond help. The ones who maneuver more or less well in the middle seem to his aristocratic prejudices to be thieving from both ends. When they bunch at the door, Angstrom puts his arm around his daughter's waist and Eccles thinks of Mrs. Angstrom silent in the kitchen with her wet cheeks and red arms, a captive queen. Yet, turning on the pavement to wave at the two of them in the doorway, he has to smile at their incongruous symmetry, the earringed Arab boy with her innocent contempt for his Christian collar, and the limp-

faced old woman of a printer, paired in slenderness, inter-
locked.

He gets into the car thirsty and vexed. There was something pleasant said in the last half-hour but he can't remember what it was. He feels scratched, hot, confused, and dry;
he's spent an afternoon in a bramble patch. He's seen half a
dozen people and a dog and nowhere did an opinion tally
with his own, that Harry Angstrom was worth saving and
could be saved. Instead down there between the brambles
there seemed to be no Harry at all: nothing but stale air and
last year's dead stalks. The day is declining through the white
afternoon to the long blue spring evening. He drives past a
corner where someone is practicing on a trumpet behind an
open upstairs window. *Du du do do da da dee. Dee dee da da
do do du.* Cars are whispering home from work. He drives
across the town, tacking on the diagonal streets along a course
parallel to the distant ridge of the mountain. Fritz Kruppenbach, Mt. Judge's Lutheran minister for twenty-seven years,
lives in a high brick house not far from the cemetery. The
motorcycle belonging to his college-age son is on its side in
the driveway, partly dismantled. The sloping lawn, graded in
fussy terraces, has the unnatural chartreuse evenness that
comes with much fertilizing, much weed-killing, and much
mowing. Mrs. Kruppenbach—will Lucy ever achieve that
dimpled, obedient look?—comes to the door in a gray dress
that makes no compromise with the season. Her gray hair
girdles her head with braids of great compactness. When
she lets all that hair down, she must be a witch. "He's mowing out back," she says.

"I'd like to talk to him for just a few minutes. It's a problem
that involves our two congregations."

"Go up to his room, why do-an tcha? I'll fetch him."

The house—foyer, halls, staircase, even the minister's leath-
ery den upstairs—is flooded with the smell of beef roasting.
Eccles sits by the window of Kruppenbach's den on an oak-
backed choir pew left over from some renovation. Seated
on the bench he feels an adolescent compulsion to pray but in-

stead peers across the valley at the green fragments of the golf course where he would like to be, with Harry. Eccles has found other partners either better or worse than he; only Harry is both, and only Harry gives the game a desperate gaiety, as if they are together engaged in an impossible quest set by a benevolent but absurd lord, a quest whose humiliations sting them almost to tears but one that is renewed at each tee, in a fresh flood of green. And for Eccles there is an additional hope, a secret determination to trounce Harry. He feels that the thing that makes Harry unsteady, that makes him unable to repeat his beautiful effortless swing every time, is the thing at the root of all the problems that he has created; and that by beating him decisively he, Eccles, will get on top of this weakness, this flaw, and hence solve the problems. In the meantime there is the pleasure of hearing Harry now and then cry, "Yes, yes," or "That's the one!" Their rapport at moments attains for Eccles a pitch of pleasure, a harmless ecstasy, that makes the world with its vicious circumstantiality seem remote and spherical and green.

The house shudders to the master's step. Kruppenbach comes up the stairs into his den, angry at being taken from his lawn-mowing. He wears old black pants and an undershirt soaked with sweat. His shoulders are coated with wiry gray wool.

"Hello, Chack," he says at pulpit volume, with no intonation of greeting. His German accent makes his words seem stones, set angrily one on top of another. "What is it?"

Eccles, not daring "Fritz" with the older man, laughs and blurts, "Hello!"

Kruppenbach grimaces. He has a massive square head, crew-cut. He is a man of brick: as if he was born as a baby literally of clay and decades of exposure have baked him to the color and hardness of brick. He repeats, "What?"

"You have a family called Angstrom."

"Yes."

"The father's a printer."

"Yes."

"Their son, Harry, deserted his wife over two months ago; her people, the Springers, are in my church."

"Yes, well. The boy. The boy's a *Schussel*."

Eccles isn't certain what that means. He supposes that Kruppenbach doesn't sit down because he doesn't want to stain his furniture with his own sweat. His continuing to stand puts Eccles in a petitionary position, sitting on the bench like a choirboy. The odor of meat cooking grows more insistent as he explains what he thinks happened: how Harry has been in a sense spoiled by his athletic successes; how the wife, to be fair, had perhaps showed little imagination in their marriage; how he himself, as minister, had tried to keep the boy's conscience in touch with his wife without pressing him into a premature reunion—for the boy's problem wasn't so much a lack of feeling as an uncontrolled excess of it; how the four parents, for various reasons, were of little help; how he had witnessed, just minutes ago, a quarrel between the Angstroms that perhaps offered a clue as to why their son—

"Do you think," Kruppenbach at last interrupts, "do you think this is your job, to meddle in these people's lives? I know what they teach you at seminary now: this psychology and that. But I don't agree with it. You think now your job is to be an unpaid doctor, to run around and plug up the holes and make everything smooth. I don't think that. I don't think that's your job."

"I only—"

"No now let me finish. I've been in Mt. Judge twenty-seven years and you've been here two. I've listened to your story but I wasn't listening to what it said about the people, I was listening to what it said about you. What I heard was this: the story of a minister of God selling his message for a few scraps of gossip and a few games of golf. What do you think now it looks like to God, one childish husband leaving one childish wife? Do you ever think any more what God sees? Or have you grown beyond that?"

"No, of course not. But it seems to me our role in a situation like this—"

"It seems to you our role is to be cops, cops without hand-cuffs, without guns, without anything but our human good nature. Isn't it right? Don't answer, just think if I'm not right. Well, I say that's a Devil's idea. I say, let the cops be cops and look after their laws that have nothing to do with us."

"I agree, up to a point—"

"There *is* no up to a point! There is no reason or measure in what we must do." His thick forefinger, woolly between the knuckles, has begun to tap emphasis on the back of a leather chair. "If Gott wants to end misery He'll declare the Kingdom now." Jack feels a blush begin to burn his face. "How big do you think your little friends look among the billions that God sees? In Bombay now they die in the streets every minute. You say role. I say you don't know what your role is or you'd be home locked in prayer. *There* is your role: to make yourself an exemplar of faith. *There* is where comfort comes from: faith, not what little finagling a body can do here and there, stirring the bucket. In running back and forth you run from the duty given you by God, to make your faith powerful, so when the call comes you can go out and tell them, "Yes, he is dead, but you will see him again in Heaven. Yes, you suffer, but you must *love* your pain, because it is *Christ's* pain." When on Sunday morning then, when we go before their faces, we must walk up not worn out with misery but full of Christ, *hot*"—he clenches his hairy fists—"with Christ, on *fire: burn* them with the force of our belief. That is why they come; why else would they pay us? Anything else we can do or say anyone can do and say. They have doctors and lawyers for that. It's all in the Book—a thief with faith is worth all the Pharisees. Make no mistake. Now I'm serious. Make no mistake. There is nothing but Christ for us. All the rest, all this decency and busyness, is nothing. It is Devil's work."

"Fritz," Mrs. Kruppenbach's voice calls carefully up the stairs. "Supper."

The red man in his undershirt looks down at Eccles and

asks, "Will you kneel a moment with me and pray for Christ to come into this room?"

"No. No I won't. I'm too angry. It would be hypocritical."

The refusal, unthinkable from a layman, makes Kruppenbach, not softer, but stiller. "Hypocrisy," he says mildly. "You have no seriousness. Don't you believe in damnation? Didn't you know when you put that collar on, what you risked?" In the brick skin of his face his eyes seem small imperfections, pink and glazed with water as if smarting in intense heat.

He turns without waiting for Jack to answer and goes downstairs for supper. Jack descends behind him and continues out the door. His heart is beating like a scolded child's and his knees are weak with fury. He had come for an exchange of information and been flagellated with an insane spiel. Unctuous old thundering Hun, no conception of the ministry as a legacy of light, probably himself scrambled into it out of a butcher's shop. Jack realizes that these are spiteful and unworthy thoughts but he can't stop them. His depression is so deep that he tries to gouge it deeper by telling himself *He's right, he's right* and thus springing tears and purging himself, however absurdly, above the perfect green circle of the Buick steering wheel. But he can't cry; he's parched. His shame and failure hang downward in him heavy but fruitless.

Though he knows that Lucy wants him home—if dinner is not quite ready he will be in time to give the children their baths—he instead drives to the drugstore in the center of town. The poodle-cut girl behind the counter is in his Youth Group and two parishioners buying medicine or contraceptives or Kleenex hail him gaily. It is here that in truth they come to find the antidotes to their lives. He feels at home; Eccles feels most at home in public places. He rests his wrists on the cold clean marble and orders a vanilla ice-cream soda with a scoop of maple-walnut ice cream, and drinks two Coca-Cola glasses full of miraculous clear water before it comes.

Club Castanet was named during the war when the South
American craze was on and occupies a triangular building
where Warren Avenue crosses Running Horse Street at an
acute angle. It's in the south side of Brewer, the Italian-Negro-
Polish side, and Rabbit distrusts it. With its glass-brick
windows grinning back from the ridge of its face it looks like
a fortress of death; the interior is furnished in the glossy low-
lit style of an up-to-date funeral parlor, potted green plants
here and there, music piping soothingly, and the same smell of
strip rugs and fluorescent tubes and Venetian-blind slats and,
the most inner secretive smell, of alcohol. You drink it and
then you're embalmed in it. Ever since a man down from them
on Jackson Road lost his job as an undertaker's assistant and
became a bartender, Rabbit thinks of the two professions as
related; men in both talk softly, look very clean, and are always seen standing up. He and Ruth sit at a booth near the
front, where they get through the window a faint fluctuation
of red light as the neon castanet on the sign outside flickers
back and forth between its two positions, that imitate clicking.

This pink tremor takes the weight off Ruth's face. She sits
across from him. He tries to picture the kind of life she was
leading; a creepy place like this probably seems as friendly to
her as a locker room would to him. But just the thought of it
that way makes him nervous; her sloppy life, like his having a
family, is something he's tried to keep behind them. He was
happy just hanging around her place at night, her reading
mysteries and him running down to the delicatessen for ginger ale and some nights going to a movie but nothing like this.
That first night he really used that Daiquiri but since then he
didn't care if he ever had another and hoped she was the same
way. For a while she was but lately something's been eating
her; she's heavy in bed and once in a while looks at him as if
he's some sort of pig. He doesn't know what he's doing different but knows that somehow the ease has gone out of it. Tonight her so-called friend Margaret called up. It scared him

out of his skin when the phone rang. He has the idea lately it's going to be the cops or his mother or somebody; he has the feeling of something growing on the other side of the mountain. A couple times after he first moved in, the phone rang and it was some thick-voiced man saying "Ruth?" or just hanging up at Rabbit's voice answering. When they hung on, Ruth just said a lot of "No's" into the receiver and that seemed to settle it. She knew how to handle them, and anyway there were only about five that ever called; the past was a vine hanging on by just these five tendrils and it tore away easily, leaving her clean and blue and blank. But tonight it was Margaret out of this past and she wanted them to come down to the Castanet and Ruth wanted to and Rabbit went along. Anything for a little change. He's bored.

He asks her, "What do you want?"

"A Daiquiri."

"You're sure? You're sure now it won't make you sick?" He's noticed that, that she seems a little sick sometimes, and won't eat, and sometimes eats the house down.

"No, I'm not sure but why the hell shouldn't I be sick?"

"Well I don't know why you shouldn't. Why shouldn't anybody?"

"Look, let's not be a philosopher for once. Just get me the drink."

A colored girl in an orange uniform that he guesses from the frills is supposed to look South American comes and he tells her two Daiquiris. She flips shut her pad and walks off and he sees her back is open halfway down her spine, so a bit of black bra shows. Compared with this her skin isn't black at all. Soft purple shadows swing on the flats of her back where the light hits. She has a pigeon-toed way of sauntering, swinging those orange frills. She doesn't care about him; he likes that, that she doesn't care. The thing about Ruth is lately she's been trying to make him feel guilty about something.

She asks him, "What are *you* looking at?"

"I'm not looking at anything."

"You can't have it, Rabbit. You're too white."

"Say you really are in a sweet mood."

She smiles defiantly. "I'm just myself."

"God I hope not."

The Negress returns and sets the Daiquiris between them as they sit there silently. The door behind them opens and Margaret comes in with the chill. On top of everything, the guy with her is, he isn't very happy to see, Ronnie Harrison. Margaret says to Rabbit, "Hello, you. Are you still hanging on?"

"Hell," Harrison says, "it's the great Angstrom," as if he's trying to take Tothero's place in every way. "I've been hearing about you," he adds slimily.

"Hearing what?"

"Oh. The word."

Harrison was never one of Rabbit's favorites and has not improved. In the locker room he was always talking about making out and playing with himself under his little hairy pot of a belly and that pot has really grown. Harrison is fat. Fat and half bald. His kinky brass-colored hair has thinned and the skin of his scalp shows, depending on how he tilts his head. This pink showing through disgusts Rabbit, like the one bald idea that is always showing through Harrison's talk. Still, he remembers one night when Harrison came back into the game after losing two teeth to somebody's elbow and tries to be glad to see him. There were just five of you out there at a time and the other four for that time were unique in the world.

But it seems long ago, and every second Harrison stands there smirking it seems longer. He is wearing a narrow-shouldered summer suit of some linen imitation and having this nifty self-satisfied cloth hanging beside his ear annoys Rabbit. He feels hemmed in. The problem is, who shall sit where? He and Ruth have gotten on opposite sides of the table, which was the mistake. Harrison decides, and ducks down to sit beside Ruth, with a little catch in the movement that betrays the old limp from his football injury. Rabbit becomes obsessed by Harrison's imperfections. He's ruined the effect of his Ivy League suit by wearing a black wool tie like a wop. When he opens his mouth the two false teeth don't quite match the others.

"Well, how's life treating the old Master?" he says. "The word is you got it made." His eyes make his meaning by flicking sideways to Ruth, who sits there like a lump, her hands folded around the Daiquiri. Her knuckles are red from washing dishes for him. She lifts the glass to drink.

Margaret wriggles at Rabbit's side. She feels somehow like Janice: jumpy. Her presence in the left corner of his vision feels like a dark damp cloth approaching that side of his face.

"Where's Tothero?" he asks her.

"Totherwho?"

Ruth giggles, damn her. Harrison bends his head toward Ruth's, pink showing, and whispers a remark. Her lips tuck up in a smile; it's just like that night in the Chinese place, anything he says will please her, except that tonight he is Harrison and Rabbit sits across from them married to this girl he hates. He's sure what Harrison whispers is about him, "the old Master." From the second there were four of them it was clear he was going to be the goat. Like Tothero that night.

"You know damn well who," he tells Margaret. "Tothero."

"Our old coach, Harry!" Harrison cries, and reaches across the table to touch Rabbit's fingertips. "The man who made us immortal!"

Rabbit curls his fingers an inch beyond Harrison's reach and Harrison, with a satisfied smirk, draws back, pulling his palms along the slick table-top so they make a slippery screech of friction.

"Me, you mean," Rabbit says. "You were nothing."

"Nothing. That seems a little stern. That seems a little stern, Harry old bunny. Let's cast our minds back. When Tothero wanted a guy roughed up, who did he send in to do it? When he wanted a hot shot like you guarded nice and close, who was his boy?" He pats his own chest. "You were too much of a queen to dirty your hands. No, you never touched anybody, did you? You didn't play football either, and get your knee scrambled, either, did you? No sir, not Harry the bird; he was on wings. Feed him the ball and watch it go in."

"It went in, you noticed."

"Sometimes. Sometimes it did. Harry now don't wrinkle your nose. Don't think we all don't appreciate your ability." From the way he's using his hands, chopping and lifting in a practiced way, Rabbit thinks he must do a lot of talking around a table. Yet there's a tremor; and in seeing that Harrison is afraid of him, Rabbit loses interest. The waitress comes —Harrison orders Bourbon-on-the-Rocks for himself and Margaret and another Daiquiri for Ruth—and Rabbit watches her back recede as if it is the one real thing in the world: the little triangle of black bra under the two blue-brown pillows of muscle. He wants Ruth to see him looking.

Harrison is losing his salesman's composure. "Did I ever tell you what Tothero once said to me about you? Ace, are you listening?"

"What did Tothero say?" God, this guy is a middle-aged bore and he's not even thirty.

"He said to me, 'This is in confidence, Ronnie, but I depend on you to spark the team. Harry is not a team player.' "

Rabbit looks down at Margaret and over at Ruth. "Now I'll tell ya what really happened," he says to them. "Old Harrison here went in to Tothero and he said, 'Hey, I'm a real spark plug, ain't I, coach? A real play-maker, huh? Not like that lousy showboat Angstrom, huh?' And Tothero was probably asleep and didn't answer, so Harrison goes through the rest of his life thinking, 'Gee, I'm a real hero. A real play-maker.' On a basketball team, you see, whenever you have a little runty clumsy guy that can't do anything he's called the play-maker. I don't know where he's supposed to be making all these plays. In his bedroom I guess." Ruth laughs; he's not sure he wanted her to.

"That's not true." Harrison's practiced palms flicker more hastily. "He volunteered it to me. Not that it was anything I didn't know; the whole school knew it."

Did it? Nobody ever told him.

Ruth says, "God, let's not talk *bas*ketball. Every time I go out with this bastard we talk nothing but."

He wonders, Did doubt show on his face, and she say that to reassure him? Does she in any part of her pity him?

Harrison perhaps thinks he's been uglier than befits his sales-conference suavity. He takes out a cigarette and a lizard-skin Ronson. They can't help but watch him, like children around a magician, while he snaps a shapely flame into being.

Rabbit turns to Margaret. Something in the way this arranges the nerves in his neck rings a bell, makes him think he turned to her exactly like this a million years ago. He says, "You never answered me."

"Nuts, I don't know where he is. I guess he went home. He was sick."

"Just sick, or—" Harrison's mouth does a funny thing, smiling and pursing both, as if he is introducing, with deference, this bit of Manhattan cleverness to his rural friends for the first time, tapping his head to make sure they will "get it" —"sick, sick, sick?"

"All ways," Margaret says. A serious shadow crosses her face that seems to remove her and Harry, who sees it, from the others, and takes them into that strange area of a million years ago from which they have wandered; a strange guilt pierces Harry at being here instead of there, where he never was. Ruth and Harrison across from them, touched by staccato red light, seem to smile from the heart of damnation.

"Dear Ruth," Harrison says, "how have you been? I often worry about you."

"Don't worry about *me*," she says, yet seems pleased.

"I just wonder," he goes on, "about the ability of our mutual friend to support you in the style to which you are accustomed."

The Negress brings their drinks and Harrison, as if flashing a badge, shows her the lizard-skin Ronson in his hand. "Real skin," he says.

"Mmm," she says, with lots of throat. "Your own?"

Rabbit laughs. He loves that woman.

When she goes, Harrison leans forward with the sweet smile you use on children. "Did you know," he asks Harry, "that Ruth and I once went to Atlantic City together?"

"There was another couple," she tells Harry.

"A disgusting pair," Harrison says, "who preferred the shabby privacy of their own bungalow to the golden sunshine outdoors. The male of this twosome later confided to me, with ill-concealed pride, that he had enjoyed the orgasmatic climax eleven times in the all-too-short period of thirty-six hours."

Margaret laughs. "Honestly, Ronnie, to hear you talk sometimes you'd think you went to Harvard."

"Princeton," he corrects. "Princeton is the effect I want to give. Harvard is suspect around here."

Rabbit looks toward Ruth and sees that the second Daiquiri is on its way and the first has been delivered. She titters. "The awful thing about them," she says, "was that they did it in the car. Here was poor Ronnie, trying to drive through all this Sunday-night traffic, and I looked back at a stoplight and Betsy's dress was up around her neck."

"I didn't drive all the way," Harrison tells her. "Remember we *fin*ally got him to drive." His head tips toward her for confirmation and his pink scalp glints.

"Yeah." Ruth looks into her glass and titters again, maybe at the thought of Betsy naked.

Harrison watches narrowly the effect of this on Rabbit. "This guy," he says, in the pushy-quiet voice of offering a deal, "had an interesting theory. He thought"—Harrison's hands grip air—"that right at the crucial, how shall I say?—development, you should *slap* your partner, as hard as you can, right in the face. If you're in a position to. Otherwise slap what you can."

Rabbit blinks; he really doesn't know what to do about this awful guy. And just there, in the space of blinking, with the alcohol vaporizing under his ribs, he feels himself pass over.

He laughs, really laughs. They can all go to Hell. "Well what did he think about biting?"

Harrison's I've-got-your-number-buddy grin grows fixed; his reflexes aren't quick enough to take this sudden turn. "Biting? I don't know."

"Well he couldn't have given it much thought. A good big bloody bite: nothing better. Of course I can see how you're handicapped, with those two false teeth."

"Do you have false teeth, Ronnie?" Margaret cries. "How exciting! You've never told."

"Of course he does," Rabbit tells her. "You didn't think those two piano keys were his, did you? They don't even come close to matching."

Harrison presses his lips together but he can't afford to give up that forced grin and it sharply strains his face. His talking is hampered too.

"Now there was this place we used to go to in Texas," Rabbit says, "where there was this girl whose backside had been bitten so often it looked like a piece of old cardboard. You know, after it's been out in the rain. It's all she did. She was a virgin otherwise." He looks around at his audience and Ruth shakes her head minutely, one brief shake, as if to say, *No, Rabbit,* and it seems extremely sad, so sad a film of grit descends on his spirit and muffles him.

Harrison says, "It's like that story about this whore that had the biggest—ah—you don't want to hear it, do you?"

"Sure. Go ahead," Ruth says.

"Well, this guy, see, was making out and he loses his, ahem, device." Harrison's face bobbles in the unsteady light. His hands start explaining. Rabbit thinks the poor guy must have to make a pitch five times a day or so. He wonders what he sells; some sort of ideas it must be, nothing as definite as the MagiPeel Peeler. ". . . up to his elbow, up to his shoulder, then he gets his whole head in, and his chest, and starts crawling along this tunnel . . ." Good old MagiPeel, Rabbit thinks, he can almost feel one in his hand. Its handle came in three colors, which the company called turquoise, scarlet, and gold.

The funny thing about it, it really did what they said, really took the skin off turnips, carrots, potatoes, radishes, neat, quick, it had a long sort of slot with razor-sharp edges. ". . . sees this *other* guy and says, 'Hey, have you seen . . .'" Ruth sits there resigned and with horror he believes it's all the same to her in her mind there's no difference between Harrison and him and for that matter *is* there a difference? The whole interior of the place muddles and runs together red like the inside of a stomach in which they're all being digested. ". . . and the other guy says, 'Stripper, hell. I've been in here three weeks looking for my *motorcycle!*'"

Harrison, waiting to join the laughter, looks up in silence. He's failed to sell it. "That's too fantastic," Margaret says.

Rabbit's skin is clammy under his clothes; this makes the draft from the door opening behind him sharp. Harrison says, "Hey, isn't that your sister?"

Ruth looks up from her drink. "Is it?" He makes no sign and she says, "They have the same horsy look."

One glance told Rabbit. Miriam and her escort luckily walk a little into the place, past their table, and wait there to see an empty booth. The place is shaped like a wedge and widens out from the entrance. The bar is in the center, and on either side there is an aisle of booths. The young couple heads for the opposite aisle. Mim wears bright white shoes with very high heels. The boy with her has woolly blond hair cut just long enough to comb and one of those smooth caramel tans people who play but don't work outdoors in summer get.

"Is that your sister?" Margaret says. "She's attractive. You and her must take after different parents."

"How do *you* know her?" Rabbit asks Harrison.

"Oh—" His hand flicks diffidently, as if his fingertips slide across a streak of grease in the air. "You see her around."

Rabbit's instinct was to freeze at first but this suggestion of Harrison's that she's a tramp makes him get up and walk across the orange tile floor and around the bar.

"Mim."

"Well, *hi*."

"What are you doing here?"

She tells the boy with her, "This is my brother. He's back from the dead."

"Hi, big brother." Rabbit doesn't like the boy's saying this and he doesn't like the way the kid is sitting on the inside of the booth with Mim on the outside in the man's place. He doesn't like the whole feel of the thing, that Mim is showing him around. The kid is wearing a seersucker coat and a narrow tie and looks, in a smirched prep-school way, too young and too old. His lips are too thick. Mim doesn't give his name.

"Harry, Pop and Mom fight all the time about you."

"Well if they knew you were in a dump like this they'd have something else to talk about."

"Its not so bad, for this section of town."

"It stinks. Why don't you and Junior get out?"

"Say. Who's in charge here?" the kid asks, drawing his shoulders up and making his lips thicker.

Harry reaches over, hooks his finger around the kid's striped necktie, and snaps it out. It flies up and hits his thick mouth and makes his manicured face go slightly fuzzy. He starts to rise and Rabbit puts his hand on top of his tidy haircut and pushes him down again and walks away, with the hardness of the kid's narrow head still tingling in his fingertips. At his back his sister half-calls "Harry."

His ears are so good he hears, as he rounds the bar, Junior explain to her, in a voice husky with cowardice, "He's in love with you."

To his own table he says, "Come on, Ruth. Get on your motorcycle."

She protests, "I'm happy."

"Come on."

She moves to collect her things and Harrison, after looking around in doubt, gets out of the booth to let her up. He stands there beside Rabbit and Rabbit on an impulse puts his hand on Ronnie's unpadded would-be-Princeton shoulder. In comparison with Mim's kid he likes him. "You're right, Ronnie," he tells him, "you were a real play-maker." It comes out nasty but he meant it well, for the sake of the old team.

Harrison, too slow to feel that he means it, knocks his hand away and says, "When are you gonna grow up?" It's telling that lousy story that has rattled him.

Outside on the summer-warm steps of the place Rabbit starts laughing. "Looking for my motorcycle," he says, and lets go, "Hwah hwah *hyaaa*," under the neon light.

Ruth is in no humor to see it. "Well you *are* a nut," she says.

It annoys him that she is too dumb to see that he is really sore. The way she shook her head "No" at him when he was gagging it up annoys him; his mind goes back over the minute again and again and every time snags on it. He is angry about so many things he doesn't know where to begin; the only thing clear is he's going to give her hell.

"So you and that bastard went to Atlantic City together."

"Why is he a bastard?"

"Oh. He's not and I am."

"I didn't say you were."

"You did too. Right back in there you did."

"It was just an expression. A *fond* expression, though I don't know why."

"You don't."

"No I don't. You see your sister come in with some boy friend and practically pee in your pants."

"Did you see the punk she was with?"

"What was the matter with him?" Ruth asks. "He looked all right."

"Just about everybody looks all right to you, don't they?"

"Well I don't see what you're doing going around like some almighty judge."

"Yes sir, just about anything with hair in its armpits looks all right to you."

They are walking up Warren Avenue. Their place is seven blocks away. People are sitting out on their steps in the early

summer air; their conversation is in this sense public and they
fight to keep their voices low.

"Boy, if this is what seeing your sister does to you I'm glad
we're not married."

"What brought that up?"

"What brought what up?"

"Marriage."

"You did, don't you remember, the first night, you kept
talking about it, and kissed my ring finger."

"That was a nice night."

"All right then."

"All right then nothing." Rabbit feels he's been worked into
a corner where he can't give her hell without giving her up
entirely, without obliterating the sweet things. But she did
that by taking him to that stinking place. "You've laid for
Harrison, haven't you?"

"I guess. Sure."

"You guess. You don't know?"

"I said sure."

"And how many others?"

"I don't know."

"A hundred?"

"It's a pointless question."

"Why is it pointless?"

"It's like asking how many times you've been to the mov·
ies."

"They're about the same to you, is that it?"

"No they're not the same but I don't see what the count
matters. You knew what I was."

"I'm not sure I did. You were a real hooer?"

"I took some money. I've told you. There were boy friends
when I was working as a stenographer and they had friends
and I lost my job because of the talk maybe I don't know and
some older men got my number I guess through Margaret, I
don't know. Look. It's by. If it's a question of being dirty or
something a lot of married women have had to take it more
often than I have."

"Did you pose for pictures?"

"You mean like for high-school kids? No."

"Did you blow guys?"

"Look, maybe we should say bye-bye." At the thought of that her chin softens and eyes burn and she hates him too much to think of sharing her secret with him. Her secret inside her seems to have no relation to him, this big body loping along with her under the street lamps, hungry as a ghost, wanting to hear the words to whip himself up. That was the thing about men, the importance they put on the mouth. Rabbit seems like another man to her, with this difference: in ignorance he has welded her to him and she can't let go.

With degrading gratitude she hears him say, "No I don't *want* to say bye-bye. I just want an answer to my question."

"The answer to your question is yes."

"Harrison?"

"Why does Harrison mean so much to you?"

"Because he stinks. And if Harrison is the same to you as me then I stink."

They are, for that moment, the same to her—in fact she would prefer Harrison, just for the change, just because he doesn't insist on being the greatest thing that ever was—but she lies. "You're not at all the same. You're not in the same league."

"Well I got a pretty funny feeling sitting across from you two in that restaurant. What all did you do with him?"

"Oh, I don't know, what *do* you do? You make love, you try to get close to somebody."

"Well, would you do everything to me that you did to him?"

This stuns her skin in a curious way, makes it contract so that her body feels squeezed and sickened inside it. "If you want me to." After being a wife a whore's skin feels tight.

His relief is boyish; his front teeth flash happily. "Just once," he promises, "honest. I'll never ask you again." He tries to put his arm around her but she pulls away. Her one hope is that they aren't talking about the same thing.

Up in the apartment he asks plaintively, "Are you going to?" She is struck by the helplessness in his posture; in the interior darkness, to which her eyes have not adjusted, he seems a suit of clothes hung from the broad white knob of his face.

She asks, "Are you sure we're talking about the same thing?"

"What do you think we're talking about?" He's too fastidious to mouth the words.

She says.

"Right," he says.

"In cold blood. You just want it."

"Uh-huh. Is it so awful for you?"

This glimmer of her gentle rabbit emboldens her. "May I ask what I've done?"

"I didn't like the way you acted tonight."

"How did I act?"

"Like what you were."

"I didn't mean to."

"Even so. I saw you that way tonight and I felt a wall between us and this is the one way through it."

"That's pretty cute. You just want it, really." She yearns to hit out at him, to tell him to go. But that time is past.

He repeats, "Is it so awful for you?"

"Well it is because you think it is."

"Maybe I don't."

"Look, I've loved you."

"Well I've loved *you*."

"And now?"

"I don't know. I want to still."

Now those damn tears again. She tries to hurry the words out before her voice crumbles. "That's good of you. That's heroic."

"Don't be smart. Listen. Tonight you turned against me. I need to see you on your knees."

"Well just that—"

"No. Not just that."

The two tall drinks have been a poor experiment; she wants

to go to sleep and her tongue tastes sour. She feels in her stomach her need to keep him and wonders, Will this frighten
him? Will this kill her in him?

"If I did it what would it prove?"

"It'd prove you're mine."

"Shall I take my clothes off?"

"Sure." He takes his off quickly and neatly and stands by
the dull wall in his brilliant body. He leans awkwardly and
brings one hand up and hangs it on his shoulder not knowing
what to do with it. His whole shy pose has these wings of tension, like he's an angel waiting for a word. Sliding her last
clothes off, her arms feel cold touching her sides. This last
month she's felt cold all the time; her temperature being divided or something. In the growing light he shifts slightly.
She closes her eyes and tells herself, they're not ugly. Not.

Mrs. Springer called the rectory a little after eight. Mrs. Eccles told her Jack had taken the young people's softball team
to a game fifteen miles away and she didn't know when he'd
be home. Mrs. Springer's panic carried over the wire and Lucy
spent nearly two hours calling numbers in an attempt to reach
him. It grew dark. She finally reached the minister of the
church whose softball team they were playing and he told her
the game had been over for an hour. The darkness thickened
outside; the window whose sill held the phone became a waxy
streaked mirror in which she could see herself, hair unpinning,
slump back and forth between the address book and the
phone. Joyce, hearing the constant ticking of the dial, came
downstairs and leaned on her mother. Three times Lucy took
her up to the bed and twice the child came down again and
leaned her damp weight against her mother's legs in frightened
silence. The whole house, room beyond room surrounding
with darkness the little island of light around the telephone,
filled with menace and when, the third time, Joyce failed to
come down from her bed, Lucy felt guilty and forsaken both,
as if she had sold her only ally to the shadows. She dialed the
number of every problem case in the parish she could think

of, tried the vestrymen, the church secretary, the three co-chairmen of the fund-raising drive, Henry the old deaf sexton, and even the organist, a piano-teaching professional who lived in Brewer.

The hour-hand has moved past ten; it's getting embarrassing. It's sounding as if she's been deserted. And in fact it frightens her, that her husband seems to be nowhere in the world. She makes coffee and weeps weakly, in her own kitchen. How did she get into this? What drew her in? His gaiety, he was always so gay. To know him back in seminary you would never think he would take all this so seriously; he and his friends sitting in their drafty old rooms lined with handsome blue exegetical works made it all seem an elegant joke. She remembers playing with them in a softball game that was the Athanasians against the Arians. And now she never saw his gaiety, it was all spent on other people, on this grim gray intangible parish, her enemy. Oh, how she hates them, all those clinging quaint quavering widows and Christing young people—the one good thing if the Russians take over is they'll make religion go extinct. It should have gone extinct a hundred years ago. Maybe it shouldn't have, maybe our minds need it, but let somebody else carry it on. On Jack it was so dreary. Sometimes she feels sorry for him and, abruptly, this is one of the times.

When he does come in, at quarter of eleven, it turns out he's been sitting in a drugstore gossiping with some of his teen-agers; the idiotic kids tell him everything, all smoking like chimneys, so he comes home titillated silly with "how far" you can "go" on dates and still love Jesus. He can't really believe it, that people want to make love.

Eccles sees at once she is furious. He had been having far too happy a time in the drugstore. He loves kids; their belief is so real to them and sits so light.

Lucy delivers her message as sufficient rebuke, but it fails as that; for, with hardly a backward glance at the horrid evening she has, implicitly, spent, he rushes to the phone.

He takes his wallet out and between his driver's license and his public-library card finds the telephone number he has been saving, the key that could be turned in the lock just once. He wonders, dialing it, if it will fit, if he was a fool to lean the entire weight of the case on the word of young Mrs. Fosnacht, with her mirroring, perhaps mocking, sunglasses. The distant phone rings often, as if electricity, that amazingly trained mouse, has scurried through miles of wire only to gnaw at the end of its errand on an impenetrable plate of metal. He prays, but it is a bad prayer, a doubting prayer; he fails to superimpose God upon the complexities of electricity. He concedes them their inviolable laws. Hope has vanished, he is hanging on out of numbness, when the gnawing ringing stops, the metal is lifted, and openness, an impression of light and air, washes back through the wires to Eccles' ear.

"Hello." A man's voice, but not Harry's. It is more sluggish and brutal than that of his friend.

"Is Harry Angstrom there?" Sunglasses mock his sunk heart; this is not the number.

"Who's this?"

"My name is Jack Eccles."

"Oh. Hi."

"Is that you, Harry? It didn't sound like you. Were you asleep?"

"In a way."

"Harry, your wife has started to have the baby. Her mother called here around eight and I just got in." Eccles closes his eyes; in the dark tipping silence he feels his ministry, sum and substance, being judged.

"Yeah," the other breathes in the far corner of the darkness. "I guess I ought to go to her."

"I wish you would."

"I guess I should. It's mine I mean too."

"Exactly. I'll meet you there. It's St. Joseph's in Brewer. You know where that is?"

"Yeah, sure. I can walk it in ten minutes."

"You want me to pick you up in the car?"

"No, I'll walk it."

"All right. If you prefer. Harry?"

"Huh?"

"I'm very proud of you."

"Yeah. O.K. I'll see you."

Eccles had reached for him, it felt like, out of the ground. Voice had sounded tinny and distant. Ruth's bedroom is dim; the street lamp like a low moon burns shadows into the inner planes of the armchair, the burdened bed, the twisted sheet he tossed back finally when it seemed the phone would never stop. The bright rose window of the church opposite is still lit: purple red blue gold like the notes of different bells struck. His body, his whole frame of nerves and bone, tingles, as if with the shaking of small bells hung up and down his silver skin. He wonders if he had been asleep, and how long, ten minutes or five hours. He finds his underclothes and trousers draped on a chair and fumbles with them; not only his fingers but his vision itself trembles in the luminous gloom. His white shirt seems to crawl, like a cluster of glow-worms in grass. He hesitates a second before poking his fingers into the nest, that turns under his touch to safe cloth, dead. He carries it in his hand to the sullen laden bed.

"Hey. Baby."

The long lump under the covers doesn't answer. Just the top of Ruth's hair peeks up out of the pillow. He doesn't feel she is asleep.

"Hey. I got to go out."

No answer. If she wasn't asleep she heard everything he said on the phone, but what did he say? He remembers nothing except this sense of being reached. Ruth lies heavy and silent and her body hidden. The night is hot enough for just a sheet but she put a blanket on the bed saying she felt cold. It was just about the only thing she did say. He shouldn't have made her do it. He doesn't know why he did except it felt right at the time. He thought she might like it or at least like the humbling. If she didn't want to, if it made her sick, why didn't she say no like he half-hoped she would anyway? He kept touching her cheeks with his fingertips. He kept wanting to lift her up and hug her in simple thanks and say *Enough you're mine again* but somehow couldn't bring himself to have it stop and kept thinking the *next* moment, until it was too late, done. With it went instantly that strange floating feeling of high pride. Shame plunged in.

"My wife's having her baby. I got to go see her through it. I'll be back in a couple hours. I love you."

Still the body under the covers and the frizzy crescent of hair peeking over the top edge of the blanket don't move. He is so sure she is not asleep he thinks, *I've killed her.* It's ridiculous, such a thing wouldn't kill her, it has nothing to do with death; but the thought paralyzes him from going forward to touch her and make her listen.

"Ruth. I got to go this once, it's my baby she's having and she's such a mutt I don't think she can do it by herself. Our first one came awfully hard. It's the least I owe her."

Perhaps this wasn't the best way to say it but he's trying to explain and her stillness frightens him and is beginning to make him sore.

"Ruth. Hey. If you don't say anything I'm not coming back. Ruth."

She lies there like some dead animal or somebody after a car accident when they put a tarpaulin over. He feels if he went over and lifted her she would come to life but he doesn't like being manipulated and is angry. He puts on his shirt and doesn't bother with a coat and necktie but it seems to take forever putting on his socks; the soles of his feet are tacky.

When the door closes the taste of seawater in her mouth is swallowed by the thick grief that mounts in her throat so fully she has to sit up to breathe. Tears slide from her blind eyes and salt the corners of her mouth as the empty walls of the room become real and then dense. It's like when she was fourteen and the whole world trees sun and stars would have swung into place if she could lose twenty pounds just twenty pounds what difference would it make to God Who guided every flower in the fields into shape? Only now it's not that she's asking she knows now that's superstitious all she wants is what she had a minute ago *him* in the room who when he was good could make her into a flower who could undress her of her flesh and turn her into sweet air Sweet Ruth he called her and if he had just said "sweet" talking to her she might have answered and he'd still be between these walls. No. She had known from the first night the wife would win they have the hooks and anyway she feels really lousy: a wave of wanting to throw up comes over her and washes away caring much about anything. She goes into the john and kneels on the tiles and watches the still oval of water in the toilet as if *it's* going to do something. She doesn't think after all she has it in her to throw up but stays there anyway because it pleases her, her bare arm resting on the icy porcelain lip, and grows used to the threat in her stomach, which doesn't dissolve, which stays with her, so in her faint state it comes to seem that this thing that's making her sick is some kind of friend.

He runs most of the way to the hospital. Up Summer one block, then down Youngquist, a street parallel to Weiser on the north, a street of brick tenements and leftover business places, shoe-repair nooks smelling secretively of leather, darkened candy stores, insurance agencies with photographs of tornado damage in the windows, real-estate offices lettered in gold, a bookshop. On an old-fashioned wooden bridge Youngquist Street crosses the railroad tracks, which slide between walls of blackened stone soft with soot like moss through the center of the city, threads of metal deep below in a darkness like a river, taking narrow sunset tints of pink from the neon lights of the dives along Railway Street. Music rises to him. The heavy boards of the old bridge, waxed black with locomotive smoke, rumble under his feet. Being a small-town boy, he always has a fear of being knifed in a city slum. He runs harder; the pavement widens, parking meters begin, and a new drive-in bank faces the antique Y.M.C.A. He cuts up the alley between the Y and a limestone church whose leaded windows show the reverse sides of Biblical scenes to the street. He can't make out what the figures are doing. From a high window in the Y.M.C.A. fall the clicks of a billiard game; otherwise the building's broad side is lifeless. Through the glass side door he sees an old Negro sweeping up in green aquarium light. Now the pulpy seeds of some tree are under his feet. Its tropically narrow leaves are black spikes against the dark yellow sky. Imported from China or Brazil or somewhere because it can live in soot and fumes. The St. Joseph's parking lot is a striped asphalt square whose sides are lined with such city trees; and above their tops, in this hard open space, he sees the moon, and for a second stops and communes with its mournful face, stops stark on his small scrabbled shadow on the asphalt to look up toward the heavenly stone that mirrors with metallic brightness the stone that has risen inside his hot skin. *Make it be all right,* he prays to it, and goes in the rear entrance.

He walks down a linoleum hall perfumed with ether to the front desk. "Angstrom," he tells the nun behind the typewriter. "I think my wife is here."

Her plump washerwoman's face is rimmed like a cupcake with scalloped linen. She surveys her cards and says "Yes" and smiles. Her little wire spectacles perch way out from her eyes on the pads of fat at the top of her cheeks. "You may wait over there." She points with a pink ball-point pen. Her other hand rests, beside the typewriter, on a string of black beads the size of the necklace of beads carved in Java he once got Janice for Christmas. He stands there staring, expecting to hear her say, *She's been here hours, where were you?* He can't believe she'll just accept him. As he stares, her nerveless white hand, that has never seen the sun, slides the black necklace off the desktop into her lap.

Two other men are already established in the waiting end of the room. This is the front entrance hall; people drift in and out. Rabbit sits down on an imitation leather chair with chrome arms and from this touch of metal and the furtive clicking quiet gets the idea he's in a police station and these other two men are the cops who made the arrest. It seems they ignore him pointedly. In his nervousness he plucks a magazine from the table. It's a Catholic magazine the size of the *Reader's Digest*. He tries to read a story about a lawyer in England who becomes so interested in how legally un*fair* it was for Henry VIII to confiscate the property of the monasteries that he becomes a Roman Catholic convert and eventually a monk. The two men whisper together; one maybe is the other's father. The younger one keeps kneading his hands together and nodding to what the older man whispers.

Eccles comes in, blinking and looking scrawny in his collar. He greets the sister behind the desk by name, Sister Bernard. Rabbit stands up on ankles of air and Eccles comes over with that familiar frown in his eyebrows made harsh by the hospital light. His forehead is etched in purple. He's had a haircut that day; as he turns his skull, the shaved planes above his ears shine like the blue throat feathers of a pigeon.

Rabbit asks, "Does she know I'm here?" He wouldn't have predicted that he would whisper too. He hates the panicked choke in his voice.

"I'll see that she's told if she's still conscious," Eccles says in a loud voice that makes the whispering men look up. He goes over to Sister Bernard. The nun seems happy to chat, and both laugh, Eccles in the startled guffaw Rabbit knows well and Sister Bernard with a pure and girlish fat woman's fluting that springs from her throat slightly retracted, curbed by the frame of stiff frills around her face. When Eccles moves away she lifts the phone by her skirted elbow.

Eccles comes back and looks him in the face, sighs, and offers him a cigarette. The effect is somehow of a wafer of repentance and Rabbit accepts. The first drag, after so many clean months, unhinges his muscles and he has to sit down. Eccles takes a hard chair near by and makes no effort at conversation. Rabbit can't think of much to say to him off the golf course and, shifting the smoking cigarette awkwardly to his left hand, pulls another magazine off the table, making sure it's unreligious, the *Saturday Evening Post*. It opens to an article in which the author, who from the photograph looks Italian, tells how he took his wife and four children *and* mother-in-law on a three-week camping trip to the Canadian Rockies that only cost them $120 not counting the initial investment of a Piper Cub. His mind can't keep with the words but keeps skidding up and branching away and flowering into little soft visions of Janice screaming, of the baby's head blooming out of blood, of the wicked ridged blue light Janice must be looking into if she's conscious, *if she's conscious* Eccles said, of the surgeon's red rubber hands and gauze face and Janice's babyish black nostrils widening to take in the antiseptic smell he smells, the smell running everywhere along the whitewashed walls, of being washed, washed, blood washed, retching washed until every surface smells like the inside of a bucket but it will never come clean because we will always fill it up again with our filth. A damp warm cloth seems wrapped around his heart. He is certain that as a consequence of his sin Janice or the baby will die. His sin a conglomerate of flight, cruelty, obscenity, and conceit; a black clot embodied in the entrails of the birth. Though his bowels twist with the will to dismiss this clot, to retract, to turn back and undo, he does not turn to the priest beside him, but instead reads the same sentence about delicious fried trout again and again.

On the extreme edge of his tree of fear Eccles perches, black bird, flipping the pages of magazines and making frowning faces to himself. He seems unreal to Rabbit, everything seems unreal that is outside of his sensations. His palms tingle; a strange impression of pressure darts over his body, seizing now his legs, now the base of his neck. His armpits itch the way they used to when he was little and late for school, running up Jackson Road.

"Where's her parents?" he asks Eccles.

Eccles looks surprised. "I don't know. I'll ask the sister." He moves to get up.

"No no, sit still for Chrissake." Eccles' acting like he half-owns the place annoys him. Harry wants to be unnoticed;

Eccles makes noise. He rattles the magazines so it sounds like he's tearing orange crates apart, and flips cigarettes around like a juggler.

A woman in white, not a nun, comes into the waiting-room and asks Sister Bernard, "Did I leave a can of furniture polish in here? I can't find it anywhere. A green can, with one of those pushy things on top that makes it spritz."

"No, dear."

She looks for it and goes out and after a minute comes back and announces, "Well that's the mystery of the world."

To the distant music of pans, wagons, and doors, one day turns through midnight into another. Sister Bernard is relieved by another nun, a very old one, dressed in dark blue. As if in her climb toward holiness she got stalled in the sky. The two whispering men go to the desk, talk, and leave, their crisis unresolved. Eccles and he are left alone. Rabbit strains his ears to catch the cry of his child somewhere deep in the hushed hospital maze. Often he thinks he hears it; the scrape of a shoe, a dog in the street, a nurse giggling—any of these are enough to fool him. He does not expect the fruit of Janice's pain to make a very human noise. His idea grows, that it will be a monster, a monster of his making. The thrust whereby it was conceived becomes confused in his mind with the perverted entry a few hours ago he made into Ruth. Momentarily drained of lust, he stares at the remembered contortions to which it has driven him. His life seems a sequence of grotesque poses assumed to no purpose, a magic dance empty of belief. *There is no God; Janice can die:* the two thoughts come at once, in one slow wave. He feels underwater, caught in chains of transparent slime, ghosts of the urgent ejaculations he has spat into the mild bodies of women. His fingers on his knees pick at persistent threads.

Mary Ann. Tired and stiff and lazily tough after a game he would find her hanging on the front steps under the school motto and they would walk across mulching wet leaves through white November fog to his father's car and drive to get the heater warmed and park. Her body a branched tree of warm nests yet always this touch of timidity. As if she wasn't sure but he was much bigger, a winner. He came to her as a winner and that's the feeling he's missed since. In the same way she was the best of them all because she was the one he brought most to, so tired. Sometimes the shouting glare of the gym would darken behind his sweat-burned eyes into a shad-owed anticipation of the careful touchings that would come under the padded gray car roof and once there the bright tri-umph of the past game flashed across her quiet skin streaked with the shadows of rain on the windshield. So that the two kinds of triumph were united in his mind. She married when he was in the Army; a P.S. in a letter from his mother shoved him out from shore. That day he was launched.

But he feels joy now; cramped from sitting on the eroded chrome-armed chair sick with cigarettes he feels joy in re-membering his girl; the water of his heart has been poured into a thin vase of joy that Eccles' voice jars and breaks.

"Well I've read this article by Jackie Jensen all the way to the end and I don't know what he said," Eccles says.

"Huh?"

"This piece by Jackie Jensen on why he wants to quit base-ball. As far as I can tell the problems of being a baseball player are the same as those of the ministry."

"Say, don't you want to go home? What time is it?"

"Around two. I'd like to stay, if I may."

"I won't run off if that's what you're afraid of."

Eccles laughs and keeps sitting there. Harry's first impres-sion of him had been tenacity and now all the intervening companionship has been erased and it's gone back to that.

Harry tells him, "When she had Nelson the poor kid was at it for twelve hours."

Eccles says, "The second child is usually easier," and looks at his watch. "It hasn't quite been six hours."

Events create events. Mrs. Springer passes through from the privileged room where she has been waiting and stiffly nods at Eccles; seeing Harry in the corner of her eye makes her stumble on her sore legs and tumbledown saddle shoes.

Eccles gets up and goes with her through the door to the outside. After a while the two of them come back in along with
Mr. Springer, who wears a tiny-knotted necktie and a laun-
dry-fresh shirt. His little sandy mustache has been trimmed
so often his upper lip has withered gray under it. He says,
"Hello, Harry."

This acknowledgment from her husband, despite some
talking-to they've probably had from Eccles, goads the fat
nag into turning on Harry and telling him, "If you're sitting
there like a buzzard young man hoping she's going to die, you
might as well go back to where you've been living because
she's doing fine without you and has been all along."

The two men hustle her away while the old nun peers with
a quaint smile across her desk, deaf? Mrs. Springer's attack,
though it ached to hurt him, is the first thing anybody has
said to Harry since this began that seems to fit the enormity
of the event going on somewhere behind the screen of hospital soap-smell. Until her words he felt alone on a dead planet
encircling the great gaseous sun of Janice's labor; her cry,
though a cry of hate, pierced his solitude. The dreadful
thought of Janice's death: hearing it voiced aloud has
halved its weight. That strange scent of death Janice breathed:
Mrs. Springer also smelled it, and this sharing seems the most
precious connection he has with anybody in the world.

Mr. Springer returns and passes through to the outside, be-
stowing upon his son-in-law a painfully complex smile, com-
pounded of a wish to apologize for his wife (we're both men;
I know), a wish to keep distant (nevertheless you've behaved
unforgivably; don't touch me), and the car salesman's mechanical reflex of politeness. Harry thinks, *You crumb;* hurls
the thought at the slammed door. *You slave.* Where is everybody going? Where are they coming from? Why can't anybody rest? Eccles comes back and feeds him another cigarette and goes away again. Smoking it makes the floor of his
stomach tremble. His throat feels like it does when you wake
up after sleeping all night with your mouth open. His own
bad breath brushes his nostrils. A doctor with a barrel chest

and unimaginably soft small hands, held curled in front of the pouch of his smock, comes into the anteroom uncertainly. He asks Harry, "Mr. Angstrom? I'm Dr. Crowe." Harry has never met him; Janice used another obstetrician for the first baby and after her hard time her father made her switch to this one. Janice used to visit him once a month and bring home tales of how gentle he was, how wonderfully soft his hands were, how he seemed to know exactly what it was like to be a pregnant woman.

"How—?"

"Congratulations. You have a beautiful little daughter."

He offers his hand so hastily Harry has only time to half-rise, and so absorbs the news in a crouching position. The scrubbed pink of the doctor's face—his sterile mask is unknotted and hangs from one ear, exposing pallid beefy lips—becomes enmeshed in the process of trying to give shape and tint to the unexpected word "daughter."

"I do? It's O.K.?"

"Seven pounds ten ounces. Your wife was conscious throughout and held the baby for a minute after delivery."

"Really? She held it? Was it—did she have a hard time?"

"No-o. It was normal. In the beginning she seemed tense, but it was normal."

"That's wonderful. Thank you. Good grief, thank you."

Crowe stands there smiling uneasily. Coming up from the pit of creation, he stammers in the open air. Strange: in these last hours he has been closer to Janice than Harry ever was, has been grubbing with his hands in her roots, riding her body like an earthquake, yet he has brought back nothing to confide, no curse, no blessing. Harry dreads that the doctor's eyes will release with thunder the mystery they have absorbed; but Crowe's gaze contains no wrath. Not even a reprimand. He seems to see Harry as just another in the parade of more or less dutiful husbands whose brainlessly sown seed he spends his life trying to reap.

Harry asks, "Can I see her?"

"Who?"

Who? That "her" is a forked word now startles him. The world is thickening. "My my wife."

"Of course, surely." Crowe seems in his mild way puzzled that Harry asks for permission. He must know the facts, yet seems unaware of the gap of guilt between Harry and humanity. "I thought you might mean the baby. I'd rather you waited until visiting hours tomorrow for that; there's not a nurse to show her right now. But your wife is conscious, as I say. We've given her some Equanil. That's just a tranquillizer. Meprobamate. Tell me"—he moves closer gently, pink skin and clean cloth—"is it all right if her mother sees her for a moment? She's been on our necks all night." He's asking *him*, him, the runner, the fornicator, the monster. He must be blind. Or maybe just being a father makes everyone forgive you, because after all it's the only sure thing we're here for.

"Sure. She can go in."

"Before or after you?"

Harry hesitates, and remembers the way Mrs. Springer came and visited him on his empty planet. "She can go in before."

"Thank you. Good. Then she can go home. We'll get her out in a minute. It'll be about ten minutes all told. Your wife is being prepared by the nurses."

"Swell." He sits down to show how docile he is and rises again. "Say, thanks by the way. Thank you very much. I don't see how you doctors do it."

Crowe shrugs. "She was a good girl."

"When we had the other kid I was scared silly. It took ages."

"Where did she have it?"

"At the other hospital. Homeopathic."

"Nn-*huh*." And the doctor, who had gone into the pit and brought back no thunder, emits a spark of spite at the thought of the rival hospital, and wags his scrubbed head sharply and, still wagging it, walks away.

Eccles comes into the room grinning like a schoolboy and Rabbit can't keep his attention on his silly face. He suggests thanksgiving and Rabbit bows his head blankly into his friend's silence. Each heartbeat seems to flatten against a wide white wall. When he looks up, objects seem infinitely solid and somehow tip, seem so full they are about to leap. His real happiness is a ladder from whose top rung he keeps trying to jump still higher, because he knows he should.

Crowe's phrase about nurses "preparing" Janice has a weird May Queen sound. When they lead him to her room he expects to find her with ribbons in her hair and paper flowers twined into the bedposts. But it's just old Janice, lying between two smooth sheets on a high metal bed. She turns her face and says, "Well look who it isn't."

"Hey," he says, and goes over to kiss her, intending it gently. He bends as you would bend to a glass flower. Her mouth swims in the sweet stink of ether. To his surprise her arms come out from the sheets and she puts them around his head and presses his face down into her soft happy swimming mouth. "Hey take it easy," he says.

"I have no legs," she says, "it's the funniest feeling." Her hair is drawn tight against her skull in a sanitary knot and she has no makeup on. Her small skull is dark against the pillow.

"No legs?" He looks down and there they are under the sheets, stretched out flat in a motionless V.

"They gave me a spinal or whatever at the end and I didn't feel anything. I was lying there hearing them say push and the next thing here's this teeny flubbly *baby* with this big moon face looking cross at me. I told Mother it looks like you and she didn't want to hear it."

"She gave me hell out there."

"I wish they hadn't let her in. I didn't want to see her. I wanted to see *you*."

"Did you, God. Why, baby? After I've been so crummy."

"No you haven't. They told me you were here and all the while I was thinking then it was your baby and it was like I was having *you*. I'm so full of ether it's just like I'm floating; without any legs. I could just talk and talk." She puts her hands on her stomach and closes her eyes and smiles. "I'm really quite drunk. See, I'm flat."

"Now you can wear your bathing suit," he says, smiling and entering the drift of her ether-talk, feeling himself as if he has no legs and is floating on his back on a great sea of cleanness light as a bubble amid the starched sheets and germless surfaces before dawn. Fear and regret are dissolved, and gratitude is blown so large it has no cutting edge. "The doctor said you were a good girl."

"Well isn't that silly; I wasn't. I was horrible. I cried and screamed and told him to keep his hands to himself. Though the thing I minded worst was when this horrible old nun shaved me with a dry razor."

"Poor Janice."

"No it was wonderful. I tried to count her toes but I was so dizzy I couldn't so I counted her eyes. Two. Did we want a girl? Say we did."

"I did." He discovers this is true, though the words discover the desire.

"Now I'll have somebody to side with me against you and Nelson."

"How is Nelson?"

"Oh. Every day, 'Daddy home day?' until I could belt him, the poor saint. Don't make me talk about it, it's too depressing."

"Oh, damn," he says, and his own tears, that it seemed didn't exist, sting the bridge of his nose. "I can't believe it was me. I don't know why I left."

"Vnnn." She sinks deeper into the pillow as a lush grin spreads her cheeks apart. "I had a little baby."

"It's terrific."

"You're lovely. You look so tall." She says this with her eyes shut, and when she opens them, they brim with an inebriated idea; he has never seen them sparkle so. She whispers, "Harry. The girl in the other bed in here went home today so why don't you sneak around when you go and come in the window and we can lie awake all night and tell each other stories? Just like you've come back from the Army or somewhere. Did you make love to lots of other women?"

"Hey I think you ought to go to sleep now."

"It's all right, now you'll make better love to me." She giggles and tries to move in the bed. "No I didn't mean that, you're a good lover you've given me a baby."

"It seems to me you're pretty sexy for somebody in your shape."

"That's how you feel," she says. "I'd invite you into bed with me but the bed's so narrow. Ooh."

"What?"

"I just got this terrible thirst for orangeade."

"Aren't you funny?"

"*You're* funny. Oh that baby looked so *cross*."

A nun fills the doorway with her wings. "Mr. Angstrom. Time."

"Come kiss," Janice says. She touches his face as he bends to inhale her ether again; her mouth is a warm cloud that suddenly splits and her teeth pinch his lower lip. "Don't leave," she says.

"Just for now. I'll be back tomorrow."

"Love you."

"Listen. I love *you*."

Waiting for him in the anteroom, Eccles asks, "How was she?"

"Terrific."

"Are you going to go back now, to uh, where you were?"

"No," Rabbit answers, horrified, "for Heaven's sake. I can't."

"Well, then, would you like to come home with me?"

"Look, you've done more than enough. I can go to my parents' place."

"It's late to get them up."

"No, really, I couldn't put you to the trouble." He has already made up his mind to accept. Every bone in his body feels slack.

"It's no trouble; I'm not asking you to live with us," Eccles says. The long night is baring his nerves. "We have *scads* of room."

"O.K. O.K. Good. Thanks."

They drive back to Mt. Judge along the familiar highway. At this hour it is empty even of trucks. Though this is the pit of the night the sky is a strangely relenting black, really a gray. Harry sits wordless staring through the windshield, rigid in body, rigid in spirit. The curving highway seems a wide straight road that has opened up in front of him. There is nothing he wants to do but go down it.

The rectory is asleep. The front hall smells like a closet. Eccles takes him upstairs to a room that has tassels on the bedspread. He uses the bathroom stealthily and in underclothes curls up between the rustling clean sheets, making the smallest possible volume of himself. Thus curled near one edge, he draws backward into sleep like a turtle drawing into his shell. Sleep this night is not a dark haunted domain the mind must consciously set itself to invade, but a cave inside himself, into which he shrinks while the claws of the bear rattle like rain outside.

Sunshine, the old clown, rims the room. Two pink chairs flank the gauze-filled window buttered with light that smears a writing desk furry with envelope-ends. Above the desk is a picture of a lady in pink stepping toward you. A woman's voice is tapping the door. "Mr. Angstrom. Mr. Angstrom."

"Yeah. Hi," he calls, hoarse.

"It's twelve-twenty. Jack told me to tell you the visiting hours at the hospital are one to three." He recognizes Eccles' wife's crisp little twitty tone, like she was adding, *And what the hell are you doing in my house anyway?*

"Yeah. O.K. I'll be right out." He puts on the cocoa-colored trousers he wore last night and, displeased by the sense of these things being dirty, he carries his shoes and socks and shirt into the bathroom with him, postponing putting them against his skin, giving them another minute to air. Still foggy despite splashing water all around, he carries them out of the bathroom and goes downstairs in bare feet and a T-shirt.

Eccles' little wife is in her big kitchen, wearing khaki shorts this time and sandals and painted toenails. "How did you sleep?" she asks from behind the refrigerator door.

"Like death. Not a dream or anything."

"It's the effect of a clear conscience," she says, and puts a glass of orange juice on the table with a smart click. He imagines that seeing how he's dressed, with just the T-shirt over his chest, makes her look away quickly.

"Hey don't go to any bother. I'll get something in Brewer."

"I won't give you eggs or anything. Do you like Cheerios?"

"Love 'em."

"All right."

The orange juice burns away some of the fuzz in his mouth. He watches the backs of her legs; the white tendons behind her knees jump as she assembles things at the counter. "How's Freud?" he asks her. He knows this could be bad, because if he brings back that afternoon he'll bring back how he nicked her fanny; but he has this ridiculous feeling with Mrs. Eccles, that he's in charge and can't make mistakes.

She turns with her tongue against her side teeth, making her mouth lopsided and thoughtful, and looks at him levelly. He smiles; her expression is that of a high-school tootsie who wants to seem to know more than she's telling. "He's the same. Do you want milk or cream on the Cheerios?"

"Milk. Cream is too sticky. Where is everybody?"

"Jack's at the church, probably playing ping-pong with one of his delinquent boys. Joyce and Bonnie are asleep, Heaven knows why. They kept wanting to look at the naughty man in the guest room all morning. It took real love to keep them out."

"Who told them I was a naughty man?"

"Jack did. He said to them at breakfast, 'I brought home a naughty man last night who's going to stop being naughty.' The children have names for all of Jack's problems—you're the Naughty Man, Mr. Carson, an alcoholic, is the Silly Man,

Mrs. MacMillan is the Woman Who Calls Up in the Night. Then there's the Droopsy Lady, Mr. Hearing-Aid, Mrs. Side-Door, and Happy Beans. Happy Beans is just about the least happy man you ever wanted to see, but once he brought the children some of those celluloid capsules with a weight in them, so they jiggle around. Ever since that he's Happy Beans."

Rabbit laughs, and Lucy, having delivered the Cheerios—too much milk; he is used to living with Ruth, who let him pour his own milk; he likes just enough to take away the dryness, so that the milk and cereal come out even—chats on gaily. "The worst thing that happened, in connection with some committee or other Jack was talking with one of the vestry-men over the phone and had the idea that it would buck this poor soul up to be given a church job so he said, 'Why not make Happy Beans the chairman of something or other?' Well, the man on the other end of the line said 'Happy Who?' and Jack realized what he'd said but instead of just sluffing it off like anybody else would have, Jack told the whole story about the children calling him Happy Beans and of course this stuffy old vestryman didn't think it was at all that funny. He was a friend, you see, of Happy Beans; they weren't exactly business associates but often had lunch to-gether over in Brewer. That's the thing about Jack; he always tells people too much. Now this vestryman is probably telling everybody how the rector pokes fun of this poor miserable Happy Beans."

He laughs again. His coffee comes, in a thin shallow cup monogrammed in gold, and Lucy sits down opposite him at the table with a cup of her own. "He said I'm going to stop being naughty," Rabbit says.

"Yes. He's overjoyed. He went out of here virtually singing. It's the first constructive thing he thinks he's done since he came to Mt. Judge."

Rabbit yawns. "Well I don't know what he did."

"I don't either," she says, "but to hear him talk the whole thing was on his shoulders."

This suggestion that he's been managed rubs him the wrong way. He feels his smile creak. "Really? Did he talk about it?"

"Oh, all the time. He's very fond of you. I don't know why."

"I'm just lovable."

"That's what I keep hearing. You have poor old Mrs. Smith wrapped around your little finger. She thinks you're marvelous."

"And you don't see it?"

"Maybe I'm not old enough. Maybe if I were seventy-three." She lifts the cup to her face and tilts it and the freckles on her narrow white nose sharpen in proximity to the steaming brown coffee. She is a naughty girl. Yes, it's very clear, a naughty-girl type. She sets the cup down and looks at him with round eyes, and the triangular white space between her eyebrows seems to look and mock too. "Well tell me. How does it feel? To be a new man. Jack's always hoping I'll reform and I want to know what to expect. Are you 'born anew'?"

"Oh, I feel about the same."

"You don't act the same."

He grunts "Well" and shifts in his chair. Why does he feel so awkward? She is trying to make him feel foolish and sissy, just because he's going to go back to his wife. It's quite true, he doesn't act the same; he doesn't feel the same with her, either; he's lost the nimbleness that led him so lightly into tapping her backside that day. He tells her, "Last night driving home I got this feeling of a straight road ahead of me; before that I was sort of in the bushes and it didn't matter which way I went."

Her small face above the coffee cup held in two hands like a soup bowl is perfectly tense with delight; he expects her to laugh and instead she smiles silently. He thinks, *She wants me.*

Then he remembers Janice with her legs paralyzed talking about toes and love and orangeade and this perhaps seals shut something in his face, for Lucy Eccles turns her head impatiently and says, "Well you better get going down that nice straight road. It's twenty of one."

"How long does it take to walk to the bus stop?"

"Not long. I'd drive you to the hospital if it weren't for the children." She listens to the stairs. "Speak of the devil: here comes one."

As he's pulling on his socks the older girl sneaks into the kitchen, dressed just in underpants.

"Joyce." Her mother halts halfway to the sink with the empty cups. "You get right back up to bed."

"Hello, Joyce," Rabbit says. "Did you come down to see the naughty man?"

Joyce stares and hugs the wall with her shoulder blades. Her long golden stomach protrudes thoughtfully.

"Joyce," Lucy says. "Didn't you hear me?"

"Why doesn't he have his shirt on?" the child asks distinctly.

"I don't know," her mother says. "I suppose he thinks he has a nice chest."

"I have a T-shirt on," he protests. It's as if neither of them see it.

"Is that his boo-zim?" Joyce asks.

"No, darling: only ladies have bosoms. We've been through that."

"Hell, if it makes everybody nervous," Rabbit says, and puts on his shirt. It's rumpled and the inside of the collar is gray; he put it on clean to go to the Club Castanet. He has no coat, he left Ruth too hastily. "O.K.," he says, tucking in the tail. "Thank you very much."

"You're very welcome," Lucy says. "Be good now." The two girls walk with him down the hall. Lucy's white legs mix in pallor with the child's naked chest. Little Joyce keeps staring up at him. He wonders what she's puzzling about. Children and dogs sense the invisible. He tries to calculate how much sarcasm was in that "Be good now" and what it meant, if anything. He wishes she could drive him; he wants, he really wants, to get into a car with her. Not so much to do anything as just feel how things set. His reluctance to leave pulls the air between them taut.

They stand at the door, he and Eccles' baby-skinned wife and under them Joyce's face looking up with her father's wide lips and arched eyebrows and under them all Lucy's painted toenails, tiny scarlet shells in a row on the carpet. He strums the air with a vague disclaimer and puts his hand on the hard doorknob. The thought that only ladies have bosoms haunts him foolishly. He looks up from the toenails to Joyce's watching face and from there to her mother's bosom, two pointed bumps under a buttoned blouse that shows through its airy summer weave the white shadow of the bra. When his eyes reach Lucy's an amazing thing enters the silence. The woman winks. Quick as light: maybe he imagined it. He turns the knob and retreats down the sunny walk with a murmur in his chest as if a string in there had snapped.

At the hospital they say Janice has the baby with her for a moment and would he please wait? He is sitting in the chair with chrome arms leafing through a *Woman's Day* backwards when a tall woman with backswept gray hair and somehow silver, finely wrinkled skin comes in and looks so familiar he stares. She sees this and has to speak; he feels she would have preferred to ignore him. Who is she? Her familiarity has touched him across a great distance. She looks into his face reluctantly and tells him, "You're an old student of Marty's. I'm Harriet Tothero. We had you to dinner once. I can almost think of your name."

Yes, of course, but it wasn't from that dinner he remembers her, it was from noticing her on the streets. The students at Mt. Judge High knew, most of them, that Tothero played around, and his wife appeared to their innocent eyes wreathed in dark flame, a walking martyr, a breathing shadow of sin. It was less pity than morbid fascination that singled her out; Tothero was himself such a clown and windbag, such a speechifier, that the stain of his own actions slid from him, oil off a duck. It was the tall, silver, serious figure of his wife that accumulated the charge of his wrongdoing, and released it to their young minds with an electrical shock that snapped their eyes away from the sight of her, in fear as much as embarrassment. Harry stands up, surprised to feel that the world she walks in is his world now. "I'm Harry Angstrom," he says.

"Yes, that's your name. He was so proud of you. He often talked to me about you. Even recently."

Recently. What did he tell her? Does she know about him? Does she blame him? Her long schoolmarmish face, as always, keeps its secrets in. "I've heard that he was sick."

"Yes, he is, Harry. Quite sick. He's had two strokes, one since he came into the hospital."

"He's here?"

"Yes. Would you like to visit him? I know it would make him very happy. For just a moment. He's had very few visitors; I suppose that's the tragedy of teaching school. You remember so many and so few remember you."

"I'd like to see him, sure."

"Come with me, then." As they walk down the halls she says, "I'm afraid you'll find him much changed." He doesn't take this in fully; he is concentrating on her skin, trying to see if it *does* look like a lot of little lizard skins sewed together. Just her hands and neck show.

Tothero is in a room alone. Like waiting presences white curtains hang expectantly around the head of his bed. Green plants on the windowsills exhale oxygen. Canted panes of glass lift the smells of summer into the room. Footsteps crunch on the gravel below.

"Dear, I've brought you someone. He was waiting outside in the most miraculous way."

"Hello, Mr. Tothero. My wife's had her baby." He speaks these words and goes toward the bed with blank momentum; the sight of the old man lying there shrunken, his tongue sliding in his lopsided mouth, has stunned him. Tothero's face, spotted with white stubble, is yellow in the pillows, and his thin wrists stick out from candy-striped pajama sleeves beside the shallow lump of his body. Rabbit offers his hand.

"He can't lift his arms, Harry," Mrs. Tothero says. "He is helpless. But talk to him. He can see and hear." Her sweet patient enunciation has a singing quality that is sinister, as if she is humming to herself.

Since he has extended his hand, Harry presses it down on the back of one of Tothero's. For all its dryness, the hand, under a faint scratchy fleece, is warm, and to Harry's horror moves, revolves stubbornly, so the palm is presented upward to Harry's touch. Harry takes his fingers back and sinks into the bedside chair. His old coach's eyeballs shift with scattered quickness as he turns his head an inch toward the visitor. The flesh under them has been so scooped that they are weakly protrusive. *Talk*, he must talk. "It's a little girl. I want to thank you"—he speaks loudly—"for the help you gave in getting me and Janice back together again. You were very kind."

Tothero retracts his tongue and shifts his face to look at his wife. A muscle under his jaw jumps, his lips pucker, and his chin crinkles repeatedly, like a pulse, as he tries to say something. A few dragged vowels come out; Harry turns to see if Mrs. Tothero can decipher them, but to his surprise she is looking elsewhere. She is looking out the window, toward an empty green courtyard. Her face is like a photograph.

Is it that she doesn't care? If so, should he tell Tothero about Margaret? But there was nothing to say about Margaret that might make Tothero happy. "I'm straightened out now, Mr. Tothero, and I hope you're up and out of this bed soon."

Tothero's head turns back with an annoyed quickness, the mouth closed, the eyes in a half-squint, and for this moment he looks so coherent Harry thinks he will speak, that the pause is just his old disciplinarian's trick of holding silent until your attention is complete. But the pause stretches, inflates, as if, used for sixty years to space out words, it at last has taken on a cancerous life of its own and swallowed the words. Yet in the first moments of the silence a certain force flows forth, a human soul emits its invisible and scentless rays with urgency. Then the point in the eyes fades, the brown lids lift and expose pink jelly, the lips part, the tip of the tongue appears.

"I better go down and visit my wife," Harry shouts. "She just had the baby last night. It's a girl." He feels claustrophobic, as if he's inside Tothero's skull; when he stands up, he has the fear he will bump his head, though the white ceiling is yards away.

"Thank you very much, Harry. I know he's enjoyed seeing you," Mrs. Tothero says. Nevertheless from her tone he feels he's flunked a recitation. He walks down the hall springingly, dismissed. His health, his reformed life, make space, even the antiseptic space in the hospital corridors, delicious. Yet his visit with Janice is disappointing. Perhaps he is still choked by seeing poor Tothero stretched out as good as dead; perhaps out of ether Janice is choked by thinking of how he's treated her. She complains a lot about how much her stitches hurt, and when he tries to express his repentance again she seems to find it boring. The difficulty of pleasing someone begins to hem him in. She asks why he hasn't brought flowers. He had no time; he tells her how he spent the night and, sure enough, she asks him to describe Mrs. Eccles.

"About your height," he answers carefully. "Freckles."

"Her husband's been wonderful," she says. "He seems to love everybody."

"He's O.K.," Rabbit says. "He makes me nervous."

"Oh, everybody makes you nervous."

"No now that's not true. Marty Tothero never made me nervous. I just saw the poor old bastard, stretched out in a bed up the hall. He can't say a word or move his head more than an inch."

"He doesn't make you nervous but I do, is that right?"

"I didn't say that."

"Oh no. Ow. These damn stitches they feel like barbed

wire. I just make you so nervous you desert me for two months. Over two months."

"Well Jesus Janice. All you did was watch television and drink all the time. I mean I'm not saying I wasn't wrong, but it felt like I had to. You get the feeling you're in your coffin before they've taken your blood out. On that first night, when I got in the car in front of your parents' place, even then I might just as easy have gone down to get Nelson and driven it home. But when I let the brake out—" Her face goes into that bored look again. Her head switches from side to side, as if to keep flies from setting. He says, "Shit."

This gets her. She says, "I see your language hasn't been improved by living with that prostitute."

"She wasn't a prostitute, exactly. She just kind of slept around. I think there are a lot of girls like her around. I mean if you're going to call everybody who isn't married a prostitute—"

"Where are you going to stay now? Until I get out of the hospital."

"I thought Nelson and me would move into our apartment."

"I'm not sure you can. We didn't pay any rent on it for two months."

"Huh? You didn't?"

"Well my *good*ness, Harry. You expect a lot. You expect Daddy to keep paying rent? *I* didn't have any money."

"Well did the landlord call? What happened to our furniture? Did he put it out on the street?"

"I don't know."

"You don't *know?* Well what *do* you know? What have you been doing all this time? Sleeping?"

"I was carrying your baby."

"Well hell, I didn't know you have to keep your whole mind on *that* all the time. The trouble with you, kid, is you just don't give a damn. Really."

"Well listen to you."

He does listen to what he's been sounding like, remembers

how he felt last night, and after a pause tries to begin all over
again. "Hey," he says, "I love you."

"I love you," she says. "Do you have a quarter?"

"I guess. I'll look. What do you want it for?"

"If you put a quarter in that"—she points toward a small
television set on a high stand, so patients can see it over the
foot of their beds—"it'll play for an hour. There's a silly program on at two that Mother and I got to watching when I
was home."

So for thirty minutes he sits by her bed watching some
crew-cut M.C. tease a lot of elderly women from Akron,
Ohio, and Oakland, California. The idea is all these women
have tragedies they tell about and then get money according to how much applause there is, but by the time the M.C.
gets done delivering commercials and kidding them about
their grandchildren and their girlish hairdos there isn't much
room for tragedy left. Rabbit keeps thinking that the M.C.,
who has that way of a Jew of pronouncing very distinctly, no
matter how fast the words, is going to start plugging the
MagiPeel Peeler but the product doesn't seem to have hit the
big time yet. It isn't too bad a show; a pair of peroxide twins
with twitchy tails push the women around to various micro-
phones and booths and applause areas. It even makes for a
kind of peace; he and Janice hold hands. The bed is almost as
high as his shoulders when he sits down, and he enjoys being
in this strange relation to a woman—as if he's carrying her
on his shoulder but without the weight. He cranks her bed up
and pours her a drink of water and these small services suit
some need he has. The program isn't over when a nurse comes
and says, "Mr. Angstrom, if you want to see your baby the
nurse is holding them to the window now."

He goes down the hall after her; her square hips swing
under the starched white. From just the thickness of her neck
he figures her for a good solid piece: haunchy. Big above the
knee. He does like women big above the knee. Also he's
worrying about what a woman from Springfield, Illinois,
was going to say happened after her son's dreadful auto-

mobile accident, in which he lost an arm. So he's quite un-
prepared when the nurse in the baby room, where little
bundles with heads like oranges lie in rows of supermarket
baskets, some tilted, brings his girl to the viewing window,
and it's like a damper being slid back in his chest. A sudden
stiff draft freezes his breath. People are always saying how
ugly new babies are, maybe this is the reason for the amazement. The baby is held by the nurse so her profile is sharp
red against the buttoned white bosom of the uniform. The
folds around the nostril, worked out on such a small scale,
seem miraculously precise; the tiny stitchless seam of the
closed eyelid runs diagonally a great length, as if the eye,
when it is opened, will be huge and see everything and know
everything. In the suggestion of pressure behind the tranquil
lid and in the tilt of the protruding upper lip he reads a de-
lightful hint of disdain. She knows she's good. What he never
expected, he can feel she's feminine, feels something both
delicate and enduring in the arc of the long pink cranium,
furred in bands with black licked swatches. Nelson's head
had been full of lumps and frightening blue veins and bald
except at the base of the neck. Rabbit looks down through
the glass with a timidity in the very act of seeing, as if rough
looking will smash the fine machinery of this sudden life.

The smile of the nurse, foreshortened and flickering cutely
between his eyes and the baby's nose, reassures him that he is
the father. Her painted lips wrinkle a question through the
glass, and he calls, "O.K., yeah," and gestures, throwing his
hands, fingers splayed, to the height of his ears. "She's great,"
he adds, in a forced voice meant to carry through glass, but
the nurse is already returning his daughter to her supermarket
basket. Rabbit turns the wrong way, into the sleepless face of
the father next in line, and laughs outright. He goes back to
Janice with the wind swirling through him and fire the red
of the baby's skin blazing. In the soap-scented hall he gets the
idea: they should call the girl June. This is June, she was
born in June. He's never known a June. It will please Janice
because of the J. But Janice has been thinking about names

too and wants to call her after her mother. Harry never thinks of Mrs. Springer as having a first name. It is Rebecca. His warm gust of pride in his child turns Janice soft in the bed, and he in turn is sweetened by her daughterly wish; it worries him at times that she does not seem to love her mother. They compromise: Rebecca June Angstrom.

The straight path is made smooth. Mr. Springer had been paying rent on the apartment all along, it turns out; he is a personal friend of the landlord and had arranged it without troubling his daughter. He always had a hunch Harry would come back but didn't want to advertise it in case he was wrong. Harry and Nelson move in and start housekeeping. Rabbit has a gift for housekeeping; the sensation of dust sucking into the vacuum cleaner, down the cloth hose, into a paper bag that when it is full of compact gray fluff will pop the cover of the Electrolux like a gentleman tipping his hat, pleases him. He was not entirely miscast as a barker for the MagiPeel Peeler; he has an instinctive taste for the small appliances of civilization, the little grinders and slicers and holders. Perhaps the oldest child should always be a girl; Mim, coming after him to the Angstrom household, was never exposed direct to the bright heart of the kitchen, but was always in his shadow with the housework, and sullen about assuming her share, which eventually became the greater share, because he was, after all, a boy. He supposes it will be the same with Nelson and Rebecca.

Nelson is a help. Closer to three now than two, the child can carry out orders that do not take him out of the room, understands that his toys belong in the bushel basket, and feels the happiness in cleanness, order, and light. The June breeze sighs at the screens of the long-closed windows. The sun dots the mesh with hundreds of sparkling T's and L's. Beyond the windows Wilbur Street falls away. The flat tin-and-tar roofs of their neighbors, weathered into gentle corrugations, glitter with mysterious twists of rubble, candy-bar wrappers and a pool of glass flakes, litter that must have fallen from the clouds or been brought by birds to this street in the sky, planted with television aerials and hooded chimneys the size of fire hydrants. There are three of these roofs on the down side, tipped like terraces for drainage, three broad dirty steps leading to a brink below which the better homes begin, the stucco and brick forts, rugged with porches and dormer windows and lightning rods, guarded by conifers, protected by treaties with banks and firms of lawyers. It was strange that a row of tenements had been set above them; they had been tricked by growth. But in a town built against a mountain, height was too common to be precious; above them all there was the primitive ridge, the dark slum of forest, separated from the decent part of town by a band of unpaved lanes, derelict farmhouses, a cemetery, and a few raw young developments. Wilbur Street was paved for a block past Rabbit's door, and then became a street of mud and gravel between two short rows of ranch-houses of alternating color erected in 1953 on scraped red earth that even now is unsteadily pinned by the blades of grass that speckle it, so that after a good rain the gutter-water flows orange down Wilbur Street. The land grows steeper still, and the woods begin.

Straight out from the windows Rabbit can look in the opposite direction across the town into the wide farm valley, with its golf course. He thinks, *My valley, my home.* The blemished green-papered walls, the scatter rugs whose corners keep turning under, the closet whose door bumps the television set, absent from his senses for months, have returned with unexpected force. Every corner locks against a remembered corner in his mind; every crevice, every irregularity in the paint clicks against a nick already in his brain. This adds another dimension of neatness to his housecleaning.

Under the sofa and chairs and behind doors and in the footspace under the kitchen cabinets he finds old fragments of toys that delight Nelson. The child has a perfect memory for his own possessions. "Mom-mom gay me dis." Holding up a plastic duck that had lost its wheels.

"She did?"

"Yop. Mom-mom did."

"Wasn't that nice of Mom-mom?"

"Yop."

"You know what?"

"What?"

"Mom-mom is Mommy's mommy!"

"Yop. Where Mommy?"

"At the hospital."

"At hop-pital? Come back Fi-day?"

"That's right. She'll come back Friday. Won't she be happy to see how clean we make everything?"

"Yop. Daddy at hop-pital?"

"No. Daddy wasn't at the hospital. Daddy was away."

"Daddy away"—the boy's eyes widen and his mouth drops open as he stares into the familiar concept of "away"; his voice deepens with the seriousness of it—"very, very *long*." His arms go out to measure the length, so far his fingers bend backward. It is as long as he can measure.

"But Daddy's not away now, is he?"

"Nope."

He takes Nelson with him in the car the day he goes to tell Mrs. Smith he has to quit working in her garden. Old man Springer has offered him a job in one of his lots. The rhododendron trees by the crunching driveway look dusty and barren with a few brown corsages still hanging to their branches. Mrs. Smith herself comes to the door. "Yes, yes," she croons, her brown face beaming.

"Mrs. Smith, this is my son Nelson."

"Yes, yes, how do you do, Nelson? You have your father's head." She pats the small head with a hand withered like a tobacco leaf. "Now let me think. Where did I put that jar of old candy? He can eat candy, can't he?"

"I guess a little but don't go looking for it."

"I will too, if I want to. The trouble with you, young man, you never gave me credit for any competence whatsoever." She totters off, plucking with one hand at the front of her dress and poking the other into the air before her, as if she's brushing away cobwebs.

While she's out of the room he and Nelson stand looking at the high ceiling of this parlor, at the tall windows with mullions as thin as chalk-lines, through whose panes, some of which are tinted lavender, they can see the pines and cypresses that guard the far rim of the estate. Paintings hang on the shining walls. One shows, in dark colors, a woman wrapped in a whipping strip of silk apparently having an argument, from the way her arms are flailing, with a big swan that just stands there pushing. On another wall there is a portrait of a young woman in a black gown sitting in a padded chair impatiently. Her face, though squarish, is fine-looking, with a triangular forehead caused by her hairdo. Round white arms curve into her lap. Rabbit moves a few steps closer to get a less oblique view. She has that short puffy little upper lip that is so good in a girl: the way it lifts to let a dab of dark come between her lips. There is this readiness about her all over. He feels that she's about to get out of the chair and step forward toward him with a frown on her triangular forehead. Mrs. Smith, returning with a crimson glass ball on a stem like a wineglass, sees where he's looking and says, "What I always minded was Why did he have to make me look so irritable? I didn't like him a whit and he knew it. A slick little Italian. Thought he knew about women. Here." She had crossed to Nelson with the candy glass. "You try one of these. They're old but good like a lot of old things in this world." She takes off the lid, a knobbed hemisphere of translucent red glass, and holds it waggling in her hand. Nelson looks over and Rabbit nods at him to go ahead and he chooses a piece wrapped in colored tinfoil.

"You won't like it," Rabbit tells him. "That's gonna have a cherry inside."

"Shoosh," Mrs. Smith says. "Let the boy have the one he wants." So the poor kid goes ahead and takes it, bewitched by the tinfoil.

"Mrs. Smith," Rabbit begins, "I don't know if Reverend

Eccles has told you, but my situation has kind of changed and I have to take another job. I won't be able to help around here any more. I'm sorry."

"Yes, yes," she says, alertly watching Nelson fumble at the tinfoil.

"I've really enjoyed it," he goes on. "It was sort of like Heaven, like that woman said."

"Oh that foolish woman Alma Foster," Mrs. Smith says. "With her lipstick half-way up to her nose. I'll never forget her, the dear soul. Not a brain in her body. Here, child. Give it to Mrs. Smith." She sets the dish down on a round marble table holding only an oriental vase full of peonies and takes the piece of candy from Nelson and with a frantic needling motion of her fingers works the paper off. The kid stands there staring up with an open mouth; she thrusts her hand down jerkily and pops the ball of chocolate between his lips. With a crease of satisfaction in one cheek she turns, drops the tinfoil on the table, and says to Rabbit, "Well, Harry. At least we brought the rhodies in."

"That's right. We did."

"It pleased *my* Harry, I know, wherever he is."

Nelson bites through to the startling syrup of the cherry and his mouth curls open in dismay; a dribble of brown creeps out one corner and his eyes dart around the immaculate palace room. Rabbit cups a hand at his side and the boy comes over and silently spits the mess into it, bits of chocolate shell and stringy warm syrup and the broken cherry.

Mrs. Smith sees none of this. Her eyes with their transparent irises of crazed crystal burn into Harry's as she says, "It's been a religious duty to me, to keep Horace's garden up."

"I'm sure you can find somebody else. Vacation's started; it'd be a perfect job for some high-school kid."

"No," she says, "no. I won't think about it. I won't be here next year to see Harry's rhodies come in again. You kept me alive, Harry; it's the truth; you did. All winter I was fighting the grave and then in April I looked out the window and here was this tall young man burning my old stalks and

√ I knew life hadn't left me. That's what you have, Harry: life. It's a strange gift and I don't know how we're supposed to use it but I know it's the only gift we get and it's a good one." Her crystal eyes have filmed with a liquid thicker than tears and she grabs his arms above his elbows with hard brown claws. "Fine strong young man," she murmurs, and her eyes come back into focus as she adds, "You have a proud son; take care."

She must mean he should be proud of his son and take care of him. He is moved by her embrace; he wants to respond and did moan "No" at her prediction of death. But his right hand is full of melting mashed candy, and he stands helpless and rigid hearing her quaver, "Good-by. I wish you well. I wish you well."

In the week that follows this blessing, he and Nelson are often happy. They go for walks around the town. One day they watch a softball game played on the high-school lot by men with dark creased faces like millworkers, dressed in gaudy felt-and-flannel uniforms, one team bearing the name of a fire hall in Brewer and the other the name of the Sunshine Athletic Association, the same uniforms, he guesses, that he saw hanging in the attic the time he slept in Tothero's bedroom. The number of spectators sitting on the dismantleable bleachers is no greater than the number of players. All around, behind the bleachers and the chicken-wire-and-pipe backstop, kids in sneakers scuffle and run and argue. He and Nelson watch a few innings, while the sun lowers into the trees. It floods Rabbit with an ancient, papery warmth, the oblique sun on his cheeks, the sparse inattentive crowd, the snarled pepper chatter, the spurts of dust on the yellow infield, the girls in shorts strolling past with chocolate popsicles. Brown adolescent legs thick at the ankle and smooth at the thigh. They know so much, at least their skins do. Boys their age scrawny sticks in dungarees and Keds arguing frantically if Williams was washed up or not. Mantle ten thousand times better. Williams ten million times better. He and Nelson share an orange soda bought from a man in a Boosters' Club apron who has established a bin in the shade. The smoke of dry ice leaking from the ice-cream section, the *ffp* of the cap being pulled from the orange. The artificial sweetness fills his heart. Nelson spills on his chest trying to get it to his lips.

Another day they go to the playground. Nelson acts frightened of the swings. Rabbit tells him to hold on and pushes very gently, from the front so the kid can see. Laughs, pleads, "Me out," begins to cry, "me out, me out, Da-dee." Dabbling in the sandbox gives Rabbit a small headache. Over at the pavilion the rubber thump of Roofball and the click of checkers call to his memory, and the forgotten smell of that narrow plastic ribbon you braid bracelets and whistle-chains out of and of glue and of the sweat on the handles on athletic equipment is blown down by a breeze laced with children's murmuring. He feels the truth: the thing that has left his life has left irrevocably; no search would recover it. No flight would reach it. It was here, beneath the town, in these smells and these voices, forever behind him. The fullness ends when we give Nature her ransom, when we make children for her. Then she is through with us, and we become, first inside, and then outside, junk. Flower stalks.

They visit Mom-mom Springer. The child is delighted; Nelson loves her, and this makes Rabbit like her. Though she tries to pick a fight with him he refuses to fight back, just admits everything; he was a crumb, a dope, he behaved terribly, he's lucky not to be in jail. Actually there's no real bite in her attack. Nelson is there for one thing, and for another she is relieved he has come back and is afraid of scaring him off. For a third, your wife's parents can't get at you the way your own can. They remain on the outside, no matter how hard they knock, and there's something relaxing and even comic about them. He and the old lady sit on the screened sunporch with iced tea; her bandaged legs are up on a stool and her little groans as she shifts her weight make him smile. It feels like one of those silly girls in high school you kind of liked without there ever being a question of love. Nelson and Billy Fosnacht are inside the house playing quietly. They're too quiet. Mrs. Springer wants to see what's happening but doesn't want to move her legs; in her torment she starts to complain about what a crude child little Billy Fosnacht is, and from this shifts over to the kid's mother. Mrs. Springer doesn't like her, doesn't trust her around the corner; it isn't just the sunglasses, though she thinks that's a ridiculous affectation; it's the girl's whole manner, the way she came cozying around to Janice just because it looked like juicy gossip. "Why, she came around here so much that I had more charge of Nelson than Janice did, with those two off to the movies every day like high-school girls that don't have the responsibility of being mothers." Now Rabbit knows from school that Peggy Fosnacht, then Peggy Gring, wears sunglasses because she is freakishly, humiliatingly wall-eyed. And Eccles has told him that her company was a great comfort to Janice during the trying period now past. But he does not make either of these objections; he listens contentedly, pleased to be united with Mrs. Springer, the two of them against the world. The cubes in the iced tea melt, making the beverage doubly bland; his mother-in-law's talk laves his ears like the swirling mutter of a brook. Lulled, he lets his lids lower and a smile creeps into his face; he sleeps badly at nights, alone, and drowses now on the grassy breadth of day, idly blissful, snug on the right side at last.

It is quite different at his own parents' home. He and Nelson go there once. His mother is angry about something; her anger hits his nostrils as soon as he's in the door, like the smell of age on everything. This house looks shabby and small after the Springers'. What ails her? He assumes she's always been on his side and tells her in a quick gust of confiding how terrific the Springers have been, how Mrs. Springer is really quite warmhearted and seems to have forgiven him everything, how Mr. Springer kept up the rent on their apartment and now has promised him a job selling cars in one of his lots. He owns four lots in Brewer and vicinity; Rabbit had no idea he was that much of an operator. He's really kind of a jerk but a successful jerk at least; at any rate he thinks he, Harry Angstrom, has got off pretty easily. His mother's hard arched nose and steamed spectacles glitter bitterly. Her disapproval nicks him whenever she turns from the sink. At first he thinks it's that he never got in touch with her but if that's so she should be getting less sore instead of more because he's in touch with her now. Then he thinks it's that she's disgusted he slept with Ruth, and committed adultery; she's getting religious as she gets older and probably thinks of him as around twelve years old anyway, but out of a clear sky she explodes that by asking abruptly, "And what's going to happen to this poor girl you lived with in ✓ Brewer?"

"Her? Oh, she can take care of herself. She didn't expect nothing." But he tastes his own saliva saying it. It makes his life seem cramped, that Ruth can be mentioned out of his mother's mouth.

Her mouth goes thin and she answers with a smug flirt of her head, "I'm not saying anything, Harry. I'm not saying one word."

But of course she is saying a great deal only he doesn't know what it is. There's some kind of clue in the way she treats Nelson. She as good as ignores him, doesn't offer him toys or hug him, just says, "Hello, Nelson," with a little nod, her glasses snapping into white circles. After Mrs. Springer's warmth this coolness seems brutal. Nelson feels it and acts hushed and frightened and leans against his father's legs. Now Rabbit doesn't know what's eating his mother but she certainly shouldn't take it out on a two-year-old kid. He never heard of a grandmother acting this way. It's true, just the poor kid's being there keeps them from having the kind of conversation they used to have, where his mother tells him something pretty funny that happened in the neighborhood and they go on to talk about him, the way he used to be as a kid, how he dribbled the basketball all afternoon until after dark and was always looking after Mim. Nelson's being half Springer seems to kill all that. For the moment he stops liking his mother; it takes insanity to snub a tiny kid that just

learned to talk. He wants to say to her, *What is this, anyway?*
You act like I've gone over to the other side. You're acting
insane. Don't you know it's the right side and why don't you
praise me?

But he doesn't say this; he has a stubborness to match hers.
He doesn't say much at all to her, after telling her what
good sports the Springers are doesn't go over. He just hangs
around, him and Nelson rolling a lemon back and forth in the
kitchen. Whenever the lemon wobbles over toward his mother's feet he has to get it; Nelson won't. The silence makes
Rabbit blush, for himself or for her he doesn't know. When
his father comes home it isn't much better. The old man isn't
angry but he looks at Harry like there isn't anything there.
His weary hunch and filthy fingernails annoy his son; it's as
if he's willfully aging them all. Why doesn't he get false teeth
that fit? His mouth works like an old woman's. But one thing
at least, his father pays some attention to Nelson, who hopefully rolls the lemon toward him. He rolls it back. "You
going to be a ballplayer like your Dad?"

"He can't, Earl," Mom interrupts, and Rabbit is happy to
hear her voice, thinks the ice has broken, until he hears what
she says. "He has those little Springer hands." These words,
spoken hard as steel, strike a flurry of sparks off Rabbit's
heart.

"For Chrissake, lay off," he says, and regrets it, being
trapped. It shouldn't matter what size hands Nelson has. Now
he discovers it does matter; he doesn't want the boy to have
his mother's hands, and, if he does—and if Mom noticed it
he probably does—he likes the kid a little less. He likes the
kid a little less, but he hates his mother for making him do it.
It's as if she wants to pull down everything, even if it falls on
her. And he admires this, her willingness to have him hate her,
so long as he gets her message. But he rejects her message,
he feels it probing at his heart and rejects it. He doesn't want
to hear it. He doesn't want to hear her say another word. He
just wants to get out with a little piece of his love of her left.

At the door he asks his father, "Where's Mim?"

"We don't see much of Mim any more," the old man says. His blurred eyes sink and he touches the pocket of his shirt, which holds two ballpoint pens and a little soiled packet of cards and papers. Just in these last few years his father has been making little bundles of things, cards and lists and receipts and tiny calendars that he wraps rubber bands around and tucks into different pockets with an elderly fussiness. Rabbit leaves his old home depressed, with a feeling of his heart having slumped off center.

The days go all right as long as Nelson is awake. But when the boy falls asleep, when his face sags asleep and his breath drags in and out of helpless lips that deposit spots of spit on the crib sheet and his hair fans in fine tufts and the perfect skin of his fat slack cheeks, drained of animation, lies sealed under a heavy flush, then a dead place opens in Harry, and he feels fear. The child's sleep is so heavy he fears it might break the membrane of life and fall through to oblivion. Sometimes he reaches into the crib and lifts the boy's body out, just to re-assure himself with its warmth and the responsive fumbling protest of the tumbled limp limbs.

He rattles around in the apartment, turning on all the lights and television, drinking ginger ale and leafing through old *Life*'s, grabbing anything to stuff into the emptiness. Before going to bed himself he stands Nelson in front of the toilet, running the faucet and stroking the taut bare bottom until wee-wee springs from the child's irritated sleep and jerkily prinkles into the bowl. Then he wraps a diaper around Nelson's middle and returns him to the crib and braces himself to leap the deep gulf between here and the moment when in the furry slant of morning sun the boy will appear, resurrected, in sopping diapers, beside the big bed, patting his father's face experimentally. Sometimes he gets into the bed, and then the clammy cold cloth shocking Rabbit's skin is like retouching a wet solid shore. The time in between is of no use to Rabbit. But the urgency of his wish to glide over it balks him. He lies in bed, diagonally, so his feet do not hang over, and fights the tipping sensation inside him. Like an

unsteered boat, he keeps scraping against the same rocks: his
mother's ugly behavior, his father's gaze of desertion, Ruth's
silence the last time he saw her, his mother's oppressive not
saying a word, what ails her? He rolls over on his stomach
and seems to look down into a bottomless sea, down and
down, to where crusty crags gesture amid blind lead. Good
old Ruth in the swimming pool. That poor jerk Harrison
sweating it out Ivy-League style the ass-crazy son of a bitch.
Margaret's weak little dirty hand flipping over into Tothero's
mouth and Tothero lying there with his tongue floating
around under twittering jellied eyes: No. He doesn't want to
think about that. He rolls over on his back in the hot dry bed
and the tipping sensation returns severely. Think of something pleasant. Basketball and cider at that little school down
at the end of the county Oriole High but it's too far back he
can't remember more than the cider and the way the crowd
sat up on the stage. Ruth at the swimming pool; the way she
lay in the water without weight, rounded by the water, slipping backwards through it, eyes shut and then out of the
water with the towel, him looking up her legs at the secret
hair and then her face lying beside him huge and yellow and
still: dead. No. He must blot Tothero and Ruth out of his
mind both remind him of death. They make on one side this
vacuum of death and on the other side the threat of Janice
coming home grows: that's what makes him feel tipped,
lopsided. Though he's lying there alone he feels crowded, all
these people troubling about him not so much their faces or
words as their mute dense presences, pushing in the dark like
crags under water and under everything like a faint high
hum Eccles' wife's wink. That wink. What was it? Just a
little joke in the tangle at the door, the kid coming down in
her underpants and maybe she conscious of him looking at
her toenails, a little click of the eye saying *On your way
Good luck* or was it a chink of light in a dark hall saying
Come in? Funny wise freckled piece he ought to have nailed
her that steady high hum bothering him ever since she wanted

him to really nail her the shadow of her bra tipped bumps, in a room full of light slips down the shorts over the child-skin thighs fat butt two globes hanging of white in the light Freud in the white-painted parlor hung with watercolors of canals; come here you primitive father canals on the sofa she sits spreads like two white gates parted—what a nice chest you have and here and here and here. He rolls over and the dry sheet is the touch of her anxious hands, himself taper-ing tall up from furred velvet, ridges through which the thick vein strains, and he does what he must with a tight knowing hand to stop the high hum and make himself slack for sleep. A woman's sweet froth. Nails her. Passes through the diamond standing on his head and comes out on the other side wet. How silly. He feels sorry. Queer where the wet is, nowhere near where you'd think, on the top sheet instead of the bottom. He puts his cheek on a fresh patch of pillow. He tips less, Lucy undone. Her white lines drift off like unraveled string. He must sleep; the thought of the far shore ap-proaching makes a stubborn lump in his glide. Think of things pleasant. Out of all his remembered life the one place that comes forward where he can stand without the ground turn-ing into faces he is treading on is that lot outside the diner in West Virginia after he went in and had a cup of coffee the night he drove down there. He remembers the mountains around him like a ring of cutouts against the moon-bleached blue of the night sky. He remembers the diner, with its golden windows like the windows of the trolley cars that used to run from Mt. Judge into Brewer when he was a kid, and the air, cold but alive with the beginnings of spring. He hears the footsteps tapping behind him on the asphalt, and sees the couple running toward their car, hands linked. One of the red-haired girls that sat inside with her hair hanging down like seaweed. And it seems right here that he made the mis-taken turning, that he should have followed, that they meant to lead him and he should have followed, and it seems to him in his disintegrating state that he did follow, that he *is* following, like a musical note that all the while it is being held seems to travel though it stays in the same place. On this note he carries into sleep.

But awakes before dawn being tipped again, frightened on the empty bed, with the fear that Nelson has died. He tries to sneak back into the dream he was having but his nightmare fear dilates and he at last gets up and goes to hear the boy breathe and then urinates with slight pain and returns to a bed whose wrinkles the first stirrings of light are etching into black lines. On this net he lies down and steals the hour left before the boy comes to him, hungry and cold.

On Friday Janice comes home. For the first days the presence of the baby fills the apartment as a little casket of incense fills a chapel. Rebecca June lies in a bassinet of plaited rushes painted white and mounted on a trundle. When Rabbit goes over to look at her, to reassure himself that she is there, he sees her somehow dimly, as if the baby has not gathered to herself the force that makes a silhouette. Her averted cheek, drained of the bright red he glimpsed at the hospital, is mottled gray, yellow, and blue, marbled like the palms of his hands when he is queasy; when Janice suckles Rebecca, yellow spots well up on her breast as if in answer to the fainter shadows of this color in the baby's skin. The union of breast and baby's face makes a globular symmetry to which both he and Nelson want to attach themselves. When Rebecca nurses, Nelson becomes agitated, climbs against them, pokes his fingers into the seam between the baby's lips and his mother's udder and, scolded and pushed away, wanders around the bed intoning, a promise he has heard on television, "Mighty Mouse is on the way." Rabbit himself loves to lie beside them watching Janice manipulate her swollen breasts, the white skin shiny from fullness. She thrusts the thick nipples like a weapon into the blind blistered mouth, that opens and grips with birdy quickness. "Ow!" Janice winces, and then the glands within the baby's lips begin to bubble in tune with her milk-making glands; the symmetry is established; her face relaxes into a downward smile. She holds a diaper against the other breast, mopping the waste milk it exudes in sympathy. Those first days, full of rest and hospital health, she has more milk than the baby takes. Between feedings she leaks; the bodices of all her nighties bear two stiff stains. When he sees her naked, naked all but for the elastic belt that holds her Modess pad in place, her belly shaved and puffed and marked with the vertical brown line only mothers have, his whole stomach stirs at the fierce sight of her breasts, braced high by the tension of their milk, jutting from her slim body like glossy green-veined fruit with coarse purple tips. Top-heavy, bandaged, Janice moves gingerly, as if she might spill, jarred. Though with the baby her breasts are used without shame, tools like her hands, before his eyes she is still shy, and quick to cover herself if he watches too openly. But he feels a difference between now and when they first loved, lying side by side on the borrowed bed, his eyes closed, to-gether making the filmy sideways descent into one another. Now, she is intermittently careless, walks out of the bath-room naked, lets her straps hang down while she burps the baby, seems to accept herself with casual gratitude as a machine, a white, pliant machine for fucking, hatching, feed-ing. He, too, leaks; thick sweet love burdens his chest, and he wants her—just a touch, he knows she's a bleeding wound, but just a touch, just enough to get rid of his milk, give it to her. Though in her ether trance she spoke of making love, she turns away from him in bed, and sleeps with a heaviness that feels sullen. He is too grateful, too proud of her, to disobey. He in a way, this week, worships her.

Eccles comes calling and says he hopes to see them in church. Their debt to him is such that they agree it would be nice of them, at least one of them, to go. The one must be Harry. Janice can't; she has been, by this Sunday, out of the hospital nine days, and, with Harry off at his new job since Monday, is beginning to feel worn out, weak, and abused. Harry is happy to go to Eccles' church. Not merely out of affection for Eccles, though there's that; but because he considers himself happy, lucky, blessed, forgiven, and wants to give thanks. His feeling that there is an unseen world is instinctive, and more of his actions than anyone suspects constitute transactions with it. He dresses in his new gray suit and steps out at quarter of eleven into a broad blue Sunday morning a day before the summer solstice. He always enjoyed those people parading into church across from Ruth's place and now he is one of them. Ahead of him is the first hour in over a week when he won't be with a Springer, either Janice at home or her father at work. The job at the lot is easy enough, if it isn't any work for you to lie. He feels exhausted by midafternoon. You see these clunkers come in with 80,000 miles on them and the pistons so loose the oil just pours through and they get a washing and the speedometer turned back and you hear yourself saying this represents a real bargain. He'll ask forgiveness.

He hates all the people on the street in dirty everyday clothes, advertising their belief that the world arches over a pit, that death is final, that the wandering thread of his feelings leads nowhere. Correspondingly he loves the ones dressed for church: the pressed business suits of portly men give substance and respectability to his furtive sensations of the invisible; the flowers in the hats of their wives seem to begin to make it visible; and their daughters are themselves whole flowers, their bodies each a single flower, petaled in gauze and frills, a bloom of faith, so that even the plainest walk in Rabbit's eyes glowing with beauty, the beauty of belief. He could kiss their feet in gratitude; they release him from fear. By the time he enters the church he is too elevated with happiness to ask forgiveness. As he kneels in the pew on a red stool that is padded but not enough to keep his weight from pinching his knees painfully, his head buzzes with joy, his blood leaps in his skull, and the few words he frames, *God, Rebecca, thank you* bob inconsecutively among senseless eddies of gladness. People who know God rustle and stir about him, upholding him in the dark. When he sinks back into sitting position the head in front of him takes his eye. A woman in a wide straw hat. She is smaller than average with narrow freckled shoulders, probably young, though women tend to look young from the back. The wide hat graciously broadcasts the gentlest tilt of her head and turns the twist of blonde hair at the nape of her neck into a kind of peeping secret he alone knows. Her neck and shoulders are given a faint, shifting lambency by their coat of fine white hairs, invisible except where the grain lies with the light. He smiles, remembering Tothero talking about women being covered all over with hair. He wonders if Tothero is dead now and quickly prays not. He becomes impatient for the woman to turn so he can see her profile under the rim of the hat, a great woven sun-wheel, garnished with an arc of paper violets. She turns to look down at something beside her; his breath catches; the thinnest crescent of cheek gleams, and is eclipsed again. Something in a pink ribbon pops up beside her shoulder. He stares into the inquisitive, delighted face of little Joyce Eccles. His fingers fumble for the hymnal as the organ heaves into the service; it is Eccles' wife rising within reach of his arm.

Eccles comes down the aisle shuffling behind a flood of acolytes and choristers. Up behind the altar rail he looks absent-minded and grouchy, remote and insubstantial and stiff, like a Japanese doll in his vestments. The affected voice, nasal-pious, in which he intones prayers affects Rabbit disagreeably; there is something disagreeable about the whole Episcopal service, with its strenuous ups and downs, its canned petitions, its cursory little chants. He has trouble with the kneeling pad; the small of his back aches; he hooks his elbows over the back of the pew in front of him to keep from falling backward. He misses the familiar Lutheran liturgy, scratched into his heart like a weathered inscription. In this service he blunders absurdly, balked by what seem willful dislocations of worship. He feels too much is made of collecting the money. He scarcely listens to the sermon at all.

It concerns the forty days in the Wilderness and Christ's

conversation with the Devil. Does this story have any relevance to *us*, here, now? In the twentieth century, in the
United States of America. Yes. There exists a sense in which
all Christians must have conversations with the Devil, must
learn his ways, must hear his voice. The tradition behind this
legend is very ancient, was passed from mouth to mouth
among the early Christians. Its larger significance, its greater
meaning, Eccles takes to be this: suffering, deprivation,
barrenness, hardship, lack are all an indispensable part of the
education, the initiation, as it were, of any of those who
would follow Jesus Christ. Eccles wrestles in the pulpit with
the squeak in his voice. His eyebrows jiggle as if on fish-
hooks. It is an unpleasant and strained performance, contorted, somehow; he drives his car with an easier piety. In his
robes he seems the sinister priest of a drab mystery. Harry
has no taste for the dark, tangled, visceral aspect of Christianity, the *going through* quality of it, the passage *into*
death and suffering that redeems and inverts these things, like
an umbrella blowing inside out. He lacks the mindful will
to walk the straight line of a paradox. His eyes turn toward the light however it glances into his retina.

Lucy Eccles' bright cheek ducks in and out of view under
its shield of straw. The child, hidden—all but her ribbon—
behind the back of the pew, whispers to her, presumably that
he is behind them. Yet the woman never turns her head
directly to see. This needless snub excites him. The most he
gets is her profile; the soft tuck of doubleness in her chin
deepens as she frowns down at the child beside her. She wears
a dress whose narrow blue stripes meet at the seams in
numerous sharp V's. The smart fabric and cut of the cloth on
her shoulders clash with the church yet submit to it; there is
something sexed in her stillness in the church, in her obedience to its manly, crusted, rigid procedure. He flatters himself that her true attention radiates backward at him. Against
the dour patchwork of subdued heads, stained glass, yellow-
ing memorial plaques on the wall, and laboriously knobbed
and beaded woodwork, her hair and skin and hat glow singly,

their differences in tint like the shades of brilliance within one flame.

So that when the sermon yields to a hymn, and her bright nape bows to receive the benediction, and the nervous moment of silence passes, and she stands and faces him, it is anticlimactic to see her face, with its pointed collection of dots—eyes and nostrils and freckles and the tight faint dimples that bring a sarcastic tension to the corners of her mouth. That she wears a facial expression at all shocks him slightly; the luminous view he had enjoyed for an hour did not seem capable of being so swiftly narrowed into one small person.

"Hey. Hi," he says.

"Hello," she says. "You're the last person I ever expected to see here."

"Why?" He is pleased that she thinks of him as an ultimate.

"I don't know. You just don't seem the institutional type."

He watches her eyes for another wink. He has lost belief in that first one, weeks ago. She returns his gaze until his eyes drop. "Hello, Joyce," he says. "How are you?"

The little girl halts and hides behind her mother, who continues to maneuver down the aisle, walking with small smooth steps brightly distributing smiles to the faces of the sheep. He has to admire her social co-ordination.

At the door Eccles clasps Harry's hand with his broad grip, a warm grip that tightens at the moment it should loosen. "It's exhilarating to see you here," he says, hanging on. Rabbit feels the whole line behind him bunch and push.

"Nice to be here," he says. "Very nice sermon."

Eccles, who has been peering at him with a feverish smile and a blush that seems apologetic, laughs; the roof of his mouth glimmers a second and he lets go.

Harry hears him tell Lucy, "In about an hour."

"The roast's in now. Do you want it cold or overdone?"

"Overdone," he says. He solemnly takes Joyce's tiny hand and says, "How do you do, Mrs. Pettigrew? How splendid you look this morning!"

Startled, Rabbit turns and sees that the fat lady next in line is startled also. His wife is right, Eccles is indiscreet. Lucy, Joyce behind her, walks up beside him. Her straw hat comes up to his shoulder. "Do you have a car?"

"No. Do you?"

"No. Walk along with us."

"O.K." Her proposition is so bold there must be nothing in it; nevertheless the harpstring in his chest tuned to her starts trembling. Sunshine quivers through the trees; in the streets and along unshaded sections of the pavement it leans down with a broad dry weight. It has lost the grainy milkiness of morning sun. Mica fragments in the pavement glitter; the hoods and windows of hurrying cars smear the air with white reflections. She pulls off her hat and shakes her hair. The church crowd thins behind them. The waxy leaves, freshly thick, of the maples planted between the pavement and curb embower them rhythmically; in the broad gaps of sun her face, his shirt, feel white, white; the rush of motors, the squeak of a tricycle, the touch of a cup and saucer inside a house are sounds conveyed to him as if along a bright steel bar. As they walk along he trembles in light that seems her light.

"How are your wife and baby?" she asks.

"Fine. They're just fine."

"Good. Do you like your new job?"

"Not much."

"Oh. That's a bad sign, isn't it?"

"I don't know. I don't suppose you're supposed to like your job. If you did, then it wouldn't be a job."

"Jack likes his job."

"Then it's not a job."

"That's what he says. He says it's not a job, which is the way I'd treat it. But I'm sure you know his line as well as I do."

He knows she's needling him, but he doesn't feel it, tingling all over anyway. "He and I in some ways I guess are alike," he says.

"I know. I know." Her odd quickness in saying this sets his

heart ticking quicker. She adds, "But naturally it's the differences that I notice." Her voice curls dryly into the end of this sentence; her lower lip goes sideways.

What is this? He has a sensation of touching glass. He doesn't know if they are talking about nothing or making code for the deepest meanings. He doesn't know if she's a conscious or unconscious flirt. He always thinks when they meet again he will speak firmly, and tell her he loves her, or something as blunt, and lay the truth bare; but in her presence he is numb; his breath fogs the glass and he has trouble thinking of anything to say and what he does say is stupid. He knows only this: underneath everything, under their minds and their situations, he possesses, like an inherited lien on a distant piece of land, a dominance over her, and that in her grain, in the lie of her hair and nerves and fine veins, she is prepared for this dominance. But between that preparedness and him everything reasonable intervenes. He asks, "Like what?"

"Oh—like the fact that you're not afraid of women."

"Who is?"

"Jack."

"You think?"

"Of course. The old ones, and the teenagers, he's fine with; the ones who see him in his collar. But the others he's very leery of; he doesn't like them. He doesn't really think they even ought to come to church. They bring a smell of babies and bed into it. That's not just in Jack; that's in Christianity. It's really a very neurotic religion."

Somehow, when she fetches out her psychology, it seems so foolish to Harry his own feeling of foolishness leaves him. Stepping down off a high curb, he takes her arm. Mt. Judge, built on its hillside, is full of high curbs difficult for little women to negotiate gracefully. Her bare arm remains cool in his fingers.

"Don't tell that to the parishioners," he says.

"See? You sound just like Jack."

"Is that good or bad?" There. This seems to him to test her bluff. She must say either good or bad, and that will be the fork in the road.

But she says nothing. He feels the effort of self-control this takes; she is accustomed to making replies. They mount the opposite curb and he lets go of her arm awkwardly. Though he is awkward, there is still this sense of being nestled against a receptive grain, of fitting.

"Mommy?" Joyce asks.

"What?"

"What's rottic?"

"Rottic. Oh. *Neu*rotic. It's when you're a little bit sick in the head."

"Like a cold in the head?"

"Well yes, in a way. It's about that serious. Don't worry about it, sweetie. It's something most everybody is. Except our friend Mr. Angstrom."

The little girl looks up at him across her mother's thighs with a spreading smile of self-conscious impudence. "He's naughty," she says.

"Not very," her mother says.

At the end of the rectory's brick wall a blue tricycle has been abandoned and Joyce runs ahead and mounts it and rides away in her aqua Sunday coat and pink hair ribbon, metal squeaking, spinning ventriloquistic threads of noise into the air. Together they watch the child a moment. Then Lucy asks, "Do you want to come in?" In waiting for his reply, she contemplates his shoulder; her white lids from his angle hide her eyes. Her lips are parted and her tongue, a movement in her jaw tells him, touches the roof of her mouth. In the noon sun her features show sharp and her lipstick looks cracked. He can see the inner lining of her lower lip wet against her teeth. A delayed gust of the sermon, its anguished exhortatory flavor, like a dusty breeze off the desert, sweeps through him, accompanied grotesquely by a vision of Janice's breasts, green-veined tender. This wicked snip wants to pluck him from them.

"No thanks, really. I can't."

"Oh come on. You've been to church, have a reward. Have some coffee."

"No, look." His words come out soft but somehow big. "You're a doll, but I got this wife now." And his hands, rising from his sides in vague explanation, cause her to take a quick step backward.

"I beg your pardon."

He is conscious of nothing but the little speckled section of her green irises like torn tissue paper around her black pupil-dots; then he is watching her tight round butt jounce up the walk. "But thanks, anyway," he calls in a hollowed, gutless voice. He dreads being hated. She slams the door behind her so hard the fish-shaped knocker clacks by itself on the empty porch.

He walks home blind to the sunlight. Was she mad because he had turned down a proposition, or because he had shown that he thought she had made one? Or was it a mixture of these opposites, that had somehow exposed her to herself? His mother, suddenly caught in some confusion of her own, would turn on the heat that way. In either case, he feels tall and elegant and potential striding along under the trees in his Sunday suit. Whether spurned or misunderstood, Eccles' wife has jazzed him, and he reaches his apartment clever and cold with lust.

His wish to make love to Janice is like a small angel to which all afternoon tiny lead weights are attached. The baby scrawks tirelessly. It lies in its crib all afternoon and makes an infuriating noise of strain, *hnnnnnah ah nnnnh,* a persistent feeble scratching at some interior door. What does it want? Why won't it sleep? He has come home from church carrying something precious for Janice and keeps being screened from giving it to her. The noise spreads fear through the apartment. It makes his stomach ache; when he picks up the baby to burp her he burps himself; the pressure in his stomach keeps breaking and re-forming into a stretched bubble as the bubble in the baby doesn't break. The tiny soft marbled body, weightless as paper, goes stiff against his chest and then floppy, its hot head rolling as if it will unjoint from its neck. "Becky, Becky, Becky" he says, "go to sleep. Sleep, sleep, sleep."

The noise makes Nelson fretful and whiny. As if, being closest to the dark gate from which the baby has recently emerged, he is most sensitive to the threat the infant is trying to warn them of. Some shadow invisible to their better-formed senses seems to grab Rebecca as soon as she is left alone. Rabbit puts her down, tiptoes into the living-room; they hold their breath. Then, with a bitter scratch, the membrane of silence breaks, and the wobbly moan begins again, *Nnnh, A-nnnnnih!*

"Oh my God," Rabbit says. "Son of a bitch. Son of a bitch."

Around five in the afternoon, Janice begins to cry. Tears burble down her dark pinched face. "I'm dry," she says. "I'm dry. I just don't have anything to feed her." The baby has been at her breasts repeatedly.

"Forget it," he says. "She'll conk out. Have a drink. There's some old whisky in the kitchen."

"Say; what is this Have a drink routine of yours? I've been trying not to drink. I thought you didn't like me to drink. All afternoon you've been smoking one cigarette after another and saying, 'Have a drink. Have a drink.' "

"I thought it might loosen you up. You're tense as hell."

"I'm no tenser than you are. What's eating you? What's on your mind?"

"What's happened to your milk? Why can't you give the kid enough milk?"

"I've fed her three times in four hours. There's nothing there any more." In a plain, impoverished gesture, she presses her breasts through her dress.

"Well have a drink of something."

"Say, what did they tell you at church? 'Go on home and get your wife soused'? *You* have a drink if that's on your mind."

"I don't need a drink."

"Well you need something. You're the one's upsetting Becky. She was fine all morning until you came home."

"Forget it. Just forget it. Just forget the whole stinking thing."

"Baby *cry!*"

Janice puts her arm around Nelson. "I know it honey. She's hot. She'll stop in a minute."

"Baby hot?"

They listen for a minute and it does not stop; the wild feeble warning, broken by tantalizing gaps of silence, goes on and on. Warned, but not knowing of what, they blunder about restlessly through the wreckage of the Sunday paper, inside the apartment, whose walls sweat like the walls of a prison. Outside, the sky holds a wide queenly state, blue through the hours, and Rabbit is further panicked by the thought that on such a day his parents used to take them on long pleasant walks, that they are wasting a beautiful Sunday. But they can't get organized enough to get out. He and Nelson could go but Nelson's strange fright makes him reluctant to leave his mother, and Rabbit, hoping to possess her eventually, hovers near her like a miser near treasure. His lust glues them together.

She feels this and is oppressed by it. "Why don't you go out? You're making the baby nervous. You're making *me* nervous."

"Don't you want a drink?"

"No. *No.* I just wish you'd sit down or stop smoking or rock the baby or something. And stop touching me. It's too hot. I think I should be back at the hospital."

"Do you hurt? I mean down there."

"Well I wouldn't if the baby would stop. I've *fed* her three times. Now I must feed you supper. Ohh. Sundays make me sick. What did you *do* in church that makes you so busy?"

"I'm not busy. I'm trying to be helpful."

"I know. That's what's so unnatural. Your skin smells funny."

"How?"

"Oh I don't know. Stop bothering me."

"I love you."

"Stop it. You can't. I'm not lovable right now."

"You just lie down on the sofa and I'll make some soup."

"No no no. You give Nelson his bath. I'll try to nurse the baby again. Poor thing there's nothing there."

They eat supper late but in broad light; the day is one of the longest of the year. They sip soup by the flickering light of Rebecca's urgent cries; her feeble voice is a thin filament burning with erratic injections of power. But as, amid the stacked dishes on the sink, under the worn and humid furniture, and in the coffin-like hollow of the plaited crib, the shadows begin to strengthen, the grip of the one with which Becky has been struggling all afternoon relaxes, and suddenly she is quiet, leaving behind a solemn guilty peace. They had failed her. A foreigner speaking no English but pregnant with a great painful worry had been placed among them and they had failed her. At last, night itself had swept in and washed her away like a broken piece of rubbish.

"It couldn't have been colic, she's too young for colic," Janice says. "Maybe she was just hungry, maybe I'm out of milk."

"How could that be, you've been like footballs."

She looks at him squinting, sensing what's up. "Well don't think you're going to play." But he thinks he spies a smile there.

Nelson goes to bed as he does when he's sick, willingly, whimpering. His sister was a drain on him today. Sunk in the pillow, Nelson's brown head looks demure and compact. As the child hungrily roots the bottle in his mouth, Rabbit hovers, seeking what you never find, the expression with which to communicate, to transfer, those fleeting burdens, ominous and affectionate, that are placed upon us and as quickly lifted, like the touch of a brush. Obscure repentance clouds his mouth, a repentance out of time and action, a mourning simply that he exists in a world where the tan heads of little boys sink gratefully into narrow beds sucking bottles of rubber and glass. He cups his hand over the bulge of Nelson's forehead. The boy drowsily tries to brush it off, waggles his head with irritation, and Harry takes it away and goes into the other room.

He persuades Janice to have a drink. He makes it—he doesn't know much about alcoholic things—of half whisky and half water. She says it tastes hateful. But after a while consumes it.

In bed he imagines that he can feel its difference in her flesh. There is that feeling of her body coming into his hand, of fitting his palm, that makes a welcome texture. All under her nightie up to the pit of her throat her body is still for him. They lie sideways, facing each other. He rubs her back, first lightly, then toughly, pushing her chest against his, and gathers such a feel of strength from her pliancy that he gets up on an elbow to be above her. He kisses her dark, hard face scented with alcohol. She does not turn her head, but he reads no rejection in this small refusal of motion, that lets him peck away awkwardly at a profile. He stifles his tide of resentment, reschooling himself in her slowness. Proud of his patience, he resumes rubbing her back. Her skin keeps its secret, as does her tongue; is she feeling it? She is mysterious against him, a sullen weight whose chemistry is impervious to ideas, impregnable to their penetration. Is he kindling the spark? His wrist aches. He dares undo the two buttons of her nightie front and lifts the leaf of cloth so a long arc is exposed in the rich gloom of the bed, and her warm breast flattens against the bare skin of his chest. She submits to this maneuver and he is filled with the joyful thought that he has brought her to this fullness. He is a good lover. He relaxes into the warmth of the bed and pulls the bow on his pajama waist. She has been shaved and scratches; he settles lower, on the cotton patch. This unnaturalness, this reminder of her wound, makes his confidence delicate, so he is totally destroyed when her voice—her thin, rasping, dumb-girl's voice—says by his ear, "Harry. Don't you know I want to go to sleep?"

"Well, why didn't you tell me before?"

"I don't know. I didn't know."

"Didn't know what?"

"I didn't know what you were doing. I thought you were just being nice."

"So this isn't nice."

"Well it's not nice when I can't *do* anything."

"You can do *some*thing."

"No I can't. Even if I wasn't all tired and confused from Rebecca's crying all day I can't. Not for six weeks. You know that."

"Yeah, I know, but I thought—" He's terribly embarrassed. "*What* did you think?"

"I thought you might love me anyway."

After a pause she says, "I *do* love you."

"Just a touch, Jan. Just let me touch you."

"Can't you go to sleep?"

"No I can't. I can't. I love you too much. Just hold still."

It would have been easy a minute ago to get it over with but all this talk has taken the fine point off. It's a bad contact and her stubborn limpness makes it worse; she's killing it by making him feel sorry for her and ashamed and foolish. The whole sweet thing is just sweat and work and his ridiculous inability to finish it against the dead hot wall of her belly. She pushes him back. "You're just using me," she says. "It feels horrible."

"Please, baby. I'm almost there."

"It feels so cheap."

Her daring to say this infuriates him; he realizes she hasn't had it for three months and in all that time has got an unreal idea of what love is. She exaggerates its importance, has imagined it into something rare and precious she's entitled to half of when all he wants is to get rid of it so he can move on, on into sleep, down the straight path, for her sake. It's for her sake.

"Roll over," he says.

"I love you," she says with relief, misunderstanding, thinking he's dismissing her. She touches his face in farewell and turns her back.

He scrunches down and fits himself between her buttocks, cool. It's beginning to work, steady, warm, when she twists her head and says over her shoulder, "Is this a trick your whore taught you?"

He thumps her shoulder with his fist and gets out of bed and his pajama bottoms fall down. The night breeze filters in through the window screen. She turns over on her back into the center of the bed and explains out of her dark face, "I'm not your whore, Harry."

"Damn it," he says, "that was the first thing I've asked from you since you came home."

"You've been wonderful," she says.

"Thanks."

"Where are you going?"

He is putting on his clothes. "I'm going out. I've been cooped up in this damn hole all day."

"You went out this morning."

He finds his suntans and puts them on. She asks, "Why can't you try to imagine how I *feel?* I've just had a baby."

"I can. I can but I don't want to, it's not the thing, the thing is how *I* feel. And I feel like getting out."

"Don't. Harry. Don't."

"You can just lie there with your precious ass. Kiss it for me."

"Oh for God's sake," she cries, and flounces under the covers, and smashes her face down into her pillow.

Even this late he might have stayed if she hadn't accepted defeat by doing this. His need to love her is by, so there's no reason to go. He's stopped loving her at last so he might as well lie down beside her and go to sleep. But she asks for it, lying there in a muddle sobbing, and outside, down in the town, a motor guns and he thinks of the air and the trees and streets stretching bare under the streetlamps and goes out the door.

The strange thing is she falls asleep soon after he goes; she's been used to sleeping alone lately and it's a physical relief not having him in bed kicking his hot legs and twisting the sheets into ropes. That business of his with her bottom made her stitches ache and she sinks down over the small pain all feathers. Around four in the morning Becky cries her awake and she gets up; her nightie taps her body lightly. Her skin feels unnaturally sensitive as she walks about. She changes the baby and lies down on the bed to nurse her. As Becky takes the milk it's as if she's sucking a hollow place into her mother's body; Harry hasn't come back.

The baby keeps slipping off the nipple because she can't keep her mind on her; she keeps listening for Harry's key to scratch at the door.

Mother's neighbors will laugh their heads off if she loses him again, she doesn't know why she should think of Mother's neighbors except that all the time she was home Mother kept reminding her of how they sneered and there was always that with Mother the feeling she was dull and plain and a disappointment, and she thought when she got a husband it would be all over, all that. She would be a woman with a house on her own. And she thought when she gave this baby her name it would settle her mother but instead it brings her mother against her breast with her blind mouth poor thing and she feels she's lying on top of a pillar where everyone in the town can see she is alone. She feels cold. The baby won't stay on the nipple nothing will hold to her.

She gets up and walks around the room with the baby on her shoulder patting to get the air up and the baby poor thing so floppy and limp keeps sliding and trying to dig its little boneless legs into her to hold tight and the nightie blown by the breeze keeps touching her calves the backs of her legs her ass as he called it. Makes you feel filthy they don't even have decent names for parts of you.

If there would be a scratch at the lock and he would come in the door he could do whatever he wanted with her have

any part of her if he wanted what did she care that was marriage. But when he tried tonight it just seemed so unfair, she
still aching and him sleeping with that prostitute all those
weeks and him just saying Roll over in that impatient voice
like it was just something he wanted to have done with and
who was she not to let him after she had let him run off what
right had she to any pride? Any self-respect. That was just
why she had to have some because he didn't think she dared
have any after she let him run off that was the funny thing it
was his bad deed yet she was supposed not to have any pride
afterwards to just be a pot for his dirt. When he did that to
her back it was so practiced and reminded her of all those
weeks he was off doing what he pleased and she was just helpless Mother and Peggy feeling sorry for her and everybody
else laughing she couldn't bear it.

And then his going off to church and coming back full of
juice. What right did he have to go to church? What did he
and God talk about behind the backs of all these women ex-
changing winks that was the thing she minded if they'd just
think about love when they make it instead of thinking about
whatever they do think about think about whatever they're
going to do whenever they've got rid of this little hot clot
that's bothering them. You can feel in their fingers if they're
thinking about you and tonight Harry was at first and that's
why she let him go on it was like lying there in an envelope
of yourself his hands going around you but then he began to
be rough and it made her mad to feel him thinking about himself what a good job he was doing sucking her along and not
at all any more about how she felt exhausted and aching, poking his thing at her belly like some elbow. It was so *rude.*

Just plain rude. Here he called her dumb when he was too
dumb to have any idea of how she felt any idea of how his
going off had changed her and how he must nurse her back
not just wade in through her skin without having any idea of
what was there. That was what made her panicky ever since
she was little this thing of nobody knowing how you felt and
whether nobody could know or nobody cared she had no

idea. She didn't like her skin, never had it was too dark made her look like an Italian even if she never did get pimples like some of the other girls and then in those days both working at Kroll's she on the salted nuts when Harry would lie down beside her on Mary Hannacher's bed the silver wallpaper he liked so much and close his eyes it seemed to melt her skin and she thought it was all over she was with somebody. But then they were married (she felt awful about being pregnant before but Harry had been talking about marriage for a year and anyway laughed when she told him and said Great she was terribly frightened and he said Great and lifted her put his arms around under her bottom and lifted her like you would a child he could be so wonderful when you didn't expect it in a way it seemed important that you didn't expect it there was so much nice in him she couldn't explain to anybody she had been so frightened about being pregnant and he made her be proud) they were married and she was still little clumsy dark-complected Janice Springer and her husband was a conceited lunk who wasn't good for anything in the world Daddy said and the feeling of being alone would melt a little with a little drink. It wasn't so much that it dissolved the lump as made the edges nice and rainbowy.

She's been walking around patting the baby until her wrists and ankles hurt and poor tiny Rebecca is asleep with her legs around the breast that still has all its milk in it. She wonders if she should try to make her take some and thinks no if she can sleep let her sleep. She lifts the poor tiny thing weighing nothing off the sweaty place on her shoulder and lays her down in the cool shadows of the crib. Already the night is dimming, dawn comes early to the town facing east on its mountainside. Janice lies down on the bed but the sense of light growing beside her on the white sheets keeps her awake. Pleasantly awake at first; the coming of morning is so clean and makes her feel like she did through the second month Harry was hiding. Mother's great Japanese cherry tree blooming below her window and the grass coming up and the ground smelling wet and ashy and warm. She had thought things out and was resigned to her marriage being finished. She would have her baby and get a divorce and never get married again. She would be like a kind of nun she had just seen that beautiful picture with Audrey Hepburn. And if he came back it would be equally simple; she would forgive him everything and stop her drinking which annoyed him so though she didn't see why and they would be very nice and simple and clean together because he would have got everything out of his system and love her so because she had forgiven him and she would know now how to be a good wife. She had gone to church every week and talked with Peggy and prayed and had come to undersand that marriage wasn't a refuge it was a sharing and she and Harry would start to share everything. And then, it was a miracle, these last two weeks had been that way.

And then Harry had suddenly put his whore's filthiness into it and asked her to love it and the unfairness makes her cry aloud softly, as if startled by something in the empty bed with her.

The last hours are like some narrow turn in a pipe that she can't force her thought through. Again and again she comes up to the sound of him saying *Roll over* and can't squeeze through it, cannot feel panicked and choked. She gets out of bed and wanders around with her one tight breast the nipple stinging and goes into the kitchen in her bare feet and sniffs the empty glass Harry made her drink whisky out of. The smell is dark and raw and soft and deep, and she thinks maybe a sip will cure her insomnia. Make her sleep until the scratch at the door awakens her and she sees his big, white body ramble in sheepishly and she can say *Come to bed, Harry, it's all right, do me, I want to share it, I really want it, really.*

She puts just an inch of whisky in, and not much water because it would take too long to drink, and no ice cubes because the noise of the tray might wake up the children. She takes this dose to the window and stands looking down past the three tar roofs at the sleeping town. Already a few kitchen and bedroom lights show pale here and there. A car, its head-lights dull discs that do not throw beams into the thinning darkness, eases down Wilbur toward the center of town. The highway, half-hidden by the silhouettes of houses, like a river between banks of trees, this early swishes with traffic. She feels the workday approaching like an army of light, feels the dark ridged houses beneath her as potentially stirring, waking, opening like castles to send forth their men, and re-grets that her own husband is unable to settle into the rhythm of which one more beat is about to sound. Why him? What was so precious about him? Anger at Harry begins to bloom, and to stifle it she drains the glass and turns in the dawn; everything in the apartment is a shade of brown. She feels lopsided; the pressure in the unused breast pulls her.

She goes into the kitchen and makes another drink, stronger than the first, thinking that after all it's about time she had a little fun. She hadn't had a moment to herself since she came back from the hospital. The thought of fun makes her move-ments quick and airy; she fairly runs in her bare feet across the gritty carpet back to the window, as if to a show ar-ranged just for her. Mounted in her white gown above every-thing she can see, she touches her fingers to her tight breast so that the milk starts to leak, stains the white cloth with slow warmth.

The wetness slides down her front and turns cold in the air by the window. Her varicose veins ache from standing. She goes and sits in the moldy brown armchair and is sick-ened by just the angle at which the mottled wall meets the pasty ceiling. The angle tips her, muddles up and down. The pattern on the wallpaper swarms; the flowers are brown spots that swim in the murk and chase each other and merge hun-grily. It's hateful. She turns her face away and studies the calm green globe of the dead television set. The front of her nightie is drying; the crusty stiffness scratches her. Baby book said *Keep nipples clean, Soap gently:* germs enter scratches. She sets the drink on the round chair arm and stands up and pulls her nightgown over her head and sits

down again. It gives her nakedness a mossy hug. She puts the
bunched nightgown in her lap on top of her Modess pad and
belt and pulls the footstool over cleverly with her toes and
rests her ankles on it and admires her legs. She always
thought she had good legs. Straight small nice even thighs.
She does have good legs. Their tapering wavering silhouettes
are white against the deep shadow of the rug. The dim light
erases the blue veins left from carrying Becky. She wonders
if her legs are going to go as bad as Mother's. She tries to imagine the ankles as thick as the knees and they do seem to
swell. She reaches down to reassure herself by feeling the
ankles' hard narrow bones and her shoulder knocks the
whisky glass off the chair arm. She jumps up, startled to feel
the air embrace her bare skin, cool space sweep around her
wobbly, knobbed body. She giggles. If Harry could see her
now. Luckily there wasn't much in the glass. She tries to walk
boldly into the kitchen with no clothes on like a whore but
the sense of somebody watching her, which began when she
stood at the window and made her milk flow, is too strong;
she ducks into the bedroom and wraps the blue bathrobe
around her and then mixes the drink. There is still a third of
the bottle left. Tiredness makes the rims of her lids dry but
she has no desire to go back to bed. She has a horror of it because Harry should be there. This absence is a hole that widens and she pours a little whisky into it but it's not enough and
when she goes to the window for the third time it is now
light enough to see how drab everything is. Someone has
smashed a bottle on one of the tar roofs. The gutters of Wilbur Street are full of mud that washes down from the new
development. While she looks the street lights, great pale
strings of them, go off in patches. She pictures the man at the
power plant pulling the switches, little and gray and hunch-
backed and very sleepy. She goes to the television set and the
band of light that suddenly flares in the green rectangle
sparks joy in her breast but it's still too early, the light is just
a speckling senseless brightness and the sound is nothing but
static. As she sits there watching the blank radiance a feeling

of some other person standing behind her makes her snap her head around several times. She is very quick about it but there is always a space she can't see which the other person could dodge into if he's there. It's the television has called him into the room but when she turns off the set she starts to cry immediately. She sits there with her face in her hands, her tears crawling out between her fingers and her sobs shaking through the apartment. She doesn't stifle them because she wants to wake somebody; she is sick of being alone. In the bleaching light the walls and furniture are clear and regain their colors and the merging brown spots have gone into herself.

She goes and looks at the baby, the poor thing lying there snuffling the crib sheet, its little hands twitching up by its ears, and reaches down and strokes its hot membranous head and lifts it out its legs all wet and takes it to nurse in the armchair that looks toward the window. The sky beyond is a pale smooth blue that looks painted on the panes. There is nothing to see but sky from this chair, they might be a hundred miles up, in the basket of a great balloon. A door on the other side of the partition slams and her heart leaps but then of course it's just another tenant maybe old Mr. Cappello who never says a civil word to anybody going off to work, the stairs rumbling reluctantly. This wakes Nelson and for a time her hands are full. In making breakfast for them she breaks an orange-juice glass, it just drifts away from her thumb into the brittle sink. When she bends over Nelson to serve him his Rice Krispies he looks up at her and wrinkles his nose; he smells sadness and its familiar odor makes him timid with her. "Daddy go way?" He's such a good boy saying this to make it easy on her, all she has to do is answer "Yes."

"No," she says. "Daddy went out to work early this morning before you got up. He'll be home for supper like he always is."

The child frowns at her and then parrots with sharp hope, "Like always is?"

Worry has stretched his head high, so his neck seems a stem

too thin to support the ball of his skull with its broad whorl
of pillow-mussed hair. "Daddy will be home," she repeats.
Having taken on herself the burden of lying, she needs a little more whisky for support. There is a murk inside her
which she must tint a bright color or collapse. She takes the
dishes out to the kitchen but they slide so in her hands she
doesn't try to wash them. She thinks she must change out of
her bathrobe into a dress but in taking the steps into the bedroom forgets her purpose and begins making the bed. But
something whose presence she feels on the wrinkled bed
frightens her so that she draws back and goes into the other
room to be with the children. It's as if in telling them Harry
would be back as normal she's put a ghost in the apartment.
But the other person does not feel like Harry, it feels like a
burglar, a teasing burglar dancing from room to room ahead
of her.

When she picks up the baby again she feels its wet legs and
thinks of changing it but cleverly realizes she is drunk and
might stab it with the pins. She is very proud of thinking this
through and tells herself to stay away from the bottle so she
can change the baby in an hour. She puts good Becky in her
crib and, wonderfully, doesn't hear her cry once. She and
Nelson sit and watch the tail end of Dave Garroway and then
a program about Elizabeth and her husband entertaining a
friend of his who is always going away on camping trips being a bachelor and turns out to be a better cook than Elizabeth. For some reason watching this makes her so nervous
that just out of television-watching habit she goes to the
kitchen and makes herself a little drink, mostly ice cubes, just
to keep sealed shut the great hole that is threatening to pull
open inside of her again. She takes just a sip and it's like a
swallow of blue light that makes everything clear. She must
just arch over this one little gap and at the end of the day
after work Harry will be back and no one will ever know, no
one will laugh at Mother. She feels like a rainbow arching pro-
tectively over Harry, who seems infinitely small under her,
like some children's toy. She thinks how good it would be to

play with Nelson; it is bad for him to watch television all morning. She turns it off and finds his coloring book and crayons and they sit on the rug and color opposite pages.

Janice repeatedly hugs him and talks to make him laugh and is very happy doing the actual coloring. In high school, art was the one subject she wasn't afraid of and she always got a B. She smiles in the delight of coloring her page, a barnyard, so well, of feeling the little rods of color in her fingers make such neat parellel strokes and her son's small body intent and hard beside hers. Her bathrobe fans out on the floor around her and her body seems beautiful and broad. She moves to get her shadow off the page and sees that she has colored one chicken partly green and not stayed within the lines at all well and her page is ugly; she starts to cry; it is so un*fair*, as if someone standing behind her without understanding a thing has told her her coloring is ugly. Nelson looks up and his quick face slides wide and he cries, "Don't! Don't, Mommy!" She prepares to have him pitch forward into her lap but instead he jumps up and runs with a lopsided almost crippled set of steps into the bedroom and falls on the floor kicking.

She pushes herself up from the floor with a calm smile and goes into the kitchen, where she thinks she left her drink. The important thing is to complete the arch to the end of the day, to be a protection for Harry, and it's silly not to have the one more sip that will make her long enough. She comes out of the kitchen and tells Nelson, "Mommy's stopped crying, sweet. It was a joke. Mommy's not crying. Mommy's very happy. She loves you very much." His rubbed stained face watches her. Like a stab from behind the phone rings. Still carrying that calmness she answers it. "Hello?"

"Darling? It's Daddy."

"Oh, Daddy!" Joy just streams through her lips.

He pauses. "Baby, is Harry sick? It's after eleven and he hasn't shown up at the lot yet."

"No, he's fine. We're all fine."

There is another pause. Her love for her father flows toward him through the silent wire. She wishes the conversation would go on forever. He asks, "Well where is he? Is he there? Let me speak to him, Janice."

"Daddy, he's not here. He went out early this morning."

"Where did he go? He's not at the lot." She's heard him say the word "lot" a million times it seems; he says it like no other man; it's dense and rich from his lips, as if all the world is concentrated in it. All the good things of her growing-up, her clothes, her toys, their house, came from the "lot."

She is inspired; car-sale talk is one thing she knows. "He went out early, Daddy, to show a station wagon to a prospect who had to go to work or something. Wait. Let me think. He said the man had to go to Allentown early this morning. He had to go to Allentown and Harry had to show him a station wagon. Everything's all right, Daddy. Harry loves his job."

The third pause is the longest. "Darling. Are you sure he's not there?"

"Daddy, aren't you funny? He's not here. See?" As if it has eyes she thrusts the receiver into the air of the empty room. It's meant as a daughter's impudent joke but unexpectedly just holding her arm out makes her feel sick. When she brings the receiver back to her ear he is saying in a remote ticky voice, "darling. All right. Don't worry about anything. Are the children there with you?"

Feeling dizzy, she hangs up. This is a mistake, but she thinks on the whole she's been clever enough. She thinks she deserves a drink. The brown liquid spills down over the smoking ice cubes and doesn't stop when she tells it to; she snaps the bottle angrily and blot-shaped drops topple into the sink. She goes into the bathroom with the glass and comes out with her hands empty and a taste of toothpaste in her mouth. She remembers looking into the mirror and patting her hair and from that she went to brushing her teeth. With Harry's toothbrush.

She discovers herself making lunch, like looking down into a food advertisement in a magazine, bacon strips sizzling in a

pan at the end of a huge blue arm. She sees the BB's of fat flying in the air like the pretty spatter of a fountain in a park
and wonders at how quick their arcs are. They prick her hand
on the handle and she turns the purple gas down. She pours a
glass of milk for Nelson and pulls some leaves off of a head
of lettuce and sets them on a yellow plastic plate and eats a
handful herself. She thinks she won't set a place for herself
and then thinks she will because maybe this trembling in her
stomach is hunger and gets another plate and stands there
holding it with two hands in front of her chest wondering
why Daddy was so sure Harry was here. There *is* another
person in the apartment she knows but it's not Harry and
the person has no business here anyway and she determines to
ignore him and continues setting lunch with a slight stiffness
operating in her body. She holds on to everything until it is
well on the table.

Nelson says the bacon is greasy and asks again if Daddy
go away and his complaining about the bacon that she was so
clever and brave to make at all annoys her so that after his
twentieth refusal to eat even a bit of lettuce she reaches over
and slaps his rude face. The stupid child can't even cry he
just sits there and stares and sucks in his breath again and again
and finally does burst forth. But luckily she is equal to the situation, very calm, she sees the unreason of his whole attempt
and refuses to be bullied. With the smoothness of a single
great wave she makes his bottle, takes him by the hand, over-
sees his urinating, and settles him in bed. Still shaking with the
aftermath of sobs, he roots the bottle in his mouth and she is
certain from the glaze on his watchful eyes that he is locked
into the channel to sleep. She stands by the bed, surprised by
her stern strength.

The telephone rings again, angrier than the first time, and
as she runs to it, running because she does not want Nelson
disturbed, she feels her strength ebb and a brown staleness
washes up the back of her throat. "Hello."

"Janice." Her mother's voice, even and harsh. "I just got
back from shopping in Brewer and your father's been trying

to reach me all morning. He thinks Harry's gone again. Is he?"

Janice closes her eyes and says, "He went to Allentown."

"What would he do there?"

"He's going to sell a car."

"Don't be silly. Janice. Are you all right?"

"What do you mean?"

"Have you been drinking?"

"Drinking what?"

"Now don't worry, I'm coming right over."

"Mother, don't. Everything is fine. I just put Nelson into his nap."

"I'll have a bite to eat out of the icebox and come right over. You lie down."

"Mother, *please* don't come over."

"Janice, now don't talk back. When did he go?"

"Stay away, Mother. He'll be back tonight." She listens and adds, "And stop crying."

Her mother says, "Yes you say stop when you keep bringing us all into disgrace. The first time I thought it was all his fault but I'm not so sure any more. Do you hear? I'm not so sure."

Hearing this speech has made the sliding sickness in her so steep she wonders if she can keep her grip on the phone. "Don't come over, Mother," she begs. "Please."

"I'll have a bite of lunch and be over in twenty minutes. You go to bed."

Janice replaces the receiver and looks around her with horror. The apartment is horrible. Coloring books on the floor, glasses, the bed unmade, dirty dishes everywhere. She runs to where she and Nelson crayoned, and tests bending over. She drops to her knees, and the baby begins to cry. Panicked with the double idea of not disturbing Nelson and of concealing Harry's absence, she runs to the crib and nightmarishly finds it smeared with orange mess. "Damn you, damn you," she moans to Rebecca, and lifts the little filthy thing out and wonders where to carry her. She takes her to the armchair and biting her lips unpins the diaper. "You little shit," she murmurs, feeling that the sound of her voice is holding off the other person who is gathering in the room. She takes the soaked daubed diaper to the bathroom and drops it in the toilet and dropping to her knees fumbles the bathtub plug into its hole. She pulls on both faucets as wide as they will go, knowing from experiment that both opened wide make the right tepid mixture. The water bangs out of the faucet like a fist. She notices the glass of watery whisky she left on the top of the toilet and takes a long stale swallow and then puzzles how to get it off her hands. All the while Rebecca screams as if she has mind enough to know she's filthy. Janice takes the glass with her and spills it on the rug with her knee while she strips the baby of its nightie and sweater. She carries the sopping clothes to the television set and puts them on top while she drops to her knees and tries to stuff the crayons back into their box. Her head aches with all this jarring up and down. She takes the crayons to the kitchen table and dumps the uneaten bacon and lettuce into the paper bag under the sink but the mouth of the bag leans partly closed and the lettuce falls behind into the darkness in back of the can and she crouches down with her head pounding to try to see it or get it with her fingers and is unable. Her knees sting from so much kneeling. She gives up and to her surprise sits flatly on a kitchen chair and looks at the gaudy soft noses of the crayons poking out of the Crayola box. Hide the whisky. Her body doesn't move for a second but when it does she sees her hands with the little lines of dirt on her fingernails put the whisky bottle into a lower cabinet with some old shirts of Harry's she was saving for rags he would never wear a mended shirt not that she was any good at mending them. She shuts the door, it bangs but doesn't catch, and on the edge of linoleum beside the sink the cork cap of the whisky bottle stares at her like a little top hat. She puts it in the garbage bag. Now the kitchen is clean enough. In the living-room Rebecca is lying naked in the fuzzy armchair with her belly puffing out sideways to yell and her lumpy curved legs clenched and red. Janice's other baby was a boy and it still seems unnatural to her, between the girl's legs, those two little buns of fat instead of a boy's triple business (when the doctor had Nelson circumcised Harry hadn't wanted him to he hadn't been and thought it was unnatural she had laughed at him he was so mad). The baby's face goes red with each squall and Janice closes her eyes and thinks how really horrible it is of Mother to come and ruin her day just to make sure she's lost Harry again. She can't wait a minute to find out and this awful baby can't wait a minute and there are the clothes on top of the television set. She takes them into the bathroom and drops them into the toilet on top of the diaper and turns off the faucets. The wavery gray line of the water is almost up to the lip of the tub. On the skin quick wrinkles wander and under it a deep mass waits colorless. She wishes she could have the bath. Brimful of composure she returns to the living-room. She tips too much trying to dig the tiny rubbery thing out of the chair so drops to her knees and scoops Rebecca into her arms and carries her into the bathroom held sideways against her breasts. She is proud to be carrying this to completion; at least the baby will be clean when Mother comes. She drops gently to her knees by the big calm tub and does not expect her sleeves to be soaked. The water wraps around her forearms like two large hands; under her eyes the pink baby sinks down like a gray stone.

With a sob of protest she grapples for the child but the water pushes up at her hands, her bathrobe tends to float, and the slippery thing squirms in the sudden opacity. She has a hold, feels a heartbeat on her thumb, and then loses it, and the skin of the water leaps with pale refracted oblongs that she can't seize the solid of; it is only a moment, but a moment dragged out in a thicker time. Then she has Becky squeezed in her hands and it is all right.

She lifts the living thing into air and hugs it against her sopping chest. Water pours off them onto the bathroom tiles. The little weightless body flops against her neck and a quick look of relief at the baby's face gives a fantastic clotted impression. A contorted memory of how they give artificial

respiration pumps Janice's cold wet arms in frantic rhythmic
hugs; under her clenched lids great scarlet prayers arise, wordless, monotonous, and she seems to be clasping the knees of a
vast third person whose name, Father, Father, beats against
her head like physical blows. Though her wild heart bathes
the universe in red, no spark kindles in the space between her
arms; for all of her pouring prayers she doesn't feel the faint-
est tremor of an answer in the darkness against her. Her sense
of the third person with them widens enormously, and she
knows, knows, while knocks sound at the door, that the worst
thing that has ever happened to any woman in the world has
happened to her.

JACK comes back from the telephone a shocking color. "Janice Angstrom has accidentally drowned their baby."

Lucy asks, "How *could* she?"

"I don't know. I'm afraid she was drunk. She's unconscious now."

"Where was *he?*"

"Nobody knows. I'm supposed to find out. That was Mrs. Springer."

He sits down in the great walnut-armed chair that had been his father's and Lucy realizes with resentment that her husband is middle-aged. His hair is thinning, his skin is dry, he looks exhausted. She cries, "Why must you spend your life chasing after that worthless heel?"

"He's not worthless. I love him."

"You love him. That's sickening. Oh I think that's sickening, Jack. Why don't you try loving me, or your children?"

"I do."

"You *don't*, Jack. Let's face it, you don't. You couldn't bear to love anybody who might return it. You're afraid of that, aren't you? Aren't you afraid?"

They had been drinking tea in the library when the phone rang and he picks his empty cup off the floor between his feet and looks into the center. "Don't be fancy, Lucy," he says. "I feel too sick."

"You feel sick, yes, and I feel sick. I've felt sick ever since you got involved with that animal. He's not even in your church."

"Any Christian is in my church."

"Christian! If he's a Christian thank God I'm not one. Christian. Kills his baby and that's what you call him."

"He didn't kill the baby. He wasn't there, it was an accident."

"Well he as good as did. Runs off and sends his idiot wife on a bender. You never should have brought them back together. The girl had adjusted and something like this never would have happened."

Eccles blinks; shock has put a great analytic distance between him and things. He's rather impressed by the way she has reconstructed what must have happened. He wonders a little why her speech is so vengeful. "Heel" was a strange word for her to have used. "So you're saying I really killed the baby," he says.

"Of course not. I didn't mean to say that at all."

"No. I think you're probably right," he says, and lifts himself out of the chair. He goes into the hall to the telephone and again draws out of his wallet the number written in pencil below the faint name, Ruth Leonard. The number worked once but this time the mouse of electricity gnaws at the remote membrane of metal in vain. He lets it ring twelve times, hangs up, dials the number again, and hangs up after seven rings. When he returns to the study Lucy is ready for him.

"Jack, I'm sorry. I didn't mean to suggest you were responsible at all. Of course you're not. Don't be silly."

"It's all right, Lucy. The truth shouldn't be able to hurt us."

These words are a shadow of his idea that if Faith is true, then nothing that is true is in conflict with Faith.

"Oh mercy, the martyr. Well I can see it's an idea you have that it's your fault and nothing I can say will change your mind. I'll save my breath."

He keeps silent to help her save her breath but after a moment she asks in a softer voice, "Jack?"

"What?"

"Why *were* you so anxious to get them back together?"

He picks the slice of lemon up from the saucer of his teacup and tries to squint through it into the room. "Marriage is a sacrament," he says.

He half-expects her to laugh but instead she asks earnestly, "Even a bad marriage?"

"Yes."

"But that's ridiculous. That's not common sense."

"I don't believe in common sense," he says. "If it'll make you happy, I don't believe in anything."

"That doesn't make me happy," she says. "You're being psychopathic. But I'm sorry this has happened. I'm truly sorry." She takes away their cups and swishes into the kitchen and leaves him alone. Afternoon shadows gather like cobwebs on the walls of books, most of them belonging not to him but to his predecessor in the rectory, the much-admired bachelor Joseph Langhorne. He sits waiting numbly but not too long. The phone rings. He hurries to answer it before Lucy can; through the window above the sill where the phone rests he can see his neighbor unpinning her wash from the line.

"Hello?"

"Hey, Jack? This is Harry Angstrom. I hope I'm not interrupting anything."

"No, you're not."

"You don't have any old ladies sitting around sewing or anything, do you?"

"No."

"Why, I've been trying to call my apartment and nobody answers and I'm kind of nervous about it. I didn't spend last

night there and I'm getting sort of a prickly feeling. I want to
go home but I want to know if Janice has done anything like
call the cops or anything. Do you know?"

"Harry, where are you?"

"Oh, at some drugstore in Brewer."

The neighbor has bundled the last sheet into her arms and
Jack's sight leans on the bare white line. One of the uses society seems to have for him is to break tragic news and the
cave of his mouth goes dry as he braces for the familiar duty.
No man, having put his hand to the plough . . . He keeps
his eyes wide open so he will not seem too close to the presence by his ear. "I guess to save time I'd better tell you over
the phone," he begins. "Harry. A terrible thing has happened
to us."

When you twist a rope and keep twisting, it begins to lose its
straight shape and suddenly a kink, a loop leaps up in it. Harry
has such a hard loop in himself after he hears Eccles out. He
doesn't know what he says to Eccles; all he is conscious of is
the stacks of merchandise in jangling packages he can see
through the windows of the phone-booth door. On the drugstore wall there is a banner bearing in red the one word
PARADICHLOROBENZENE. All the while he is trying to
understand Eccles he is rereading this word, trying to see
where it breaks, wondering if it can be pronounced. Right
when he finally understands, right at the pit of his life, a fat
woman comes up to the counter and pays for two boxes of
Kleenex. He steps into the sunshine outside the drugstore
swallowing, to keep the loop from rising in his body and choking him. It's a hot day, the first of summer; the heat comes up
off the glittering pavement into the faces of pedestrians,
strikes them sideways off the store windows and hot stone
façades. In the white light faces wear the American expression,
eyes squinting and mouths sagging open in a scowl, that
makes them look as if they are about to say something menacing and cruel. In the street under glaring hardtops drivers
bake in stalled traffic. Above, milk hangs in a sky that seems

too exhausted to clear. Harry waits at a corner with some red sweating shoppers for a Mt. Judge bus, number 16A; when it hisses to a stop it is already packed. He hangs from a steel bar in the rear, fighting to keep from doubling up with the kink inside. Curved posters advertise filtered cigarettes and suntan lotion and C.A.R.E.

He had ridden one of these buses last night into Brewer and gone to Ruth's apartment but there was no light on and nobody answered his ring, though there was a dim light behind the frosted glass lettered F. X. PELLIGRINI. He sat around on the steps, looking down at the delicatessen until the lights went out and then looking at the bright church window. When the lights went out behind that he felt cramped and hopeless and thought of going home. He wandered up to Weiser Street and looked down at all the lights and the great sunflower and couldn't see a bus and kept walking, over to the side, and became afraid of getting knifed and robbed and went into a low-looking hotel and bought a room. He didn't sleep very well with a neon tube with a taped connection buzzing outside and some woman laughing and woke up early enough to go back to Mt. Judge and get a suit and go to work but something held him back. Something held him back all day. He tries to think of what it was because whatever it was murdered his daughter. Wanting to see Ruth again was some of it but it was clear after he went around to her address in the morning that she wasn't there probably off to Atlantic City with some madman and still he wandered around Brewer, going in and out of department stores with music piping from the walls and eating a hot dog at the five and ten and hesitating outside a movie house but not going in and keeping an eye out for Ruth. He kept expecting to see her shoulders that he kissed jostle out of a crowd and the ginger hair he used to beg to unpin shining on the other side of a rack of birthday cards. But it was a city of over a hundred thousand and the odds were totally against him and anyway there was tons of time he could find her another day. No, what kept him in the city despite the increasing twisting inside that told him something was wrong back home, what kept him walking through the cold air breathed from the doors of movie houses and up and down between counters of perfumed lingerie and tinny jewelry and salted nuts (poor old Jan) and up into the park along paths he walked once with Ruth to watch from under a horsechestnut tree five mangy kids play cat with a tennis ball and a broomstick and then finally back down Weiser to the drugstore he called from, what kept him walking was the idea that somewhere he'd find an opening. For what made him mad at Janice wasn't so much that she was in the right for once and he was wrong and stupid but the closed feeling of it, the feeling of being closed in. He had gone to church and brought back this little flame and had nowhere to put it on the dark damp walls of the apartment, so it had flickered and gone out. And he realized that he wouldn't always be able to produce this flame. What held him back all day was the feeling that somewhere there was something better for him than listening to babies cry and cheating people in used-car lots and it's this feeling he tries to kill, right there on the bus, he grips the chrome bar and leans far over two women with white pleated blouses and laps of packages and closes his eyes and tries to kill it. The kink in his stomach starts to take the form of nausea and he clings to the icy bar bitterly as the bus swings around the mountain. He gets off, in a sweat, blocks too soon. Here in Mt. Judge the shadows have begun to grow deep, the sun baking Brewer rides the crest of the mountain, and his sweat congeals, shortening his breath. He runs to keep his body occupied, to joggle his mind blank. Past a dry-cleaning plant with a little pipe hissing steam at the side. Through the oil and rubber smells riding above the asphalt pond around the red pumps of an Esso station. Past the Mt. Judge townhall lawn and the World War II honor roll with the name plaques crumbled and blistered behind glass. His chest begins to hurt and he slows to a walk.

When he gets to the Springers' house Mrs. comes to the door and shuts it in his face. But he knows from the olive Buick parked outside that Eccles is in there and in a little while Jack comes to the door and lets him in. He says softly in the dim hall, "Your wife has been given a sedative and is asleep."

"The baby . . ."

"The undertaker has her."

Rabbit wants to cry out, it seems indecent, for the undertaker to be taking such a tiny body, that they ought to bury it in its own simplicity, like the body of a bird, in a small hole dug in the grass. But he nods. He feels he will never resist anything again.

Eccles goes upstairs and Harry sits in a chair and watches the light from the window play across an iron table of ferns and African violets and baby cacti. Where it hits the leaves they are bright yellow-green; the leaves in shadow in front of them look like black-green holes cut in this golden color. Somebody comes down the stairs with an erratic step. He doesn't turn his head to see who it is; he doesn't want to risk looking anybody in the face. A furry touch on his forearm and he meets Nelson's eyes. The child's face is stretched shiny with curiosity. "Mommy sleep," he says in a deep voice imitating the tragedy-struck voices he has been hearing.

Rabbit pulls him up into his lap. He's heavier and longer than he used to be. His body acts as a covering; he pulls the boy's head down against his neck. Nelson asks, "Baby sick?"

"Baby sick."

"Big, big water in tub," Nelson says, and struggles to sit up so he can explain with his arms, which go wide. "Many, many water," he says. He must have seen it. He wants to get off his father's lap but Harry holds him fast with a kind of terror; the house is thick with a grief that seems to threaten the boy. Also the boy's body wriggles with an energy that threatens the grief, might tip it and bring the whole house crashing down on them. It is himself he is protecting by imprisoning the child.

Eccles comes downstairs and stands there studying them. "Why don't you take him outside?" he asks. "He's had a nightmare of a day."

They all three go outdoors. Eccles takes Harry's hand in a long quiet grip and says, "Stay here. You're needed, even if they don't tell you." After Eccles pulls away in his Buick, he and Nelson sit in the grass by the driveway and throw bits of gravel down toward the pavement. The boy laughs and talks in excitement but out here the sound is not so loud. Harry feels thinly protected by the fact that this is what Eccles told him to do. Men are walking home from work along the pavement; Nelson tosses a pebble too near the feet of one and the man looks up. This unknown face seems to stare at Harry from deep in another world, the world of the blameless. They change their target to a green lawn-seeder leaning against the wall of the garage. Harry hits it four times running. Though the air is still light the sunshine has shrunk to a few scraps in the tops of trees. The grass is growing damp and he wonders if he should sneak Nelson in the door and go.

Mr. Springer comes to the door and calls, "Harry." They go over. "Becky's made a few sandwiches in place of supper," he says. "You and the boy come in." They go into the kitchen and Nelson eats. Harry refuses everything except a glass of water. Mrs. Springer is not in the kitchen and Harry is grateful for her absence. "Harry," Mr. Springer says, and stands up, patting his mustache with two fingers, like he's about to make a financial concession, "Reverend Eccles and Becky and I have had a talk. I won't say I don't blame you because of course I do. But you're not the only one to blame. Her mother and I somehow never made her feel secure, never perhaps you might say made her welcome, I don't know"—his little pink crafty eyes are not crafty now, blurred and chafed—"we tried, I'd like to think. At any rate"—this comes out harsh and crackly; he pauses to regain quietness in his voice—"life must go on. Am I making any sense to you?"

"Yes sir."

"Life must go on. We must go ahead with what we have left. Though Becky's too upset to see you now, she agrees. We had a talk and agree that it's the only way. I mean, what I mean to say, I can see you're puzzled, is that we consider you in our family, Harry, despite"—he lifts an arm vaguely toward the stairs—"this." His arms slumps back and he adds the word "accident."

Harry shields his eyes with his hand. They feel hot and vulnerable to light. "Thank you," he says, and almost moans in his gratitude to this man, whom he has always despised, for making a speech so generous. He tries to frame, in accordance with an etiquette that continues to operate in the thick of grief as if underwater, a counter-speech. "I promise I'll keep my end of the bargain," he brings out, and stops, stifled by the abject sound of his voice. What made him say bargain?

"I know you will," Springer says. "Reverend Eccles assures us you will."

"Dessert," Nelson says distinctly.

"Nelly, why don't you take a cookie to bed?" Springer speaks with a familiar jollity that, though strained, reminds Rabbit that the kid lived here for months. "Isn't it your bedtime? Shall Mom-mom take you up?"

"Daddy," Nelson says, and slides off his chair and comes to his father.

Both men are embarrassed. "O.K.," Rabbit says. "You show me your room."

Springer gets two Oreo cookies out of the pantry and unexpectedly Nelson runs forward to hug him. He stoops to accept the hug and his withered dandy's face goes blank against the boy's cheek; his unfocused eyes stare at Rabbit's shoes, and big black square cufflinks, thinly rimmed and initialed S in gold, creep out of his coat sleeves as his arms tighten the hug.

As Nelson leads his father to the stairs they pass the room where Mrs. Springer is sitting. Rabbit has a glimpse of a puffed face slippery with tears like an interior organ surgically exposed, and averts his eyes. He whispers to Nelson to go in and kiss her good night. When the boy returns to him they go upstairs and down a smooth corridor papered with a design of old-style cars into a little room whose white curtains are tinted green by a tree outside. On either side of the window symmetrical pictures, one of kittens and one of puppies, are hung. He wonders if this was the room where Janice was little. It has a musty innocence, and a suspense, as if it stood empty for years. An old teddy-bear, the fur worn down to cloth and one eye void, sits in a broken child's rocker. Has it been Janice's? Who pulled the eye out? Nelson becomes queerly passive in this room. Harry undresses the sleepy body, brown all but the narrow bottom, puts it into pajamas and into bed and arranges the covers over it. He tells him, "You're a good boy."

"Yop."

"I'm going to go now. Don't be scared."

"Daddy go way?"

"So you can sleep. I'll be back."

"O.K. Good."

"Good."

"Daddy?"

"What?"

"Is baby Becky dead?"

"Yes."

"Was she frightened?"

"Oh no. No. She wasn't frightened."

"Is she happy?"

"Yeah, she's very happy now."

"Good."

"Don't you worry about it."

"O.K."

"You snuggle up."

"Yop."

"Think about throwing stones."

"When I grow up, I'll throw them very *far*."

"That's right. You can throw them pretty far now."

"I know it."

"O.K. Go to sleep."

Downstairs he asks Springer, who is washing dishes in the kitchen, "You don't want me to stay here tonight, do you?"

"Not tonight, Harry. I'm sorry. I think it would be better not tonight."

"O.K., sure. I'll go back to the apartment. Shall I come over in the morning?"

"Yes, please. We'll give you breakfast."

"No, I don't want any. I mean, to see Janice when she wakes up."

"Yes of course."

"You think she'll sleep the night through."

"I think so."

"Uh—I'm sorry I wasn't at the lot today."

"Oh, that's nothing. That's negligible."

"You don't want me to work tomorrow, do you?"

"Of course not."

"I still have the job, don't I?"

"Of course." His talk is gingerly; his eyes fidget; he feels his wife is listening.

"You're being awfully good to me."

Springer doesn't answer; Harry goes out through the sun-porch, so he won't have to glimpse Mrs. Springer's face again, and around the house and walks home in the soupy summer dark, tinkling with the sounds of supper dishes being washed. He climbs Wilbur Street and goes in his old door and up the stairs, which still smell faintly of something like cabbage cooking. He lets himself into the apartment with his key and turns on all the lights as rapidly as he can. He goes into the bathroom and the water is still in the tub. Some of it has seeped away so the top of the water is an inch below a faint gray line on the porcelain but the tub is still more than half full. A heavy, calm volume, odorless, tasteless, colorless, the water shocks him like the presence of a silent person in the bathroom. Stillness makes a dead skin on its unstirred surface. There's even a kind of dust on it. He rolls back his sleeve and reaches down and pulls the plug; the water swings and the drain gasps. He watches the line of water slide slowly and evenly down the wall of the tub, and then with a crazed vortical cry the last of it is sucked away. He thinks how easy it was, yet in all His strength God did nothing. Just that little rubber stopper to lift.

In bed he discovers that his legs ache from all the walking he did in Brewer today. His shins feel splintered; no matter how he twists, the pain, after a moment of relief gained by the movement, sneaks back. He tries praying to relax him but it doesn't do it. There's no connection. He opens his eyes to look at the ceiling and the darkness is mottled with an unsteady network of veins like the net of yellow and blue that mottled the skin of his baby. He remembers seeing her neat red profile through the window at the hospital and a great draft of horror sweeps through him, brings him struggling out of bed to turn on the lights. The electric glare seems thin. His groin aches to weep. He is afraid to stick even his hand into the bathroom; he fears if he turns on the light he will see a tiny wrinkled blue corpse lying face up on the floor of the drained tub. Dread presses on his kidneys and he is at last forced to dare; the dark bottom of the tub leaps up blank and white.

He expects never to go to sleep and, awaking with the slant of sunshine and the noise of doors slamming downstairs, feels his body has betrayed his soul. He dresses in haste, more panicked now than at any time yesterday. The event is realer. Invisible cushions press against his throat and slow his legs and arms; the kink in his chest has grown thick and crusty. *Forgive me, forgive me*, he keeps saying silently to no one.

He goes over to the Springers' and the tone of the house has changed; he feels everything has been rearranged slightly to make a space into which he can fit by making himself small. Mrs. Springer serves him orange juice and coffee and even speaks, cautiously.

"Do you want cream?"

"No. No. I'll drink it black."

"We have cream if you want it."

"No, really. It's fine."

Janice is awake. He goes upstairs and lies down on the bed

beside her; she clings to him and sobs into the cup between his neck and jaw and the sheet. Her face has been shrunk; her body seems small as a child's, and hot and hard. She tells him, "I can't stand to look at anyone except you. I can't bear to look at the others."

"It wasn't your fault," he tells her. "It was mine."

"I've got my milk back," she says, "and every time my breasts sting I think she must be in the next room."

They cling together in a common darkness; he feels the walls between them dissolve in a flood of black; but the heavy knot of apprehension remains in his chest, his own.

He stays in the house all that day. Visitors come, and tip-toe about. Their manner suggests that Janice upstairs is very sick. They sit, these women, over coffee in the kitchen with Mrs. Springer, whose petite rounded voice, oddly girlish divorced from the sight of her body, sighs on and on like an indistinct, rising and falling song. Peggy Fosnacht comes, her sunglasses off, her wall eyes wild, wide to the world, and goes upstairs. Her son Billy plays with Nelson, and no one moves to halt their squeals of anger and pain in the back yard, which, neglected, in time die, and revive, after a pause, in the form of laughter. Even Harry has a visitor. The doorbell rings and Mrs. Springer goes and comes into the dim room where Harry is sitting looking at magazines and says, in a surprised and injured voice, "A man for you."

She leaves the doorway and he gets up and walks a few steps forward to greet the man coming into the room, Tothero, leaning on a cane and his face half-paralyzed; but talking, walking, alive. And the baby dead. "Hi! Gee, how are you?"

"Harry." With the hand that is not on the cane he grips Harry's arm. He brings a long look to bear on Harry's face; his mouth is tweaked downward on one side and the skin over his eye on this side is dragged down diagonally so it nearly curtains the glitter. The gouging grip of his fingers trembles.

"Let's sit down," Rabbit says, and helps him into an easy chair. Tothero knocks off a doily in arranging his arms. Rabbit brings over a straight chair and sits close so he won't have to raise his voice. "Should you be running around?" he asks when Tothero says nothing.

"My wife brought me. In the car. Outside, Harry. We heard your terrible news. Didn't I warn you?" Already his eyes are bulging with water.

"When?"

"When?" The stricken side of his face is turned away, perhaps consciously, into shadow, so his smile seems wholly alive, wise, and sure. "That first night. I said go back. I begged you."

"I guess you did. I've forgotten."

"No you haven't. No you haven't, Harry." His breath chuffs on the "Ha" of "Harry." "Let me tell you something. Will you listen?"

"Sure."

"Right and wrong," he says, and stops; his big head shifts, and the stiff downward lines of his mouth and bad eye show. "Right and wrong aren't dropped from the sky. We. We make them. Against misery. Invariably, Harry, invariably"— he grows confident of his ability to negotiate long words— "misery follows their disobedience. Not our own, often at first not our own. Now you've had an example of that in your own life." Rabbit wonders when the tear-trails appeared on Tothero's cheeks; there they are. "Do you believe me?"

"Sure. Sure. Look, I know this has been my fault. I've felt like a, like an insect ever since that thing happened."

Tothero's tranquil smile deepens; a faint rasping purr comes out of his face. "I warned you," he says, "I warned you, Harry, but youth is deaf. Youth is careless."

Harry blurts, "But what can I do?"

Tothero doesn't seem to hear. "Don't you remember? My begging you to go back?"

"I don't know, I guess so."

"Good. Ah. You're still a fine man, Harry. You have a healthy body. When I'm dead and gone, remember how your old coach told you to avoid suffering. Remember." The last word is intoned coyly, with a little wag of the head; on the thrust of this incongruous vivacity he rises from his chair, and prevents himself from pitching forward by quick use of his cane. Harry jumps up in alarm, and the two of them stand for the moment very close. The old man's big head breathes a distressing scent, not so much medicine as a sweet vegetable staleness. "You young people," he says with a rising intonation, a schoolteacher's tone, scolding yet sly, "tend to forget. Don't you? Now don't you?"

He wants this admission mysteriously much. "Sure," Rabbit says, praying he'll go.

Harry helps him to his car, a '57 blue-and-cream Dodge waiting in front of the orange fire hydrant. Mrs. Tothero offers, rather coolly, her regrets at the death of his infant daughter. She looks harried and noble. Gray hair straggles down across her finely wrinkled silver temple. She wants to get away from him, away with her prize. Beside her on the front seat Tothero looks like a smirking gnome, brainlessly stroking the curve of his cane. Rabbit returns to the house feeling depressed and dirtied by the visit. Tothero's revelation chilled him. He wants to believe in the sky as the source of all things.

Eccles comes later in the afternoon, to complete the arrangements for the funeral: it will be held tomorrow afternoon, Wednesday. As he leaves Rabbit catches his attention and they talk in the front hall a moment. "What do you think?" Rabbit asks.

"About what?"

"What shall I do?"

Eccles glances up nervously. His face has that pale babyish look of someone who has not slept enough. "Do what you are doing," he says. "Be a good husband. A good father. Love what you have left."

"And that's enough?"

"You mean to earn forgiveness? I'm sure it is, carried out through a lifetime."

"I mean"—he's never before felt *pleading* with Eccles—"remember that thing we used to talk about? The thing behind everything."

"Harry, you know I don't think that thing exists in the way you think it does."

"O.K." He realizes that Eccles wants to get away too, that the sight of himself is painful, disgusting.

Eccles must see that he senses this, for he curtly summons up mercy and makes an attempt. "Harry, it's not for me to forgive you. You've done nothing to me *to* forgive. I'm equal with you in guilt. We must work for forgiveness; we must *earn* the right to see that thing behind everything. Harry, I *know* that people are brought to Christ. I've seen it with my eyes and tasted it with my mouth. And I do think this. I think marriage is a sacrament, and that this tragedy, terrible as it is, has at last united you and Janice in a sacred way."

Through the next hours Rabbit clings to this belief, though it seems to bear no relation to the colors and sounds of the big sorrowing house, the dabs and arcs of late sunshine in the little jungle of plants on the glass table, or the almost wordless supper he and Janice share in her bedroom.

He spends that night in the Springers' house, sleeping with Janice. Her sleep is so solid. A thin snore out of her black mouth sharpens the moonlight and keeps him awake. He gets up on an elbow and studies her face; it is frightening in the moonlight, small and smeared by patches of dark cut it seems in a soft substance that lacks the edges of a human presence. He resents her sleep. When, in first light, he feels her weight stir and slide off the bed, he turns his face deeper into the pillow, retracts his head half under the covers, and goes back to sleep stubbornly. The thought that today is the day of the funeral somehow makes this possible.

During this stolen doze he has a vivid dream. He is alone on a large sporting field, or vacant lot, littered with small pebbles. In the sky two perfect disks, identical in size but the one a dense white and the other slightly transparent, move toward each other slowly; the pale one is directly above the

dense one. At the moment they touch he feels frightened and
a voice like over a loudspeaker at a track meet announces,
"*The cowslip swallows up the elder.*" The downward gliding
of the top one continues steadily until the other, though the
stronger, is totally eclipsed, and just one circle is before his
eyes, pale and pure. He understands: "the cowslip" is the
moon, and "the elder" the sun, and that what he has witnessed
is the explanation of death: lovely life eclipsed by lovely
death. Intensely relieved and excited, he realizes he must go
forth from this field and found a new religion. There is a feeling of the disks, and the echo of the voice, bending over him
importunately, and he opens his eyes. Janice stands by the
bed in a brown skirt and a pink sleeveless blouse. There is a
drab thickness of fat under her chin he has never noticed before. He is surprised to be on his back; he almost always
sleeps on his stomach. He realizes it was a dream, that he has
nothing to tell the world, and the knot regathers in his chest.
In getting out of bed he kisses the back of her hand, which is
hanging by her side helpless and raw.

She makes him breakfast, the cereal drowned in milk, the
coffee scalded in her style. With Nelson they walk over to the
apartment to get clothes for the funeral. Rabbit resents her
being able to walk; he liked her best when she was unconscious. What kind of second-rate grief is it that permits them
to walk? The sense of their thick bodies just going on, wrap-
ping their hearts in numbness and small needs, angers him.
They walk with their child through streets they walked as
children. The gutter along Potter Avenue where the slime-
rimmed ice-plant water used to run is dry. The houses, many
of them no longer lived in by the people whose faces he all
knew, are like the houses in a town you see from the train,
their brick faces blank in posing the riddle, Why does anyone
live here? Why was he set down here, why is this town, a dull
suburb of a third-rate city, for him the center and index of a
universe that contains immense prairies, mountains, deserts,
forests, cities, seas? This childish mystery—the mystery of
"any place," prelude to the ultimate, "Why am I me?"—ignites

panic in his heart. Coldness spreads through his body and he feels detached, as if at last he is, what he's always dreaded, walking on air. The details of the street—the ragged margin where the pavement and grass struggle, the tarry scarred trunks of the telephone poles—no longer speak to him. He is no one; it is as if he stepped outside of his body and brain a moment to watch the engine run and stepped into nothingness, for this "he" had been merely a refraction, a vibration within the engine, and now can't get back in. He feels he is behind the windows of the houses they walk by, watching this three-cornered family stroll along solidly with no sign that their universe has convulsed other than the woman's quiet tears. Janice's tears have come as gently as dew comes; the sight of the morning-fresh streets seems to have sprung them.

When they get inside the apartment she gives a sharp sigh and collapses against him. Perhaps she didn't expect the place to be full of sunshine; buttresses of dust drifting in milky light slant from the middle of the floor to the tops of the windows and stripe everything with innocence. The door to his closet is near the entry door so they needn't go very deep into the apartment at first. He opens the closet door as far as he can without bumping the television set and reaches far in and unzips a plastic zippered storage bag and takes out his blue suit, a winter suit made of wool, but the only dark one he owns. Nelson, happy to be here, ranges through the apartment, going wee-wee in the bathroom, finding an old rubber panda in his bedroom that he wants to take along. His exploring drains enough of the menace from the rooms for them to go into their bedroom, where Janice's clothes hang. On the way she indicates a chair. "Here I sat," she says, "yesterday morning, watching the sun come up." Her voice is lifeless; he doesn't know what she wants him to say and says nothing. He is holding his breath.

Yet in the bedroom there is a pretty moment. She takes off her skirt and blouse to try on an old black suit she has, and as she moves about in her slip, barefoot on the carpet, she reminds him of the girl he knew, with her narrow ankles and wrists and small shy head. The black suit, bought when she was in high school, doesn't fit; her stomach is still too big from having the baby. And maybe her mother's plumpness is beginning. Standing there trying to get the waist of the suit skirt to link at her side, the tops of her breasts, swollen with untaken milk, pushing above her bra, she does have a plumpness, a fullness that call to him. He thinks *Mine, my woman*, but then she turns and her smeared frantic face blots out his pride of possession. She becomes a liability that painfully weights the knot below his chest. This is the wild woman he must steer with care down a lifelong path, away from yesterday. "It won't *do* it!" she screams, and jerks her legs out of the skirt and flings it, great twirling bat, across the room.

"You have nothing else?"

"What am I going to *do?*"

"Come on. Let's get out of here and go back to your place. This place is making you nervous."

"But we're going to have to *live* here!"

"Yeah, but not today. Come on."

"We *can't* live here," she says.

"I know we can't."

"But where *can* we live?"

"We'll figure it out. Come on."

She stumbles into her skirt and puts her blouse over her arms and turns away from him meekly and asks, "Button my back." Buttoning the pink cloth down her quiet spine makes him cry; the hotness in his eyes works up to a sting and he sees the little babyish buttons through a cluster of disks of watery light like petals of apple blossoms. Water hesitates on his lids and then runs down his cheeks; the wetness is delicious. He wishes he could cry for hours, for just this tiny spill relieves him. But a man's tears are rare and his stop before they are out of the apartment. As he closes the door he feels he has already spent his whole dry life opening and closing this door.

Nelson takes the rubber panda along and every time he makes it squeak Rabbit's stomach aches. The town now is bleached by a sun nearing the height of noon.

. . .

The hours that follow are so long they seem to contain the same incidents over and over. Back in the house, Janice and her mother merge and re-merge in soft little conversations that take them from room to room. They seem to be worrying what Janice will wear. The two of them go upstairs and in half an hour Janice comes down in a pinned-in black dress of her mother's that makes her look like her mother. "Harry. Does it look all right?"

"What in hell do you think this is going to be? A fashion show?" He adds regretfully, "You look fine," but the damage is done. Janice emits a long startled whimper and goes upstairs and collapses into her mother. Mrs. Springer revokes the small measure of pardon she had extended him. The house again fills with the unspoken thought that he is a murderer. He accepts the thought gratefully; it's true, he is, he is, and hate suits him better than forgiveness. Immersed in hate he doesn't have to do anything; he can be paralyzed, and the rigidity of hatred makes a kind of shelter for him.

It becomes one o'clock. Mrs. Springer comes into the room where he is sitting and asks, "Do you want a sandwich?"

"Thanks, I can't eat anything."

"You better have something." He finds this insistence so strange he goes into the kitchen to see what is there. Nelson is having soup and raw carrots and a Lebanon baloney sandwich by himself at the table. He seems uncertain if he should smile at his father or not. Mrs. Springer keeps her back turned.

Harry asks, "Has the kid had a nap?"

"You might take him up," she says, without turning. Upstairs in the room with the one-eyed teddy-bear Harry reads the boy a Little Golden Book about a little choo-choo who was afraid of tunnels. By the time the choo-choo has proved he is no longer afraid Nelson has fallen asleep under his father's arm. Harry goes downstairs again. Janice is having a rest in her room and the sound of Mrs. Springer's sewing machine, as it adjusts the dress for Janice to wear, spins out into the birdsong and murmur of the early afternoon.

The front door slams and Springer comes into the living-room. None of the shades have been pulled up and he starts at seeing Harry in a chair, "Harry! Hello!"

"Hello."

"Harry, I've been down at Town Hall talking to Al Horst. He's the coroner. He's promised me there won't be a man-slaughter charge; they're satisfied. Accidental. He's been talk-ing to just about everybody and wants to talk to you some-time. Unofficially."

"O.K." Springer hangs there, expecting some kind of con-gratulation. "Why don't they just lock me up?" Harry adds.

"Harry, that's a very negative way to think. The question is, How do we cut the losses from here on in?"

"You're right. I'm sorry." It disgusts him to feel the net of law slither from him. They just won't do it for you, they just won't take you off the hook.

Springer trots upstairs to his women. Footfalls pad above. Fancy dishes in the glass-fronted cupboard behind Harry vi-brate. It's not yet two o'clock, he sees by the little silver-faced clock on the mantel of the fake fireplace.

He wonders if the pain in his stomach comes from eating so little in the last two days and goes out to the kitchen and eats two crackers. He can feel each bite hit a scraped floor inside. The pain increases. The bright porcelain fixtures, the steel doors, all seem charged with a negative magnetism that pushes against him and makes him extremely thin. He goes into the shadowy living-room and pulls the shade and at the front window watches two teenage girls in snug shorts shuffle by on the sunny sidewalk. Their bodies are already there but their faces are still this side of being good. Funny about girls about fourteen, their faces have this kind of eager bunchy business. Too much candy, sours their skin. They walk as slowly as time to the funeral passes, as if if they go slow enough some magic transformation will meet them at the corner. Daughters, these are daughters, would June—? He chokes the thought. The two girls passing, with their perky butts and expectant sex, seem distasteful and unreal. He himself, watching them behind the window, seems a smudge on the glass. He wonders why the universe doesn't just erase a thing so dirty and small. He looks at his hands and they seem fantastically ugly.

He goes upstairs and with intense care washes his hands and face and neck. He doesn't dare use one of their fancy towels. Coming out with wet hands he meets Springer in the muted hallway and says, "I don't have a clean shirt." Springer whispers "Wait" and brings him a shirt and black cufflinks. Harry dresses in the room where Nelson sleeps. Sunlight creeps under the drawn shades, which flap softly back and forth almost in time to the boy's heavy breathing. Though he spaces the stages of dressing carefully, and fumbles for minutes with the unaccustomed cufflinks, it takes less time to dress than he hoped it would. The wool suit is uncomfortably hot, and doesn't fit as well as he remembered. But he refuses to take off the coat, refuses to give somebody, he doesn't know who, the satisfaction. He tiptoes downstairs and sits, immaculately dressed, the shirt too tight, in the living-room looking at the tropical plants on the glass table, moving his head so that now this leaf eclipses that, now that this, and wondering if he is going to throw up. His insides are a clenched mass of dread, a tough bubble that can't be pricked. The clock says only 2:25.

Of the things he dreads, seeing his parents is foremost. He hasn't had the courage to call them or see them since it happened; Mrs. Springer called Mom Monday night and asked her to the funeral. The silence from his home since then has frightened him. It's one thing to get hell from other people and another from your own parents. Ever since he came back from the Army Pop had been nibbling at a grudge because he wouldn't go to work in the print shop and in a way had nibbled himself right into nothing in Harry's heart. All the mildness and kindness the old man had ever shown him had faded into nothing. But his mother was something else; she was still alive and still attached to the cord of his life. If she comes in and gives him hell he thinks he'll die rather than take it. And of course what else is there to give him? Whatever Mrs. Springer says he can slip away from because in the end she has to stick with him and anyway he feels somehow she wants to like him but with his mother there's no question of liking him they're not even in a way separate people he began in her stomach and if she gave him life she can take it away and if he feels that withdrawal it will be the grave itself. Of all the people in the world he wants to see her least. Sitting there by himself he comes to the conclusion that either he or his mother must die. It is a weird conclusion, but he keeps coming to it, again and again, until the sounds of stirring above him, of the Springers getting dressed, lift his mind out of himself a little.

He wonders if he should go up but he doesn't want to surprise anyone undressed and one by one they come down, dressed, Mr. Springer in a spiffy graphite-gray drip-and-dry and Nelson in a corduroy sissy suit with straps and Mrs. in a black felt hat with a veil and a stiff stem of artificial berries and Janice looking lost and shapeless in the pinned and tucked dress of her mother's. "You look fine," he tells her again.

"Whez big black cah?" Nelson asks in a loud voice.

There is something undignified about waiting and as they mill around in the living-room watching the minutes ebb in the silver-faced clock they become uncomfortably costumed children nervous for the party to begin. They all press around the window when the undertaker's Cadillac stops out front, though by the time the man has come up the walk and rings the doorbell they have scattered to the corners of the room as if a bomb of contagion has been dropped among them.

The funeral parlor was once a home but now is furnished the way no home ever was. Unworn carpets of a very pale green deaden their footsteps. Little silver half-tubes on the walls shield a weak glow. The colors of the curtains and walls are atonal half-colors, colors no one would live with, salmon and aqua and a violet like the violet that kills germs on toilet seats in gas stations. They are ushered into a little pink side-room. Harry can see into the main room; on a few rows of auditorium chairs about six people sit, five of them women. The only one he knows is Peggy Gring. Her little boy wriggling beside her makes seven. It was meant to be at first nobody but the families, but the Springers then asked a few close friends. His parents are not here. Invisible hands bonelessly trail up and down the keys of an electric organ. The unnatural coloring of the interior comes to a violent head in the hothouse flowers arranged around a little white coffin. The coffin, with handles of painted gold, rests on a platform draped with a deep purple curtain; he thinks the curtain might draw apart and reveal, like a magician's trick, the living baby underneath. Janice looks in and yields a whimper and an undertaker's man, blond and young with an unnaturally red face, conjures a bottle of spirits of ammonia out of his side pocket. Her mother holds it under her nose and Janice suppresses a face of disgust; her eyebrows stretch up, showing the bumps her eyeballs make under the thin membrane. Harry takes her arm and turns her so she can't see into the next room.

The side-room has a window through which they can look at the street, where children and cars are running. "Hope the minister hasn't forgotten," the young red-faced man says, and to his own embarrassment chuckles. He can't help being at his ease here. His face seems lightly rouged.

"Does that happen often?" Mr. Springer asks. He is standing behind his wife, and his face tips forward with curiosity, a birdy black gash beneath his pale mustache. Mrs. Springer has sat down on a chair and is pressing her palms against her face through the veil. The purple berries quiver on their stem of wire.

"About twice a year," is the answer.

A familiar old Plymouth slows against the curb outside. Rabbit's mother gets out and looks up and down the sidewalk angrily. His heart leaps and trips his tongue: "Here come my parents." They all come to attention. Mrs. Springer gets up and Harry places himself between her and Janice. Standing in formation with the Springers like this, he can at least show his mother that he's reformed, that he's accepted and been accepted. The undertaker's man goes out to bring them in; Harry can see them standing on the bright sidewalk, arguing which door to go into, Mim a little to one side. Dressed in a church sort of dress and with no make-up, she reminds him of the little sister he once had. The sight of his parents makes him wonder why he was afraid of them.

His mother comes through the door first; her eyes sweep the line of them and she steps toward him with reaching curved arms. "Hassy—what have they done to you?" She asks this out loud and wraps him in a hug as if she would carry him back to the sky from which they have fallen.

This quick it opens, and seals shut again. In a boyish reflex of embarrassment he pushes her away and stands to his full height. As if unaware of what she has said, his mother turns and embraces Janice. Pop, murmuring, shakes Springer's hand. Mim comes and touches Harry on the shoulder and then squats and whispers to Nelson, these two the youngest. All under him Harry feels these humans knit together. His wife and mother cling together. His mother began the embrace automatically but has breathed a great life of grief into it. Her face creases in pain; Janice, rumpled and smothered, yet responds; her weak black arms try to encircle the great frame yearning against her. Mrs. Angstrom yields up two words to her. The others are puzzled; only Harry from his tall cool height understands. His mother had been propelled by the instinct that makes us embrace those we wound, and then she had felt this girl in her arms as a member with her of an ancient abused slave race, and then she had realized that, having restored her son to herself, she too must be deserted.

He had felt in himself these stages of grief unfold in her as her arms tightened. Now she releases Janice, and speaks, sadly and properly, to the Springers. They have let her first outcry pass as madness. They of course have done nothing to Harry, what has been done he has done to them. His liberation is unseen by them. They become remote beside him. The words his mother spoke to Janice, "My daughter," recede. Mim rises from squatting; his father takes Nelson into his arms. Their motions softly jostle him.

And meanwhile his heart completes its turn and turns again, a wider turn in a thinning medium to which the outer world bears a decreasing relevance.

Eccles has arrived by some other entrance and from a far doorway beckons them. The seven of them file with Nelson into the room where the flowers wait and take their seats on the front row. Black Eccles reads before the white casket. It annoys Rabbit that Eccles should stand between him and his daughter. It occurs to him, what no one has mentioned, the child was never baptized. Eccles reads. "I am the resurrection and the life, saith the Lord: he that believeth in me, though he were dead, yet shall he live: and whosoever liveth and believeth in me, shall never die."

The angular words walk in Harry's head like clumsy blackbirds; he feels their possibility. Eccles doesn't; his face is humorless and taut. His voice is false. All these people are false: except his dead daughter, the white box with gold trim.

"He shall feed his flock like a shepherd: he shall gather the lambs with his arms, and carry them in his bosom."

Shepherd, lamb, arms: Harry's eyes fill with tears. It is as if at first the tears are everywhere about him, a sea, and that at last the saltwater gets into his eyes. His daughter is dead; June gone from him; his heart swims in grief, that had skimmed over it before, dives deeper and deeper into the limitless volume of loss. Never hear her cry again, never see her marbled skin again, never cup her faint weight in his arms again and watch the blue of her eyes wander in search of the source of his voice. Never, the word never stops, there is never a gap in its thickness.

They go to the cemetery. He and his father and Janice's father and the undertaker's man carry the white box to the hearse. There is weight to it but the weight is all wood. They get into their cars and drive through the streets uphill. The town hushes around them; a woman comes out on her porch

with a basket of wash and waits there, a small boy stops himself in the middle of throwing a ball to watch them pass. They
pass between two granite pillars linked by an arch of wrought
iron. The cemetery is beautiful at four o'clock. Its nurtured
green nap slopes down somewhat parallel to the rays of the
sun. Tombstones cast long slate shadows. Up a crunching blue
gravel lane the procession moves in second gear, its destination a meek green canopy smelling of earth and ferns. The
cars stop; they get out. Beyond them at a distance stands a
crescent sweep of black woods; the cemetery is high on the
hill, between the town and the forest. Below their feet chimneys smoke. A man on a power lawnmower rides between the
worn teeth of tombstones near the far hedge. Swallows in a
wide ball dip and toss themselves above a stone cottage, a
crypt. The white coffin is artfully rolled on casters from the
hearse's deep body onto crimson straps that hold it above the
small nearly square-mouthed but deep-dug grave. The small
creaks and breaths of effort scratch on a pane of silence. Silence. A cough. The flowers have followed them; here they
are, densely banked within the tent. Behind Harry's feet a
neat mound of dirt topped with squares of sod waits to be replaced and meanwhile breathes a deep word of earth. The
undertaking men look pleased, their job near done, fold their
pink hands in front of their flies. Silence.

"The Lord is my shepherd; therefore can I lack nothing."

Eccles' voice is fragile outdoors. The distant buzz of the
power mower halts respectfully. Rabbit's chest vibrates with
excitement and strength; he is sure his girl has ascended to
Heaven. This feeling fills Eccles' recited words like a living
body a skin. "O God, whose most dear Son did take little children into his arms and bless them; Give us Grace, we beseech
thee, to entrust the soul of this child to thy never-failing care
and love, and bring us all to the heavenly kingdom; through
the same thy Son, Jesus Christ, our Lord. Amen."

"Amen," Mrs. Springer whispers.

Yes. That is how it is. He feels them all, the heads as still
around him as tombstones, he feels them all one, all one with

the grass, with the hothouse flowers, all, the undertaker's men, the unseen caretaker who has halted his mower, all gathered into one here to give his unbaptized baby force to leap to Heaven.

An electric switch is turned, the straps begin to lower the casket into the grave and stop. Eccles makes a cross of sand on the lid. Stray grains roll one by one down the curved lid into the hole. A pink hand throws crumpled petals. "Deal graciously, we pray thee, with all those who mourn, that, casting every care on thee . . ." The straps whine again. Janice at his side staggers. He holds her arm and even through the cloth it feels hot. A small breath of wind makes the canopy fill and luff. The smell of flowers rises toward them. ". . . and the Holy Ghost, bless you and keep you, now and for evermore. Amen."

Eccles closes his book. Harry's father and Janice's, standing side by side, look up and blink. The undertaker's men begin to be busy with their equipment, retrieving the straps from the hole. Mourners move into the sunshine. *Casting every care on thee.* . . . The sky greets him. A strange strength sinks down into him. It is as if he has been crawling in a cave and now at last beyond the dark recession of crowding rocks he has seen a patch of light; he turns, and Janice's face, dumb with grief, blocks the light. "Don't look at *me*," he says. "I didn't kill her."

This comes out of his mouth clearly, in tune with the simplicity he feels now in everything. Heads talking softly snap around at a voice so sudden and cruel.

They misunderstand. He just wants this straight. He explains to the heads, "You all keep acting as if *I* did it. I wasn't anywhere near. *She's* the one." He turns to her, and her face, slack as if slapped, seems hopelessly removed from him. "Hey it's O.K.," he tells her. "You didn't mean to." He tries to take her hand but she snatches it back like from a trap and looks toward her parents, who step toward her.

His face burns. His embarrassment is savage. Forgiveness had been big in his heart and now it's hate. He hates his wife's face. She doesn't *see*. She had a chance to join him in truth, just the simplest factual truth, and she turned away. He sees that among the heads even his own mother's is horrified, blank with shock, a wall against him; she asks him what have they done to him and then she does it too. A suffocating sense of injustice blinds him. He turns and runs.

Uphill exultantly. He dodges among gravestones. Dandelions grow bright as butter among the graves. Behind him his name is called in Eccles' voice: "Harry! Harry!" He feels Eccles chasing him but does not turn to look. He cuts diagonally through the stones across the grass toward the woods. The distance to the dark crescent of trees is greater than it seemed from beside the grave. The romping of his body turns heavy; the slope of land grows steeper. Yet there is a softness in the burial ground that sustains his flight, a gentle settled bumpiness that buoys him up with its reminiscence of the dodging spurting runs down a crowded court. He arrives between the arms of the woods and aims for the center of the crescent. Once inside, he is less sheltered than he expected; turning, he can see through the leaves back down the graveyard to where, beside the small green tent, the human beings he had left cluster. Eccles is halfway between them and him. He has stopped running. His black chest heaves. His wide-set eyes concentrate into the woods. The others, thick stalks in dark clothes, jiggle: maneuvering, planning, testing each other's strengths, holding each other up. Their pale faces flash mute signals toward the woods and turn away, in disgust or despair, and then flash again full in the declining sun, fascinated. Only Eccles' gaze is steady. He may be gathering energy to renew the chase.

Rabbit crouches and runs raggedly. His hands and face are scratched from plowing through the bushes and saplings that rim the woods. Deeper inside there is more space. The pine trees smother all other growth. Their brown needles muffle the rough earth with a slippery blanket; sunshine falls in narrow slots on this dead floor. It is dim but hot in here, like an attic; the unseen afternoon sun bakes the dark shingles of green above his head. Dead lower branches thrust at the level of his eyes. His hands and face feel hot where they were scratched. He turns to see if he has left the people behind. No one is following. Far off, down at the end of the aisle of pines he is in, a green glows which is perhaps the green of the cemetery; but it seems as far off as the patches of sky that flicker through the treetops. In turning he loses some sense of direction. But the tree-trunks are at first in neat rows that carry him along between them, and he walks always against the slope of the land. If he walks far enough uphill he will in time reach the scenic drive that runs along the ridge. Only by going downhill can he be returned to the others.

The trees cease to march in rows and grow together more thickly. These are older trees. The darkness under them is denser and the ground is steeper. Rocks jut up through the blanket of needles, scabby with lichen; collapsed trunks hold intricate claws across the path. At places where a hole has been opened up in a roof of evergreen, berrying bushes and yellow grass grow in a hasty sweet-smelling tumble, and midges swarm. These patches, some of them broad enough to catch a bit of the sun slanting down the mountainside, make the surrounding darkness darker, and in pausing in them Rabbit becomes conscious, by its cessation, of a whisper that fills the brown caverns all around him. The surrounding trees are too tall for him to see any sign, even a remote cleared landscape, of civilization. Islanded in light he becomes frightened. He is conspicuous; the bears and nameless menaces that whisper through the forest can see him clearly. Rather than hang vulnerable in these wells of visibility he rushes toward the menaces across the rocks and rotting trunks and slithering needles. Insects follow him out of the sun; his sweat is a strong perfume. His chest binds and his shins hurt from jarring uphill into pits and flat rocks that the needles conceal. He takes off his binding blue coat and carries it in a twisted bundle. He struggles against his impulse to keep turning his head, to see what is behind him; there is never anything, just the hushed, deathly life of the woods, but his fear fills the winding space between the tree-trunks with agile threats, that just dodge out of the corner of his eye each time he whips his head around. He must hold his head rigid. He's terrorizing himself. As a kid he often went up through the woods. But maybe as a kid he walked under a protection that has now been lifted; he can't believe the woods were this dark then. They too have grown. Such an unnatural darkness, clogged with spider-fine twigs that finger his face incessantly, darkness in defiance of the broad daylight whose sky leaps in jagged patches from treetop to treetop above him like a silent monkey.

The small of his back aches from crouching. He begins to doubt his method. As a kid he never entered from the cemetery. Perhaps walking against the steepest slope is stupid, carrying him along below the ridge of the mountain when a few yards to his left the road is running. He bears to his left, trying to keep himself in a straight path; the whisper of woods seems to swell louder and his heart lifts with hope: he was right, he is near a road. He hurries on, scrambling ruthlessly, expecting the road to appear with every step, its white posts and speeding metal to gleam. The slope of the ground dies unnoticed under his feet. He stops, stunned, on the edge of a precipitate hollow whose near bank is strewn with the hairy bodies of dead trees locked against trunks that have managed to cling erect to the steep soil and that cast into the hollow a shadow as deep as the last stage of twilight. Something rectangular troubles this gloom; it dawns on him that on the floor of the hollow lie the cellarhole and the crumbled sandstone walls of a forgotten house. To his shrill annoyance at having lost his way and headed himself downhill again is added a clangorous horror, as if this ruined evidence of a human intrusion into a world of blind life tolls bells that ring to the edges of the universe. The thought that this place was once self-conscious, that its land was tramped and cleared and known, blackens the air with ghosts that climb the ferny bank toward him like children clambering up from a grave. Perhaps there were children, fat girls in calico fetching water from a spring, scarring the trees with marks of play, growing old on boards stretched above the cellarhole, dying with a last look out the window at the bank where Harry stands. He feels more conspicuous and vulnerable than in the little clearings of sunshine; he obscurely feels lit by a great spark, the spark whereby the blind tumble of matter recognized itself, a spark struck in the collision of two opposed realms, an encounter a terrible God willed. His stomach slides; his ears seem suddenly open to the sound of a voice. He scrambles back uphill, thrashing noisily in the deepening darkness to drown out the voice that wants to cry out to him from a source that flits from tree to tree in the shadows. In the treacherous light the slope of land is like some fleeing, twisting thing.

The light widens enough for him to spy off to his right a nest of old tin cans and bottles sunken into the needles. He is safe. He strikes the road. He jacks his long legs over the guard fence and straightens up. Gold spots are switching on and off in the corners of his eyes. The asphalt scrapes under his shoes and he seems entered, with the wonderful resonant hollowness of exhaustion, on a new life. Cold air strokes his shoulder blades; somewhere in there he split old man Springer's shirt right down the back. He has come out of the woods about a half-mile below the Pinnacle Hotel. As he swings along, jauntily hanging his blue coat over his shoulder on the hook of one finger, Janice and Eccles and his mother and his sins seem a thousand miles behind. He decides to call Eccles, like you'd send somebody a postcard. Eccles had liked him and put a lot of trust in him and deserves at least a phone call. Rabbit rehearses what he'll say. *It's O.K.*, he'll tell him, *I'm on the way. I mean, I think there are several ways; don't worry. Thanks for everything.* What he wants to get across is that Eccles shouldn't be discouraged.

On top of the mountain it is still broad day. Up in the sea of sky a lake of fragmented mackerel clouds drifts in one piece like a school of fish. There are only a couple cars

parked around the hotel, jalopies, '52 Pontiacs and '51 Mercs
like Springer Motors sells to these blotchy kids that come in
with a stripper in their wallets and a hundred dollars in the
bank. Inside the cafeteria a few of them are playing a pinball
machine called BOUNCING BETSY. They look at him and make
wise faces and one of the boys even calls, "Did she rip your
shirt?" But, it's strange, they don't really know anything
about him except he looks mussed. You do things and do
things and nobody really has a clue. The clock says twenty of
six. He goes to the pay phone on the butterscotch wall and
looks up Eccles' number in the book.

His wife answers dryly, "Hello?" Rabbit shuts his eyes and
her freckles dance in the red of his lids.

"Hi. Could I speak to Reverend Eccles please?"

"Who is that?" Her voice has gotten up on a hard little high
horse; she knows who.

"Hey, this is Harry Angstrom. Is Jack there?"

The receiver at the other end of the line is replaced. That
bitch. Poor Eccles probably sitting there his heart bleeding
to hear the word and she going back and telling him wrong
number, that poor bastard being married to that bitch. He
hangs up himself, hears the dime rattle down, and feels
simplified by this failure. He goes out across the parking lot.

From the edge of the parking lot, Brewer is spread out
like a carpet, its flowerpot red going dusty. Some lights are
already turned on. The great neon sunflower at the center of
the city looks small as a daisy. Now the low clouds are pink
but up above, high in the dome, tails of cirrus still hang pale
and pure. As he starts down the steps he wonders, Would she
have? Lucy. Are ministers' wives frigid?

He goes down the mountainside on the flight of log stairs
and through the park, where some people are still playing
tennis, and down Weiser Street. He puts his coat back on
and walks up Summer. His heart is murmuring in suspense
but it is in the center of his chest. That lopsided kink about
Becky is gone, he has put her in Heaven, he felt her go. If

Janice had felt it he would have stayed. Or would he? The
outer door is open and an old lady in a Polish sort of ker-
chief is coming mumbling out of F. X. Pelligrini's door.
He rings Ruth's bell.

The buzzer answers and he quickly snaps open the inner
door and starts up the steps. Ruth comes to the banister and
looks down and says, "Go away."

"Huh? How'd you know it was me?"

"Go back to your wife."

"I can't. I just left her."

She laughs; he has climbed to the step next to the top one,
and their faces are on a level. "You're always leaving her,"
she says.

"No, this time it's different. It's really bad."

"You're bad all around. You're bad with me, too."

"Why?" He has come up the last step and stands there a
yard away from her, excited and helpless. He thought when
he saw her, instinct would tell him what to do but in a way
it's all new, though it's only been a few weeks. She is changed,
graver in her motions and thicker in the waist. The blue of
her eyes is no longer blank.

She looks at him with a contempt that is totally new.
"*Why?*" she repeats in an incredulous hard voice.

"Let me guess," he says. "You're pregnant."

Surprise softens the hardness a moment.

"That's great," he says, and takes advantage of her softness
to push her ahead of him into the room. Just from the
touches of pushing he remembers what Ruth feels like in his
arms. "Great," he repeats, closing the door. He tries to embrace her and she fights him successfully and backs away behind a chair. She had meant that fight; his neck is scraped.

"Go away," she says. "Go *away*."

"Don't you need me?"

"*Need* you," she cries, and he squints in pain at the straining note of hysteria; he feels she has imagined this encounter
so often she is determined to say everything, which will be

too much. He sits down in an easy chair. His legs ache. She says, "I needed you that night you walked out. Remember how much I needed you? Remember what you made me do?"

"She was in the hospital," he says. "I had to go."

"God, you're cute. God, you're so holy. You had to go. You had to stay, too, didn't you? You know, I was stupid enough to think you'd at least call."

"I wanted to but I was trying to start clean. I didn't know you were pregnant."

"You didn't, why not? Anybody else would have. I was sick enough."

"When, with me?"

"God, yes. Why don't you look outside your own pretty skin once in a while?"

"Well why didn't you tell me?"

"Why should I? What would that have done? You're no help. You're nothing. You know why I didn't? You'll laugh, but I didn't because I thought you'd leave me if you knew. You wouldn't ever let me do anything to prevent it but I figured once it happened you'd leave me. You left me anyway so there you are. Why don't you get out? Please get out. I begged you to get out the first time. The damn first time I begged you. Why are you *here?*"

"I want to be here. It's right. Look. I'm happy you're pregnant."

"It's too late to be happy."

"Why? Why is it too late?" He's frightened, remembering how she wasn't here when he came before. She's here now, she had been away then. Women went away to have it done, he knew. There was a place in Philadelphia.

"How can you sit there?" she asks him. "I can't understand it, how you can sit there; you just killed your baby and there you sit."

"Who told you that?"

"Your ministerial friend. Your fellow saint. He called about a half-hour ago."

"God. He's still trying."

"I said you weren't here. I said you'd never be here."

"I didn't kill the poor kid. Janice did. I got mad at her one night and came looking for you and she got drunk and drowned the poor kid in the bathtub. Don't make me talk about it. Where *were* you, anyway?"

She looks at him with dull wonder and says softly, "Boy, you really have the touch of death, don't you?"

"Hey; have you done something?"

"Hold still. Just sit there. I see you very clear all of a sudden. You're Mr. Death himself. You're not just nothing, you're worse than nothing. You're not a rat, you don't stink, you're not enough to stink."

"Look, I didn't do anything. I was coming to see you when it happened."

"No, you don't do anything. You just wander around with the kiss of death. Get out. Honest to God, Rabbit, just looking at you makes me sick." Her sincerity in saying this leaves her kind of limp, and she grips the top slat of a straight chair bearing a Pennsylvania Dutch design stenciled in faded flowers.

He, who always took pride in dressing neatly, who had always been led to think he was all right to look at, blushes to feel this sincerity. The sensation he had counted on, of being by nature her master, of getting on top of her, hasn't come. He looks at his fingernails, with their big cuticle moons. His hands and legs are suffused with a paralyzing sensation of reality; his child is really dead, his day is really done, this woman is really sickened by him. Realizing this much makes him anxious to have all of it, to go as far in this direction as he can. He asks her flat, "Did you get an abortion?"

She smirks and says hoarsely, "What do *you* think?"

He closes his eyes and while the gritty grained fur of the chair arms rushes up against his fingertips prays, *God, dear God, no, not another, you have one, let this one go.* A dirty knife turns in his intricate inner darkness. When he opens his eyes he sees, from the tentative hovering way she is standing there, trying to bring off a hard swagger in her stance, that she means to torment him. His voice goes sharp with hope: "Have you?"

A crumbling film comes over her face. "No," she says, "*no*. I should but I keep not doing it. I don't want to do it."

Up he gets and his arms go around her, without squeezing, like a magic ring, and though she stiffens at his touch and twists her head sideways on her muscled white throat, he has regained that feeling, of being on top. "Oh," he says, "good. That's so good."

"It was too ugly," she says. "Margaret had it all rigged up but I kept—thinking about—"

"Yes," he says. "Yes. You're so good. I'm so glad," and tries to nuzzle the side of her face. His nose touches wet. "You have it," he coaxes. "Have it." She is still a moment, staring at her thoughts, and then jerks out of his arms and says, "Don't touch me!" Her face flares; her body is bent forward like a threatened animal's. As if his touch *is* death.

"I love you," he says.

"That means nothing from you. Have it, have it, you say: how? Will you marry me?"

"I'd love to."

"You'd love to, you'd love to do anything. What about your wife? What about the boy you already have?"

"I don't know."

"Will you divorce her? No. You love being married to her too. You love being married to everybody. Why can't you make up your mind what you want to *do?*"

"Can't I? I don't know."

"How would you support me? How many wives can you support? Your jobs are a joke. You aren't worth hiring. Maybe once you could play basketball but you can't do *any-* thing now. What the hell do you think the world is?"

"Please have the baby," he says. "You got to have it."

"Why? Why do you *care?*"

"I don't know. I don't know any of these answers. All I know is what feels right. You feel right to me. Sometimes Janice used to. Sometimes nothing does."

"Who cares? That's the thing. Who cares *what* you feel?"

"I don't know," he says again.

She groans—from her face he feared she would spit—and turns and looks at the wall that is all in bumps from being painted over peeling previous coats so often.

He says, "I'm hungry. Why don't I go out to the delicatessen and get us something. Then we can think."

She turns, steadier. "I've *been* thinking," she says. "You know where I was when you came here the other day? I was with my parents. You know I have parents. They're pretty poor parents but that's what they are. They live in West Brewer. They know. I mean they know some things. They know I'm pregnant. Pregnant's a nice word, it happens to everybody, you don't have to think too much what you must do to get that way. Now I'd like to marry you. I would. I mean whatever I said but if we're married it'll be all right. Now you work it out. You divorce that wife you feel so sorry for about once a month, you divorce her or forget me. If you can't work it out, I'm dead to you; I'm dead to you and this baby of yours is dead too. Now; get out if you want to." Saying all this unsteadies her and makes her cry, but she pretends she's not. She grips the back of the chair, the sides of her nose shining, and looks at him to say something. The way she is fighting for control of herself repels him; he doesn't like people who manage things. He likes things to happen of themselves.

He has nervously felt her watching him for some sign of resolution inspired by her speech. In fact he has hardly listened; it is too complicated and, compared to the vision of a sandwich, unreal. He stands up, he hopes with soldierly effect, and says, "That's fair. I'll work it out. What do you want at the store?" A sandwich and a glass of milk, and then undressing her, getting her out of that cotton dress harried into wrinkles and seeing that thickened waist calm in its pale cool skin. He loves women when they're first pregnant; a kind of dawn comes into their bodies. If he can just once more bury himself in her he knows he'll come up with his nerves all combed.

"I don't want anything," she says.

"Oh you got to eat," he says.

"I've eaten," she says.

He tries to go kiss her but she says "No" and does not look inviting, fat and flushed and her many-colored hair straggled and damp.

"I'll be right back," he says.

As he goes down the stairs worries come as quick as the clicks of his footsteps. Janice, money, Eccles' phone call, the look on his mother's face all clatter together in sharp dark waves; guilt and responsibility slide together like two substantial shadows inside his chest. The mere engineering of it—the conversations, the phone calls, the lawyers, the finances—seems to complicate, physically, in front of his mouth, so he is conscious of the effort of breathing, and every action, just reaching for the doorknob, feels like a precarious extension of a long mechanical sequence insecurely linked to his heart. The doorknob's solidity answers his touch, and turns nicely.

Outside in the air his fears condense. Globes of ether, pure nervousness, slide down his legs. The sense of outside space scoops at his chest. Standing on the step he tries to sort his worries, tries to analyze the machinery behind him in the house, put his finger on what makes it so loud. Two thoughts comfort him, let a little light through the dense pack of impossible alternatives. Ruth has parents, and she will let his baby live; two thoughts that are perhaps the same thought, the vertical order of parenthood, a kind of thin tube upright in time in which our solitude is somewhat diluted. Ruth and Janice both have parents: with this thought he dissolves both of them. Nelson remains: here is a hardness he must carry with him. On this small fulcrum he tries to balance the rest, weighing opposites against each other: Janice and Ruth, Eccles and his mother, the right way and the good way, the way to the delicatessen—gaudy with stacked fruit lit by a naked bulb—and the other way, down Summer Street to where the city ends. He tries to picture how it will end, with an empty baseball field, a dark factory, and then over a brook into a dirt road, he doesn't know. He pictures a huge vacant field of cinders and his heart goes hollow.

Afraid, really afraid, he remembers what once consoled him by seeming to make a hole where he looked through into underlying brightness, and lifts his eyes to the church window. It is, because of church poverty or the late summer nights or just carelessness, unlit, a dark circle in a stone façade.

There is light, though, in the streetlights; muffled by trees their mingling cones retreat to the unseen end of Summer Street. Nearby, to his left, directly under one, the rough asphalt looks like dimpled snow. He decides to walk around the block, to clear his head and pick his path. Funny, how what makes you move is so simple and the field you must move in is so crowded. His legs take strength from the distinction, scissor along evenly. Goodness lies inside, there is nothing outside, those things he was trying to balance have no weight. He feels his inside as very real suddenly, a pure blank space in the middle of a dense net. *I don't know*, he kept telling Ruth; he doesn't know, what to do, where to go, what will happen, the thought that he doesn't know seems to make him infinitely small and impossible to capture. Its smallness fills him like a vastness. It's like when they heard you were great and put two men on you and no matter which way you turned you bumped into one of them and the only thing to do was pass. So you passed and the ball belonged to the others and your hands were empty and the men on you looked foolish because in effect there was nobody there.

Rabbit comes to the curb but instead of going to his right and around the block he steps down, with as big a feeling as if this little side-street is a wide river, and crosses. He wants to travel to the next patch of snow. Although this block of brick three-stories is just like the one he left, something in it makes him happy; the steps and window sills seem to twitch and shift in the corner of his eye, alive. This illusion trips him. His hands lift of their own and he feels the wind on his ears even before, his heels hitting heavily on the pavement at first but with an effortless gathering out of a kind of sweet panic growing lighter and quicker and quieter, he runs. Ah: runs. Runs.

MODERN LIBRARY GIANTS

A series of sturdily bound and handsomely printed, full-sized library editions of books formerly available only in expensive sets. These volumes contain from 600 to 1,400 pages each.

THE MODERN LIBRARY GIANTS REPRESENT A
SELECTION OF THE WORLD'S GREATEST BOOKS